$2

PERFECTION

A Novel

To Sally,
Love,
Kathy

by

KATHLEEN WADE

Copyright Notice

Publisher: Jesse Krieger

If you are interested in publishing through Lifestyle Entrepreneurs Press, write to Jesse@JesseKrieger.com.

Publications or foreign rights acquisitions of our catalogue books.
Learn More: www.LifestyleEntrepreneursPress.com

ISBN: 978-1-946697-77-6

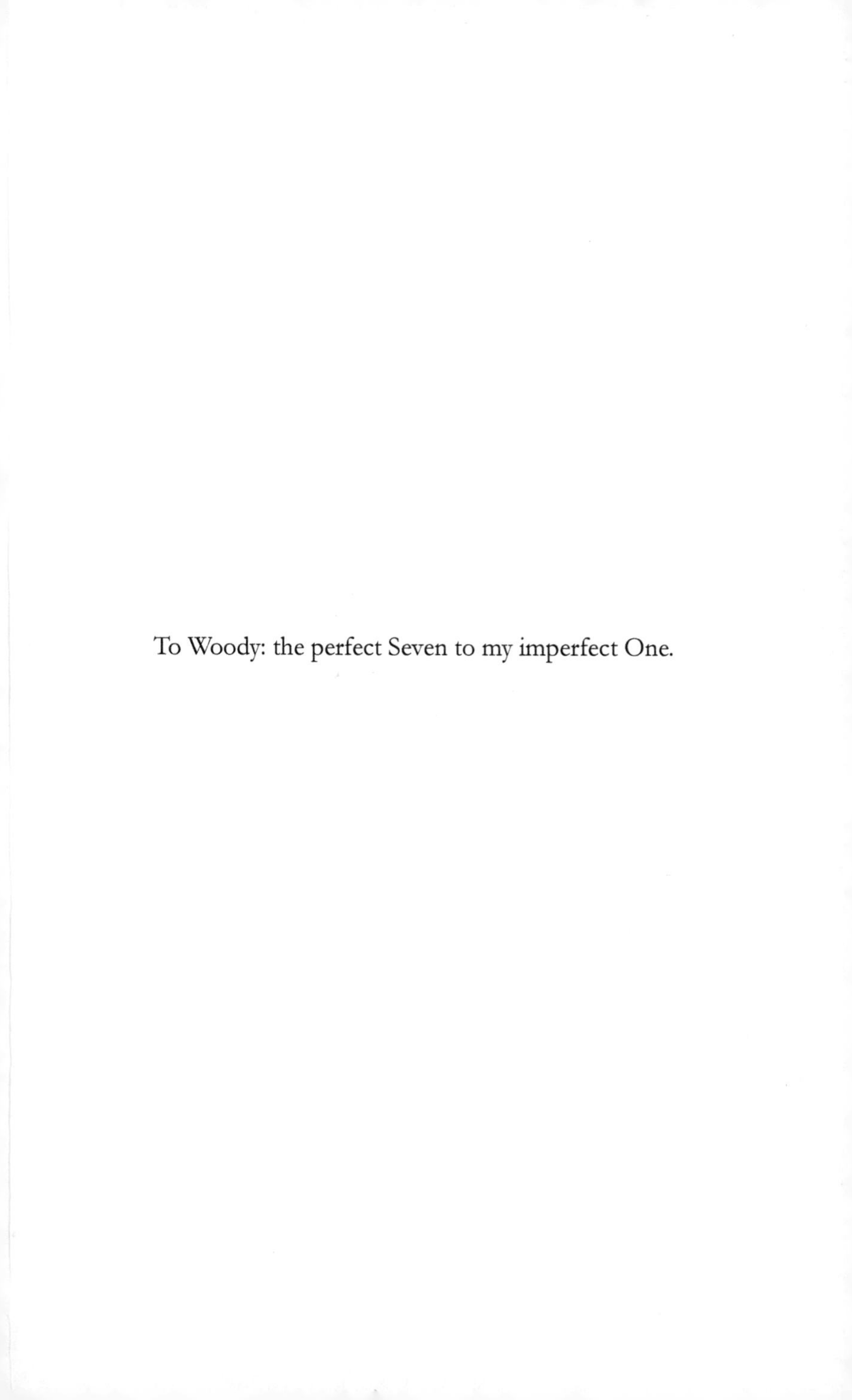

To Woody: the perfect Seven to my imperfect One.

There would be no need for love if perfection were possible. Love arises from our imperfection, from our being different and always in need of the forgiveness, encouragement and that missing half of ourselves that we are searching for, as the Greek myth tells us, in order to complete ourselves.
—Eugene Kennedy

While this story is based loosely on historic events, this is entirely a work of fiction. Names, characters, places, and incidents are the product of the author's imagination or are used fictitiously, and any resemblance to actual persons, living or dead, business establishments, events, or locales is entirely coincidental.

PART ONE

June 1960 - August 1962

CHAPTER 1

I waited for him on our front porch—something I'd done a hundred times. His old blue Ford chugged down our street of modest, red-brick houses. He parked and slid through the opening in the boxwood shrubs—a shortcut he'd created during the two years we'd been going together.

The sight of Stan gave me butterflies—his wavy hair, flashy smile, broad shoulders, and tanned arms. This time, though—on this June day a week before my high school graduation—it would be different. He took our front steps two at a time and planted a kiss on my forehead.

I didn't kiss him back.

"Stan," I said. I looked him in the eyes—those beautiful blue-green eyes. "I have something...."

He interrupted, out of breath. "Don't say a word."

"But wait, I want to...."

He held up a hand to silence me. "Close your eyes."

"Stan. I need...."

"Come on, Maggie." He smiled, his face full of mischief. "Close. Your. Eyes." He was gentle, but it was a command.

I obeyed. I could feel him close, smell his Old Spice aftershave, hear his breathing, quick and heavy.

"Now—give me your hand."

I held up my right hand.

"No," he said. "Your left hand. No peeking."

"Stan, what are you…?"

I held up my left hand. He hummed as he slipped a ring on my ring finger. "There! Open your eyes."

He was beaming.

I looked down at my hand. "An opal. It's my...."

"Birthstone—I do pay attention. Your sister helped me with the size." He seemed pleased with himself. "Do you like it?"

"Stan, it's…just...beautiful."

"It's not technically an engagement ring—couldn't afford a diamond. But the jeweler said it's the finest opal he's ever seen. It's not flashy, but...."

"Stan…I don't know what to say."

"Say you'll wear it." He leaned in, twining his fingers into mine, and whispered, "Think of me…how much you mean to me. How much…I love you."

I couldn't speak. I could hardly breathe. I nodded.

"Something's…what is it? Maggie?"

"Oh, Stan." His fingers were still locked in mine. I led him to the porch swing. "Here, sit down."

We glided back and forth, our bodies touching, the way we'd done on so many summer nights. The chains holding the swing creaked and groaned rhythmically from their hooks in the porch ceiling. My throat tightened. The tears I'd promised not to cry welled up.

"Something's wrong." He loosened his hand.

"Stan, it isn't you." I couldn't look at him. "It's me. I need to tell you something. You need to listen."

"Jesus, Maggie, you're crying. What's happened?"

I caught my breath. "I've made a decision…about my future." I felt the tears and took a few deep breaths.

Stan pulled out his handkerchief and handed it to me. Telling my family had been one thing—that hadn't been easy. But telling Stan—how many times I'd tried. I'd put it off for too long.

"There's no easy way, so I'm just going to say it. I've decided to enter the convent."

"Yeah, right." He laughed. "And I'm going to be the next Pope."

"I'm not kidding." I met his gaze.

Stan's smile faded, his eyes darkened. "You have to be kidding."

"I'm sorry. I'm not. On September 8, I'll enter the convent of the Sisters of Saint Mary."

The swing stopped abruptly—he planted his feet on the floor. "You're not joking?"

I shook my head.

"Don't you think you owe me an explanation?" His voice rose. "When did you decide this—*big decision*?"

I didn't answer.

"How long have you been stringing me along?"

"I only just decided—for sure—a few weeks ago."

"A few *weeks* ago?" The anger in his voice startled me.

"I told Sister Helen first—my drama teacher—then my parents, then yesterday we met with the Mother Superior at the Motherhouse. There are papers to sign and stuff to order in the next two months. It's been really fast." I tried to get the swing moving again.

"All this time, you've kept this little secret from me? How could you?"

"I can't explain it, even to myself," I said, swallowing hard and dabbing at my eyes with the handkerchief. "You're the first one I've told—after the Sisters and my family."

"Great. Is that supposed to make me feel better?" He got quiet, then stood up and paced back and forth, his hands in his jeans pockets. "You've told Jack?"

"He's my brother, Stan, of course I told him."

"He's my best friend. Why couldn't he…?"

"I made him swear—don't think he didn't want to. Jack's not exactly happy about this."

"You thought I would be? Jesus, I've been a fool. Your whole family knew and I didn't? Your sister helped me pick out the ring. Why?" He stopped pacing and faced me. "You owe me more than *I can't explain it, Stan.*" He was deliberate, demanding. "I thought you and I were…come on, Maggie. Give me *something.*"

My mind was racing. *What could I say that would make sense? That I loved God more than I loved him? That I'd been thinking about this since sixth grade but had never told a soul? That I'd been called by God to be a nun—not in so many words, but still, a real call? That my Catholic religion taught that I needed to answer that call? All those things were true—at least I thought they were—but how could I say any of it to Stan?*

He stared at me, his brow furrowed, eyes squinting, as if I were a stranger. "How long have we been going together?"

"Two years, I guess."

"You *guess*?" He looked up, as if he were calculating. "Two years, three months, and seventeen days."

"You count the days?"

"It's an estimate." He leaned over me. "In all this time, you couldn't give me a *hint* that this was coming? I took you to prom, for God's sake." He sighed. "Maggie, look at me." He brushed his hair off his forehead.

I looked at him. His bright eyes were clouded. "The most I can say is—I've always known I had this calling," I said. "If I don't follow it, I'll never know who I am."

"God is calling you to be a nun? How in hell do you know that?"

"I told you—I can't explain. I've prayed about it. I've just got to do this. If I don't…."

"What? You'll go to hell?"

"Don't mock me, Stan—not you."

"Mock *you*? Who's mocking who here?"

Chapter 1

"Please. Listen. Like I told Mother Superior, I've tried to ignore the call for years," I said. "But in the last year, I've felt it at Mass, walking in the woods, during prayers. I finally feel ready." Stan wasn't Catholic—so he didn't understand my religious upbringing. Besides, what if this was all my imagination? "During the last two years, I put the idea aside. We've made such a good pair."

He scoffed.

"But I can't ignore it any longer. I wish I could—I don't know how to make you understand."

He looked confused, sad, angry. It broke my heart. I reached for his hand, he pulled away. "Come on, sit down next to me," I begged, wiping tears away.

Finally, he sat down. We glided back and forth without saying anything, without touching.

"You've always said you wanted to be a writer," Stan said.

"I do—at least I did—but this is a calling on a much higher level."

"What about college? Your dream to major in theater?"

A million thoughts were running through my head. Stan didn't know how my Mom laughed at my dreams of becoming a writer or an actress—or how she held up my older sister, Marianne, as the perfect daughter. But I was not a *summa cum laude* student like Marianne. I didn't want to go to nursing school like she had done.

"You know I'd need a scholarship to go to college," I said. "I'm not scholarship material—not like Marianne."

"That's bull," Stan said. "You're just as smart as your sister."

"Then why did I fail the math part of the test?" I hadn't planned to tell him that.

"I'm surprised. I don't understand...." Stan looked out to the street and watched three neighborhood kids tossing a ball.

"I'd have to wait a whole year to take that test again—and fail. So now I'm following a different dream. I heard a voice, months ago, at church."

"Now you're hearing voices?" He sounded cynical, scornful.

"I don't expect you to understand." I couldn't explain how I'd been praying—asking God to show me what to do. *Give me your whole self—nothing less*, the voice had said. Was it God—or my imagination? I needed to find out. "There's only one way for me to know if I'm being called to give my whole self to God—and that's to become a nun," I said. "I don't know what else to say." I managed to squeak out.

"I thought you loved me—that we were—was that a dream?"

"No! I did." I sniffed and drew in a deep breath. "I do love you." I touched his face. Seeing the sadness in his eyes, I was tempted to say it was all a big mistake. But I'd committed—been accepted by—the Sisters. I couldn't go back on my word.

"If you love me, call it off."

He must be reading my mind. "I can't. I have to do this."

We sat together without speaking. I stopped crying, listened to his breathing, felt the warmth of his body next to me.

He sat up straight. "Remember when we saw that movie—*The Nun's Story*—not more than six months ago?"

I remembered—Stan's shock and anger after that movie had taken me by surprise.

"Audrey Hepburn…joins a convent and gets sent to some God-awful place."

"The Congo."

"Where she's humiliated, mistreated—not by the natives, but by the other nuns." Stan's voice was rising, gaining energy. "What happens to her? She leaves—broken." He looked at me. "Am I right?"

"That was different—the story was set forty years ago." I felt more sobs catch in my throat. "It was just a movie. Things aren't like that—where I'm going."

"How do you know?"

"I just do," I said, stifling sobs. *Did I know?*

Minutes passed. Stan took a deep breath. "I know you, Megs," he said. "You're so damn stubborn. I'm not going to try to change your mind—not right now." He looked at the opal on my finger. "I've been saving that, for just the right moment." His laugh came from deep inside. "I rehearsed a speech. I was thinking of it as a pre-engagement ring. The joke's on me, isn't it?"

"Stan. I'm so sorry." I started to slip the ring off. "Maybe it's better if I…."

"Don't insult me!" It was the first time Stan had raised his voice to me. Immediately he regained his composure. "The ring is for you. Only you."

He took my hands, his eyes filling with tears. "I'm leaving now, Megs."

"Please—don't go."

"You haven't seen the last of me." He squeezed my hands so tight it hurt. I winced. He let go, stood up, and hurried down the steps. He slipped through the hedges, slammed his car door, and roared off down the street.

Stan called me twice a week—from mid-June until early August. Could we go for a ride, get a pizza, catch a concert in the park? Could he just come over and talk? Each time, I begged off—then hung up and cried my eyes out. My parents and my sister and brother tried to convince me to see him. I was afraid I wouldn't stay firm. Finally, I told Stan it was no use—I wasn't going to change my mind.

Most Saturday afternoons, I heard his voice in our back yard as he shot baskets with Jack. I watched from my bedroom window, tears falling, as he and Jack jostled. I admired his strong arms and bare back, his golden tan, his gentle laugh, his graceful athletic leaps, twists, and turns. The more I tried to separate myself from him, the more helplessly in love I fell.

I remembered the first day I'd ever seen Stan—paired with Jack in a tennis tournament at the Y. I was finishing sophomore year, Jack and Stan were about to graduate. Stan had returned Jack's final serve with a volley, beating Jack, and advancing in the tournament.

I'd liked Stan's smile, how his sandy hair fell in waves in the sunlight. But it wasn't just his perfect tan and clean good looks. Was it his eyes? Or the way he leaned in to speak with Jack, face to face?

I'd followed Jack off the court. "Who was that guy?"

"Wouldn't you like to know?" Jack loved to tease me. "Interested in him, little sister?"

"You know I am."

"We made a pact," Jack had said, "there at the net, to team up as doubles partners and win the next tournament. We're unbeatable." Jack wasn't boasting—just stating a fact.

Before long, Stan was spending his free time at our house. I was shy at first, then glad to be invited into their conversations, as Jack's friends hung out on our front porch or shot baskets in our back yard. I avoided playing tennis opposite Stan—but he insisted and I finally gave in. He was a good teacher, never lording his talent or strength over me.

"I'll never be able to play like you. What's the use?" I said one day, after losing badly in three sets.

"Don't you want to get better? Besides, it's just fun to be with you. Next time, I promise to let you win."

I loved how Stan could say, "It's fun to be with you," and not sound phony or turn red in the neck. By the end of summer, we were holding hands as we walked from the Y to my house most evenings before supper.

"You're the first non-Catholic I've ever been around," I told Stan one day, as we sat on the porch swing. "My Dad thinks I should convert you."

Stan took my hand in his. "Is that so? Do I need converting?"

"No, you're fine. It's just—Catholics aren't supposed to date Protestants. The mixed-marriage stigma and all that."

He dropped my hand. "That hits a nerve."

"I'm sorry. It was stupid—I don't know what I'm talking about." I knew little about Stan's home life, except that his father did not live with them and his mother had to work to support them. "If you don't want to talk about it, I understand."

Stan sighed, then picked up my hand again. "My Dad was brought up Catholic, my Mom wasn't, so when they married, she had to promise to bring us up in the Catholic Church."

When he didn't continue, I risked asking, "What happened?"

"My Dad showed his true colors as a cheat and a liar. I don't blame my Mom for giving him the boot. I just wish he'd left before he spent everything on booze and gambling."

"I didn't know." I held his hand tightly.

"Now you do."

That explained why Stan had not made plans for college, why he worked full-time at the bowling alley—so he could go to classes at night. We'd dated for over two years, but we were not love-struck teenagers. We took walks together, went to football games, listened to music. On Saturday nights, Stan would come over and we'd play records, sneak a few beers from my parents' fridge, and slow-dance in our basement.

I was walking away from my best friend. Every night I lay in bed, praying for strength. I missed Stan—the life we had together. If I trusted the call was real—and I did—then I needed to go through with it.

One Sunday afternoon, a week before I was off to the convent, I heard our Irish Setter, Danny, barking at the front door.

"Hey Boy, it's only me," Stan said.

My heart pounded. I opened the door and invited him in.

"I know you don't want to see me, but I have something to tell you." He avoided making eye contact. Danny loved Stan and sat obediently while Stan scratched his ears.

"It's good to see you." I stumbled over my words. "I've missed you...."

He cut me off. "I won't stay long."

We stood awkwardly in the living room. I was glad I was the only one home.

Stan eyed my opal ring. I'd worn it all summer.

"Come and sit down." I tried to take his arm and lead him to our sofa but he pulled away.

"I've enlisted in the Navy. It's the only way I'll be able to afford an education. My Mom is in tears." He smiled gently, then his face turned serious. "She'll get over it. It isn't as if I'm walling myself up inside a convent."

"Is that supposed to be funny?"

"Sorry—I shouldn't have said that."

We looked at each other. The upward curve of Stan's mouth was permanent, even when he was angry. The sight of him—his blue-green eyes and wavy hair, streaked blond from the sun, made my stomach dance.

"When do you leave? Where will you go?"

He took a step back, looking down at Danny, sprawled at his feet. "I leave next week for Boot Camp—Great Lakes Training Station in Chicago. After that, who knows?" He smiled. "*Join the Navy. See the world.*" His smile turned to a frown. "Funny—I'm going to see the world, and you're going to leave it."

"Will you write me?"

"Will *you* write *me*?" Stan shot back.

Just like the tennis volleys he is so good at, I thought. *Would I write him?*

"Probably not," I said. "Maybe—I don't know—if I'm allowed."

"I thought as much. I hope Jack will. I hope I haven't lost both my best friends."

"Stan, I'm so sorry. I wish...."

He cut me off. "Listen," he said. "I've got to go. Mom wants to make up for all the time we never spent together while I was growing up and she was working at the Post Office."

What a beautiful guy, how lucky some girl is going to be, I thought.

He looked at me, his eyes narrowing. "This isn't over, Megs. I'm not giving up on us." He leaned in, put his arms around my waist, and drew me toward him. He held me tight and kissed me harder and longer than he ever had before.

I locked my arms around his neck. I kissed him back. I felt his heartbeat, the rise and fall of his breathing. He must have felt my heart thumping.

Eventually, he pulled away. His fingers brushed my cheek. "You see?" he said. "*This* is how I know it isn't over. Not by a long shot." Then he was gone.

I don't know how long it was before I could move. I had no words to describe the sensation I felt. I'd never lived through an earthquake, but I was feeling one inside of me—a series of tremors and ripples. I had to sit down.

The days before leaving home were a confusing mix of anticipation and heartbreak, knowing I might never see Stan again.

CHAPTER 2

It was a twenty-minute ride to the Convent of St. Mary, on the edge of downtown. Nobody said a word. Dad drove. Jack sulked in the back seat next to me. In the front seat, Mom blew her nose and dabbed at her eyes. The last thing she'd wanted was for one of her daughters to enter the convent.

"You need to go to college," Mom used to say. "I never had the chance—none of my sisters did either." She'd had hopes that her girls would get a good education—make money. "Be a teacher—a nurse—even a secretary," she'd told us. "You have so many advantages we didn't have." That stemmed from the years she'd spent motherless, during the Great Depression, her German immigrant father always trying to make ends meet. Mom had given up her secretarial job to marry my gentle, fun-loving Irish father and raise a family. My father's accounting business paid the bills, but there never seemed to be enough income to suit Mom.

I knew she'd hoped I'd marry well ("Stan is a nice boy, but how ambitious is he?") and have kids. Mom was a church-goer, but she questioned many Church practices. "Men have all the power—the Church is no exception," she used to say. No wonder she didn't warm to my decision.

Even Dad—he understood—was silent. Proud of his Irish heritage, he was happy that one of his girls would become a nun. Not only was the foundress of the Sisters of St. Mary Irish—but Dad was constantly boasting about his two Irish aunts who were nuns—one still alive and kicking in Ireland. He loved the idea of keeping it in the family. I was fulfilling one of his dreams. Still, now that the day had arrived, he was unusually quiet.

My older sister, Marianne, met us at the convent with her husband, Ted. I tried to convince her it wasn't necessary but she'd insisted. Jack worked late at the bowling alley, and because I'd insisted Jack be there, we were cutting it close.

I was trying to balance the dread I felt at leaving my family with the anxiety around being on time. While Dad parked the car, I went ahead up the front steps of the main building—a yellow-brick fortress with a shiny copper dome, shaded by majestic oak trees. A tall brick wall surrounded the convent grounds—an entire city block—with wrought iron gates guarding the entrance. I was eager to get on with it, whatever *it* might be. I'd brought along my overnight case—everything else had already been shipped in a steamer trunk.

I spotted Marianne and Ted near the front door. "We got nervous when everyone else went inside and you still hadn't shown up," Marianne said. "We thought you got cold feet."

Ted rolled his eyes and forced a smile, as if to say, "She said it, not me."

Marianne saw Mom and Dad and Jack coming up the steps. "Don't cry, Mom," she said. "Knowing Maggie, it may be a short stay. Right, Jack?"

Jack frowned. "Don't ask me, Marianne. I'm just along for the ride."

I had never understood why Marianne—five years my senior—did not get along with me. She was much smarter and always brought home a perfect report card. That should have made her feel secure about herself. Instead, she seemed to delight in pointing out my limitations. Nothing I did met her approval. Eventually I'd given up trying to be her friend and settled for peaceful co-existence—I wasn't successful at that either.

"All right, let's go in," Dad said. "We're late."

My father, the peacemaker.

A sister waited for us inside the leaded-glass front door. She introduced herself but I was so distracted I didn't get her name. "You must be Margaret Ann," she said, reaching out to take my hand.

"I'm Maggie—Maggie Walsh." I followed her inside to a large foyer tiled in marble and dominated by a larger-than-life statue of the Blessed Virgin.

My parents caught up with me. "This is my family," I said.

Mom managed a smile as she shook the nun's hand.

Dad adopted his businessman's demeanor. "Ed Walsh, Maggie's dad. Good to meet you."

Marianne, seven months pregnant, locked arms with Ted, while Jack hung to one side, hands sunk in his pockets.

"We weren't sure you were coming," the sister said, her words echoing in the foyer. "You're the last one, so we'll need to move quickly if you're to be on time for vespers. She looked at my parents. "That's our prayer before supper."

"We got here as soon as we could," I said. Was I already in trouble?

The sister ushered my family towards the cloister garden. "It's such a warm day, all the families are outside." She looked back at me. "Sister Anita will take you to your cell to get dressed."

"Dressed? Now?"

I watched my family walking away, down a long hallway. Jack looked back with his "What-the-hell-is-going-on?" face.

A tall novice with a long, oval face and dark, bushy eyebrows tapped me on the shoulder. By the time I looked back, my family had disappeared.

"Margaret Ann?" the tall sister asked. "I should call you Sister Clare. I'm Sister Anita, your senior novice." She picked up my overnight case. "Follow me. We don't have a lot of time."

"Excuse me, Sister Anita. I'm not Sister Clare. Clare is my Mom's name."

"Didn't they tell you? That's your name now." She glided down the hallway and up a flight of wide, marble steps. I was out of breath keeping up with her. "There's another postulant named Margaret higher in seniority. We choose your mother's name—as long as that is not already taken."

How would Mom react? Probably more tears. We climbed another flight and reached a corridor leading to a room the size of a walk-in closet.

"This is the cell you'll be sharing with a first-year novice. Normally you'd share it with me, but there aren't enough of us senior novices to go around—your class is the largest one yet." She pointed to the bed. "So. Your postulant dress is there, stockings and petticoat on the chair, shoes underneath. Cuffs and collar, on the dresser. Once you've changed, I'll help you pin on the veil. I'll wait outside. Open the door when you're ready."

The hem of Sister Anita's habit swept the hardwood floor; her white veil lifted in the breeze she created as she left the room.

I sat down on the bed to catch my breath. It was quiet, except for the creaking of the narrow bed. On the pillow lay a nameplate in black lettering: *Sister Clare.*

"Oh my God," I said out loud. It was happening too fast. The postulant outfit, the black stockings, the cape. A new name? Sister?

Then, I spotted the shoes. At my going-away party, I'd held up the long underwear, the black robe, the granny shoes. I'd modeled them for my girlfriends, my aunts and cousins, Marianne and Mom. We'd laughed till our sides hurt. Mom and I had picked out the shoes in the heat of summer. We thought they were hilarious then—now I had to put them on.

Chapter 2

When Sister Anita tapped at the door, I was still sitting in my blue shirtwaist dress, sheer nylons, and navy pumps. "Be right there," I said. I slipped out of my dress, unsnapped the clasps on my garter belt and peeled my nylons off, pulled up the black stockings, and snapped them in place. They would hide my tan (not good) and absolve me from shaving my legs (not bad).

I slipped into the petticoat and postulant dress, zipping it up the front. It had long sleeves with white cuffs that buttoned at the wrist and a separate cape that snapped at the neck. I sat on the creaky chair, stepped into the shoes, and tied the laces.

Sister Anita peeked in, sized up the situation, and came in. She fastened the white cuffs and collar. The veil, like my first-communion veil, only black, was gathered into a ruffled crown. "Do you have naturally curly hair?" Sister Anita asked as she pulled hairpins from the drawer.

I got a close-up view of Sister Anita's fair face, her hazel eyes, and long, dark lashes. Her thick, un-plucked eyebrows were partly obscured by a white headpiece that covered her forehead and stood up like a tiny, starched mountain peak. Her face flushed as she balanced the bobby pins between her teeth. "The curls are lovely," she said.

Days earlier, Mom had given me my last home permanent—tight curls—they'd have to last a while. "No, I'm afraid not," I said. "Poker straight, ditchwater blonde—that's me." I laughed. "My Mom gave me a perm." A jolt of sadness spiraled up my spine. I missed Mom's touch already.

"She did a good job," Sister Anita said. "It looks natural." She turned me around. "Let's look at you." She eyed me from head to toe. "Good. You're ready. Follow me, Sister."

Halfway down the last flight of stairs, Sister Anita said, "I almost forgot. You'll need to give your class ring to your mother. And your wrist watch."

I fingered my high school class ring. Stan's ring flashed into my mind. It was tucked away in the top drawer of my dresser at home. "What will happen to my clothes?" I asked.

"You won't need them. They'll be safe in your trunk—in the attic. Eventually, we'll send them to our missions in the Philippines."

I followed Sister Anita down another flight of steps and along a series of corridors. She flung open a heavy door and we stepped into the garden. Mom and Dad were perched on a bench, holding hands, of all things. Marianne sat next to them, Ted stood behind her, massaging her shoulders. Jack was near the garden entrance, pacing, smoking a cigarette. He looked in my direction, then past me.

He doesn't recognize me, I thought. "Jack!" I caught his eye.

Jack stubbed out his cigarette and came toward me. "You have got to be kidding."

There was no time to ease him into the shock. "You have to help Mom through this. She listens to you."

"Why me? You're the one leaving home." He noticed my pleading look. "Okay, I'll do what I can—but don't ask me to like that outfit."

"You don't know the first thing about fashion."

I walked with Jack to the bench and stood there for a few seconds before the rest of my family recognized me.

For once, Marianne was speechless.

"Here I am. How do I look?"

Mom was the first to speak. "Those shoes. Oh my."

"Excuse me," Sister Anita said, "I'm needed inside. Five minutes, Sister." She left, her habit sweeping the sidewalk as she walked.

"Sister Anita is my senior novice," I said, "like a big sister. She helped me get dressed."

Marianne emitted a cry at the mention of *big sister*. "I hope you won't forget about *me*, Maggie." She pulled a hankie from her purse and dabbed at her eyes.

"Marianne! Not in a million years."

"What did they do with your clothes?" Jack asked.

"In my trunk."

"You'd better keep them somewhere where you can find them when you bust out of this place. You don't want to be seen on the street in that costume."

"Jack," Dad broke in, "you're not helping." He stood up and put his arm around me. "You look fine, kid. Just fine. We're so proud of you."

"Thanks, Dad." I squeezed his hand, then sat down between Mom and Marianne on the bench. "Mom," I said, a lump forming in my throat, "I want you to take my class ring—and my watch." I slid the ring off and unlatched the watch my parents had given me on my sixteenth birthday.

Mom nodded, took the ring and watch, then brushed tears away with the back of her hand.

"Mom. Please don't cry." How many times had she said that to me? *"Don't cry, Maggie. Be strong."*

Mom had been practicing how to be strong since she was twelve, when her own mother had died of cancer. She and her older sister, my Aunt Frances, had helped raise a younger sister. Mom dropped out of high school to take a business course so she could get a job as a stenographer.

I could remember only one other time I'd seen Mom cry—when Aunt Frances died suddenly of a heart attack. Mom had turned to me after the funeral and said, "A part of me is lost forever."

Does she feel that way now?

I squeezed Mom's hand and put my other hand over Marianne's. She grabbed it. "Be sure to let me know the minute it's time for the baby," I said. "I'll pray for you every day."

Marianne sucked in a sob. "I'll miss you, Maggie. Really. You don't know how much."

Seriously? Maybe she really meant it. Or maybe it was the hormones or the fear of becoming a mother. The years of sibling rivalry had jaded us both.

Just then, a group of sisters in black veils, called "professed sisters" because they had professed their vows, approached us. I recognized them as our teachers from Marywood High.

"Look at you!" It was Sister Helen, my high school drama teacher. "The day has finally come, hasn't it?" She shook Mom and Dad's hands. "We hoped Marianne would be the one to join us. Such a dedicated student. So cooperative." She smiled, took my hands, and nodded to Marianne, then Jack.

"We never dreamed Maggie would do this, Sister," Marianne said. "I mean, she was in trouble more than she was on the honor roll, wasn't she?"

"Maggie's one and only love was drama. All four years, isn't that right, dear?" Sister Helen said. "Her decision has delighted us all—she seems determined, and I have no doubt she'll succeed."

At least Sister Helen believes I can do this, I thought.

Jack hung in the background, his hands in his pockets, looking uncomfortable. Jack and I might never again have time to ourselves. At least for the next three years, I would see my family for only a few hours on visiting day, one Sunday a month. Could I make that sacrifice? Only God knew.

"We will pray for you every day," Sister Helen said. "Though we won't be able to talk to one another for the next three years—until you wear the black veil."

"Why not?"

"It's the Rule," Sister Helen answered, as if that explained everything. "But we'll pray for you, dear, and your family. As a matter of fact," Sister Helen said pointedly to my parents, "your daughter will be part of *our* family now."

That was enough to start Mom crying again. I decided not to tell her I'd been given her name. I'd save it for a letter. She could cry in private.

Sister Anita reappeared. "Vespers will begin soon. Time to say good-bye to your folks, Sister." She stepped back and waited.

I felt nailed to the concrete.

Dad gave me a strong hug and kissed my forehead. "Bye, Megs. Don't take any wooden nickels, kid. Be sure to write if you get work."

Dad—always quoting his favorite radio comedians, Bob and Ray. It was a relief to laugh.

I turned to Mom. "I'll write as often as I can. I'll see you in a few weeks." We hugged. "I love you, Mom," I whispered.

She nodded and stepped away, linking arms with Dad.

Marianne was tearing up too. She held me, her bulging stomach between us. We hadn't hugged since her wedding. "Good luck," she said. "I hope this is what you want."

Would Marianne ever stop doubting me?

"Hey, big brother." I gave Jack a gentle punch in the chest. He didn't punch me back. We hugged for a long time.

He whispered, "I'll never forgive you for this."

I couldn't look at him.

In the distance, a bell chimed. Sister Anita touched my arm. "We need to go. That bell means vespers is about to start."

I turned to see my family leaving through the side gate.

CHAPTER 3

Before I could give in to tears, Sister Anita led me to the hallway outside chapel. I got in line with the other postulants. The professed sisters and novices were already kneeling in their places as we processed up the aisle to our pews in the center of chapel. I was struck by the towering pillars surrounding the altar, the white marble sanctuary, the polished wooden pews, the rows of choir stalls lining the sides of the chapel—a scene from the Middle Ages.

I listened to the women's voices chanting Latin verses back and forth—Old Testament verses called psalms, chosen to fit the time of day and the seasons of the year. As I settled into my place, I lifted the top of the pew to reveal a storage bin for books. Its hinges creaked softly. I found a black leather prayer book and opened it—my new name had been written on the inside cover in pencil. I flipped to a ribbon marker and found the Latin verses.

The nuns' lovely voices spread over the chapel like a soft blanket. With each new psalm, the sisters would stand, bow, and sit down again.

The chanting, the graceful movements, women's voices praying in unison—was this what I'd been longing for—without even knowing it? I felt transported to another world. I forgot the separation from my family, the scratchy wool outfit I was wearing. I was about to lose my identity, yet in the midst of all this strangeness and uncertainty, I felt I'd come home.

The nuns' soft chants reverberated around the chapel and the late-afternoon sun streamed through the stained-glass windows, casting an amber glow across the choir stalls and spilling onto the yellow and white squares of tile on the polished floor. It was comforting—exciting—to think I would spend hours, days, years absorbed in the beauty, the mystery of this place.

After vespers, a novice led us down a flight of steps to a ground-floor classroom painted a drab olive green, crowded with rows of student desks. Mother Loretta, the Mistress of Novices, stood behind a podium, smiling. She directed us to sit at the desks.

"Sisters," Mother Loretta said, "there is much to learn about our customs—beginning with meals. They may not be what you're used to, but you'll feel at home in no time." She looked around the room. "There will be time tomorrow to tour the convent—the classrooms and labs, the music room, the hair-washing room…." She winked. "Next to this classroom you'll find the mission room—we collect items for our sisters working in the Philippines. You'll want to see the laundry—one of the novices will give you a tour of that when it's in full force. And our library—we have one of the few Braille libraries in the city. You'll notice people—seculars—using it often. Be cordial but not too friendly."

Mother Loretta's steady hand-tapping on the podium made me wonder if she was nervous.

"For now, though, let's talk about the proper behavior for the refectory. Can anyone tell me the meaning of *refectory*?"

Dead silence.

"*Refectory* refers to the dining room. It's a monastic term. The Latin means, roughly, *a place to be restored*." She leaned over the podium and poked at the air with her index finger. "Here's another phrase I want you all to remember: 'The perfection of our ordinary actions.' Repeat it, everyone."

"The perfection of our ordinary actions," we all said, mostly in unison.

"Good!" Mother smiled. "Saying the words aloud is the first step."

As she spoke, I noticed how her expressions changed quickly—serious, penetrating eyes one minute, a smile the next—sometimes a wink. "From now on, Sisters, everything you do will become part of your path to perfection and holiness." She looked toward a frowning postulant seated across from me. "That's right, Sister Angela. No need to frown. Even an ordinary act such as eating what's on your plate can lead to perfection."

Sister Angela's cheeks turned bright red. She hung her head.

Expect to have Mother embarrass you in public, I thought, feeling bad for poor Sister Angela and reminding myself to be careful. I knew how it felt to be publicly shamed. Marianne had made fun of my poems. A few of my teachers, too, had played that game over the years, comparing Marianne and me, me never quite measuring up.

"Most meals are taken in silence, accompanied by spiritual reading," Mother said. "Only those serving the meal are permitted to talk, and only in a whisper. We've become good at sign language. You'll pick it up quickly. But today is a special day, so you may talk at supper. I'm sure you all have a lot to say." Another wink.

"You are asked to take something of everything passed to you," she said. "In the spirit of poverty, take only what you can finish." Mother looked at Sister Angela, who shrunk in her seat. "Observe the novices," she said, "they will help you learn the routines."

Mother put her finger to her lips to signal it was time to keep silence. The novices floated by us in the hallway and Mother motioned us to follow. We marched into the refectory behind them.

The novices stood straight and still at their places. I was puzzled by the absence of chairs, until I noticed a stool under each place-setting at the table. We searched the tables for our names. With some relief, I found my name taped to a napkin ring. I was between Sister Angela and Mary, now "Sister Pauline," who had lost her name to another postulant named Mary further up the line of seniority.

Once we were at our places, Mother rang a hand bell, cleared her throat, and led us in prayer. There was a loud rumble as the stools were pulled out, followed by a swish of habits and a clicking of the rosary beads that hung at the novices' sides, as they slid onto their stools with effortless grace. We new postulants followed suit and sat down, too, though not being nearly as orderly—bumping each other, getting our skirts caught under the legs of the stools, dragging our veils across the place-settings. A few of us stifled giggles—some more successfully than others.

We all settled, everyone arranging themselves perfectly, sitting up straight, facing forward. I was fascinated by the regimented movements, the order and neatness of it all. My Mom would have loved this part. For her, knowing what to expect and being sure how to act had its merits. Mother Loretta's explanation that we needed *to be about perfection of our ordinary actions* meant small actions as well as big ones. *I can do this*, I thought.

Mother stood and tapped on the table with her ring. The novices rose. Everyone stood if Mother stood, sat if Mother sat—as if she were royalty. "Stay seated, Sisters. I simply wish to say we have permission to talk this evening, in honor of our thirty new postulants. Welcome to the Convent of Our Lady."

The novices turned to us. We gazed at the smiling faces surrounded in white. There must have been forty or more of them, in their white veils. It was like something out of a movie. Surreal. Or, 'heavenly,' maybe that was the word.

The server novices brought out large platters, steaming with slices of roast beef, and started them down both sides of the refectory table. They brought bowls of mashed potatoes with little lakes of butter, lima beans, corn, homemade bread, and plates of butter patties. Real butter—not like the margarine at home. I filled my plate and passed the dishes on to Sister Angela.

"No one's gonna mind if I skip these lima beans," Sister Angela grumbled as she passed the plate along. Already, she was cutting corners in the perfection of *her* ordinary actions.

I slid a shimmering block of red Jell-O onto my already-full plate and daubed a spoonful of gravy on the potatoes, trying to keep it from running into the bread or Jell-O. But it all swam together. It tasted good.

Once most of the sisters had cleaned their plates, the servers delivered homemade apple pie on dessert plates, followed by hot coffee—black or with cream—and more water. I was full but found room for pie. I was glad my postulant dress had an elastic waist.

Sister Angela jabbed me with her elbow. Tears were falling down her cheeks. "Apple pie," she stuttered, pointing to her dessert. "My Mom's favorite. Big ol' apple tree on our farm." She sniffed and wiped her cheeks on her cape. "God help me," she said.

I couldn't console Angela. I was welling up with tears too. We pierced the warm pie crust and swallowed the apple slices in silence.

Just as I was wondering what to do with my dishes, I felt a warm hand on my shoulder. I turned to find Sister Anita, my senior novice, leaning over to take my plate.

"Let me help you with these," she said. She led me to a side table holding a dishpan of soapy water, next to another filled with clear, hot water. In between was another bowl with a spatula for food scraps. "Once you're finished washing," Sister Anita said, "dry the next sister's dishes. Efficient, isn't it?" It was.

I couldn't wait to tell Marianne and Jack about this system. We had always squabbled over doing the dishes. Marianne insisted on washing, meaning she didn't have to put anything away. When Jack—who set and cleared the table—was back outside shooting baskets, I was still in the kitchen. Jack would hate this convent system—but then, Jack would hate everything here.

I hadn't thought about Jack or my family for over two hours. What were they doing? Were Jack and my parents at our favorite restaurant overlooking the Ohio River? Was Marianne elevating her swollen feet, watching the news about John F. Kennedy's run for president? That had become a big story, and like all Catholics, our family was following the race closely.

If I were home, I thought, I'd probably be sitting on the porch with Jack, listening to him talk politics. Jack still had another year before he could vote—but he was involved, pinning his hopes on JFK. Kennedy leaned toward civil rights issues dear to Jack's heart.

I wondered about Stan too, somewhere far away, training to be a sailor. If it hadn't been for me, he'd be sitting with Jack on our front porch at this moment. "You only have yourself to blame, Megs," Jack had said about Stan's snap decision to join the Navy.

Did Jack miss me? Would he pass by my room on his way to bed, see it empty and dark? Would he finally shed a tear?

"Sister Clare, did you hear me?" Sister Anita said.

"Sorry?"

"Take the clean dishes back to your place. It's almost time to go up to the community room," she said. "I usually stop in chapel for a short visit, if there's time. Would you like to come?"

"Yes." For the second time on what was becoming a very long day, I tried to keep up with Sister Anita as she took the steps to chapel without effort. She slipped into her stall.

There were several other nuns kneeling in silent prayer. I stood looking at them for a few seconds, not sure where to go. Then I remembered I had a pew of my own, way up in front. I walked the long center aisle, knelt on one knee to honor the presence of God—known as genuflecting—and knelt on the cushioned kneeler in my pew.

I folded my hands and waited. An occasional cough echoed in the chapel's vaulted ceiling. Otherwise, not a sound. I knelt there, staring at the flickering red sanctuary light hanging above the altar.

"I don't know what I'm doing here, God," I prayed. "But I want to please you. I'm here—the rest is up to you. Amen."

I made the sign of the cross to seal my prayer, noticing from the corner of my eye that my novice was leaving her stall. I stood in the aisle and looked up at the larger-than-life marble statue of Jesus on the cross, suspended over the altar. What cross would God ask me to carry? I touched my knee to the floor, stood, turned, and followed Sister Anita out of chapel, ready for whatever came next.

CHAPTER 4

Sister Anita led me upstairs for recreation. The community room was large and long, filled with tables and buzzing with activity—novices getting out sewing baskets, setting up game boards or playing cards, and introducing themselves to the new postulants. Still, I felt strangely alone—aware I was in a different time zone—no radio, television, or telephones, no friends or family—none of my own, familiar things. Sister Anita led me to a spot in the middle of the long rows of tables.

"Get acquainted with Sister Delores," she said, pulling out a chair for me. "I'm going to get my sewing basket."

"This isn't the recreation I had in mind," Sister Delores whispered to me. I noticed her Southern accent. "Where's the badminton? Volley ball courts? I'd even settle for ping-pong." She slid her thick, horned-rimmed glasses up on her nose and fluffed her jet-black pageboy.

Where are you from?" I sat down next to her.

"Nashville," she said, a look of sadness in her face. "I've been cooped up in a train since yesterday."

"You rode the train—by yourself—all that way?"

"All that way, honey-bun. So, I'm in need of some exercise."

"Maybe they're taking it easy on the first night," I said.

"You think? Sewing baskets? I don't know about you, but I'll need to run around the block a few times."

When Sister Anita returned with her sewing basket, she sat down beside us and pulled out several pieces of clothing, a thimble, thread, and a small pair of scissors.

"Sister Anita," I said, "what do we do at recreation?"

"I know what you're thinking, Sister Clare." Sister Anita smiled. "I guess darning stockings and mending underwear seems boring, doesn't it?" She held up her threadbare stockings in one hand, and pulled a darning egg from her sewing basket with the other. "But don't worry. We also do lots of fun things. We sing, play cards. Do you play cards? Some sisters like to play board games. Or we just talk. To be honest," she pointed to her worn underwear, "sometimes we really do need to mend our clothes."

"I play cards," I said. "I spent a summer learning bridge. My brother, Jack, said that once I got to college, I couldn't survive without it. I guess I surprised him, didn't I? I won't be going to college, but at least I learned bridge."

"You'll be going to college," Sister Anita said, "taking classes here for the first few years, until you move up to the college campus for the last two years. Didn't you know that?"

"I guess I did." I was too embarrassed to say I didn't.

"There's a group of bridge players—hoping for a fourth," Sister Anita said, looking around the room. "There's Sister Julia." She waved Sister Julia over to our table.

A short novice with a round face came over and stood next to me.

"Sister Julia, this is Sister Clare," Sister Anita said.

Sister Julia clasped my shoulder. "Nice to finally meet you, Sister."

"You too," I said.

"This is going to work out well," Sister Anita said, "you'll be sharing a cell with Sister Julia. She'll help you get ready for bed, the bathroom—all that." She turned to Julia. "Sister Clare plays bridge."

"Really? Come, join us."

"Sorry for deserting you, Sister Delores," I said, as Julia whisked me across the room. Over my shoulder, I called out, "I hope you get to exercise before bedtime."

"Our fourth!" Sister Julia said as she delivered me to her table. "Sister Clare!"

The two other novices looked overjoyed to see me.

"Welcome," a bubbly novice said. "We've been waiting months for another player. Ever since we lost Sister....Ouch!" Suddenly she leaned down to rub her shin. "Ouch!"

It looked as if one of the novices had kicked her under the table.

"What do you mean—someone got lost?" I asked, wondering what could have precipitated the kick.

"Nothing. That is, we don't," the novice stuttered, "we're not supposed to...."

"She's no longer with us," Sister Julia whispered. "She left."

"Where did she go?"

"Home, of course," Sister Julia said. "We don't talk about them—the ones who leave." She whispered, "They're essentially dead to us."

Good God, I thought. *That can't be right.*

"You'll understand better, after you've been here a while," Sister Julia said, patting my hand.

Understand what? I thought. *Will I ever feel that way? If I decide to leave, will I be dead too?*

"Sister Clare is my new cell-mate," Julia said, giving me a once-over as she sat down. "We weren't sure you were coming."

"We just got here a little late. My brother...."

"Never mind. We're just glad you're here. A fourth at last! Sit, Sister Clare."

I sat down at the table to discover my hand had already been dealt.

"Let's start the bidding," Sister Julia said. "You open, Sister. What'll you bid?"

The novices knew their bridge but they were rusty on scoring, so they put me to work as scorekeeper. The time went by fast. At 8:25, in unison, the novices closed their sewing baskets, packed up their games, and folded their hands on their laps. We didn't finish our game, and put the cards away in the order of our hands. Sister Julia tucked the tally into her sewing basket, ready for us to pick up tomorrow evening. Playing in stages…one more thing to get used to.

One of the novices sat at the piano and played a hymn everyone knew. They sang in perfect, three-part harmony—it gave me goose bumps.

After the hymn, Mother Loretta stood and announced, "Postulants, your senior novices will take you to your cells and help you prepare for bed. When I ring this bell, the Grand Silence begins. All talking will cease for tonight."

The bell reverberating, I followed Sister Julia out of the community room and down the hallway to our cell. My blue dress and pumps had disappeared. "Has Sister Anita taken my clothes to my trunk in the attic?" I asked.

"Shhhhh!" Julia said sharply. "Grand Silence!"

"Sorry!"

Sister Julia disappeared behind the white curtain separating our beds. I stood in my cramped space, under the glaring fluorescent light, looking at the narrow bed, the creaky chair, and the small nightstand, wondering what to do next.

Grand Silence was anything but quiet. Water ran in the bathtubs across the hall from our cell. Novices in their nightcaps, eyes cast down, lined up in the hallway for a bath. The tubs were partitioned with plywood and the doors squeaked open and slammed shut, while sisters in black robes slipped in and out for their baths—all without a word. The novices padded along, clinking their toothbrushes in their drinking glasses.

Curtain rings jangled along the iron rods that held starched white curtains between each bed in the cells—a thin veil of privacy.

Sister Julia jingled the curtain between our beds, then peeked around it. At first, I didn't recognize her in her white nightgown and black robe. A night cap covered her head and forehead, spilled onto her shoulders, and tied under her chin.

Did the novices ever uncover their heads? Surely in the bathtub?

I opened the middle drawer of my nightstand to find six sets of cotton underwear—white tee shirts with undershorts that reached almost to my knees. There were garter belts and black stockings and, in the bottom drawer, nightgowns and black leather slippers. When I'd ordered them all from the nun's catalogue in the summer, I had never seen anything like it except in the movies. Until this moment, I'd forgotten I'd shipped them all off in the steamer trunk.

Everything in the drawers, even the towels, had a number stitched on—my number was 800—white tape with red embroidered numbers. *How nice,* I thought, *Sister Anita put so much time and work into sewing all these. I need to thank her.*

I hung up my postulant dress. Jack had hated it. Mom hadn't said anything, but I could imagine the conversation during their ride home. Mom: "How could she?" Dad: "It's going to be okay, Clare." Jack: "I give her thirty days."

I might just surprise them, I thought. *One small comfort: I don't have to worry about what to wear here—not for a long while—maybe never.*

During the Grand Silence, I bumped into Sister Julia during her trips in and out of the cell, but she never once acknowledged me. None of the sisters smiled or laughed or even made eye contact. The novices I'd played bridge with had called it "custody of the eyes"—to block out distractions and end the day prayerfully. I tried my best to ignore everyone and everything during that hour—especially Sister Julia. The harder I tried, the more I noticed—down to her every move and intake of breath.

At one point, I heard commotion coming from the bathroom. I peeked in. There stood Sister Delores, her black hair now in rollers, her glasses riding the tip of her nose. "Why doesn't somebody say something?" Her outburst was followed by a chorus of "Shush!" as novices and postulants scattered out of the bathroom, giggling and snorting. It was going to be a long night for Delores. No run around the block for her.

Since our cell was right across from the bathroom, I got in line early and was in and out of the tub in no time, ready for bed with twenty-five minutes to go before lights out. Sister Julia was still busy, God knows with what.

"To avoid taking up time in the evening," Sister Anita had explained, "all postulants are to wash and dry their hair during the day in the hair-washing room. We have no showers, just tubs, so washing your hair gets tricky. A perfect opportunity to strive for perfection."

What about the novices—didn't they have hair to wash? I felt glad for my short haircut and home perm. I still needed rollers after I washed my hair, for a softer look—at least for the next few months.

I wondered if I'd have to turn in my overnight case. I clicked it open. It smelled like hair spray and *White Shoulders* perfume—it had leaked during a slumber party last year. I touched my rollers and manicure set, my hand mirror. Mom, bless her, must have packed it at the last minute.

I took a quick peek at myself. I had a new name, a new outfit, a new life—but except for the fact that I'd washed off my makeup, I looked the same. I put the manicure set, the rollers, and the mirror in the top drawer of my little nightstand. I took out the books—an anthology of plays and a collection of Robert Frost's poems—and the journal Jack had given me. *All the stories I'll write! My fantasy of being a writer becomes a reality, starting today.* I examined the fancy fountain pen my aunt and uncle had given me, then put my rosary on top of the nightstand, so I could pray myself to sleep. *How can I possibly fall sleep at nine-thirty?*

"No books, papers, pens, or pencils allowed in your cells," Mother had said. I couldn't imagine not writing in my journal before bedtime—not reading myself to sleep.

Sister Julia pointed to the books and my journal. "Outside," she whispered. I got up and placed them on the floor outside our cell.

Later, while Sister Julia was in the bathroom, I snuck out—heart pounding, hands sweating—and slipped my journal and pen under my bathrobe, then hid them under the pillow. I felt guilty, but I had to believe God did not want me to stop writing—it was the one God-given talent I was sure of.

What else should I be doing? If I were home, I'd be writing in my journal—but I was afraid Sister Julia might report me to Mother Loretta. With no radio, no books, no writing, what could I do?

I waited for a signal. I counted the eighty-six squares in the bedspread pattern. I counted the rods along the foot of the iron bed, imagined the make and color of the cars whizzing by outside. Johnny Mathis singing "Chances Are" kept looping in my head. I tried to block it out: *Our Father, who art in heaven, hallowed be thy name….*

I opened the drawer again and looked at myself in the hand mirror. I fought back tears. I missed Stan. I missed Jack. I missed Danny, our crazy Irish Setter. He'd be sleeping with me if I were at home. I missed my girlfriends—even the ones who'd accused me of going off the deep end. I even missed my favorite TV shows. *Dad and Jack are watching Jack Paar without me.*

I picked up my manicure set and clipped my toenails—hadn't had time to do that before leaving home. I almost laughed out loud at my bright red nail polish.

What *was* Sister Julia doing on the other side of that white curtain?

At twenty-five past nine, the bell rang again—the five-minute warning for lights out. Sister Julia shuffled to the door, clicked off the overhead light, opened the top shutters, then the bottom ones. At last, fresh air.

It was September, but humidity clung to the walls. With the shutters open, the traffic noise was magnified. I was just a few miles from home, but a world away from my quiet, tree-lined street.

I was spending my first night in this new world with a total stranger, and we couldn't even speak to one another. In the darkness with the curtain pulled back, I could see Sister Julia kneeling at her bedside. She slipped into bed and lay there, coughing and sniffing. I cleared my throat—it echoed against the empty walls. Shadows climbed across the ceiling—the headlights from cars passing below on the street. In a building packed with young—and some old—women, I felt strange and alone.

It was just past nine-thirty. I'd left my rosary on the night stand. *Was I allowed to get out of bed to get it? Would I wake Sister Julia?* She was snoring softly. *What if I had to go to the bathroom during the night? She'd said I'd have to wake up her up!* I didn't want to make a mistake and get off to a bad start. Being late getting here was trouble enough for one day.

I felt for my journal and pen under the pillow. I was desperate to write down how I was feeling, but it was too dark to see. I felt like a criminal.

Chapter 4

How had I landed in a convent full of strangers on a Thursday night in September, a month before my eighteenth birthday? I didn't want to cry, but I didn't try to stop the tears when they came. No one had forced me to come here. Plenty had tried to talk me out of it. I slipped out of bed, scooped up my rosary and eased back into bed, trying to keep the bedsprings from squeaking. I lay there, eyes closed, tears rolling out, praying, *Hail Mary full of grace, get me through this night. Amen.*

The first wake-up bell rang at five o'clock for the novices. It was still dark. I was wide awake, listening to Sister Julia dressing before leaving for a half-hour meditation in chapel. A bell rang at five-thirty for us, and by six we needed to be dressed and lined up in the corridor outside chapel, ready to process in together.

We listened as the novices chanted the Divine Office—a set of prayers, psalms, and songs that hadn't changed in centuries. Mother Loretta explained that this was the official prayer of the Church—with so many souls united at every hour of the day and night, God could not refuse this prayer. It gave me chills just to think of it.

I was glad I'd suffered through Latin class—it made chanting easier—but it didn't hurt that the English translation was on the opposite page in the manual. The psalms, composed by David—an ancient poet and king—had been Jesus' daily prayers. Now they were mine too.

I took to the psalms right away. "*My strength, my song is the Lord….*" That was the opening line of chant for Matins and Lauds. A prayer was forming in my mind: *For years, I've resisted this call. I thought it was for much holier people. I'm not special. Yet here I am, in this sacred place, chanting the psalms of David—surrounded by others like me, trying to reach holiness.*

I looked up at the marble altar and the flickering candles. "Give thanks, for the Lord is good," I whispered. *God was my song.*

That grabbed me—like a sweet ache in my chest. I loved to sing and act—to be on stage. But I was ready to give all that up. Now God would be my song.

I watched a novice glide around the altar in the sanctuary, smoothing out the altar linens, lighting the candles, setting up the water and wine in crystal cruets, opening the missal to the right page for the day's service. She was called the *sacristan*; she cared for the sanctuary. She was so close to the tabernacle, the focus of our daily adoration. I wanted to be up there, in the sanctuary. It seemed like theater at its most sacred.

Watching the sacristan reminded me of how I envied the altar boys in our parish church. Only boys and men were allowed to get that close. *When I become a full-fledged nun*, I thought, *maybe I can be the sacristan—like the novice up there. Maybe that's why I've been called.*

The sanctuary glowed with spotlights and candles. We all stood as Mass began. On my first full day in the convent, I opened my hymn book and sang my heart out.

CHAPTER 5

After breakfast, we met in our postulant meeting room for lecture with Mother Loretta. "You have brought worldly possessions with you," she said. "But we share everything in common here, so you'll be asked to turn those things over to the community—a practice known as detachment."

After the shock wore off, I thought: *It just makes sense. When the time comes, I will be ready to practice detachment.*

The time came that afternoon. I sat at my desk, fingering the things I'd received as going-away gifts—the books, the expensive fountain pen, still in its box. I'd left the journal from Jack tucked under my pillow. It had a tan leather cover and my initials, MAW, embossed in gold on the front—the initials already obsolete, since I had a new title and a new first name: *Sister Clare.* My last name seemed to disappear altogether. I thought about my journal—there was no point giving it up—with the monogram, no one else would be able to use it anyway.

The thought of my journal led me to missing Jack, which led me to thinking about Stan. Before long, I was overcome with homesickness—a stabbing in my stomach and heaviness in my heart. From the base of my spine, it twisted up, turning my stomach over and spilling into my throat. *Not now.* I swallowed, stuffing the pain back down.

I tried to distract myself. What kind of a day was it outside? The shutters on the bottom windows of our classroom were closed, but the top shutters had been folded back, allowing a slit of sunlight into the yellow room.

A patch of sun landed on my hands...*Was it a sign from God? Could I—should I—give up the journal?* I imagined that the strip of sunlight was God saying, "Don't worry, you'll be allowed to keep your journal. Show it to Mother. She'll understand."

Mother appeared at the podium. "Sisters, this afternoon, we begin practicing poverty. You will give over any items you consider your personal belongings—other than your necessary toiletries. This will be your first practice of detachment." She looked out at us. "I see some confused—even sad—faces. Sisters, let us remember the story of the rich young man in the Gospel who desired to follow Jesus."

I remembered that New Testament story all too well. The young man wants to get to heaven—observes the commandments—knows that's not enough. He asks Jesus: "Teacher, what more should I do?" Jesus says: "Sell everything, give to the poor, follow me." The man's face falls, he turns away, sad, because he has many possessions.

I'd grown up doing both: giving to the poor and if not owning, at least living with many possessions. Was I really ready for *detachment*—giving up everything? I was about to find out.

"We are not physically poor, Sisters. Our practice of poverty requires generosity of spirit. Things are here only for our use. Remember, Sisters, in heaven, only God will satisfy you." She looked at each of us with her piercing eyes. "Let's have a little bit of heaven on earth, shall we?"

She would have made a good preacher, I thought.

"If you learn nothing else as a Sister of Saint Mary, may it be this: Only God can fill you," Mother said.

Inspired by Mother's words, I made another trip to my cell to look at the toiletry items in the top drawer of my chest. *Okay*...

the cosmetic kit and eyebrow tweezers can go, I told myself. *I need my hair rollers until I take the veil and become a novice in a year.* I was overcome with guilt about hiding my journal—I didn't want to be like the rich young man. I removed the journal from under my pillow, telling myself to trust in God—Mother would understand and let me keep it—she wasn't that unreasonable.

I was one of the first to get back to my desk. Others trailed in, some somber or surly, some smiling—making the supreme sacrifice. Sister Angela, who was near the bottom of seniority with me, sat stone-faced. She'd shown her rebellious nature by refusing to eat lima beans.

Mother waited at the podium, watching carefully, until all of us were seated.

"Sisters, there is special language for all we do, based on a long tradition of monastic practices. Each time we offer belongings to the community in the person of the superior—we are *showing up.* Think seriously, Sisters, about what you are about to do. Ask for grace. If you cannot release these possessions, in the spirit of poverty, then you will not be fully practicing this life of vowed service to the poor."

I was not going to be like the rich young man. I prayed: *I'm ready—only God can fill me.*

"Come to my office when you are ready—not according to seniority—to show up your possessions." She smiled—then winked.

That wink was so demeaning—can she be trusted?

I was ready. The minute Mother left the room and crossed the hall to her office, I gathered my belongings. I paused, looking at the leather-bound journal with my initials in gold. I hadn't written anything in it yet, but Jack's inscription dedicated and personalized it—I couldn't imagine anyone else writing in it. Jack had written: *To Maggie: The best writer I know.*

My journals—hidden in my cedar chest at home—were my best friends. They held my dreams, desires, creative ideas—without judging. I had thought this leather journal—my new friend—would walk with me on the next leg of my journey. *Could I—should I—give it up*? I lifted the lid of my desk—*I'll hide it here*. My hands felt sweaty—my mouth dry. I prayed for grace. I remembered that spot of sun. I swallowed hard. I'd trust God, hand over the journal—then Mother would let me keep it.

I got in line behind Rosemary, one of the two girls from high school who'd entered with me. "We never get a chance to talk, Rosemary," I whispered. "This seniority thing…I'm at the end of the line, you're closer to the front."

"I know," she said. "Just because I was born a few months earlier. Do you think we'll ever have time to just—visit?"

We were supposed to be keeping quiet, so I whispered: "I hope so!" By the time I entered Mother's office, the items—books, fountain pen, cosmetic bag, journal—felt heavy.

Mother looked up and waved me in. "Sister Clare. Set your things on the side table. What treasures have you come to show up?"

"Mother, I was wondering about...."

Mother cleared her throat. "Sister, this might be an appropriate time for you to kneel. You are practicing poverty, as well as obedience to the Rule."

I plopped down on my knees in front of the table.

"No, Sister—here, next to me." She looked amused.

Am I being toyed with? I could take just about anything but ridicule. I moved closer, still on my knees. I was facing her, my back to the table holding the disposed-of treasures.

"Now then. You were saying, Sister?"

I had lost track of what I was saying. The situation in which I found myself—dressed in an outfit that was turn-of-the-century at best—on my knees before a stranger I was calling "Mother"—all of this on a sunny September day when I could be doing—what? Anything but this. I could not think of what to say.

"The proper way to begin, since it appears you are tongue-tied, is: 'Mother, in the spirit of poverty, I humbly show up these items, for the use of the community.' Are you prepared to say that, Sister Clare?"

I heard the automatic response come out of my mouth: "Yes."

She corrected me. "Yes, Mother."

"Yes, Mother."

"Well?" She tapped on her desk. "Go ahead."

I stumbled over the words but got them out, with a little coaching. After a pause, I asked, "The books, Mother? Where will they go? My journal…."

"I suggest you practice radical poverty, Sister. One who is striving for true detachment relinquishes everything, including control over how those things will be used. That was the spirit in which Mother Mary Dolan gave away her possessions. She is our Foundress—a model for all of us—even you who are only a few days old in this Community."

She was right. If I started putting conditions on my practice of the vows, there would be no end to what I would eventually want to take back. So, I would show up everything, even my beloved journal. The fountain pen—I could use any old pen—that was fine with me. My aunt and uncle didn't need to know.

"Is there anything else you want to say, Sister, before you go?"

"It's just that the journal—it has my initials on it, Mother. I was hoping…."

"There's nothing wrong with my eyesight, Sister." Wink.

I felt my hands clenching. "Yes, Mother. Thank you, Mother."

I stood up, my knees aching. I was light-headed—silver dots danced in front of me. I waited until I was in the hallway to take a deep breath and exhale. I was angry and disappointed, but I tried not to give in to self-pity. I would not turn away, sad, like the rich man. Surely Mother would reconsider—I would see my journal again. Hadn't God spoken to me through the flash of sunlight that had rested on my hands?

The next morning, I rushed to my desk, expecting to see my journal. It wasn't there. For more than a week, when I went to my desk, I hoped the journal would appear. It never did.

What did it mean? Had God ignored my prayer? Was I being asked to give up writing? That I could never accept.

CHAPTER 6

Postulants washed and dried their hair during the day in a damp, windowless basement room. A makeshift countertop with sinks stretched out below a few filmy mirrors—the only ones in the whole Novitiate, as far as I knew. The lime green walls did not mask its dingy atmosphere and low-hanging heating pipes. Only the sweet-smelling shampoos and gels, combs and curlers, brushes and hair dryers hinted of the world outside. Silence was required in this secular den of iniquity, but since novices seldom visited, most postulants took advantage of the fact that it was unsupervised.

I found a spot at the sink and wet my hair, using the hand-held hose over the sink. I nodded to Sister Angela, who had just finished rinsing the shampoo suds from her shoulder-length, strawberry-blonde hair and was putting in the first of four large pink rollers.

"Know what?" Sister Angela said. "My whole family is fixin' to be at our family reunion this weekend—even my brother. He's a priest. I help Mama with the apple pies. My younger brother is king of the horseshoe contest. All my cousins sing and play guitar—it's like bein' at the Grand Ol' Opry." She started to sob. "Everyone will be there but me."

I tried to whisper—we were supposed to keep silence. "I'm sorry. Maybe you could think about something else."

Angela got louder. "Like what?" She blew her nose, then ran her comb through her hair.

I envied her tight curls. *If I had natural curls like hers, I'd never need another perm,* I thought. "I don't know," I whispered, hoping to shush her. "Maybe go to chapel and meditate." *Pitiful*, I thought, scowling at myself in the mirror.

"Sweet Jesus." Looking at me in disbelief, she clamped another roller in her hair. "Aren't you even the tiniest bit homesick?" She searched my face in the mirror and reached for a roller.

"I've had my moments." I finished rinsing the shampoo from my hair, wrapped a towel around my head. *How much could I confide in Angela?* She seemed a bit rebellious, but I liked her. "Sometimes I imagine what's going on at home. Right now, Dad's on the phone with a client. Mom's ironing. Or weeding, getting the garden ready for winter. Or shopping for baby things with my sister, who's expecting. My brother Jack's...." I felt my throat tighten.

"Don't you just miss your family to *death*?" Angela asked, as she fastened the roller.

"Not *to death*. I was the one who decided to leave home. God will help me live with that decision." *Did I believe my own advice? Was I being too preachy?*

"I don't know how you can be so rational," she said, securing the final roller. She tucked the dryer cap over her head, cutting me off.

My perm had started to turn frizzy, so I was using rollers for a soft wave. I rolled and clipped my hair, then slipped the dryer cap down over my ears. *Was I too rational? The truth was, if I started thinking about home, I'd be three times worse than Angela.* With the dryer humming in my ears, I couldn't stop the song lyrics from swirling inside my head. Bobby Freeman singing, "Do You Want To Dance." It reminded me of Stan.

Reflected in the mirror, I noticed Frances and Barbara at the other end of the room. They didn't see me watching them. Even through the dryer cap, I could hear them giggling. *Wasn't anyone concerned that this is a place of silence?*

Chapter 6

Frances pulled a photo from her pocket and propped it up on the counter—Frances and Barbara in prom dresses, flanked by two boys in white suits, their arms slung around the girls' shoulders.

"I'm going to send Pete a letter," Frances said.

"How? Have you seen a mailbox around here?" Barbara asked.

"I don't care. I'll find a way," Frances snapped. "Mom gave me an envelope full of stamps. I hid them in my trunk. I'm going to do it."

"If you're going to write Pete, I'm going to write Tommy." Barbara frowned. "He told me he'd write me every day. Do you think Mother would keep his letters from me?"

They looked at one another, then shook their heads. "She wouldn't!"

I gave up my efforts to be silent. "Sorry," I said. "I couldn't help but overhear. It's early to expect mail, don't you think?" *I suspect our mail gets censored,* I thought.

"Sister Clare—you have a guy back home to write to?" Barbara asked.

"Maybe there's a prom photo still on *your* mirror at home?" Frances added.

"Not anymore." I'd packed all my photos in a shoebox and buried it in my cedar chest. I could remember everything about senior prom night. I'd worn my powder-blue taffeta dress with the jewel neckline and the gardenia corsage from Stan. His hands had trembled when he'd pinned it on my dress. I could remember the scent of gardenias, his aftershave. He'd kissed me on the forehead. "Beautiful as ever, Blue Eyes," he'd said.

"You broke up?" Barbara asked, but didn't wait for my answer. "Pete and I sort of did. But he promised to wait—you know, in case I decide this isn't right for me. That is so sweet, don't you think?"

"But that sounds like...." I caught myself before saying something judgmental. I wanted to say: *You don't have any intention of giving your life to God, do you? Is this some kind of game for you?* I didn't tell them about that final parting kiss. How Stan had insisted he would wait for me. I didn't mention the ache in my heart when I thought about him. We'd gone from being inseparable to being strangers. *How was he doing? Was he writing? Would I ever receive letters from him? I couldn't write to him even if I wanted to—we were only allowed one letter home each month. I had no idea where he was—Jack would have to fill me in.*

"Penny for your thoughts, Sister Clare," Barbara teased.

"I hope you won't be offended." I took a risk. "I'm wondering why you would enter the convent and still be carrying a picture of your boyfriend, or be thinking about writing to him." I hadn't smuggled in photos or postage stamps.

"I'm sorry you feel that way," Barbara said. She came over to me. "You won't tell Mother, will you?"

"Heavens, no!"

I watched Frances and Barbara leave and made a mental note not to sign up with those two again—I could easily start acting just like them.

Sister Angela removed her dryer cap. I noticed her cosmetic bag with comb, brush, curling iron, and other goodies. "Hey," she said, "want to use my eyebrow tweezers? Looks like you could do with a plucking."

"Where did you get them?" I whispered.

"I brought them with me, silly." She leaned close to the mirror.

"But Mother told us to hand in—show up—items like that."

"Come on. Y'all can't be serious." She winced as she pulled out a hair. "How'm I gonna pluck these suckers without my tweezers? Y'all can use them after me, if you want."

"No thanks. I'm fine." *If I gave in to tweezers, what next?*

"Suit yourself. I've got a razor too, honey-bun, in case you ever want to borrow it."

"No thanks." *What other contraband items had Angela smuggled in?*

"Okay then," Angela eyed me. "I can take a hint." She returned her focus to her eyebrows.

"You seem a little better," I said, "about being homesick, I mean."

"Comes and goes," Angela said. "My Daddy always says, 'That which doesn't kill us makes us stronger.'" She yanked out a hair. "That's what I'm hoping for."

Sister Carla and Sister Janet arrived, chatting in loud whispers and carrying their cosmetic bags. "Can you believe how naïve that novice is?" Carla said. "She didn't know half my hints during the quiz game. We could've won!"

"I had it just as bad with my novice," Janet said. "Don't play Scrabble with her. She's cutthroat! Challenged every word I put down." They both groaned.

"Look at this." Carla held out her hands. "My nail polish is almost completely worn off. My favorite color."

"That's the least of my worries," Janet said. "I haven't had a good night's sleep since I got here. I just know I got the lumpiest bed in this place."

"And the food—overcooked and literally swimming in gravy."

Angela frowned and whispered, "Those two act like this is some fancy resort—what did they expect?"

"What? Sorry, I'm trying to keep silence." I started to pack up my things. I wanted to say: *What about the spirit of charity Mother mentioned in her first lecture? Those two don't have the vaguest idea.* I was clinging to the belief that even though I was new at this, I could follow the path to holiness if I just followed the rules—not an easy thing to do in this hair-washing room. I wasn't a saint—anything but. It wasn't my place to correct or lecture anyone. But I'd have to be more careful—some postulants could be a bad influence.

From then on, I looked to see when Rosemary—my classmate from high school—was signed up for the hair-washing room. She wasn't a goody-goody, but I noticed she was following the rules. It amounted to excluding myself from the worldliness I saw in some of the postulants. That wasn't the same as being exclusive…was it?

I thought I'd be escaping temptation by entering the convent—that the road to holiness would become easier. Instead, temptation lurked around every corner.

CHAPTER 7

I prided myself on my writing ability, but writing my first letter home to my family turned out to be torture. How was I going to fit everything I wanted to say on two small sheets of stationery? I wrote in small letters and had to use the back side of the second sheet to fit everything in. I handed it in, feeling moderately satisfied.

The next evening, when I went to my desk, there was my letter. On the envelope, Mother had written, "See me." She'd littered the letter with red marks and comments. I felt sick to my stomach. I could be destroyed by criticism of my writing. It had begun with Marianne snooping in my diary, then her making fun of my poetry, then the comments of unappreciative teachers. *But to rip apart a letter to my parents?*

I knocked on Mother's door.

She looked up, saw I was holding my letter, and smiled.

How dare she smile?

"Sister Clare…come in. This might be an appropriate time to kneel—in humility."

Why?

"In imitation of Christ," she said, as if she'd read my thoughts. Her green eyes were penetrating.

My hands were sweating—the stationery I was holding started to curl—the blue ink bleeding into my palms. My knees hit the cold floor.

Mother took my letter and held it as if it were contaminated. "You have a lot to learn about letter-writing." She held it up to the light. "Your writing is so small it's not readable." Wink.

I wanted to protest—*how could I fit everything on two pieces of paper?* I said nothing.

"Your slang expressions, Sister. How many times have you used the word *Hi* in this letter?"

"I didn't know *Hi* was slang," I squeaked, fighting tears.

"You can *send greetings*, or offer your thoughts and prayers. But *Hi* is not an option. It isn't suitable for someone aspiring to be a religious sister." She had the audacity to smile again.

I wanted to tell Mother that my family would suspect someone else wrote my letter. I was shocked at my anger—I didn't dare speak. I knelt there, staring at the red marks and smeared ink.

After a painful pause, she sighed. "Take two more pieces of stationery from the table, so that you may send home a proper letter. One side only, mind you. Please—get rid of the X's and O's. 'Your loving daughter' is more suitable, don't you think?"

Your loving daughter? I can't write that. "Yes, Mother," I said. I stood up, my back aching, knees numb, ears ringing. I stuffed the letter in my pocket and practically ran down the corridor. I wasn't allowed to go to my cell—only at bedtime—unless I asked permission, which I would not do. I locked myself in one of the toilet stalls.

I had promised myself no more tears, but I couldn't stop them from dropping onto my cape. I sat on the toilet seat, lid down, wishing I had a mirror—like a child who needs to witness her own misery. I drew in a half-dozen gasps and let the tears fall. Finally, I blew my nose on the thin toilet paper, stood up, and straightened my cape. My first impulse was to open my journal and pour out my heart in writing. But my journal was gone. I clenched my jaw. *It isn't fair!*

I made my way down the steps to chapel. An elderly nun was shuffling along, stopping to pray at each of the Stations of the Cross. She gripped a crucifix—the one that all Sisters of Saint Mary tucked into their leather belts—and gazed up at the suffering Jesus depicted in each of the Stations. I doused myself in holy water—fingertips, forehead, chest, both shoulders—and knelt in my pew on my sore knees. More tears.

The altar was dark, except for the red sanctuary light flickering above the tabernacle. I told God how unfairly I was being treated. The flame flickered, then flared brightly. *Had my prayer been heard?* I needed to be strong—I could not do this on my own.

The elderly sister had made her way to the fourteenth station: Jesus laid in the tomb. I watched her sink to her knees in front of me at the communion railing. *How many years had this sister spent on her knees? If she could kneel, I could too.*

I left chapel, ready to try again with two new sheets of stationery, determined that future letters would pass Mother's inspection. She would never criticize my writing again.

Back in our classroom, I sat at my desk, staring down at the two pieces of blank paper. The excitement of writing home had left me. A tear splotched on the page. I wiped it dry with my cape. *No more tears!*

Across the aisle, a postulant was weeping—she'd done little else since entrance day. Why had the poor girl entered in the first place—and why was she still here? Not a single postulant acknowledged her crying. Like me, they probably feared going down that slippery slope. Then, I glimpsed my attitude of superiority—my lack of compassion. *Poor girl,* I thought. *That could easily be me.*

I steeled myself to the task of writing. I'd gotten enough A's in English. Marianne and Jack and I had entertained our relatives at family get-togethers, putting on the skits I created—I'd been writing plays ever since I could remember. In high school, it was parodies for variety shows. In sixth grade, Dad had given me his old Olympia typewriter. A few keys stuck—I didn't care—it made me feel like a real writer.

How could I fit all my feelings, thoughts, and impressions about this dramatically different life on two tiny sheets of stationery, using one side of the paper? I decided to write about *them* instead. *How was Marianne feeling? How were Jack's classes going? Was Mom enjoying her bridge club? Had Dad gotten the old Chevy repaired, now that I wasn't there to drive it? What did they know about plans for our cousin's wedding?* I jazzed it up with my best cheery language.

It wasn't great writing, but it wasn't bad. I had much more to say, but if I wrote any smaller, I was sure to suffer a rewrite and more time on my knees in Mother's office. I wanted to close with hugs and kisses—but X's and O's were banned. I wrote: "*I'm busy and happy. Your loving daughter, Sister Clare.*" Marianne would scream, Dad would smile, and Jack would howl with laughter... Mom would cry because I'd taken her name.

As I wrote our home address on a new envelope, I pictured our red-brick bungalow with its front porch and my favorite maple tree hiding the second-floor dormer that was my room. So many conversations had taken place on that porch. I pictured Stan shooting baskets in our back yard driveway—remembered Stan's final kiss. *Would I ever see him again?* The Everly Brothers were filling my head with verses of "Bye Bye Love." Once I caught myself humming out loud. As I put my sanitized letter—unsealed—in the IN box outside Mother's office, I noticed a thick stack of blank stationery in the box. I looked around. I was alone. I picked up a dozen or more sheets, and slipped them under my cape. *My substitute journal*, I thought.

Heart pounding, I hid the papers in my classroom desk. I'd taken something that wasn't mine, without permission. I felt like a petty thief. But I also felt a sense of liberation. Maybe it was the writer in me—she'd been gasping for breath—beginning to breathe. I'd written my first letter home and wouldn't have to face that task again until the third Sunday in October. I'd cleared another hurdle in my vocation—and lost a small part of myself. I hurried to the bathroom, locked myself in a stall, and cried.

On the second Sunday of each month, Mother or her assistant spread out letters in small stacks on the community room tables. We had only been there less than a week, so we didn't get any letters yet, but we watched our senior novices walk into the community room, as quickly as they could—without violating religious decorum—to search for their names among the stacks. Mother told us we'd get mail soon. I told myself not to get my hopes up, so when the day came, I was overjoyed to find three letters in my stack.

Mom and Dad had both signed their letter, but Mom had written it. It was predictable: they missed me but hoped I was happy; my friends asked about me; the neighbors still hadn't found a babysitter to replace me. Marianne's letter was a combination of questions about my life in the convent, followed by a list of all the gifts she'd received at a baby shower.

I saved Jack's letter for last. Like all Jack's writing, he'd typed it on his trusty Olivetti.

After he'd written that he missed me, he typed a warning to my censor, saying he made carbon copies of all his letters. I laughed. Jack not only assumed my letters would be censored by Mother Loretta—he'd confronted her. That was so him. (My mail was opened before I got it; I had to assume it was read.) He wrote that Mom visited my room every night, then joked that if I weren't home in six months, it would become Mom's sewing room.

Jack was keeping a close watch on the Kennedy-Nixon debates. I admired how he wanted to get involved in politics and envied him his position on the staff of the University's student newspaper. If I were still home, I would most likely wander into his room and ask his opinion on—well, just about anything. He read constantly. We'd make jokes and listen to music. I felt sick, realizing none of that would happen ever again.

Jack wrote that Stan was asking when I was coming home. He had good intentions—but I knew I had to block Stan out. I couldn't stop him from using Jack as a link between us—I was secretly grateful—but I had to ignore it.

He closed his letter with a PS: "Hope you're enjoying the journal."

Oh Jack, I'm aching to write to you, I thought. *But, only one letter home a month allowed, so it's not an option.*

Could I ever tell Jack I'd lost his journal on the first day?

By the time the fourth Sunday came around for visiting day, I ached to see my family—especially Jack. I had so much to tell them—things that didn't fit on two pieces of stationery. It was a struggle to cram it all in.

Finally, one o'clock on September 25 arrived. My family was sitting in a circle of folding chairs in the auditorium when I walked in. The auditorium was dimly lit and stuffy. Five other postulants and their families shared the hall, denying any of us privacy and ratcheting up the noise level. The room was already vibrating with the hum of several fans.

My father was holding my banjo—my favorite uncle had taught me to play a few chords—then had given it to me for graduation. I knew enough chords to sing and strum along to "Oh Susanna" and "Camptown Races."

"Gee, thanks, Dad." I couldn't bear to tell him I would have to show it up and probably never see it again—though I couldn't imagine it being of much use to the poor in the Philippines.

Eight of my girlfriends made a surprise appearance—I lost fifteen minutes just scaring up more folding chairs. They asked questions and talked about their lives.

"We still can't believe you entered," Brenda Taylor said. "What do you do on weekends?"

Why had she even come? We were in drama together but we'd never been close. *Curious to see the inside of a convent,* I decided. She'd been voted "Mary-like" at our school—I'd wondered what the nuns saw in her.

"I'm off to college," Brenda bragged to everyone. "Northwestern—a full scholarship!"

Brenda was the only one going to a select university. One friend had a new job; another was flashing an engagement ring; one was planning her wedding; one was attending a local college.

The questions flew: "Don't you miss home?" "Are you happy?" "Have you heard from Stan?" "Did you know he's broken-hearted?" "Do you like it here?" I couldn't answer their questions fast enough, so I smiled and nodded. The questions about Stan I pretended not to hear.

"What do you *do* all day?" Brenda asked.

"I pray and work and study and eat and sleep and go to classes and…." *Please go*, I thought. *All of you, please, I need to spend this precious time with my family.*

Marianne was about six weeks away from her due date—she and Mom told me all about the baby's room and the lovely baby showers. The race between Kennedy and Nixon kept Dad and Jack arguing. Everything reminded me of how much I was missing.

At one point, Jack stood up, patted his pocket in search of his cigarettes, and headed for the door.

Desperate to escape the chatter of everyone talking at once, desperate to tell Jack why I couldn't write to him, I jumped up and said, "Sorry, I don't mean to be rude, but it's easy to get lost here. I'll just be a minute." I ran after him. "Jack!"

When I caught up with him in the hallway, he looked relieved.

"You know I can't write just to you, Jack," I said. "Tell me you understand?"

"Stupid rule." He gave me his 'disapproving' look. "My consolation is that you're writing it all down in your journal. It'll make a great memoir."

He noticed my frown. "What?"

I couldn't lie. "I'm not really writing…."

"What? The journal I gave you...."

"I had to give it up." I tried to make it sound unimportant.

Jack saw through me. "I'm getting you another one, Megs. Promise to keep it." He was so furious, he started pacing in the hallway.

"Don't ask me to promise, Jack. I have to practice obedience."

"You know you can't survive without it—you'll die if you don't. Good God, Megs. I can't believe this."

I fought back tears. "I'm begging you. Don't tell everybody."

He gave me a long look, then nodded.

I grabbed his arm, "Come on. Please. Forget the journal." I pulled him along the corridor.

"I picked it out special," he said between clenched teeth. "I had it monogramed." As we neared the door of the auditorium, he whispered, "Who the hell else could even use it? I'm buying you one. Your obedience will be to yourself... and to me."

The visitor groups had swelled, the auditorium was overflowing. The noise was deafening. The clock on the wall read 3:40. We had twenty minutes before everyone had to leave.

One of my girlfriends said, "Tell us everything about this place. We're so curious."

I raved about the food. I told them all about my classes, about waking up at 5:30, getting dressed in the dark, making it to chapel in time for prayers.

"At least you don't have to worry what to put on in the morning," Brenda joked as everyone got up to leave.

I must look ridiculous in this outfit, straight out of the 1890's, I thought. I hugged my girlfriends good-bye, then hugged Mom, Dad, Marianne, and Ted. Jack waited till last.

"We didn't get to talk, Jack. I'm sorry."

"Not your fault. But next month, when I come with a new journal, don't tell me you're going to turn it in." He hugged me tight. "*That* I will not forgive." He followed the rest of my family to the door, turned and waved, and was gone.

That evening, before recreation in the community room, Mother announced she would be in her office in case we had gifts to show up. I would lose my banjo, but what choice did I have? I couldn't hide a banjo under my pillow.

I knelt in Mother's office with the banjo. Its round drum pinged, the silver neck gleamed in the light—it was beautiful. "My uncle taught me how to play a little," I said. "He thought we could use it." *It was useful, not selfish, to keep it.*

Mother stared at the banjo, then at me. "A musician, Sister Clare? I didn't know…."

"Not really—but I like to sing and make music." *Why was she hesitating?* "Maybe we could use it for recreation?"

"Take it to the music room." Mother's expression softened. "See the sister in charge of choir. She'll find a spot for it." Mother lifted the banjo, turned it in the light. "This is a fine instrument. See that you care for it."

"Yes, Mother. Thank you, Mother."

I carried the banjo back to my desk. Had I just peered through a crack in Mother Loretta's stony façade?

The choir director was a sweet, older professed sister. We were permitted to talk with her—but only on music matters. She'd already discovered my second-soprano voice and placed me strategically next to a tone-deaf postulant during choir practice… *no need to invent penance.*

"A banjo—a nice one, Sister." She placed it on a table in the choir room. "There's a guitar here too—doesn't Sister Pauline play guitar?"

"Piano, organ—guitar too, I think. Pauline's had a lot of musical training. I remember her playing in high school. I'll ask her."

"Some years, the postulants form a little band—entertainment for feast days and such." Her eyes lit up. "Talk it up, Sister. Our foundress loved music—did you know that?"

"No, I didn't. I'll ask around."

"Maybe a little show for Thanksgiving—or Christmas?" She smiled. "Just planting a seed."

I thought I'd be visiting my favorite bathroom stall after visiting day, to cry my eyes out. Thanks to the banjo, today, my eyes were dry.

Chapter 7

When October's visiting day approached, I adjusted my expectations—success would mean two or three sentences spoken with each person in my circle of chairs. It was a bonus that none of my girlfriends came.

Elections were only two weeks away—much of our conversation centered on that. At the convent, we had no access to newspapers, radio, or TV, so I listened with interest. My birthday had been a week earlier. We didn't celebrate birthdays, but Mom and Marianne brought my favorite chocolate brownies.

"Mom made them," Marianne said. "I sat and supervised." She rubbed her pregnant belly. "I can't wait for this baby to come."

When everyone was leaving, Jack slipped me a parcel wrapped in brown paper. "I don't know what to call you anymore," he said, his expression a cross between sadness and frustration. "So, this isn't monogramed. I have no use for a place that changes your name arbitrarily." He sighed. "But that's not up for discussion, is it?"

"What can I say?"

"Tell me you're going to keep this—that you'll write in it—write letters to me, if that helps. Write poems. Write to Stan, whose heart is cracked in a hundred pieces." He gave me his serious look. "Promise me, Megs."

I knew I would have to violate detachment to do it and that the guilt would torture me—but my desire to write was strong. "I promise."

"Another thing," Jack said. "Stan tells me the two letters he wrote to you were returned to him, opened—then resealed. He's going to send them to me in the future."

"Are you serious?" The words flew out of my mouth, too loud. "I don't believe this," I whispered. But I wanted to scream: *Where is your charity, Mother Loretta?*

"Don't try to defend your Mother Superior," Jack said.

"I'm not—I don't—believe me." I struggled to hold back tears.

Jack patted my shoulder. "From now on, you can count on me to deliver." He gave me his look again. "Honestly, Megs. Do you know what you're doing?" He turned to leave. "Do you?"

After my family had gone, I snuck into the classroom, lifted my desktop, and slid the journal under my other textbooks. I tucked the pieces of stationery I'd stolen inside it. I'd been keeping track of my thoughts, even the beginnings of a few poems. This journal would stay with me—no showing up this time. I owed that to Jack.

The rich young man popped into my head. *It's just a journal—something to write in—not riches or wealth.* But in my heart, I knew I had compromised my principles. I had side-stepped *perfection.* Could I handle the guilt—would it ever subside? I had to believe that it was okay to cherish my journal as an enduring connection to Jack, to my family—though I knew that in large part, the Sisters of St. Mary were my new family now.

On November 8th—Election Day—Mom called Mother Loretta with the message that Marianne had given birth to a healthy boy. They were naming him "Jeffrey Edward." Mother explained that as a Sister in formation, I had given up the possibility of being a godmother—or attending the Baptism. I was both happy and heartbroken at the news.

CHAPTER 8

When visiting day came around in November, my new nephew, Jeffrey, became the center of attention. Mother Loretta had warned us not to hold babies (too much of a temptation against our vow of chastity). I violated that rule, holding this adorable newborn and covering him with kisses. But I had to share Jeffrey with everyone else, especially his beaming grandparents. This gave me an opportunity to spend some private time with Jack—my best friend, my confidante.

I'd been assigned to clean the library every day, and since seculars often used the Braille section of the library, I made an excuse to show Jack the Braille equipment. I'd rehearsed a plausible excuse, in case one of the professed sisters caught us: "My brother is researching Braille printing; I thought we might be able to help him."

Jack and I walked into the library and noticed two young men near the Braille equipment in the rear of the room. They were dressed in black cassocks; they weren't wearing clerical collars—the backward white collar—so I assumed they were seminarians.

"Can I help you?" I asked.

"We're not disturbing you, are we?" the short, stout man asked.

The other man was seated at a table. He stood and smiled.

"We're working on a project," said the talkative one. "For our Jesuit mission, for the blind in the Philippines—to open a Braille library there. Our novice director checked it out with your novice director."

So, they were Jesuit novices. "We have missions in the Philippines too!" I said. I was taken with the quiet one's good looks—dark hair and high cheekbones—he and Jack might have been mistaken for brothers, except Jack didn't wear glasses.

The quiet one held up a Braille book. "This is excellent. Mind if we keep working?"

"Not at all," I said. "You'd need to see the sister in charge of the Braille section for more details. I just clean the room."

"We'll be fine," said the stout one. "By the way, I'm John and that's Bill."

Bill, the quiet one, waved and smiled again. His smile lit up the room.

I felt myself blushing a bit so I looked at the one named John. "I'm Sister Clare," I said, "and this is my brother, Jack. Stay as long as you need to."

"We promise not to get in the way," John said.

Jack and I sat down at a table a distance from them. I couldn't help noticing the good-looking novice snatching glances in our direction. I focused on Jack to avoid glancing back.

"You wanted to ask me something, Jack?"

"Don't you get homesick, Megs?"

"Only once a day." We both laughed. "I get lonely—even though I'm surrounded by people day and night."

"Have you gotten to know anyone?"

"A few postulants. My cell-mate, Sister Julia, works and sweats all day in the laundry—it takes her a half-hour to sponge the salt streaks off her habit every night."

"What do you talk about with her—in your cell?"

I laughed. "We don't talk in the cell. But we play bridge most nights at recreation—just like college."

"Yeah—except for the beer and loud music."

Jack, master of sarcasm.

"We did give a show for everyone on Thanksgiving," I said, not mentioning how much I'd missed Thanksgiving dinner at home. "I wrote a parody to 'Over the River and Through the Woods'—making fun, nicely, of life here. My friend Pauline played piano—another friend, Angela, played guitar. Everyone thought it was funny—even Mother."

"You're writing, good. And your journal?"

"I am—it's hidden in this library," I said, leaning forward to whisper. "You could search for hours, never find it."

Jack got up and scanned the bookshelves—then pulled out a book. "Merton—I've heard of this guy. He's way ahead of the Church in his thinking."

"That's *my* book! I'm reading it—and taking notes. I won't go into how boring the spiritual books Mother assigns are. Merton speaks to me."

"You're saying you have to hide in here—to read and write? That's bull!"

"Shhhhh," I said, glancing over to make sure the Jesuits hadn't heard. They were both concentrating on the books in front of them. "Never mind," I said, "I'm dealing with it."

"I can see the guilt on your face. When will you come to your senses?"

"Let's not argue. There's so much I love about being here—really."

Jack grumbled. I was telling him too much—but I couldn't stop myself.

"We'd better get back," I said.

Jack was reluctant but resigned. We slid our chairs back into place and moved toward the door.

"Good-bye," the stout Jesuit called out. The shy one waved politely.

I waved back.

"I think the quiet guy, the one with the glasses, has eyes for you," Jack whispered, as we walked along the corridor. "Did you see how he stared?"

"Don't be ridiculous!" I punched Jack in the arm.

We rejoined my family in their circle of chairs in the auditorium. I was already fantasizing about running into the shy seminarian again. *Stop it, Clare!*

Sundays during the season of Advent (from the first Sunday of December until Christmas Eve) were days of silence and prayer. I was just as glad—I could sneak in a little study time. We had very little time during the day to study (Mass, Divine Office three times a day, lecture with Mother, our chores—along with three classes a day). Evenings were taken up with recreation, then the Grand Silence and lights out.

I was upset about my grades—76% in French (a D+) and C's in Natural Science, Theology, Psychology, and Western Civilization. The only bright spot was English class—I had a solid A.

My frustrations came out when Delores, Angela, and I walked together during afternoon recreation. Along with Pauline, we were the four "juniors" or youngest in our group, so we sat together—in chapel, the refectory, our classes, our postulant classroom. It was only natural that we'd become friends. My friend Rosemary had joined up with a few others who had a passion for volleyball. We preferred walking rather than playing volleyball—never enough time to finish a game, and the ball was impossibly flat.

"I've always been an A student," Delores said. "Our schedule's so tight, no time to study. What do they expect?"

Angela had no qualms about smuggling in contraband. "I'm going to ask my brother the priest to bring me one of those special compact flashlights." Because Angela's brother was a priest, she could visit him anytime, in one of the private parlors. "Then I can study in my cell after Grand Silence."

"Angela!" Delores and I said in unison.

"What about obedience, poverty, rules of silence?" I asked.

"I won't break silence," Angela said, grinning. "I don't say a word when I'm studying. I can't sleep before eleven o'clock anyway."

Delores and I both frowned. We weren't that daring—not yet, anyway.

From the first night—when Delores got everyone giggling during Grand Silence, I knew I wanted to be her friend. I loved her Southern accent; she thought my Midwest twang was amusing.

"We should petition Mother to give us more study time," Delores said, as we rounded a bend on the garden walkway. Her pageboy cut was growing out; the afternoon light highlighted her dark hair. "She needs to shorten her lectures. God knows we should be allowed to study in our cells."

"Imagine Mother taking kindly to a petition from us. We'd get more than a wink."

"I do not take kindly to poor grades, especially when it's not my fault." She grabbed my arm. "Listen. If we don't stand up for ourselves, who will?"

"We're not supposed to be talking about grades, comparing ourselves to others—it shows a lack of humility."

"Rubbish! We're supposed to be students—whatever happened to *perfection of our ordinary actions*? How fair is it to make us attend college-level classes, then fill up our schedule with hours of lecture and housework?"

"Count me out of your petition idea. It feels too risky."

Delores stopped walking. Her frown was almost comical—though I didn't dare laugh. I noticed some of the novices walking ahead of us turn around. I didn't want to attract their attention. Delores could get overly emotional.

"Come on—let's keep walking," I said. "I'll ask you French verb forms, we'll study while we're recreating."

"Y'all are weak-kneed, y'know that? What's French for *lily-livered?*"

Our laughter rose slowly; we were doubled over by the time we'd circled the garden.

It was December, but Delores and I—and sometimes Angela—still took walks outside in the garden most afternoons—wrapped in shawls and wearing gloves. Delores and I looked forward to this time. We tried not to be exclusive—at evening recreation we were rarely together—but these thirty-minute walks gave us the chance to talk about what was going on, without being overheard. Delores had a bone to pick with the senior novices.

"I'm downright miffed," she said, "with the big deal they're making over Advent—as if for the four weeks before Christmas we should drag ourselves around in sackcloth and ashes." She swirled her shawl and draped it around her.

"I know," I said. "No decorations? No Christmas tree? They claim all the showy stuff is worldly, distracting."

We sat down on a bench and wrapped our shawls tighter around our shivering bodies.

"I want Christmas to be jolly," Delores said. "Time for a petition?"

"We're not the only postulants up in arms about this," I said, "but you know by now that signing a petition is not the way to Mother's heart." *If she has one,* I thought. "We just need to keep our spirits up and stick together."

"If we don't have a tree by Christmas Eve, I'm going to...."

"Do what? Ask Santa for one?" I was joking, but Delores didn't laugh. "Come on, this too shall pass."

"Not without a Christmas tree. If there's a tree, count me in."

"If there isn't?"

She paused, gave me a look, and said, "Count me out."

I grabbed her arm. "Look at me." I was hoping to see playfulness on her face. She looked dead serious. "You wouldn't leave the convent over something like this?"

Delores didn't respond.

If she leaves, I thought, *I have to consider her 'dead to us.' I couldn't bear that.*

At breakfast on Christmas morning we were allowed to talk—it was a feast of the first class. I was looking forward to visiting with my family that afternoon.

Pauline, Delores, Angela, and I sat across from one another in the refectory.

"I don't like that the novices were fooling us," Delores said as she spooned her oatmeal. "Did they have to treat us like children?"

Pauline ignored Delores' grumbling. "That is the biggest tree I've ever seen."

"Poinsettias everywhere!" I said.

"When did the novices find time to make all those angel ornaments?" Pauline asked.

"I cried during the whole Mass! The carols, the candles. I've never seen the chapel so beautiful," I said.

"I have to say," Angela said as she passed the coffee cake, "this turned out better than I expected. Just the right balance, Christmas lights, inspiring scripture, heavenly music—and delicious cake!"

Delores said no more about being upset with the way we'd been treated. Neither did I. The novices had lied to us, but their hearts had been in the right place. I'd done a bit of concealing myself since I'd arrived here, so I was more than forgiving.

We celebrated the New Year with eggnog and cookies. Classes wouldn't resume for another week. Once they did, I settled into a routine: First Sunday: Day of Recollection; Second Sunday: receive letters; Third Sunday: write letters; Fourth Sunday: visitors. I looked forward to some Sundays more than others.

"What did you give up for Lent?" Delores asked, as we walked around the garden in early April, just before Easter. "We've already given up everything else, just being here. I had a little trouble searching for something more."

I could see from her expression that she was only partly joking.

"It used to be chocolate," I said, "or Sunday afternoons at the movies, or eating between meals, or...." *Going out on Sundays with Stan,* I was about to say, but didn't. "But being here," I said, "I've had to dig deeper—being next to that tone-deaf sister in choir practice ranks right up there."

"What new penance did you dig up?" Delores asked.

"I've given up the need to be perfect—though I'm a long way from that. No comments from you, thank you. I'm critical enough."

"Is that *all* you're giving up? Just your entire personality?"

I loved Delores' sarcasm. "For now." *What were my strong points? I no longer knew.* Stan told me once that he thought the two of us would complete one another. *How could I become complete, having given up loving Stan—or anyone else—exclusively?* "I thought about giving up afternoon walks with you, Delores," I said, "but then I'd have no penance at all in my life."

"Funny." She socked me in the arm. "You'd be lost without me and you know it."

I knew it.

Each month as visiting day approached, I'd plot: *How do I steal time away to talk privately with Jack, without offending the rest of my family?* Sometimes I'd ask him to come with me to the Braille room—or to the garden—anything so we could have time together.

Jack wanted to tell me about his plans to travel to DC—to support a group fighting for civil rights called the Freedom Riders. "They want the government to enforce the laws against segregation on interstate buses—Supreme Court rulings that have been on the books as far back as the forties. The idea is to ride buses throughout the South, protesting discrimination."

"Is it dangerous—what you're doing?"

"There's strength in numbers—they expect thousands to be on the Mall. We're hoping for some cameras to cover the rally. The Freedom Riders leave May 4 from the bus stations." He looked at me. "How about adding these brave people to your prayer list?"

"I will," I said. "You inspire me, big brother."

"I'll tell you who's inspiring—those Black leaders who are risking their lives in sit-ins and marches. I just wish you could…."

We both got quiet. "I don't want to argue with you, Jack."

"Mom says you're going to take the habit in August. When you finish your training—whenever that is—why not join me on this crusade?"

"I've got years to go, Jack." I felt guilty—I was doing nothing, compared to Jack, to change the world. "Is it enough that I've chosen a life of prayer? I have to believe it is."

"I know you've got it in you, Megs—that fire for doing right. I've seen it. Remember all those trips downtown with your mission club? Don't let it die—don't cover yourself in that medieval outfit."

"My calling requires me to be cloistered." *Did that even sound like me?* "In a few years—who knows? For now, I need to focus on my spiritual life. Is that self-centered and selfish?"

"Want my honest opinion?"

"We'd better get back to the group," I said.

"One more thing, then I'll shut up. Every time Stan writes to me he asks: *Will she ever write? Tell her I love her and miss her.* So…would a kind word kill you?"

"It wouldn't be good—or even possible—for me to write to Stan. For that matter, it wouldn't be good for *him*. That's not to say I don't think of him—I do."

"You loved each other."

Jack had never said that before—I was touched how much he cared. I couldn't talk about it without risking tears.

As we walked towards the auditorium to join our family, I thought, *I do love Stan—as much as I am capable of love. Maybe I will always love him. But how can I love God completely and love Stan at the same time?*

June 15, 1961
Dear Journal,

First year college is finished. I didn't cover myself with glory, like Marianne. But I did better than Jack. There I go, comparing. I accept my lack of brilliance. Next year, as a first-year novice (God willing), I will only have classes in theology and philosophy. The rest will be work, solitude, prayer. I'm ready.

Merton says: "...to settle down in the quiet of our own being we must learn to be detached from the results of our own activity." What's keeping me here? It's mysterious. I'm learning to pray, meditate, live in community. It's not easy—I'm far from perfect—but I want to know what it's like, to wear the habit, to "settle down in the quiet of my own being." Soon, I'll get my wish.

CHAPTER 9

Bless me, Father, for I have sinned. Ever since second grade, I'd been reciting those words to a shadowy silhouette—the priest—on the other side of the confessional screen. As a child, I had to dig deep to come up with sins to confess: Selfishness. Disobeying my parents. Being mean to my sister. Sometimes I'd borrow a quarter from Dad's change tray and not replace it, so, stealing.

Now I was almost nineteen—about to put on the holy habit of religion. During our very first thirty-day retreat, we learned about making a General Confession—I'd be dredging up all the sins committed during my past life. Extraordinary grace would come to my soul. Mother Loretta explained it was an essential—though voluntary—practice before taking the habit and becoming a novice.

If I was serious about my vocation, I felt I needed to make a General Confession. I went over and over the list of sins contained in a little black book for just this purpose. From that, I made my own list, as far as I could remember. In my journal, I divided my life into segments, beginning with what I thought was probably my first sin—I was six when I tore a page out of my sister's favorite book—revenge for her tearing a page out of my favorite book. Honestly, I couldn't remember why, or even which books we were fighting over.

Growing up, confession meant being herded into church and waiting in line to go into the dark, creaky confessional booth to recite our sins to the priest. I wasn't a goody-goody, but in my family at least, there were so many checks and balances against serious sinfulness, that sometimes I had to invent sins, just to make the exercise worthwhile. I was greedy for sacramental grace.

As far as I could tell, I hadn't broken the Ten Commandments. I hadn't blasphemed, taken anyone's life—or their spouse—or coveted anyone's goods (though I did lust after Marianne's cashmere sweaters and rhinestone earrings). I honored the Sabbath and my parents.

I was a good girl.

One time in sixth grade Mom overheard me whining that I wished I were dead—probably some angst over being left out of the popular group of girls. She sat me down on the living room sofa and held my hand. "It's a sin to wish that. I don't ever want to hear you say that again."

I reported it to the priest.

"I'm sure you didn't really mean it," he said. "Say three Hail Marys and three Our Fathers and go in peace." Through the gauzy grill, the priest raised his hand and made the sign of the cross to bless me, whispering the words in Latin: *In nomine Patris, et Filii, et Spiritus Sancti. Amen.*"

There was one teaching about confession in the Catechism that I really liked: The three milk bottles—one pure white, one white with a few black spots (signifying a few venial sins), the third solid black (one mortal sin could blacken the entire bottle!). After confession and the sacrament of penance, the milk bottle was clean and white again—sin had been erased.

Even as a child, I disliked getting dirty.

My high school religion classes warned against sins of the flesh, especially since boys pressured girls for sex. This, of course, was a threat to our sacred virginity, which was not to be violated prior to the sacrament of marriage under any circumstances. There was even talk about "how far to go," including the "forbidden zones" of our bodies—information presented in hushed tones and veiled language. We got the message.

Mom had a hard time talking to me about sex, though she did prepare me for my menstrual period. I suspect she'd learned about sex from her older sister, Aunt Frances—their mother had died before Mom had reached puberty.

Stan had never pressured me to be sexually active, though he held me close when we slow-danced. Some of my girlfriends got pressured to "play around"—even to "go all the way." Stan never did that. The last time I'd been with Stan—that final kiss—something had come alive within me. I couldn't name it—but I didn't think it was sinful.

Then there were the "sins of omission"—not what you did, but what you *didn't* do. For instance, when my girlfriends ridiculed an awkward, obnoxious, or painfully insecure classmate, I faulted myself for not intervening on behalf of the girl. I told myself I ought to drop such girlfriends and embrace the ostracized girl—but I didn't do that often enough. (In retrospect, I felt small and ashamed, so I added that to my General Confession list.)

The pastor of the parish where I'd grown up was an elderly and ill-tempered Monsignor, who never seemed to be listening. He would mumble something, then dole out the same penance—three Hail Marys and three Our Fathers. Confession became an altogether unsatisfactory experience.

Until now. So much more was at stake for my soul. The lists of transgressions and omissions stacked up in my journal, until I felt overwhelmed with the failure I was spiritually—I had become selfish, critical, self-centered. Was I supposed to read everything on this list to the priest? Mother Loretta had told us that the more thorough we could be, the purer our conversion would be. No matter how long it took, I'd unburden myself of my sins.

I knelt in chapel an extra-long time each day during retreat, wondering how I could measure up to this life as a nun. At night, I lay in bed, my rosary beads slipping through my fingers, worrying about my unworthiness—I had not done anything even close to religiously heroic in my life. On the contrary. I had sneaked Jack's journal in and had written in it faithfully—taking care not to get caught—and I wasn't sorry. Countless times, it had saved me from loneliness. I wasn't writing a memoir as Jack had once joked—but the journal was a companion and friend that never judged me. I had no intention of giving it up—and no intention of confessing it. In my mind, it wasn't a sin.

I worried that the priest would think I was becoming scrupulous—concentrating too much on my faults and not enough on my virtues—since my list was so long. Inside the confessional, I could see his profile through the screen, hear his steady breathing. The confessional booth was tight and stuffy—I felt a bit dizzy kneeling there. I rattled off my rehearsed speech.

"Bless me, Father, for I have sinned. I've been uncharitable, disobedient, untruthful, stingy, selfish, vengeful, envious, and silent when I should have acted." I went on to give some specific times and details, then waited.

He paused and whispered, "You have opened yourself to unimaginable graces, Sister. God cannot help but fill you with a deep love and desire to do His will. You have been forgiven all your sins, and your soul is as pure as the day you were baptized. Go, and sin no more."

I left the confessional in a daze and knelt in my pew—surprised by the flood of tears. To be embraced so completely... it was overwhelming. I knelt there, gazing at the crucified Jesus hanging over the altar. It struck me that I had not really noticed his face before—he looked kind and forgiving. Tears streamed down my cheeks. I wiped them with my handkerchief, then buried my face in my hands.

There were others in chapel—I didn't care. I prayed for guidance. A feeling of peace settled over me—for the first time in a long time, I felt ready to take the next step in my vocation.

After the first few dropouts, our postulant group leveled off at twenty-six—until the Fourth of July. At morning prayers, there were six empty places. Could that many postulants be sick? At breakfast in the refectory, Pauline nudged me to move up six place-settings closer to head table.

By the time we assembled in our lecture room, six desks had disappeared, the room had been rearranged, and the nameplates of the departed had been removed. No chance to say good-bye or give them our blessing.

I remembered what Sister Julia had said to me on the first night: "They're dead to us." Why be so secretive? Maybe they felt shame. Maybe Mother didn't want them to upset us or tempt us in their direction. No explanation was given. This seemed inhuman to me.

Delores agreed. "The ones with incurable homesickness—I can understand. But what about the others?"

"I don't know," I said. "They seemed happy to me."

"We're not allowed to talk about anything personal," Delores whispered. "It's no wonder we have no idea how people feel." She stopped and grabbed my arm. "I'm so glad I have you, Clare. I'd go nuts otherwise."

I wanted to hug her but knew I shouldn't.

"There," Delores said as we walked outside during recreation, "I said it. I have no idea what a Particular Friendship is—the thing we're supposed to dread here. But I know this: you're my friend, and I'm glad of it."

Tears welled up—I didn't know why. I loved Delores—like a sister—but I was afraid to tell her that. I grabbed her hand, squeezed it hard, then let it go.

That night I lay in bed, lights out, holding my rosary beads. So many novices and postulants had disappeared. I didn't want that to happen to me. I wanted desperately to belong—to be accepted. There was so much I wanted to prove—about myself. Tears slid down my cheeks—sadness for those who were gone—and gratitude that I hadn't been asked to leave with them.

During our silent retreat, the canonical novices—the worker bees—handled the cooking and cleaning, laundering and folding. It was summer so we had no college classes—plenty of time to keep silence, attend lectures with Mother, meditate, and read spiritual books. Each afternoon a priest came to give us a lecture in chapel.

A month before the ceremony, I wrote to my parents:

> *"Dear Family,*
>
> *It has been a time of joy and excitement here, as we prepare for this holy event. My time has been divided between prayer, study of the vows with Mother, and sewing, sewing, sewing!"*

How could I tell them how satisfying it felt—to be accepted as a Sister of St. Mary? Our lectures focused on the sacredness of the vows of poverty, chastity, and obedience. "Jesus had no place to lay his head," the retreat priest said. "Can you be that detached from the world?"

My answer was always the same: "Only with the grace of God."

I glanced around the chapel I loved—stained-glass windows glowing with afternoon sunlight; gleaming brass candlesticks; white marble sanctuary—and the lovely tile floor where I would soon lie face-down in my new habit, promising to live a life of poverty, chastity, and obedience. I loved the beauty I saw around me in chapel.

Sometimes I imagined myself a player in an elaborate, unfolding drama. If I had to give up all that, would I still want to be a Sister of St. Mary? Just about once a week, I was tortured by the thought that I had been wrong about my *call* to religious life. Was I really supposed to be here?

My conferences with Mother had left me shaken. Did she or didn't she think I was worthy to take the habit? "Sister Clare," she'd said at our last meeting, using her authoritarian tone, "What makes you think you will make a good Sister of St. Mary?"

"I believe I am called, Mother." It seemed that simple to me. "I won't be happy unless I answer that call."

"But are you fit to live this life? You seem often to be at odds with the Rule and customs."

How did she know that? I thought I was doing a good job of complying.

Not for the first time, she seemed to be reading my mind. "I'm good at reading faces, Sister Clare." She winked.

My stomach did a flip.

"Your expression is not one of embracing—I would even go so far as to say I see defiance."

"No, Mother...."

"Case in point—your letters home—you don't deny you disagreed with me?"

I didn't answer.

"I hear you are reading in your cell—a flashlight? Am I correct?"

"No, Mother—that isn't...." I almost mentioned Angela but stopped in time. *Was one of the novices reporting on us?*

"I will need to see an effort on your part to embrace this life more fully—and that includes the customs and rules."

I was trembling—with fear or fury, I didn't know. "Yes, Mother," I managed to say.

I wondered why she was so hard on me. Was it because she was demanding and high-principled? Or was she trying to *break* me? I was determined *not* to be broken. I did want to please her but felt I never measured up. Her harsh manner confused me—could anyone be that hard-hearted? *Trying to please Mother was one thing; was I pleasing God?*

I decided to meet with the retreat priest. He invited me to sit in the overstuffed chair opposite him in the small parlor outside chapel.

"I have doubts, Father," I began.

As a Jesuit, he'd professed vows and lived a communal life, so he understood the commitment I was about to make.

"I want to do what's right, but how can I be sure I have what it takes?" I asked.

"How can you be sure you do *not*, if you don't give the life a try?" He seemed to be distracted, looking at the painting of the beheading of John the Baptist behind me. "Is there something specific which causes you to doubt your vocation? A relationship? A practice or part of the Rule that you cannot accept?"

The thought crept in: *Should I tell him about my secret journal-writing—that I often took time to write when I should have been cleaning the library? That I'd run into that cute Jesuit, Bill, in the library and felt an attraction to him? That he'd shown up in one of my dreams? That I sought out time alone with Delores, when I should've been inclusive? Did it matter? Was any of it wrong?*

"No, Father," I said. "I believe I've been called. I'm not even a little bit holy, compared to the novices. I just wonder…."

What did I wonder? Could I live for God alone? Would I be satisfied? Did I trust God to provide whatever I needed to fulfill my obligations? If God had called me, He would give me strength.

Suddenly I was ashamed, wanted to end the conversation gracefully. "I see now, Father, that if I trust in God's love, I *will* be a good sister."

"Good," he smiled, his hands folded on his lap. He slouched back in his chair. "You've answered your own question. It's dangerous comparing yourself to others. You may be on your way, then, Sister. Let me give you a blessing."

We both stood up. I bowed my head. He raised his right hand over me and recited a blessing in Latin.

I felt the urge to cry. *Was this a sign that God was with me?* I swallowed and concentrated on the oriental carpet, as if I were seeing the golden swirls and crimson flowers for the first time. I looked up. He smiled and motioned to the door.

"Thank you, Father." I swallowed again—grateful I'd pushed back the tears.

"I hope my lectures aren't putting you to sleep," he joked as we neared the door.

"No, Father—not at all." *Was that all he could say?* I felt disappointed that he hadn't given me theological guidance, assured me I was doing the right thing. Instead, he was worried about his lectures—more evidence that I would have to depend on my own wits to figure out my spiritual life.

CHAPTER 10

I spent the summer in the sewing room, pleating, hemming, sewing together the intricate linen pieces that comprised the headdress. *Perfection of my ordinary actions,* I kept repeating to myself, as I stitched—and ripped out—and stitched—and ripped out again—until each piece of the habit passed Mother Loretta's inspection.

Some nights, I went to bed sure I was doing the right thing. Other nights, I was wide awake hours after lights out, worrying about how to measure up. I'd fall asleep fingering my rosary beads.

I wondered about the six postulants in my group who'd disappeared. Was it their decision? Were they too attached to their families? Two had been secretly writing to their boyfriends—one had turned up her nose at everything—no surprise there.

Before the reception ceremony, we gathered in our classroom. I glanced around at the twenty classmates still left. I looked at Angela, Delores, Pauline, Rosemary…I could see the excitement in their faces. My heart expanded—I loved these women—they were like family.

I'd debated what name I wanted to be called in religion. "Sister Margaret Ann" was already taken, so my baptismal name wasn't an option. Mom liked that I'd been named after her—so I'd chosen "Sister Clare Marie"—her first and middle names. I'd surprise everyone at the reception ceremony. Mom would probably need three handkerchiefs.

On reception day, people from "the outside world" arrived, bringing the unmistakable scents that seculars bring—perfume, hairspray, stale cigarettes. Pauline and I—she got to keep her postulant name since no other sister had taken it—were leading the procession into chapel. I could feel the energy as we processed up the aisle.

I noticed Mom sitting on the aisle, her hands folded in her lap—the same hands that had sewn my clothes and braided, curled, and permed my hair, tying it up with ribbons. My hair had been such an important part of my image. I was about to have it cut off. *Without it, who would I be?*

The Archbishop stood at the communion rail where we knelt. "My children, what do you demand?" he asked.

"Your Excellency, the mercy of God and the holy habit of religion," we answered in unison.

I didn't like being called the Archbishop's *children*—but I did like the fact that we were demanding recognition by the Church. Power…status…I liked that part.

"Is it with your own free will you demand this?"

"Yes, Your Excellency."

The Archbishop asked about our intention to take up the yoke of a crucified Jesus.

"Relying on the mercy of God," we recited, "we hope to be able to do so." Our habits—stacked on tables in the sanctuary—would be blessed—a sacred garment to guide us on our path to perfection and holiness.

I felt light-headed—from the incense or from the fact that I was holding my breath in anticipation. Pauline and I led the procession out of chapel, practically running to the community room, where our habits were to be delivered. Novices stood ready to dress us.

"We'll need to cut your hair, of course, to fit under the coif," Mother had told us. But when we asked, "How much hair will they cut?" her response was "How much hair would you want under a coif all day?"

Someone removed my veil and helped me out of my postulant dress, and with firm hands on my shoulders, sat me down.

In a flash, I remembered being seven, gazing into Mom's mirror as she slipped the white taffeta First Communion dress over my head and hair-pinned the white veil to my hair. Today she waited in chapel while someone else dressed me.

Mother Loretta and her assistant—armed with electric clippers—swooped from one of us to the next—as if we were sheep being shorn or lambs being brought to slaughter. "… That thou mayest follow the lamb without spot / and walk with him in white…." Those were the words of the reception ceremony.

The sight of heads being shaved, clumps of hair flying—it was surreal.

Delores sat in front of me. A novice had already removed Delores' glasses. As the buzzing shaver moved closer, she swiveled to face me, terror in her eyes, her half-open mouth whispering: "Oh no. Dear God."

Our eyes locked. I felt my heart beating, my palms were hot and sweaty.

"I can't do this, Clare." Delores got up from her chair—still in her white, long-sleeved undershirt, undershorts, and slip—and dashed toward the door.

I followed her and grabbed her arm to stop her. "We have to," I said. "We said we would. Our families are waiting...."

"I don't care," she said. "I didn't sign up for this—to have my hair shaved off? No, I did not sign up for this." She had tears in her eyes. "Come on—let's get out of here." She ran out of the community room, into the main hall.

I ran after her. "Delores! Where would we go—dressed like this?" Suddenly I felt trapped. I could hear the music trailing from the chapel—the novices singing "Ave Maria."

"I'm not doing this, Clare. Come on, let's go down the back stairs. We can hide in the laundry."

I snuck a look out the window, just in time to see Marianne and Ted walking up the front steps—Ted carrying little Jeffrey. I could almost hear what Marianne would say: "See? I knew she couldn't last. She doesn't have it in her."

I grabbed Delores by both shoulders. "Look at me. Delores!"

She squinted at me.

"You can't run away—you don't have your glasses."

"I can see okay. They can mail them to me."

We both found that funny. She stifled a laugh.

"We can always leave later," I said, "when we're not in our underwear."

That made us laugh even more.

"Leave here without my hair?" she squeaked.

"Hair grows back. Now come on, turn around. Let's calmly return to our seats." I turned her around. "You first. Act as if nothing's happened."

"You're the dramatic one, Clare. You go first."

"Only if you're with me. Are you?"

Delores nodded.

We returned to the community room. The snake of extension cord that powered the electric clippers slid across the waxed floor, scooping up clumps of hair, gathering them into a kind of furry, multi-colored rodent.

"I might throw up," Delores whispered.

Mother stared at Delores and me. "Sisters? Return to your seats. There's no time to waste."

Delores stared back at Mother.

I watched the standoff. *Would Delores sit down?*

Mother placed her hand on Delores' shoulder. "Sit down, Sister."

"Yes, Mother." Delores slid into her chair.

I sat too, watching with detachment—a numbness—that left me questioning whether I was physically in the room.

Mother applied the razor to Delores' head. Straight, square paths blazed a trail from the nape of her neck to the top of her crown. I didn't know a scalp could be that white. The paths crossed one another randomly, as if a careless mower had lost control. Plop! Clumps of her shiny black hair flew from the shaver and settled on my shoe.

It was my turn. I closed my eyes. Gone…the hours of rolling, combing, teasing, fluffing…the torture of trying to sleep on hard plastic rollers and sharp pointed clips—at least there was that. The razor vibrated and tugged at my scalp. I watched my hair drift to the floor. I was dusted with a starchy white towel.

"Stand up, Sister!" A novice held up the wool habit. Weeks earlier, I'd tried it on for a final fitting, anticipating this moment. "Kiss it," the novice said, reminding me of the ritual of kissing each piece of the habit and reciting a prayer as we dressed.

> *Bless this habit, symbolizing humility of heart*
> *and contempt of the world….*

The fabric smelled familiar and comforting as I pressed the garment to my lips. I slipped it over my shoulders, reached my arms through the tailored sleeves. Hooks and eyes snapped the front shut. A coiled leather belt—the cincture—was thrust into my face: "Kiss...." The belt circled my waist through a ring and snapped tight.

When thou wast younger, thou didst gird thyself
and didst walk where thou wouldst....

I kissed the rosary that hung at my side—from then on, I would hear the beads clicking whenever I moved. Then I kissed the crucifix and tucked it into the leather cincture. *Would the crucifix always jab my ribs? Maybe that was the point. Would I get used to it?*

Clumps of hair were still falling when another dresser approached me. She placed a white starched cap or *coif* over my shaved head. Put your chin through the opening first," she said.

I did it.

"Now," the Sister said, "I'm going to pull the coif tight and tie the strings in the back."

The white veil was secured with white-headed pins that stabbed my temples before finally piercing the cap. It sounded like thunder over my ears. I thought again of Delores' bare head—like some disjointed Mohawk cut. If my head looked like that, I was glad it would stay covered.

Only my hands and the space between my eyebrows and chin were left exposed. Trickles of perspiration were forming in recesses under the layers of cotton, wool, nylon, silk, and starch.

We were led back to chapel and knelt before the Archbishop as he placed the outer white veil on our heads: *The emblem of inward purity....*

After the ceremony, I couldn't recognize anyone—we all looked alike. I caught a glimpse of Delores and tugged at her sleeve. She twisted to face me, her glasses perched again on her nose. Her tears had dried, her eyes were glowing. Her mouth curved into a broad smile.

"I didn't recognize you," she whispered. "Whew! Almost didn't make it through that, did we?"

I tried to smile inside the tight headdress. In the stifling heat, I had goose bumps. "You look beautiful."

"So do you." She beamed.

My family met me in the crowded courtyard. The layers of wool, the veil, and the starched headdress made it difficult to get close enough for hugging.

"What's it feel like?" Marianne asked. "Can you hear me?"

I assured everyone I could—though it echoed and rumbled inside.

I was afraid Jack may have left—he so disapproved of my choice. Then I spotted him, across the courtyard, puffing on a cigarette, staring at each of the white-veiled novices, searching their faces, looking for me, panic in his face.

I waved to him and led everyone to the cloister garden where chairs had been set up for us—practically in the same spot where, a year earlier, I had rushed out to them dressed in my postulant outfit.

"You're looking at the new Sister Clare Marie!" I announced. I hugged Mom first—then everyone else.

"Oh my," Mom said, teary-eyed. "I don't know what to say. I never liked my name much, but on you it sounds...." She leaned in close. "They didn't cut off your hair, did they? Tell me you've still got your hair."

I swallowed. "I've got hair, Mom." I didn't say how much—or how little.

CHAPTER 11

Each morning I put on the habit, reciting: *Clothe my soul, O Lord, with the nuptial robe of charity, that I may carry it pure and undefiled before your judgment seat.*

I memorized the prayers for each part of the habit. For the veil, it was: *Place on my head, O Lord, the helmet of salvation, and give me power against my enemies.* A helmet—power—I liked that.

As a novice, I felt I was on the doorstep of perfection. I'd stumbled upon it. But here I was, just the same. I had a new religious name, with the initials SSM after it: Sister of Saint Mary. Novices got their own choir stall—lining the chapel walls and facing center. They were majestic, ornately carved, medieval—elevated a few feet off the floor. There were drawbacks—it took me much longer to get dressed—but now I could devote myself to my spiritual development in a way I'd never dreamed possible before. I was no saint…but I felt I was living like one.

My first year as a novice, I took on *the helmet of salvation*—making each day as perfect as I could. That included meditating, chanting the Divine Office, praying the Mass, and learning Gregorian chant—the ancient music of the Church. Whether I was working in the laundry or kitchen, reading spiritual books, or at evening recreation, I did it all to the best of my ability.

Spiritual reading should have been easy because I loved to read. The first book Mother assigned me to read was *The Story of a Soul*—a life of St. Therese of Lisieux, the Little Flower. On one hand, it was inspiring to read about a young woman my age so completely in love with God. On the other, I felt even more inadequate—I wanted to love God like that. But I was much more in love with people—my parents, Jack, Stan—I even felt I loved Delores, Angela, and Pauline more than I loved God. My constant prayer was that I would grow more perfect—but I didn't want to give up loving everyone else.

I spent so much of my day working in the laundry or kitchen, then rushing to a theology or philosophy lecture, that by the time I got to chapel, I could easily have fallen asleep during spiritual reading—lighting in chapel was dim and it was late afternoon. But I was pursuing perfection, so I struggled to stay awake in class and managed to cover an impressive number of books, in my humble opinion—though as soon as I'd read the last page and turned it in to the library, each book became forgettable. The exception was Thomas Merton. When his book, *Seeds of Contemplation*, appeared in the convent library, I "borrowed" it and kept it in my chapel stall.

My private conferences with Mother Loretta did not get easier. "I'm finding the books assigned to me a bit dry," I confessed.

"Perhaps you need to re-read them, Sister—take more time," Mother said.

Mother seemed bent on making my life as a novice miserable. During a conference in early September, just a few weeks after I'd taken the habit, Mother said, "I'm noticing you're a bit too *familiar* with a few sisters."

I suspected she meant my friendships with Delores and Angela—or even Pauline. Our mail was intercepted and censored. It was no stretch to imagine that our interactions with one another were under scrutiny too.

I wasn't sure what to do about it—but giving up my friends was not an option. Maybe I just needed to be more discreet.

Every first Friday of the month, our chaplain and another priest offered confession. After my General Confession, monthly confession took on new significance. Our chaplain seemed like a good source for spiritual direction—actually asking questions from time to time.

"Are you finding solace in the Mass? Is your spiritual reading satisfactory? Do you have questions about practicing the vows?"

Occasionally I did have questions, but I didn't feel comfortable asking them during confession. *What would everyone think if I took too long in confession*? What I really longed for, especially as I learned more about the vows during this first year as a canonical novice, was a spiritual director—a confidante—who'd listen to my doubts, instruct me, and walk with me on this path to perfection.

I had felt Mother Loretta's sting—censoring my letters, criticizing my writing—even humiliating me in public. *Was she just doing her job*? She inflicted a penance on me after I'd accidentally dropped a tray of small plates while serving in the refectory. I went to Mother's office after dinner, knelt, and held up one of the broken plates, saying: "I carelessly broke this butter dish."

"How did this happen?"

"I got bumped and the tray of dishes slid to the floor, Mother, before I could...."

"A whole tray? You show me one splintered dish, then you tell me it's a whole tray? Next you'll be saying the butter landed on the floor too."

"Yes, Mother." Tears were falling—I could barely breathe.

"Sister, you have not been honest about this."

"No—yes, Mother—I didn't get a chance to say...."

"Didn't get a chance? When were you going to disclose the full extent of your carelessness?"

I was out of breath, couldn't make a sound.

"So." She tapped her fingers on her desk. "For your duplicity, you will spend recreation tonight kneeling before the Blessed Virgin in the center of the community room. Is that clear?"

I nodded, daring to wipe my runny nose with my left sleeve—unable to let go of the broken dish turning hot and sharp in my right hand.

Mother wasn't through. "Furthermore," she said, "you will kneel with your arms extended, for thirty minutes."

Was I dreaming? I was dizzy, not sure I could stand. I focused on the calendar on Mother's desk: October 15, 1961. There was a world outside the convent walls; the sun was setting on my red-brick house; Kennedy was president; the sisters in our Philippine mission were starting their day.

"Sister? What are you waiting for? Go on." She pointed to the door. "To recreation."

Mother's voice brought me back. My knees were sore, my face tear-stained. *How long had I been there?*

"Yes, Mother." I handed the broken dish to her and stood up, still dizzy. I walked into the community room filled with novices, talking and laughing as they played cards or rummaged in their sewing baskets. I plopped down on the kneeler before the statue of Mary, who gazed at me with her serene smile.

I spread my arms, suspending them in air. They felt detached from my shoulders, and before long they grew heavy. My neck stiffened, my jaws clenched—as if tightening everything would keep my trembling arms afloat. I longed to ease my aching back, but there was nowhere to lean. My knees drilled into the wooden kneeler.

The outrage churning in my stomach was nothing compared to the searing pain in my knees. It spiraled up my back, into my shoulders. My arms went numb.

You will not cry, I told myself. I prayed—not for forgiveness—I had done nothing wrong. My prayer to the smiling virgin had two parts: *Please, Mother Mary, let me bear this pain. Please, Blessed Virgin, make me invisible for the next thirty minutes.*

An eternity later, the clock struck eight. I rose, stiff, dizzy, and moved as if in a daze to the nearest chair. No one acknowledged me. I folded my hands and sat, stunned, pretending to listen to the idle conversation. Thirty long minutes passed. Then, mercifully, the bell rang for Grand Silence.

Once in my cell, I cried bitterly. It took me days before I was ready to accept this penance as a gift from God—a test. Did I have what it took to stay? In my journal, I wrote: *I think I have passed another hurdle, God willing.*

I was no longer cleaning the library—I was now assigned to kitchen duty—so I had to find a new hiding place for my journal. Eventually I hid it in my chapel stall, the one place I did not think Mother would look. Sitting in chapel, I'd gaze at the sanctuary—the gold candelabra and tabernacle, the soft light filtering through the stained-glass, the sweet beeswax burning—and I'd feel inspired to write. Surely no one would find fault with my writing if I were doing it in chapel.

I had filled up the pages of one journal and Jack had supplied me with more. I stored my completed journals in my trunk in the attic. Dreams, desires, and questions spilled onto the pages. My journal had become my spiritual director, even as I longed for another person who understood me on that deeper level—one who could hear and accept me without judgment.

One afternoon, I walked outside for recreation—thinking Delores and I would take our customary stroll around the cloister garden. Sister Ellen, the chronically homesick one, approached me.

"Sister Clare, I wonder if you'd walk with me?" She seemed shy and unsure, her thin face searching mine for acceptance. "I know you and Delores like to walk together, but I would really appreciate it…."

"Sure," I said, glancing toward Delores waiting near the door. I raised my eyebrows and leaned toward Sister Ellen. Delores read my body language—then turned to walk with Angela and Pauline.

"I'm not supposed to say anything, but I trust you to keep it to yourself."

From the first day, I'd pegged Ellen as a weak, homesick girl who couldn't stop crying—her fair, freckled face was almost always blotchy. Though her tears had lessened, her downturned mouth told me she was not happy.

"What is it, Ellen?"

"I'm leaving, Clare," she said, as we walked along. "My Dad is driving in from Pittsburgh. I'll sleep in my own bed tonight." She saw the shock on my face. "I know what everyone will think. 'Poor Ellen—so homesick—couldn't measure up.'"

I wanted to object, but I couldn't deny it—that's what I thought too.

"My mother picked out a nice wig—in case you're wondering. It'll be months before I can appear in public without it."

I pictured the bright red curls Ellen had lost to the evil razor on reception day. We both shook our heads—even laughed a little—remembering the shock.

"I want you to know, Clare, that it isn't just homesickness, though I had it bad at first."

"What, then?"

"It's the lack of charity, beginning with Mother. The way she treats us, it's like tacit permission to treat ourselves and one another with the same disrespect." She stopped and looked at me.

For the first time, I noticed her kind, engaging eyes.

"Our greatest commandment, Clare—you know it: Love one another. But if we actually *do* love one another, we have to hide it from Mother."

I picked up the pace so no one would hear us; Ellen kept in step. I felt guilty talking about Mother behind her back, but I didn't disagree with Ellen. "What will you do once you're home?"

"First thing I'm going to do is meet with my friend who encouraged me to enter, a senior Sister, close to Mother Provincial. She's going to get an earful, believe me. Someone needs to know what is happening here."

"You mean, *report* Mother Loretta?"

"You could say that." She stopped me again. "Would you like to know what put me over the line, Clare?"

"If you're willing to tell me, yes."

"The night I walked into the community room and saw you kneeling in the center, your arms open wide. I saw the accident happen—and I was outside Mother's office when you showed up that broken plate. I heard it all. None of it was your fault. Mother refused to listen to you—made a public spectacle of you. For what?"

"To practice humility," I said. *Feeble.*

"I don't see it that way." We had stopped walking; Ellen was searching my face. "It's meaningless—misdirected. That might have worked in the old days, but it's out of place now. This life has enough built-in sacrifice, without dreaming up cruel and unusual punishments for us."

"You're kind, Ellen—I'm grateful that you told me."

"This business of disappearing in the middle of the night… without so much as a good-bye…." She shook her head. "I'm not going to be a part of it anymore." We continued walking.

"I know you thought my tears were from homesickness—some were—but honestly, my heart broke. The lack of charity here...."

"Why are you telling *me* this, Ellen?"

"Like I said—I trust you. I think you're made of strong stuff, Clare. But you also know how to love. I can see that. I hope you'll choose love." She squeezed my hand. "Now, I'm going to walk on, and into the building, where my clothes—and my wig—will be waiting for me in a first-floor parlor. Daddy and I will leave while you're all having supper. Once I'm gone, you can tell whoever you want what I said—anyone but Mother."

"What are your plans?"

"College, of course. Daddy's a Duquesne alum, so I'll probably start out there, maybe major in psychology. I need to see how many credits will transfer." She sounded excited. "I'll still have a vocation—just not to this way of life."

"I'll pray for you, Ellen."

"Thanks." Her eyes narrowed. "Don't be offended, but I'll pray for *you*, Clare. You're the one who's going to need it."

Tears fell as I watched her disappear. The irony—that I was weeping and Ellen was dry-eyed—did not escape me.

We had two classes during our first year as novices—theology and philosophy. The rest of the time we worked in the kitchen or the laundry, read spiritual books, or knelt in adoration in chapel. Whenever I could, I'd slip into the library and read the Romantic poets. I was so tired each night, I fell asleep before the bell rang at nine-thirty.

Poems spilled out of me. I loved John Donne's sonnets. He addressed God as a real person. In Sonnet XIV, he'd written: "... *for I / Except you enthrall me, never shall be free / Nor ever chaste, except you ravish me."* I felt this paradoxical relationship—the sensation of being *enthralled* by God—and *ravished,* deep within my soul.

I didn't share my poems with anyone—they felt too raw, unfinished. Except once, that is, when I was hiding in the library stacks, reading Donne and working on a poem of my own. The Jesuit novice, Bill, was doing research in the library, and I noticed he was watching me.

"You like John Donne?" he whispered, leaving his spot and pulling out a chair to sit across from me. "I couldn't help but notice."

"I do!" I blurted, remembering I shouldn't even have been in the library, and realizing I was violating custody of the eyes by even looking at him. He still reminded me of Jack, even with his black cassock, black-rimmed glasses, and flat-top haircut.

"Me too," he said. "I should be doing Braille research but…." He glanced at my journal.

The pounding in my heart took me by surprise. I avoided making eye contact with him.

"So, you write poetry too," he said. "Mind if I have a look?"

I blushed at being asked such a personal question.

"Only if you want to share," he said, apologetic. "I'd love to read it."

All I could do was slide my journal toward him. He picked it up, read silently, then handed my journal back.

"Beautiful. John Donne would be proud. You're Clare, right?"

I nodded, closing my journal.

"Bill," he said.

"I remember, hello again."

Bill looked at his watch, then slid his chair back and stood up. "Better go. My ride's waiting outside. Thanks for letting me read your poem. Maybe someday…well, bye."

I didn't look up until he was out the door. Suddenly I felt drained of energy. *What was I doing, sharing my poetry with a stranger who did not feel like a stranger?* I reread Sonnet XIV and stopped at the lines: "*Yet dearly I love you, and would be loved fain / But am betrothed unto your enemy....*" Loving God...what a complicated affair.

Mother Loretta had warned us against *Particular Friendships*—attachments would *infect*—was that the word? Yes, *infect the spirit of unity* among us. *Infect. Infiltrate. Destroy. Jeopardize*...all terms attached to friendship. I understood why being exclusive could be damaging to the group, but this fear meant never getting close to anyone.

Delores and I had never been in the same cell—until we were. We arrived from kitchen charge and saw the new cell list posted outside the community room. We stifled a laugh.

"Isn't it enough I have to put up with you in charge after charge," Delores whispered. "Now I have to put up with your snoring too!"

"I do *not* snore," I whispered back. "You probably do, though."

"Do not!" Delores elbowed me—our way to express affection—minimal and unnoticeable.

Once we moved into the cell together, I needed to practice custody of the eyes and ears with even more resolve. I knew Delores so well that I could identify—even categorize—every little sound she made. I could imagine the salt stains on her habit; could hear her sponging and brushing it clean. I even knew when Delores was having her period, she slept more soundly and talked in her sleep.

"Familiarity breeds contempt," Mother had said.

Would Delores and I grow to despise one another?

Instead, our fondness for one another grew deeper.

One day Mother called us all together to announce the departure of two first-year and two senior novices. It was the first time she'd spoken to us about departures—she had never mentioned Ellen's leaving, but then I hadn't expected her to.

Mother didn't say so, but it was obvious that the two first-year novices had been chronically ill, off and on, since they had entered—no surprise they were going home. It was also obvious that the two senior novices had been best of friends. Mother didn't mention this either, though everyone could see it. Whenever she lectured us about Particular Friendships, I'd thought of these two novices.

With every departure, I reexamined my call. I felt sad for them—and uneasy about my own closeness to Delores. *Would the same thing happen to us?* No—I would not lose my vocation, simply because we were good friends. "God is love," I repeated to myself, as I prayed for greater love. In everything I did, I sought perfection. I trusted I could have both.

The departures created imbalances in the dormitories, and soon a new cell list appeared. Dolores and I were in different dorms—I wondered if Mother had seen the error of placing us together.

"Don't be ridiculous," Delores said, when I mentioned it to her. "We are not guilty of a PF, for goodness sakes. We work together, we live together, we study together, we pray together. We're friends—sisters. We are not exclusive." She reminded me of our philosophy class: "Platonic love," she said. "Sublimation."

Our philosophy professor—a priest—used to say that Plato's symposium—the word in Greek really meant *drinking party*—was a fictional collection of men each delivering a speech in praise of love. "Some insisted that the reason for love was to satisfy man's desire for material beauty," he'd lectured. "That level of love we call *Eros.* Others believed the purpose of love was to become a philosopher—a lover of wisdom or *Sophia.* The highest form of love seeks Supreme Beauty, thus love of the Divine." He'd raised his hand in proclamation: "*Ergo*, my Sisters, that is the love that gathers you and me together in hot pursuit."

This explanation of love consoled me—especially when that familiar ache welled up inside me. I had decided to open one of Stan's letters—smuggled in by Jack on visiting days. I'd gone to my trunk and read one, and before long, I'd read them all. I told myself I'd loved Stan and he'd loved me, it wasn't wrong to care about him. I prayed for him every day. What could be wrong with reading his letters? It seemed cruel not to.

They were predictable—opening with *My dearest Maggie*—then a page or two about what he was learning, how lonely his life in the Navy was, how he waited anxiously for Jack's news of me after each visiting day. In one letter, he wrote: *What did I do wrong?* Poor Stan. His closing was always the same: *I will always love you.*

Sometimes, when I couldn't get to sleep, I'd imagine writing to him. *My dearest Stan*.... But that was as far as I allowed myself to go. Songs we used to slow-dance to played in my head: Gershwin's "Embraceable You" was one of our favorites. The music carried me back to Stan's arms.

I wanted to be a loving person—like the person of Jesus in the Gospels. I had chosen chastity, so it would have to be platonic love. I would dedicate myself to that. Plato wrote: "Love that is genuine, including physical attraction, is a means to reach contemplation of the Divine." In other words: *Perfection.*

It was a relief when summer break arrived. As first-year novices, we'd taken only two classes—theology and philosophy. Fall semester, we'd be busy again with English, French, science, theology and something called epistemology. *Savor the summer*, I told myself, *even if it is unbearably hot under all the layers of this habit.*

PART TWO

August 1962 - June 1965

CHAPTER 12

I was on my way to spiritual reading in chapel—taking the short cut through the cloister walk—when I heard music from the other end of the corridor. I followed it to the auditorium and peeked through a crack in the door. The room was dark, except for a beam of late-afternoon sunlight highlighting a figure seated at the piano on the stage. It was Mother Loretta. I'd seen her accompany choir practice during the rare occasion when Sister Bernadette could not be there, but I'd never heard her play like this. I leaned against the wall, listening.

Pauline appeared from around the corner. "What's going on?"

"Listen," I whispered. "Isn't it beautiful?"

"Who's playing?"

"It's Mother."

"Are you serious?" Pauline tiptoed to the door and peeked in. "Do you have any idea what this means?"

"What?"

"She's playing Beethoven. His *Pathétique*. Sonata Number Eight in C Minor, Opus Thirteen, to be exact." She took another peek, then leaned against the wall next to me. "It's a *very* complex piece."

"So?"

"She's playing it by heart—without sheet music," Pauline said. "Getting it exactly right."

We listened together without a word.

Pauline seemed in a trance. Then suddenly, she looked up at the hallway clock. "Come on, we're late for chapel. I'll explain on the way."

We hurried along the dim corridor.

"Have you ever heard Mother play like that?" I asked.

"Never—I had no idea. There's a lot more to Mother than I ever gave her credit for."

"Meaning what?" I said, thinking about the harsh treatment I'd received.

"Amazing," Pauline said. "She could easily have been a concert pianist, Clare. Not only does she have a heart—and soul—she's given up an incredible career." All the way to the chapel door, Pauline kept repeating: "Amazing…just amazing."

The next day at breakfast, Mother was missing from the head table.

Was she sick? That would be a first.

Sister Dominic, Mother's assistant, rang the little hand bell at the head table and stood up. She seemed uneasy. "Finish your charge duties, Sisters," she said. "We'll meet in the community room at nine-thirty." It was a silence day, so we could only look at one another and guess what was going on.

The community room filled up. Mother was not in her office as we passed by it on our way, and she was not at the podium.

Mother Provincial stood behind the podium. "Good morning, Sisters," she said, her intense eyes peering out at us. From the first meeting I'd ever had with Mother Provincial—months before entering—I'd felt she could look straight through me. "I am sure you are wondering why I stand before you this morning. I have news which only I should deliver."

Mother Provincial was, in many aspects, the epitome of a Sister of St. Mary—spotless, wrinkleless, erect in her posture, precise in her speech and diction, a placid smile never leaving her face with its milky complexion and pink cheeks. But today, her dark eyebrows—though perfect—were compressed.

"I see puzzled looks, worry on your faces, Sisters. There is no need. My news, though it may cause you some concern, is of

God." She cleared her throat. "Beginning today, Sisters, you will have a new Mistress of Novices. Mother Loretta has been asked to direct our mission in the Philippines. She has many gifts which are needed at the mission school for girls. She left this morning to begin her new ministry."

A collective gasp rippled through the room. No one moved.

Were they forcibly removing Mother Loretta? Had Ellen actually succeeded in reporting on her? Was it her choice to go to the Philippines—our poorest mission? Why so soon?

None of us dared to ask.

"My dear Novices," Mother Provincial said as she looked to the rear of the room and motioned for a strange sister to come forward. "May I introduce Sister Vivian—excuse me—I should say, *Mother* Vivian, the new Mistress of Novices of the Sisters of St. Mary. I know you will make Mother Vivian welcome. Applause is not part of religious decorum, so let us stand to welcome her."

We all stood up and stared silently at this stranger. She walked to the front of the room, glancing sideways at us through the film of her black veil. She was tall and graceful, without being stiff.

Once she reached the podium, she said, "Please, Sisters, do sit down." She waited for the noise to settle. "I know this may be a shock for you all—I'm sorry for that. It's a shock to me too, to be honest. But it seems God has brought us together. I trust in Grace that we will continue the good work Mother Loretta has done—maybe even learn new ways to build community together."

She glanced at Mother Provincial standing next to her, sighed, and stepped from behind the podium. "I've never been comfortable behind a podium." She laughed softly—her round cheeks punctuated by dimples. "Let's have a real conversation, shall we? I know it's a silence day but...ask me anything. I'll try to tell you the truth—as I know it."

Ask her *anything*? I was stunned—everything we'd been taught was being erased—as if all the rules we'd been schooled in had been struck from the book.

"It's okay. I won't bite."

She'd said '*okay.*' What other sins against convent training might this new Novice Mistress commit? Was she too new to know that her superiors would frown upon the use of slang?

Angela—probably the most rebellious among us—raised her hand. Mother Vivian looked relieved. She walked to Angela, extended her hand, and touched her shoulder. I had never seen Mother Loretta touch any of us. "Tell me your name, Sister."

"Angela, Mother."

"Sister Angela—what's on your mind?"

"I'm wondering," Angela hesitated—something she rarely did. "What are your thoughts on the Second Vatican Council? What changes do you think Pope John XXIII is hoping for? Are you in favor of them?"

"I see you've been keeping up with the times." Mother Vivian raised her eyebrows and glanced toward Mother Provincial. "I do indeed favor change. Don't you? Change, after all, is a sign that we're alive. We all want to live life to the fullest, don't we?"

Angela grinned from ear to ear. "Yes. We do, Mother."

Mother Provincial, still behind the podium, broke in. "Sisters, I think we will give Mother Vivian some time to get settled. You will see her again at lunch in the refectory. In the meantime, we will resume today's schedule."

I caught Angela's eye and motioned for her to follow me. We walked down the steps and stood outside the refectory, where Angela was on server duty. "What's going on?" Angela asked. "Who is that woman? Did we wake up this morning on another planet?"

"It's confusing," I said. "I thought novice mistresses held their posts for life."

Angela raised her eyebrows. "Do you think Mother Loretta got in trouble with Mother Provincial?"

I thought of Sister Ellen—had she reported Mother Loretta to the Mother Superior in Pittsburgh?

Angela looked triumphant. "Do you understand the significance of this appointment?"

"No. Tell me."

"You and I and the rest of the Sisters of St. Mary *may* have just joined the 20th century. I can't wait to tell my brother."

"Why him?"

"He studied in Rome, remember? He's the one who got me so excited about the progressive movement in the Church—more liberal theology is just around the corner."

"It sounds like Mother Vivian knows something about this new movement, don't you think?" I asked.

"I'll ask my brother—I'm seeing him this weekend."

"Angela, if I didn't love you, I'd be insanely jealous."

"Why? You have a brother, Clare."

"But I never get to see him—much less write to him. You're lucky you can see your brother whenever you like."

"Someday…maybe sooner than you think, we may all have more freedom." Angela's eyes sparkled. "I think Mother Loretta's *style*—if I can use that word—was losing its appeal. It's a new age, and I, for one, am going to give Mother Vivian all the help she needs to feel welcome here. We'll talk later. Gotta set the refectory for lunch."

On my way to the kitchen for lunch duty, I thought about how I'd tried to avoid criticizing Mother Loretta—out loud. Accepting the journals from Jack was my *silent* protest against her decision to keep my journal from me. I was constantly striking a balance between self-denial—following the rules—and preserving my sanity. Was self-denial making me a better nun? That was all I really wanted—to be a good Sister of St. Mary.

I caught my reflection in the corridor glass; seeing myself in my habit took me by surprise, even after a whole year. I knew it was vain, but I had never felt so beautiful. I loved the flowing pleats, the rippling rosary, the filmy white veil, even the starched headdress that itched and cut into my skin. There were times when, as a novice, I felt complete. I'd endured a lot to become worthy of this habit. In sewing and ripping hours alone, my habit was like a trophy. How would it feel to trade it in for something *modern?*

During lunch, Mother Provincial sat at the head table, with Mother Vivian on her right, and Sister Dominic on her left. It was a silence day but we were given permission to talk, in honor of our new Mistress of Novices. We all clapped too—so what if it was worldly?

A few days later, Mother Vivian called a meeting. Delores complained: "She wants us to meet in the rec room—that awful place—a rec room in name only. Why not in the community room, or in one of the classrooms?"

I couldn't think of a good reason why our new Mistress of Novices would choose the rec room in the convent's basement—an unattractive, musty space with low ceilings and hard wooden chairs lining the walls.

"All we do in there is polish our shoes Saturday afternoons," Delores said. "The lighting is awful, the concrete floors all scuffed. God forbid you have to bring family there on visiting days."

"It does seem odd," I said.

"Why has it been off-limits since yesterday?"

"I don't know, Sister Mary Sherlock Holmes—why don't you tell me?"

"Something's going on," Delores declared.

"Brilliant. Something's always going on around here," I said.

That evening, after supper and evening prayer, we all processed out as usual. But when we got outside chapel, Mother Vivian pressed a finger to her lips, then gestured for us to follow her down the back stairway, to the hallway outside the rec room. She swung open the double metal doors.

I spotted the rocking chairs first, even a glider or two, arranged in little seating circles, each with a coffee table in the center. Occasional tables held lamps casting amber light over oriental rugs strategically placed to create seating groups. Along the walls, upholstered chairs stood ready to be moved into a circle—enough to seat just about everyone. Large pillows scattered on the floor suggested the unthinkable: some of us would even be invited to sit on the floor.

After the first oooh's and ahhh's, laughter and spontaneous applause erupted.

"Your reaction is all the reward I need, Sisters," Mother Vivian said, her face beaming, her dimples deepening. "Come in, and don't fight over the reclining chairs. Let's move the side chairs into a circle so we can have a dialogue."

For seconds, no one moved—then a few sisters took Mother's cue and gathered the side chairs to form one large circle. "No fluorescent lights, please," Mother said. "If it's too dark, we'll find more lamps."

The differences were stunning—the first being that Mother Vivian did not place herself in the center, but in one of the rocking chairs in the circle. Once all of us had found chairs—and a few brave novices had settled onto the floor pillows—she spoke.

"Tomorrow, in the light of day, you'll see that these walls need painting, so I'll be looking for volunteers. I have a few colors in mind, but I'd love to know what you all think."

There was silence again, as we studied our folded hands.

Finally, Angela spoke up. "Anything but lime green!"

Everyone laughed.

"Mother, how did you do it?" one of the novices asked. "Where did all these chairs come from?"

"One of our nursing homes had just completed a remodeling project and had lots of furniture in storage, so I made a few phone calls—promising our novices would pray for them for a whole year."

We laughed and promised we would.

"The next day, a moving van arrived, like magic," Mother was smiling. "You are all so practiced at not looking outside—you didn't even see them." She pointed to the worn area rugs. "I had the oriental carpets moved from the upstairs parlors—until we can get some of our own." She rocked back and forth, then suddenly leaned forward. "Now, Sisters, listen carefully. We are at a crossroads here. Do you sense it?"

A few heads nodded. Most of the sisters stared at Mother as if she were an alien.

"What has come before is blessed. It's as it needed to be, for the time. But we are in a new time and space." She looked around the room. "The Church is asking us as religious women to awaken, to step into the present—while honoring the past—and to prepare for the future." She stood up and walked around, looking each of us in the eye. "We are being called to something new, Sisters. I hope you can feel it."

Heads nodded, and a few sisters said, "Yes, Mother."

"Tomorrow, we'll begin a series of conversations together," she continued. "We'll talk about the vows, the Church, sexuality."

Heads jerked and several sisters sat up straighter.

"That's right—we're sexual beings, and it's time we embrace it. We'll talk about the Council—Vatican II—just opening in Rome, where Pope John has begun opening the windows of the Church and letting in the fresh air." She looked around the room. "I know the windows in this room have rarely been opened, but we're going to change that. Like the Church, we're going to breathe fresh air. I hope you can feel it…smell it…taste it."

Did that mean we would finally be allowed to look out the windows? What would happen to custody of the eyes?

"We'll be listening to writers who will help us to understand the reforms being asked of us—as new leaders in the Church. We will draw from the wisdom of the past and the energy of the present. We will open our minds and hearts—seek dialogue in an ecumenical spirit with Protestants and Buddhists, people of all faiths. Sisters, we will become women of the Church in a more public way." She paused and smiled. "Beginning tomorrow evening, I'm going to have a look under those night coifs."

Gasps rippled around the room.

"Your heads need airing out. I have it on good authority that sooner than you might imagine, we may be uncovering our heads as we step from the 19th into the 20th century—as nuns in the modern world. We mustn't do it with diseased scalps."

I'm not sure which novice started clapping—but before long, applause echoed off the ceiling and walls. Mother Vivian seemed surprised, then genuinely moved. Her tears left damp spots on her habit.

She held up her hand to ask for silence. "Thank you—but our task ahead will not be easy. For some of you, it may not be what you had in mind. Let's be mindful of the words of our Foundress, Mother Mary Dolan, who cautioned that we must trust God alone, who is guiding each of our vocations as Sisters of St. Mary. God alone, Sisters, will guide us as we step into a whole new world." She opened her arms wide. "Please stand," she said. "Let us hold hands and pray."

The rockers slowed to a stop. Those sprawled out on the pillows pulled themselves up onto their black-robed knees, then stood. Everyone gathered in a tight circle. It was awkward at first, we had never been invited to hold hands with our sister novices—touching had been discouraged. We all bowed our heads.

"Spirit of Love," Mother Vivian prayed, "teach us how to be ourselves—to see that we are the gift You have given the world. Let us not deny that gift."

In one voice, we answered, "Amen!"

We held hands for a few seconds, before one of the senior novices dropped her hands to her sides, then rubbed her palms, as if cleansing them. I'd been holding hands with Delores on one side and Angela on the other. I didn't *want* to let go. Both Angela and Delores must have felt the same, because they held on tight.

A charge of energy ran directly to my chest and my heart pumped wildly. It traveled deeper down my body, to the place my girlfriends and I used to call "down there." It was a muscle contraction—the ripple I'd felt when Stan and I had held one another and kissed for the last time. I couldn't define what I was feeling, but I knew it was good.

In that moment, holding hands with Angela and Delores, I felt so alive—maybe even as alive as I'd felt in Stan's arms. This new feeling was different. Was it the ecstasy the saints wrote about? If so, I longed for more.

That night, as I knelt to pray before getting into bed, I thanked God for sending Mother Vivian, thanked God for opening me to this feeling.

CHAPTER 13

When we met in our classroom with Mother Vivian for our first lecture, she introduced more changes. "We only have three weeks before a whole new group of postulants arrives," she told us. "First, let's move the flip-top desks to the side walls, bring your chairs into a circle. Get used to dialogue—not lecture. I'm relegating the podium to that corner alcove—under the statue of St. Catherine of Siena."

Before Mother began with the vows—poverty, chastity, obedience—she said, "Let's get the topic of sex out of the way first, shall we?"

We all developed nervous coughs and shortness of breath.

"I know, you think that once you put on the religious habit, you can be free from sex. But I'm here to tell you you're mistaken."

I was terrified—and thrilled.

"You are sexual beings," she went on. "Women with ovaries and hormones—you need to acknowledge that your body has been designed by God to give you intense pleasure."

She stopped and looked at each one of us.

I stared at my folded hands—knowing that my face was beet red.

"Some—not all—of you have experienced that pleasure. Some of you may know little about sexual pleasure or masturbation."

There was an audible gasp. That was a word that had only been whispered about at slumber parties, in my experience, and only in a male context. As far as I knew, girls didn't masturbate. How could they?

"If you're going to willingly give that pleasure up," Mother continued, "then for the love of God, you'd better know exactly what it is you are foregoing. We'll take time to explore human sexuality in some detail. Before I entered, I completed nurses' training, so while I'm not an expert, I do know a thing or two about human anatomy."

Mother stopped and looked around. "I notice that some of you are uncomfortable. Why is that? Do you know why your body is reacting as it is?"

No one said a word.

"Sisters, do not fool yourselves into believing that the habit and veil you are wearing will silence those urges—those feelings that make you human. During our reception ceremony, we pray: *Clothe me in the garment of salvation.* But pleated wool and starched linen can only do so much."

I glanced around but didn't dare make eye contact with Angela, Delores, or Pauline.

Mother went on. "Underneath those pleats and folds of wool there beats a heart that desperately wants to love and be loved—our ovaries are producing eggs—every month—ready to be fertilized. Each of us bears a womb longing to turn an embryo into an infant, a vagina wanting to feel pleasure."

I could not believe what I was hearing.

"How will you answer those longings, my dear novices? You had better know how you can," she said, her brown eyes wide, "and still remain faithful to your human sexuality *and* to your vow of chastity. It may seem easy for you now, but believe me when I tell you that it is not."

A pin dropping would have made us all jump.

Mother Vivian moved to a bookcase and asked two novices to pass out journals. "Sisters, I am presuming that some of you keep a journal. But I am also presuming that some of you do not. I am hoping that those of you who have not will begin today."

Each of us received a journal.

My heart was beating wildly—I felt like dancing around the room.

"Now, this journal will be for your own use—you're not obligated, and you do not violate obedience if you choose not to."

She walked over to a novice and held up her journal for all to see. "I will not censor you. I won't read your journals—unless you ask me to. They're an opportunity to be in dialogue with your body, your spirit, your soul, as you form your spiritual life. Find a place to write that's comfortable for you—your cell, the library, chapel even."

"We're allowed to write and read in our cells, Mother?" a sister asked.

"Of course, you are—why?" She looked at our faces. "I see. I'm sure there was good reason for such a rule, but let's experiment. Just don't keep one another up with the lights on past your bedtime, okay? Charity first."

I had been vindicated. My two years of contraband journals had been sanctioned. I was no longer a sinner or a sneak. In fact, I prided myself a little on being ahead of the game, at least in this respect.

"You may be wondering what to write," she said.

I needed no coaching.

"Write about what you're feeling regarding your own sexuality. What do you want from the vow of chastity? How will you manage your sexual urges? What has worked for you, so far?" She glanced around the room. "I can imagine that some of you may be angry with me for bringing the subject up at all. Write about that." She paused, and looked around. "I see the skepticism on your faces. I don't blame you. You've been censored—perhaps with good intentions. I am not here to judge the past. But this is a new day, Sisters. Until I do something to betray your trust, I ask you to trust me. Can you do that?"

We turned in surprise when the oldest member of our class said, "Yes, Mother." She had volunteered next to nothing of herself over the entire two years she had been part of our group. I'd had her pegged as shy, then as surly, and finally, as mature. The transformation in her face at this moment startled me. She was smiling, and her eyes lit up. She said it again: "Yes, Mother. Thank you."

Others chimed in. I nodded but couldn't bring myself to say anything out loud. What was holding me back? Maybe I feared that if I ever tapped into my own pleasure source, I would never be able to turn the spigot off.

It had only been one week since Mother Vivian's arrival, and already the Novitiate felt different—not just because she'd rearranged the furniture. We were seeing one another with a warmth I'd never noticed before. With Delores, Angela, and Pauline, my closest friends, I felt more free to touch—even hug them.

Sometimes it made me uncomfortable. I'd had close girlfriends, but I'd never felt the urge for close physical contact with them. Of course, there had always been men and boys around for that. This was new. It reminded me that beneath the yards of habit, I was a live human being. Sometimes, I worried that the four of us were becoming a spectacle.

When the postulants arrived in September 1962, we instinctively toned down our play and shows of affection. We built up an artificial distance between us. A period of abstinence followed—we gave ourselves a mock lecture about "religious decorum," glibly quoting the Customs Guidebook which stated, among other things: *It is unsuitable to run giddily throughout the Convent.*

From time to time, I wrote about our relationship in my journal, wondering if others were scandalized by our behavior. But mostly, I just knew I wanted to be close to them. Was it from God, this longing and appreciation I felt for my sisters? Of course it was: God is love.

During the next few days, before the new postulants were to arrive on September 8, Mother called each of us into her cell during the Grand Silence. It felt sacrilegious to be talking, but Mother Vivian explained that the rule of silence was to encourage recollection, to quiet the mind, so we could be free and open to the Spirit. The rule of silence is a guideline—not an end in itself. Mother Vivian said this so often, it became a common saying.

Before her arrival, the rules had never been challenged. Now, we reminded ourselves often: *The rules are a guideline, not an end in themselves.* I felt mature enough to know this required a fine line, and immature enough to cross it occasionally.

During one of Mother Vivian's first lectures—*dialogues*—she'd explained the fine line: "The Rule—the official Constitutions of our Order approved by Rome—can only be changed by Rome. The rules—that's an entirely different story." She'd sat up straight, slid her veil back off her forehead as far as it would go, then looked around at each one of us. "The rules need to be flexible, Sisters, because we are all evolving, aren't we?"

I was one of the first to visit Mother's cell for scalp inspection. I was surprised to see her without her night coif. Her light-brown hair was thick and wavy, combed back off her forehead, tapered around her ears, and closely cropped. "Don't be shocked, Sister—I'm still the same person. I'm just doing my scalp a favor—exposing it to the air. Come in—sit down. Take off your coif, let's have a look."

I hadn't taken a close look at my butchered scalp since Reception Day. I'd used my sewing scissors to trim my hair in the privacy of my cell. Without the luxury of shampoo, we'd been using bar soap to wash our heads. If the soap left a scum or film, how would we know?

"Ah—we'll need to treat your scalp, I'm afraid." Mother Vivian spoke softly. "I see some dandruff—a little eczema—not too serious. A few treatments should do it." She handed me a tube labeled *Medicated Shampoo.* "Every night now, for at least two weeks—no exceptions. No night coif—you need to air out."

"Yes, Mother." I couldn't imagine the humiliation of exposing my crudely clipped head.

"Wait. Before you go—let me patch you up." On her dresser sat an array of tools—combs, scissors, shaving blades, electric shaver, even special scissors for thinning. "Don't worry—you won't look like a movie star, but you won't scare anyone either." She laughed softly.

I was too nervous to laugh.

By the time Mother was finished, I looked a little like I had when I'd turned sixteen and defied fashion by getting a short haircut.

"I bet you wore bangs as a girl, didn't you?" she asked, after attempting to brush back the hair on my forehead.

I nodded. I felt teary. "My Mom used to trim my bangs and curl my hair. It was our time together."

"Of course," Mother Vivian whispered. "How you must miss your mother."

I couldn't hold the tears in. My shoulders shook. I drew deep breaths to stem what felt like a rushing tide.

"Go ahead, dear. Tears can be cleansing." She rested a hand on my shoulder.

I sat in the chair, wiping my eyes. Mother Vivian handed me a hanky. My breathing eventually returned to near-normal.

Mother lifted my bowed head, her hand under my chin. "There now," she whispered, "I think you've pulled together nicely. I've done a passable job on your hair. It's going to be up to you to rescue your scalp."

I nodded, still sniffling.

"If you could manage a smile, walking out of here, it might encourage the other novices. I've noticed how they look up to you. Can you do that for me—for them?"

"Yes, Mother." I was touched by Mother Vivian's tenderness. At the same time, I struggled to believe I could trust it.

After Mother Vivian's arrival, books and magazines appeared in a newly-formed corner of our classroom—a corner with rockers and reading lamps. It seemed to me that all the book titles had the word "Change" in them. Delores, Angela, Pauline, Rosemary, and I loved meeting in the magazine-reading corner. We all took turns reading *America*, a Jesuit magazine. It published articles on formerly taboo topics—politics, the voice of women, the morality of war. It was both exciting and confusing. I could see how this new movement in the Church could divide us.

Mother scheduled regular one-on-one conversations with each of us. I entered Mother's office to find that the desk had been moved to one side, leaving room for two comfortable chairs with a table and lamp between them. I looked around the room, for a space where I could kneel.

"There's no need to kneel—unless you're here to ask for forgiveness," Mother said.

I was stunned. Was I supposed to sit in one of the chairs next to Mother?

"This arrangement allows for better conversation—don't you think so?"

"Yes, Mother," I settled into one of the chairs. Since when did the Mistress of Novices ask her novices what they thought?

"You look surprised. Is this arrangement going to be okay for you?"

That the Mistress of Novices was using the word "okay" was so out of the ordinary that I had to suppress a laugh. "Yes, Mother. It's more than…." I paused before saying, "okay," trying to rid myself of the feeling that I'd just spoken a curse word.

"Fine. Now, what would you like to talk about?"

I'd been thinking about the books and writers Angela had been raving about. "I love Thomas Merton, the Trappist monk—there are several books by him I want to read," I said. "If I ask my family for some, would I be able to keep them, write in them?" (I didn't tell her I was keeping a library copy for my own use, or that I hid away in the library—especially that I'd shared a poem with a seminarian!)

"Of course," Mother answered. "Merton is a fine writer and thinker—some say even a modern-day mystic—any of his books would make excellent reading. You know the titles—*No Man Is an Island; Seeds of Contemplation; The Living Bread.* By all means, ask for them. Yes—keep them for as long as they serve you in your spiritual life. I can suggest a few other writers—I'll get back to you." She reached out to pat my hand. "You seem relieved."

"Yes, Mother." *How much should I reveal to her?* "I've liked the books assigned to me so far," I said (*not entirely true*), "but they've been a little dry. I get more out of reading when I can underline and make notes. Does that violate the vow of poverty?"

"Not if the books and notes support your spiritual development—which I assume they do." She cleared a stack of magazines and newspapers from her desk and set them on a side shelf. "By the way, I understand some of you have formed a little band—you on the banjo, Sister Pauline on guitar. Any chance we might have a show soon?"

I wanted to hug her. "I think that can be arranged, Mother."

"Are you enjoying classes this semester?" she asked.

"I love English Lit and French...Epistemology and Sociology...very dry." *We work hard at getting those professors off topic,* I thought but did not say.

"I hear you were active in drama in high school—any thoughts about your major, once you move on to classes on the college campus? You'll need to declare a major, you know."

I was taken by surprise again—the new norm with Mother Vivian. "I think I *would* like to major in theater." *Could I actually say what I wanted to be and do?*

"There's time to make that decision," Mother said. "But let's give it some thought."

"Thank you, Mother."

We sat in silence. I searched for the words to express my joy, without crying or laughing, or both. "I like the way you speak matter-of-factly to us," I said.

"You don't think I'm too blunt? I expect some do."

"No, Mother."

I often thought of Sister Ellen who had left us, determined to report the lack of charity under Mother Loretta's reign. Ellen's sacrificial leaving had rescued us.

Angela and I were assigned to clean the classrooms on the ground floor—something we did after supper and before recreation. We were supposed to keep silence during our charges, but no one was around to report us.

"Everyone in my family—except my Dad—wants to know when I'm going to start wearing a modern habit," I said, scooping dust into a dustpan. "They think Mother Vivian is the best thing. My brother is thrilled that we're allowed to watch the evening news. He shouted, 'Welcome to the 20th century!'"

"My brother the priest says it's only a matter of time—that we're living in a bubble here—that once that new Council in Rome gets going…."

"I love the changes, Angela…but how are we going to…." I wasn't sure how to say it. "The Rule says we need to be *in* the world but not *of* the world."

"Clare…you and your ideal, perfect path." She handed me a dust cloth. We raced to see who could wipe the most desktops. "Let's concentrate on being 'in the world'—and worry about the 'not' part later."

"We'll call it *The Novitiate Follies*," I told Pauline, as we sat at the upright piano in the rec room one afternoon before spiritual reading and Divine Office. "We'll start with our first week as postulants, then maybe a skit in the sewing room—you know, ripping out stitches and trying to learn how to operate the sewing-machine treadle, then maybe a scene during the Grand Silence, where we invent a new form of sign language."

Pauline was tapping out songs on the piano: "Sisters, Sisters" followed by "What's The Matter With Kids Today," while I turned the words into parodies. We created a repertoire and recruited others to be in the show—especially Rosemary, who had been in the drama club with me at school.

"This is tons more fun than studyin' for classes," Delores said, as she rummaged for costumes—most were borrowed from the used-clothing collections donated for our missions in the Philippines.

"We'll all flunk French together," Pauline said.

Pauline had convinced another novice to type up the song sheets and program and Angela had dreamed up a makeshift lighting system. One of the postulant's fathers, an electrician, had donated three strips of footlights and two side spots, and Angela supplemented the system using all the available lamps in the parlors.

"We may not be scholars," Angela said, "but we sure can put on a good show!"

We staged the show on the feast of All Saints. Under Mother's guidance, the new postulants had taken on the dingy auditorium as their remodeling project—and had painted it in warm gold and aqua blue. Mother invited the professed sisters—an historic first. They sat in front of the auditorium and the novices and postulants sat in the rear—things were changing, but we still weren't allowed to mingle with the professed sisters.

Mother pulled me aside after the *Follies*. "You seem to have found your calling, Sister Clare Marie," she said. "I hope we can expect more shows before we send you off to the House of Studies."

I was exhilarated—thrilled to be creating and working with my friends Pauline and Delores, Angela, and Rosemary. I had succeeded in bringing our most senior novice—and a sister we called "the philosopher"—into our project. I was humbled. It gave me status within our little community and helped me appreciate my talents—something I'd thought I'd have to keep buried forever in a life of humility and self-sacrifice.

Long after the Grand Silence bell, I hummed tunes in my head and rewrote lyrics, satirizing the serious life we were trying to live. Mother Vivian had given me hope that I could retain that part of myself—and still be holy.

CHAPTER 14

Mother Vivian's lectures moved from sexuality to the vow of poverty.

"Poverty is easy," I told Rosemary as we folded linens in the laundry. "I've trained myself to say *ours*, not *mine*."

Rosemary smoothed out a wrinkle in a sheet. "I'm one of seven—had to grab whenever I could. Sharing is harder for me." She set the folded sheet on a table.

"We're not lacking for anything—clothing, textbooks, plenty of food—and a place to lay our heads, as scripture says."

Rosemary wheeled an empty laundry cart between us. "Doesn't it bother you—asking for everything?"

"It used to—especially Mother Loretta's third degree." I remembered giving up my journal. "But now we write a billet and things end up on our desks." I placed folded sheets in the cart. "Poverty is not the hardest vow for me."

Rosemary handed me one end of a sheet; we folded it together. "I think there's a lot more to practicing poverty," she said. "It's about what you give—not give up."

"I think about everything we have, Rosemary. We're not poor."

"Detachment." She dropped the folded sheet into the laundry cart. "Practicing poverty means letting go…not what you have *to your use,* but *how* you use it."

"You're a good influence on me," I said.

Rosemary laughed. "Let me influence you to help wheel this cart so the sheets can be delivered to the dorms."

"Done!" We bent over and pushed. The cart's metal wheels rumbled along the concrete floor.

After the vow of poverty, Mother focused on chastity, which the Rule of the Sisters of St. Mary described as "the most angelic virtue." I objected to the wording—none of us were angels. During my first two years in the Novitiate, Mother Loretta had emphasized that "nothing is more precious than the gift of chastity," saying we should observe the strictest guard on our senses. "The enemy, Sisters, is constantly trying to penetrate the senses and tarnish the purity of your heart and soul."

Besides observing celibacy—defined as abstaining from sexual relations and marriage—we had been instructed to avoid any internal or external acts contrary to chastity. Internal acts could include thoughts, fantasies, and desires. External acts—any of the senses but especially touching, seeing, listening, and speaking in any way that would violate purity of intention—were a sacrilege, since we were temples of the Holy Spirit consecrated to God.

We were told to guard against undue familiarity, to be "modest in all actions, modifying the senses." But by the time I'd become a senior novice, I had become aware of the many ways I could skirt around the practice of modesty—from rubbing elbows with Delores, to basking in the applause after a successful *Follies* show, to admiring my reflection in a window.

Though Mother Vivian's first lecture on sexuality was shocking, it opened me to a deeper appreciation of the vow of chastity. I could love others—and myself—as long as I learned how to sublimate my desires and direct them to the ultimate source of love—the Divine. I could allow myself to be familiar—to love other human beings, as long as I learned how to channel that love to God. I was only beginning to test this out with my sister friends. I had no words to explain this to Jack or Marianne, or my parents.

I was learning that not sharing myself with others was just as much a violation of the vow of chastity as going to the other extreme. Mother Vivian tried to show us that chastity allowed us to give unconditionally, without expecting anything in return. That was comforting. Some days I wished Sister Ellen had stuck it out—she would have loved Mother Vivian.

Over time, I realized that Mother Vivian always had our best interests at heart and I consented to anything she asked of me. But I was no longer naïve enough to believe that all superiors would be so easy to trust and obey. What if my conscience conflicted with something a superior told me to do—as it had in the case of keeping my journal?

Mother Vivian's lectures on obedience carried a different slant. "Your vow of obedience requires you, first and foremost, Sisters, to be open to the Spirit, to be obedient to what this loving God is calling you to do. When you have perfected that kind of loving response, then you can say you are obedient."

There was a story that had become one of the folk myths mentioned in most books about monastic life. It told about a virtuous monk who was so obedient that, when his superior requested he water a stick, he did it.

Mother Vivian objected. "God is not asking you to water a stick—but to listen, be open, to say yes…and follow the example of Jesus, his Son, who was obedient, even to death on the cross." She paused. "But why was he willing to go that far? Out of love—the only reason to say yes."

Obedient, even to death…. I tried to imagine myself, years from now, yielding my will to my superiors, *Doing what I am told and going where I am sent*, as the Rule put it. How hard would it be?

God would never ask me to do anything without giving me the grace to accomplish it. I took courage in the fact that I wasn't alone—my friends Pauline and Delores, Rosemary and Angela, and all the others who had become my sisters in Christ were on this path with me.

"Don't look so worried," Mother Vivian said when she called me into her office one morning. "Sit down. I have good news. My friend, the Novice Master at the Jesuit seminary, invited us to take part in a symposium at their college in two weeks. It's a few miles across town. Novices don't normally leave the cloister, but I've gotten permission for you and Sister Pauline to go."

"What for?"

"As part of a panel. You'll be speaking—you on Thomas Merton; Pauline on Mother Mary Dolan."

"You want me to speak? On Thomas Merton? But...."

"You've studied his writings. You know him. You have a theater background. The symposium theme is 'The Voices of Modern Mystics.' Mother Dolan, our Foundress, was a modern mystic. So is Merton."

"But Mother!"

"Write something up—five hundred words or less," she said. "I have no doubt you can do it."

Finally, someone who recognizes I'm a writer. But speak at a symposium? With scholars?

That afternoon during outdoor recreation, I handed Pauline a badminton racquet and led her to a grassy spot where we could volley the birdie. "Did Mother talk to you about...."

"The symposium? Yes! I'm terrified," Pauline said, whacking the birdie to me. "How can I speak in Mother Dolan's voice?"

"We've been reading her letters. Pull out some lines, a few quotes." I swung and missed, then picked up the birdie and hit it to her.

"I hear you're going to speak in Thomas Merton's voice." Pauline returned my serve. "Sounds scary."

"Mother Vivian has faith in us. We can do this!"

We volleyed for a while, but when Pauline finally missed a fast-flying birdie and her racquet went flying, we met at the imaginary net, and, out of breath, walked into the rec room to return the racquets.

On the way to chapel, Pauline started laughing. "I keep thinking of Plato's definition of a *symposium*. Remember?"

"A drinking party where men sit around telling stories," I said. "Let's hope this isn't going to be that." I nudged her. "Or... let's hope it is!"

"Clare! I'm scandalized." Pauline struck a pose of pretend shock and folded her hands in prayer. We giggled all the way to chapel.

The day of the symposium, we were ushered to the stage and seated at a long row of tables. The college auditorium was packed with sisters, brothers, priests, and seminarians. The panel consisted of four women and four men: Pauline and me at one end of the table, two novices from the Sisters of St. Francis next to us, then two Brothers of St. Paul, and at the far end of the table, two Jesuit novices. I was so nervous all I could do was stare at my notes or look straight out above the heads of the audience and try to remember to breathe. I barely heard the other presenters, my heart was pounding so hard.

When it was my turn, I spoke Merton's words as best I could, praying that I wouldn't embarrass myself or misrepresent his theology. Pauline quoted eloquently from Mother Dolan's letters and used quotes to explain her theology.

When it was over, Pauline and I rushed to Mother Vivian's side. "Seeing you in the front row helped calm my nerves," I told Mother Vivian.

"You were both scholarly and articulate," Mother Vivian said. "I'm proud of you!"

"*You* had drama classes in high school," Pauline said. "I had to depend on dumb luck—and Mother Dolan's spirit, of course."

"What did you think of the Jesuit novices on the panel?" Pauline asked when we sat down to recreation that evening.

"I was so nervous I hardly noticed anyone else," I said, "though now that you mention it, one Jesuit seemed familiar." (He'd reminded me of the shy seminarian I'd met in the Braille room, but since I'd violated any number of rules just talking to him, I decided not to mention it to Pauline.)

"One of them was a guy from my grade school. Billy McBride."

"Which one was he?" I opened my sewing basket and pulled out three pairs of stockings needing darning. *Could it be the same guy?*

"The one with the glasses and the crew cut," Pauline said. "He spoke about Teilhard de Chardin, the Jesuit geologist and theologian." Pauline squinted to thread her darning needle. "Chardin's writings have been banned by the Vatican—it took courage to stand up and talk about him. I was impressed."

"Now that I think about it, maybe I did recognize him…he and another novice have been using our Braille library. I ran into him—them." (I didn't admit that I'd been taking Jack there on visiting days. Or that I'd actually talked to Bill—shared my poetry with him, even dreamed about him once!)

"Really? Jesuit novices in our library? You'd better keep custody of the eyes, Clare!"

"You went to school with him? Did he remember you?"

"I don't think so." Pauline stuffed her darning egg into her stocking. "Most girls had a crush on him. We went to different high schools, but I saw him at a few dances. Never had a steady girlfriend, not even a date—so shy. His Dad died while he was in high school. He broke a lot of hearts when he entered the seminary."

I elbowed Pauline. "Were you one of those heartbroken girls?"

"No. I was busy falling in love with Beethoven. Mere mortal boys didn't hold a candle to Ludwig."

We laughed, but Pauline was serious.

I can see how "Billy" might be a heart-breaker, I thought. *Not for me, of course.* I felt a little disloyal to Stan, even though I knew it was over between us. *Was I being unfaithful to God too? What was the harm in looking, in being friendly?*

Toward the end of my year as a senior novice I was chosen to be sacristan—my dream job. I loved dressing the altar, setting out the gold chalice, lighting the candles. I didn't even mind ironing linens, or mopping the marble sanctuary. I kept long lists—make a mistake and everyone saw it. Still, I was comfortable in that sacred space, on stage, in the spotlight.

As summer approached, I took stock: I'd finished my second full year of college classes with a solid B average. I'd written faithfully in my journal. I'd represented Merton at a scholarly symposium—I was ready for summer break!

CHAPTER 15

The thirty-day retreat in preparation for our first profession ceremony opened in mid-July with a scorching heat wave—which we sweated through without air conditioning, covered in wool and linen. There would be no visitors, letters, or contact with the outside world.

Mother told us that even though we would be professing temporary vows, we should open our hearts to the prospect that we were professing for life. I could imagine next year—maybe even five years from now. It would be 1968, I would be twenty-six. But I began to wonder if I could commit for life.

"I can't tell you what to do, Sister Clare," Mother said when I shared my questions with her. "It's between you and your God. I will only say that—from where I stand—you have what it takes. The decision—that's yours alone."

I wrote page after page in my journal—trying to discern whether I could be faithful to the vows. I prayed and meditated, asked for some kind of sign. I searched the faces of my novice friends—did they have doubts, as I did? I loved them and couldn't imagine losing them.

I knew not to ask my family—only my father would have encouraged me to go on.

During the final week of retreat, Mother led us through rehearsals in chapel for our ceremony. We would recite together our Profession of Vows:

I, Margaret Ann Walsh, called in religion Sister Clare Marie, do promise to God that I shall observe the vows of poverty, chastity, and obedience. I promise to persevere for three years in the Community of the Sisters of Saint Mary, according to the Holy Rule, and in the presence of you, Mother Mary Thomasina, Mother Provincial. I pronounce these vows this fifteenth day of August, in the year of Our Lord, nineteen hundred and sixty-three."

After three years as temporary-professed sisters, we would renew our vows—in a quiet ceremony—for two more years. Then it would be time for final profession. I memorized the words, reciting them to myself throughout the days leading up to the ceremony.

During the last few days, I'd re-read my journal—there were questions on nearly every other page. *How could I go through with this, when my heart and mind were so full of questions?* Only God could answer that. I had to trust that the call was still there, that my response was genuine—that I was in God's hands. Just days before the ceremony, I wrote to my family. I had given up trying to make my letters sound like great literature. I explained that my vows—like a second baptism—meant I would now belong to Christ. I thanked them for supporting me in my vocation. I reassured them that I was excited and happy to profess my vows as a Sister of St. Mary. I could only imagine their consternation, receiving a letter so brief and so serious.

Mother Vivian called one last gathering in the rec room. "Thank you," she said, "for your acceptance of me. You will do great things." She wiped tears from her cheeks. "I know you will not disappoint. You're my first group—you will never be forgotten."

We all sat dabbing our eyes, our rockers slowing to a halt. Each of us waited for the others to break the circle first—there would never be another moment like this.

Chapter 15

We were saying good-bye to the walled cloister, the garden, the stunning chapel with its stained glass and marble. How I would miss the medieval-style choir stalls, the refectory with its black and white tiled floor, the kitchen I had lovingly scrubbed, the library shelves I had dusted with care. *Perfection of my ordinary actions*—that's what had inspired me. But there had been nothing ordinary about these three years I'd spent discovering myself. Tonight, I was a "professed-elect." Tomorrow, I would become a full-fledged member of the community—a professed Sister of St. Mary.

That evening Pauline and I cleaned out our sewing baskets.

"I'll never be a concert pianist." Pauline looked sad. "You'll never be a writer."

"I don't believe in that dream anymore."

"What dream do you believe in, then?"

I couldn't think of an answer.

"See?" Pauline said. "That's the doubt that creeps in for me. Was I supposed to give up my dream? Because deep down, I know I can be that pianist."

"We were both supposed to give up those dreams—this is a higher call. Don't you believe that, Pauline?"

"Convince me."

That night I dreamed Pauline performed to a standing ovation at Carnegie Hall. I stood in the audience, applauding, with Stan on one side, Bill-the-novice on the other.

CHAPTER 16

The profession ceremony was a profound act of faith and abandonment. Even so, it was less dramatic than the reception ceremony—a simple replacement of the white veil with the black one. We pronounced our vows in unison, then signed our vows. We lay face down on the chapel floor, our prostration a symbol of the submission of our will, in all things, to the will of God. I pressed my nose and flattened my palms against the floor in an act of humility for all to witness.

I was now a professed sister, with all the privileges: traveling outside the cloister, interacting with other professed sisters, living on a college campus, attending classes with lay students—and, most importantly, acceptance as a Sister of St. Mary.

At last, I felt grown up. I was almost twenty-one. In a few months, I'd officially be an adult, eligible to vote.

I spotted Jack waiting in the courtyard. My excitement turned to concern when I saw his wrinkled brow and tight mouth. "You look worried. What's happened?"

"It's you, Megs. You're the one I'm worried about."

"Me? Jack, this is the happiest day of my life. I've made it! See this black veil? I'm a professed sister."

"Exactly, Megs." He raised his voice. "Damn it," he said. "I hate to see you vowing yourself to a life that's going to close you off from everything. Is this what you want?"

I squeezed his hand. "Don't worry. I know what I'm doing. I've been studying, praying, working toward this day for three years. It's here, be happy with me—please?"

Jack heaved a sigh. "I can't say I'm happy—unless you want me to lie." He wiped his eyes with the back of his hand. "I'm not going to change your mind, not today anyway."

"You'll see. This is what I want. I couldn't possibly be happy if I didn't answer this call. Tell me you understand."

"I don't," he retorted. "But, you see it as your calling, so I'll shut up—for now."

I admired his high cheek bones; his thick, dark hair; his serious, searching eyes. I touched his cheek. "Thanks for that, Jack."

"I have something for you." He reached into his pocket and handed me an envelope addressed to him. I recognized Stan's handwriting.

I slipped it into my pocket. "I guess I should say thank you," I sighed. The rest of Stan's letters lay at the bottom of my trunk.

"I'm only doing the kind thing, Maggie."

"I know." Now that I was a professed sister, I didn't have to hide Stan's letters. "I'm professed now—you could help by not encouraging Stan."

"Stan hasn't given up hope—and neither have I."

I sighed. "Come on. Let's find Mom and Dad—and Marianne, Ted, and little Jeffrey—they'll think they've been abandoned."

We found them sitting in the garden.

"This is the same circle of chairs we sat in three years ago," Mom said, reaching for Marianne's toddler, Jeffrey. She perched him on her lap. "I guess there's no talking you out of this, is there Maggie?"

"No, Mom." I leaned over to hug her and Jeffrey, then Dad and Marianne.

"I'm so excited for you, Marianne," I said, patting her pregnant belly. "You look really well."

"I am. Pregnancy isn't a disease, you know."

I ignored Marianne's remark—I could only imagine what she felt.

Soon, Jeffrey was scrambling off Mom's lap and running toward another toddler—a niece of Angela's—with Ted in pursuit.

"Can you be happy for me, Mom?"

"Your father is. Not only is his youngest a nun, but finally, one of you is going to a Catholic college."

"You'll see, Mom. I'll make you proud."

She nodded and gave me a faint smile. "I know you will, Maggie—give me time."

"It was a lovely ceremony, Megs," Dad said.

We talked about what everyone could expect once I moved to the House of Studies.

"It's a block or two from the college," Marianne said. "You'll finally be on a real campus. Better watch out—you don't want to be corrupted."

"It's close, Marianne, but far enough that we can still live our religious life." I was determined to keep it light, even though I was thinking: *Will she ever stop judging me?*

The House of Studies was a collection of buildings where the temporary professed sisters—known as "junior professed"—lived. Like the college campus, the style was red-brick colonial, surrounded by mature trees and winding sidewalks. The largest of the buildings housed the Mistress of Juniors' office, a dining room, a community room with a library, and a recreation room on the lower level.

"What'll it be like," Marianne asked, "going to class with *real* people?"

I nearly bit my tongue—I suspected my smile looked forced. "Marianne, we're *all* real people. Don't let this black veil fool you."

Marianne bounced Jeffrey on her knees. "I just meant—the invasion of *men* into your all-female world." There was an awkward silence. "I don't mean to sound critical, Megs, but I hope Mom will let you re-read some of the letters you've sent home. I had a hard time recognizing my own sister."

Dad interrupted. "Okay. Let's save that discussion for another time."

Good old Dad. Would there ever be a time when Marianne and I wouldn't be locking horns?

"Say, Megs," Dad said, "tell us about the classes you'll be taking. You'll be declaring a major?"

"Yes," I said, "A major in theater, a minor in English. It's perfect. If all goes well, I'll eventually teach English or theater in one of our high schools." I'd just made a public vow to be obedient, to go wherever I was sent and do whatever I was told. "Whatever is decided," I added, "it'll be the right decision."

Although Mt. St. Mary's—MSM—was a small college, it was strong in liberal arts, and especially in the performing arts. I remembered how Sister Helen, my high school drama teacher, had encouraged me to consider going to MSM. "You won't find a better drama department in the city," she'd said. "Maybe at the Conservatory, but then, you'd be a small fish in a big pond. At St. Mary's, you'd have more opportunity. Our college president is a visionary."

"We'll have monthly visiting days, Mom," I said. "But you can drop by anytime—another advantage of being a professed sister."

"That's wonderful, dear," Mom said.

It was a day of triumph for me, tarnished only by the fact that Jack spent much of the time pacing nervously and smoking cigarettes. I forgot about the letter in my pocket until later in the evening, after we'd arrived at the House of Studies. Once I'd settled in my cell, I slit open the envelope and unfolded the thin, light-blue stationery with the red, white, and blue edging. I sat on my bed in my nightgown and read his letter.

Stan wrote that he hoped I was happy…that he couldn't imagine me in a black veil. He wrote about his promotion to petty officer—his plans to become an engineer. He wrote that he hoped to avoid being sent to Southeast Asia, where trouble was brewing. He closed with… *I miss you with all my heart. Maybe someday we'll meet again. It's up to you. My question still stands: Will you write to me? I will always love you. Yours, Stan.*

I read Stan's letter over and over, then put it back in the envelope. What should I do with the letter and the others at the bottom of my trunk—tear them up and throw them in the trash? Even though I'd received them illegally, I couldn't destroy them. There was something special about the mere act of writing—one human reaching out to another—it felt sacred. I wanted to honor Stan and his words. When I was reunited with my trunk, I would deposit his letter there, with the others.

CHAPTER 17

"Walsh?" Dr. Wickham rattled off the names on his attendance list—alphabetical, so mine was last—on the first day of Acting I class. I'd gone so long without using my last name that I didn't recognize it at first.

"Here." I was crouched in the last row of the theater—trying to make myself invisible.

"Walsh!" Louder this time, irritated.

I got up and moved closer to the stage, where the rest of the class was gathered. "I'm here—Sister Clare Marie Walsh."

"You?" He glared at me—everyone glared. "I'm not accustomed to having nuns in my acting classes."

"But…." I held up my class schedule and admit slip.

"Very well. Now—all of you—pick up these scripts, *Oedipus Rex*. "Divide into groups of four. Read over Scene One. By the end of class I want to hear how you'd stage it." He looked at me. "Go—don't stand around."

I did a quick head count—twenty of us—*someone* had to work with me.

"Sister?" A group of three girls approached me. They must have seen the relief on my face. We plotted Scene One—I was the only one who hadn't read the play, so I kept quiet.

The rest of the day was less harrowing—classes in History of the Theater, Stagecraft, and Sociology. None of them required leaving my seat or choosing a partner.

Pauline and I walked back to the House of Studies at the end of the day. We ignored the rule to keep silence while walking to and from classes. We had too much to share.

"Looks like our schedules are identical, Clare." She seemed tired but happy. "The music department is in the same building as the theater. This is going to work out well."

I was disappointed that classes for Angela, Delores, and Rosemary would be on the opposite end of campus. I missed them already.

"My day was great," Pauline said. "I love my professors, the girls I met were nice. How about you?"

"My theater professor makes Mother Loretta seem like the Fairy Godmother. It can only get better—I hope."

"You'll do fine. How about the other students?"

"Theater majors…." I laughed. "Long hair, thick eyelashes, tie-dyed shirts, black is the fashionable color. They break into song at the drop of a hat."

Pauline laughed. "You should fit in."

"I wish. Oh. And there are three men in my acting class—a first."

"What are they like? Friendly?"

"None of them have spoken to me yet. I'm keeping my distance." We rounded the corner and headed up the front steps of the House of Studies. "But I have to hand it to Mt. St. Mary's," I said as I held the door open. "I'm proud of our liberal academic program—and that we've opened our women's college to male students."

Pauline hesitated. "Fine. But I'd like to see more women on our faculty, wouldn't you?"

Jack took advantage of the relaxed visiting rules to show up on campus in late September. We sat down in the library. He had pictures of Marianne and Ted's baby, a girl born the last day of August.

"They wanted you to be godmother, but your convent rules don't allow it."

Chapter 17

I tried to hide my disappointment at not being Jennifer's godmother but Jack saw the pain on my face.

"Well," he said, "they'll be coming to visit soon."

"She's beautiful. I can't wait to meet her!"

Jack had news of his own. "I've changed my major to Pre-Law—with a minor in Poly Sci," he said. "Dad is covering tuition, so I've moved into a place near campus with three other guys."

"Didn't Dad want you to get a degree in business? His heart was set on you taking over his business."

Jack's turned-up nose said it all. "He finally heard me, Megs. A law degree is the only way I'm going to make a difference for the cause of civil rights. Talk about a slow road."

"I admire you Jack. You never give up."

"Did you know there are entire states south of the Mason-Dixon Line insisting that only white people have the right to vote, eat in restaurants, ride buses, earn a living, get a decent education, or drink from a water fountain—to name a few civil rights you and I take for granted?"

I didn't know—but I was ashamed to say so.

"But enough about me." Jack leaned in. "I came to apologize for my outburst at your vow ceremony."

"You don't need to."

"It's just that it tears me up to see you wrapped up in that nun habit. Still, I'm proud of you—you chose this life, professed your vows, stuck it out. I wanted to say this on your big vow day. I never get to say much on those God-awful visiting days."

"Jack—sometimes you just break my heart."

"You're as courageous, in my eyes, as the brave civil rights workers I admire. It's a different kind of courage, but I value your determination. I don't understand this life you've chosen—but I promise to stop picking on you…."

"If we weren't sitting in a library, I'd jump up and hug you."

He reached over and held my hand.

We smiled. A nun and a handsome young man together—I didn't care how it looked.

It was Friday, November 22, 1963. Pauline and I were just getting settled in our seats and opening our Western Civ notebooks, when our professor walked to the podium.

"The President has been shot!"

Screams erupted.

"That's all we know," he said. "All classes are dismissed." He raised his voice over the din. "Please get home safely. Let us pray for our President."

We practically ran the two blocks from the college to the House of Studies, in tears and in shock. For the first time since I had entered the convent, there were no restrictions on watching television. Beginning that afternoon, and concluding on Monday evening with the state funeral, we stared in disbelief at the TV in the community room. We even took our meals in front of the screen.

On Saturday evening, Jack called. "What can I say?" he said, holding back tears. "Such a waste of a great life. I'm sad one minute, confused, hopeless, angry the next. We haven't been able to stop watching."

"The weekend has been a blur here at the House of Studies too," I said. "Mother Regina, our Mistress, cancelled everything so that we could watch TV. No one feels like eating or doing anything. It's just utter shock."

"For guys who like to think we're tough, we've shed our share of tears," Jack said. "I will not let the dream die—the ideals Kennedy stood for." I heard his voice catch.

"We've lost our innocence, Jack. Nothing will ever be the same."

We were front and center when the assassin, Lee Harvey Oswald, was shot and killed before our eyes. The next day, we watched the President's funeral: the toddler saluting his father, the riderless horse, the eulogy by Robert Kennedy, the burial and lighting of the "eternal flame" in Arlington Cemetery.

Soon after dealing with this terrible blow to the nation, we entered the season of Advent—preparing for Christmas. My heart wasn't in it. The idealism and youthful spirit that Kennedy symbolized had been struck down, along with the hope we'd placed in him.

The four of us juniors sat together at breakfast after Mass on Christmas morning.

"Something is missing this Christmas," Angela said, "but I can't put my finger on it."

"I can. Visiting day," Delores said, "dealing with parents who aren't getting along—that's what I've got to look forward to."

"I've got a few chapters in philosophy to look forward to—and memorizing a scene from *Antigone*," I said, taking a sip of coffee. "But I can't wait to see my family—especially Marianne's new baby, Jennifer. My brother's changed, though—since Kennedy's death—he's lost his spark."

"We all have," said Pauline. "If you hear Chopin's Étude No. 3 in E Major coming from the music room—that'll be me, practicing. It's the saddest piece. And no visits for me over the holidays, my parents are away."

It was Christmas…but none of us felt merry.

Jack and I met in the college library in early February. It was a new year—1964—and our fragile hopes had been restored.

"It's strange—Kennedy's death has given me a new purpose," Jack said. "I'm getting good grades. For once, Mom and Dad are not on my back."

"What brought this about?" I was glad to see Jack not brooding.

"For one thing, the Vietnam War—which no one has declared—but let's face it, a war it is."

"Wait a minute. Jack—you could be drafted?"

"My status as a full-time student puts my draft number on the back burner—so they say. You know I love my country, but I am also dead set against this 'undeclared aggression' as they call it."

"If you continue to be a full-time student—you'll be safe, right?"

"You know me, Megs, never one to leave well enough alone. I've decided to do something that might move me to the draft board's front burner."

"What now?"

"My history prof is talking about taking part in a program called Freedom Summer at Western College in Oxford—Ohio that is. Are you familiar with Western?"

"Tell me."

"It's a liberal arts college for women near Miami U, they plan to train volunteers to campaign for voting rights for Blacks. Turns out Western was originally a women's seminary—how about that? You should have looked into going there."

"There you go, orchestrating my life again. But seriously, Freedom Summer sounds dangerous."

"This is big. All the major civil rights organizations will be involved. The training takes a week over the summer, then we're sent south as Freedom Riders on buses—probably to Mississippi." He paused and whispered, "Now don't pass this on to our parents, please, but there are horror stories—folks being hauled off to jail for standing up for civil rights, all over the south—especially in Mississippi."

"Dear God, Jack."

"Don't worry—there'll be lawyers, the National Council of Churches, all kinds of civil-rights organizations taking part. It's safe and supervised, so my room-mate Ray and I are going to do it—the training, at least. We'll see if we get chosen."

"I admire your convictions, Jack, but I might be in Mom and Dad's camp…must you be a Freedom Rider to make a difference?"

"At this moment in time, yes."

I sighed. "I've made a radical choice too…I shouldn't talk. Keep me posted?"

"Will do," he said. "Speaking of *posted*, I had a letter from Stan. He's thinking about re-upping for another three years in the Navy. Every letter asks about you. So you know."

I sighed, deeply this time. "When are you going to give up on Stan?"

"When you write the poor guy one measly letter. Is that so much to ask?"

"Yes. We've talked about this. It isn't good for me—or Stan. It's pointless."

"I take your *point*, Megs." Jack loved playing with words.

"I've got a class. We'll talk again soon. Please. Don't do anything rash."

"Rash? That's my middle name."

I stopped in the college chapel for a quick prayer. I was thinking how devoted Jack was to righting social wrongs—how self-centered I was being, worrying about carrying twenty credit hours and doing it perfectly. Should I have joined an order of nuns devoted to missionary work? Was I in the wrong place? How was being a theater major going to change the world?

CHAPTER 18

"Pre-Cana" arrived at the House of Studies to raised eyebrows. Why was Mother Regina bringing the Church's marriage-preparation course for couples to a bunch of nuns?

Despite objections, Mother Regina insisted we young sisters needed to be educated.

Some secretly cheered—others groaned—more interference to our study time.

The jury was still out on Mother Regina. Those of us who'd had the advantage of Mother Vivian feared turning back the clock under Mother Regina's reign. I wanted to give her the benefit of the doubt. That she favored the Pre-Cana meetings gave me hope.

The Wedding Feast of Cana, where water was reportedly turned into wine, was justification by biblical scholars that, because Jesus and his Mother were present, God intended marriage as a sacrament. But I always felt the *real* story was that Jesus and Mary loved good wine, enjoyed a party, and didn't want to see the wedding couple publicly embarrassed for lack of wine.

Pauline was skeptical, which surprised me. "So, you think you know all you need to about love, sex, and marriage?" I asked. "I don't." It seemed reasonable that before we left the House of Studies, we should learn more about those we would be serving, whether in a hospital, school, or social service setting.

The couple teaching—in their late forties—had never given the marriage course to nuns before. Mr. Lake, looking uncomfortable in a too-tight suit, came forward with his wife, who wore a pale-yellow suit jacket and skirt with matching pumps.

Mrs. Lake—Sylvia—began. "We're here to talk about love and marriage. I'm the woman, so I get to go first."

We all laughed.

"But really, John and I hope to model for you the kind of give-and-take that makes for a good marriage."

She rattled off their list of topics: everything from The Marriage Bond as a Sacred Contract to Natural Family Planning to The Role of Finances and—if there was time—Planning Your Wedding Ceremony.

"It's a little warm in here," John said, removing his tie. "Or is it just me, the only man surrounded by so many women?"

He laughed. No one else did.

I sat up when he said *women*. I was used to being referred to as a nun—not as a *woman*.

"I had a speech prepared but…." John motioned for his wife to join him in the center of the room and took her hand. He spoke as if inspired, praising Sylvia as the person who had taught him the true meaning of love and marriage as a sacrament.

I was touched by the way their eyes met—the tender way he held her hand. He reminded me of Stan…the way he'd hold my hand and look at me, the way he could talk about his feelings. Something stirred in me. I felt the urge to go to my trunk and re-read Stan's letters.

I glanced sideways at Delores. Her eyes were wide open.

John looked at his wife. "The greatest gift God has given me," he said, choking up, "is Sylvia…my soul mate. Until I met her, I didn't know what that meant."

Sylvia took a deep breath. "This is not the speech we rehearsed on the way over here," she said. She shared how she'd learned about sex—from her older sister, her friends, a few pamphlets, books in the public library.

I could relate. I remembered slumber parties in high school where the topic of sex often came up. Once, one of my girlfriends had snuck in a *Playboy Magazine* she'd found when cleaning her brother's room. I'd felt embarrassed. Should I be looking at these near-naked women? What did it feel like to be sexy? To be naked and pose for the camera like that? To be aroused?

I remembered how another, older girlfriend had dropped in on our sleepover one Friday night, intent on telling us the facts of life. "You need to know your own anatomy, ladies," she'd said. "Use a mirror. Try it out and see!"

I'd felt a little insulted by her attitude. She'd sat in the middle of the floor where we were stretched out with our pillows and proclaimed: "This is the Fifties, girls! Get with it." I already *was* "with it." Using my babysitting money, I had a collection of records with the latest hits by Elvis Presley, The Platters, The Kingston Trio, Johnny Mathis, and The Everly Brothers. Jack had even convinced me to sample Dave Brubeck. I knew the songs by heart, and I could dance to the latest dances—the Bop, Stroll, Cha-Cha, Jitterbug. Jack wasn't a good dancer but Stan was—one more reason I was attracted to him. I was definitely with it. I just wasn't sexually active.

The Fifties were all about freedom and fun for me, but not about exploring my sexuality. Maybe it was the warnings nuns and priests doled out, from seventh grade all through high school—the cautionary tales about girls having babies out of wedlock—soiled reputations—and the most damning warning of all: sex outside wedlock was a mortal sin. I would have to confess it to the priest or burn in hell.

Sylvia and John gathered their materials and said they'd see us next week. We all stood and applauded.

Pauline followed me out of the community room and across the yard to our building. "I wouldn't be surprised if Mother doesn't invite those two back," Pauline whispered.

"Why not?" I asked.

"It's a waste of time. I could've been studying for my music theory class tomorrow."

Delores caught up with us. "What'd y'all think of John and Sylvia?"

"What did *you* think?" I asked Delores.

"It was worth the ninety minutes. It's so sweet the way they looked at each other, held hands. He was brave, admitting what an imbecile he'd been, how much he'd learned from her."

"What about you, Clare?" Pauline asked.

"I don't think it was a waste of time—but it did leave me with questions."

"Such as?" Pauline asked.

"What is a soul mate?" *As a nun, will I ever have one?*

Mother called the second meeting of the Pre-Cana session to order with a Hail Mary. Sylvia quoted passages from Genesis throughout her talk, "*...and God blessed them: and God said unto them, Be fruitful, and multiply, and replenish the earth,*" explaining God's plan that a man and a woman should marry and have children.

All this talk about seeds and being fruitful—as sisters, we were not following God's commandment to increase and multiply. Granted, there were also lines from scripture and theology defending a life of chastity—the theology dating back to St. Augustine in the fourth and fifth centuries. Most of the scriptural quotes were lifted from the letters of St. Paul; most involved avoiding the temptation to "sexual immorality," as St. Paul put it. The model for choosing a life of virginity and chastity, of course, rested with Mary, the mother of Jesus. But Mary had gotten pregnant, married, and given birth. Her "Yes" to God—her *Fiat*—had changed the world.

"Some mysteries cannot be understood"—so said Catholic teaching. But I'd always wondered about the virgin birth and the whole concept of the holy family. How could Joseph and Mary be the ideal, if they had never touched one another? That I had been chosen by God to embrace a life of chastity, never experiencing marriage, sex, procreation, motherhood, parenting—this was a mystery I struggled to understand. And explain to my family… and to Stan.

Regarding "Natural Family Planning," John joked that he didn't have "good rhythm." We didn't get the word play, so Sylvia explained that the Church's natural family planning—known as "the rhythm method"—depended on a woman's cycle.

"I can show you how well the rhythm method worked," John said, reaching in his pocket and fishing out photos of their seven children. "Don't get me wrong—we love them all—but only three were planned. The other four—chalk them up to poor rhythm."

Sylvia and John treated the fact that the rhythm method hadn't worked with humor. I didn't think it was funny. I knew families in our parish with too many kids; I'd grown up feeling sorry for the Bennett children. Mrs. Bennett was constantly pregnant, looked unwell and unkempt most of the time, and her kids were dressed in shabby hand-me-downs. They never had money for school field trips or extras that most parents could give their children.

Once, when I was about thirteen, I knelt on one side of the confessional while Mrs. Bennett was on the other side. She was crying. I overheard the priest say she was obligated to do her husband's bidding. I had only a vague idea what that meant. Now, suddenly, it clicked. She was asking to be dispensed from having more children, asking for birth-control help, whether that meant saying no to her husband or using contraceptives. The priest, as God's representative, was telling her she had no recourse.

John and Sylvia had made the best of their marriage. But what about poor Mrs. Bennett?

After Pre-Cana, I had new questions. "Do you ever wonder who you'd be if you hadn't become a nun?" I asked Pauline one afternoon.

"I don't have time to think about it," Pauline said. We were walking to campus—one of the rare times Pauline and I could have a private conversation.

"I mean, if you'd married and had kids, how different would you be?" I asked.

"I wouldn't be getting a degree and majoring in music," Pauline said. "I wouldn't be writing my own music, or playing the violin, or learning to conduct an orchestra, or direct a choir."

"I meant—you know—what kind of a *person* you'd be?"

"We'll never know, will we? Because we're not going to marry and have kids," Pauline said. "We're Sisters of St. Mary."

"It's that easy for you, is it?" I asked. Pauline was good at masking her real feelings.

"I didn't say it was easy—just—that's who we are."

"You're not curious? Don't you ever imagine there's a soul mate out there just for you?"

Pauline stopped and looked at me. "Soul mate? You mean a guy? No guy could possibly measure up."

You haven't met Stan, I thought. I envied Pauline her certainty. Was I the only one curious about the person I was becoming? Would I ever know myself as anyone other than Sister Clare Marie? Was that enough? I remembered Mother Vivian's warning—at least it had felt like a warning—that each of us carried deep within ourselves a longing to be loved, to belong to another person. For us—for me—that other person would be God.

I changed the subject. "What courses are you taking this summer?"

"Music theory—violin—a private lesson in piano. You?"

"Shakespeare's comedies—can you imagine reading one play each week? I'm not exactly on the Dean's List, but my grades have improved. I'll finish out this first year with a solid B+."

Pauline stopped and shook my hand. "Me too, Clare. Hooray for us!"

CHAPTER 19

Jack had been out of town—in Oxford at the Freedom Summer training—most of the summer, so I was especially glad to get a phone call from him in mid-July.

"I didn't get chosen for the project, Megs." He sounded glum. "There were hundreds of people—mostly Whites—who applied; the screening was intense. My chances were slim."

"What was it like?"

"Trainees partnered with Black leaders, mostly in Mississippi. You had to accept abuse without striking back, and work with local leaders."

"You can do those things, Jack—but I'm glad you didn't get chosen. What kind of trainees did they choose?"

"My room-mate Ray, for one," Jack said. "He has credentials as a Press photographer—he's a stringer for our local paper. He's going to Jackson, Mississippi." He paused. "Truth is, once Dad heard the project was headed for Mississippi, he ordered me to drop out."

"Is it that bad there?"

"Volunteers getting beaten, reports of church bombings and burnings," he said. "Blacks' homes and businesses burned to the ground. Hundreds of people arrested. Three Freedom volunteers jailed, then released, now missing and feared dead."

"Dear God! That's terrible. No wonder Dad insisted."

Jack grunted.

"Listen, Jack—you need to be careful. There are plenty of ways for you to help the cause. You're a writer. Get writing!"

"Maybe writing is the best thing. I'm going to apply myself—as Dad would say—get into law school. This civil rights battle will be fought in the courts." He laughed. "Dad has let up on his dream that I take over his business."

"Our poor parents...their dreams dashed," I sighed. "Except for Marianne, of course," I said. "The perfect daughter."

"That's ridiculous, Megs."

"All right. I'll drop the rivalry with Marianne. What else is new?"

"One positive thing came out of my time at Western...."

"What?"

"I met a girl—Amy. She's getting her degree in education—wants to be an elementary teacher. She didn't make the Freedom cut either."

"What's she like?"

"You know, when you're sure you've met the right person? Don't get mad. You said that once about Stan, remember?"

I growled.

"We share the same ideals. I've been burning rubber, driving to Oxford to see her. She has another year at Western—unless I can convince her to transfer to UC. We'll see where it goes."

"When can I meet her?"

"I've told her I've got one sister who's a perfect housewife and mother, and another who's a perfect nun. She's in awe."

I laughed. "You're setting Amy up for bitter disappointment, when she discovers how flawed I am."

"You said that—not me. What's your August like? Maybe I can bring her by."

"August is full," I said. "A full load of summer courses, then a thirty-day retreat."

"Yikes! Thirty days? How do you do it?"

"Practice—and the grace of God." I paused. "After retreat, right into senior year. It's a heavy load, including senior thesis."

"Let me know when you've got time for company," Jack said. "I'd better sign off, I'm expecting a call from Ray in

Mississippi. Hoping there's news about those missing guys. Say some prayers, huh?"

"Count on it. I'll let the sisters know. If you can't reach me, write. I love your letters. And my censor? Gone."

At the end of August, Jack called again. "Those missing Freedom volunteers—found. Buried in Mississippi."

"How terrible! What are you going to do?"

"You'll find this surprising—I went to church—downtown, a Black church. It was the only place I felt at home." He went silent.

"Jack? You there?"

"I don't know what I'd do if I came face to face with the bastards who killed those men, Megs. Loving, forgiving such atrocities—the Black leaders joined hands and sang 'We Shall Overcome.'" His voice cracked. "How do they do it? I wish I could live it, just a little."

My heart felt heavy. "I don't know what to say."

"Nothing, Megs. You're listening. That means everything." He cleared his throat. "To change the subject entirely…I ran into Stan's Mom. Stan's re-enlisted, another Navy tour, stationed in Virginia. I have his address—say the word, I'll give it to you."

"No comment, Jack—except—I love you."

CHAPTER 20

"Some days I envy Angela and Delores," I said to Pauline, on a walk from the House of Studies to campus. "Even Rosemary. They have normal majors—Angela in philosophy, a minor in theology, Delores in education. And Rosemary—she's in her element in biology and chemistry."

"Back in high school, being an actress was your dream," Pauline said. "Hasn't your dream come true?"

I laughed. "Not the way I thought it would. My Dad used to discourage me, saying theater was too competitive—I'd never survive. Some days the competition gets to me."

"The performing arts—they're all like that. But would we trade our majors to teach first grade? Not me."

"You know what Dr. Wickham said to me—last week—in front of the whole class?"

"What?" Pauline stopped to listen.

I stopped and faced Pauline. "He said: 'I don't know why you're majoring in theater, Sister. I can't help you—I can't even see your feet.'" I felt like crying, just thinking about it. "It makes me so mad. Who does he think he is?"

"What a—I can't say what I'm thinking." Pauline shook her head. "Ignore him, Clare."

"How? He's my advisor—he teaches nearly half my classes." I took a few breaths. "My biggest fear is that I'll make a fool of myself. I've made friends with a few girls—but at the end of the day, I'm alone."

"We've got each other, Clare."

"Yes, we do," I said, taking her arm. We started walking again.

"We're not supposed to want praise—but as a performer, it's what I thrive on. You understand," Pauline said.

"How can I tell everyone at the House of Studies that I'm reading Greek dramas like *Lysistrata,* where the women refuse to have sex with their husbands until they give up war—and the men walk around with wildly exaggerated phallic erections?"

Pauline laughed out loud. "You can't tell them."

"Then there are the bawdy jokes all over Shakespeare's plays. Sometimes I have to recite them as if I believe it all."

Pauline stopped when we got close to the music department on campus. "Anytime you want to rehearse those bawdy scenes, just let me know." She fluttered her thick eyelashes.

It was good to laugh. But I still had to feel and act out those emotions, be those characters if I wanted to fulfill my theater degree.

As I watched Pauline entering the music department, it struck me how close we'd become. But I didn't want to get too close. Pauline and I weren't exclusive, but whenever she chose someone else to sit and talk with, play cards with, walk with, I wondered why she hadn't chosen me. Was I getting too dependent? I thought I'd sorted all that out as a senior novice, under the guidance of Mother Vivian.

One day Mother Regina called me into her office. "I think you and Sister Pauline need to consider your behavior—do you think you're excluding others?"

"Has someone complained?" I could feel my fists clench, my stomach tighten.

"Just a warning, Sister Clare. My own observations, nothing more." She folded her hands on her desk. "I know your group thinks you have all the answers—after a year with Mother Vivian, but.... That's all I wanted to say. You may go."

Who was talking about us? I struggled to contain my anger—my disappointment that our whole group was being judged.

I turned to one of my teachers, Sister Audrey, who lived on campus and taught psychology. Practically from the first day I'd attended her *Intro to Psychology* class, I felt she was a wise teacher—someone I could talk to. I stopped by her office one afternoon. I found her reading *The Art of Loving* by Erich Fromm.

"Ah, the age-old question of Particular Friendships," Sister Audrey said with a sigh, after I'd explained my doubts. "My dear, I think it's important to ask yourself some questions. First, if you share yourself with a variety of people, over and above the person or persons of your affections, it's a good sign you are not being exclusive."

I gave myself above-average marks on that score.

"Second, I would be worried about any human being—religious sister or otherwise—who was not forming a bond with a few individuals she felt close to. It's normal." She leaned forward in her chair. "Consider the fact that this communal life we lead—all women, all the time—is anything *but* normal. There are bound to be power struggles, jealousies—yes, jealousies—and the possibility our affections could lead us to behavior which—to most lay people—would not be considered the norm."

"You're not saying, are you, that my attachment to another sister is abnormal?"

"Not at all—especially under the circumstances," Sister Audrey said. "Friendships among women are some of the most rewarding and sacred liaisons I know. Unfortunately, our society is not open to such friendships between women—not just in the convent—I'm talking about all women. There's some force in our society that wants to pit women against one another."

She fanned through *The Art of Loving* and set it down. "As for Mother Regina's comment about your group being different—take it as a compliment. I find the lot of you refreshing—you give me hope for the future. As religious women, let's show society that we know how to love. But there is a caveat: our vow of chastity doesn't allow for us to consummate any union—with a man or woman—and that is where we need to be watchful."

Sister Audrey must have sensed my hesitation to talk about my sexuality. "You don't need to confide in me," she said, "though I promise you confidentiality. You are at a fragile stage in your development—I'm sure you know that."

"There is so much I need to learn—about myself—about others—about forming relationships," I said. "But thank you, Sister. You've helped me."

"Good. Don't hesitate to visit again. And Sister—don't worry about what other people think. That can be crippling. I know you're striving to do everything perfectly, but don't choose perfection over freedom."

I was so grateful to her—I felt we'd bridged a gap. From then on, I called her *Audrey*—unless we were in a formal setting. She had eased my anxiety about close friendships. But there was an even bigger issue—someone was watching and reporting me to Mother Regina. Whoever it was could snoop all they wanted—I was not going to change my behavior.

CHAPTER 21

I had survived my first fall semester as a theater major on a college campus. I hadn't made a lot of friends but at least Dr. Wickham had stopped embarrassing me in public. I began the winter-spring semester with an Acting II class. One day, a few weeks into the semester, I entered the theater. Students were milling around, waiting for Dr. Wickham to breeze in. I sat down and opened my copy of *Taming of the Shrew*. A male student sat down next to me. He smiled and glanced at my playbook.

"I'm Will," he said and held out his hand.

"Sister Clare," I said, shaking his hand.

"I know," he said. "We've been in this class together for a few weeks, sorry I didn't introduce myself earlier." He let go of my hand and gestured to my playbook. "I see you're ready for the *Shrew*, Sister?"

He reminded me a little of Jack—high cheekbones, straight nose, and thick, dark hair that fell in wavy locks over his forehead. He had a neatly trimmed beard—not my favorite look on a guy, but it didn't look bad on him. He wasn't tall—just a few inches taller than me—but he was slim, strong. He had nice eyes—in the theater's dim light, I couldn't tell exactly what color they were—brown? He didn't seem egotistical like the other two men in the class, who deliberately avoided making contact with me.

"Most people just call me Clare—I mean—you know, it's easier."

"Okay…*Clare*. I'm a transfer student. This is my first experience with Dr. Wickham." He leaned in to whisper, "I've heard the horror stories—but I hear he's a genius. What do you think?"

"The horror part—not an exaggeration," I whispered back. "The genius part—the jury is still out, in my opinion."

Professor Wickham rushed in, came to a dead stop, looked around and called out, "Sister! You—next to Sister—step forward."

"He could have asked your name," I whispered to Will as we rose from our seats. "But he probably doesn't know my name either."

"I want you two to play Act Two, Scene One. Start where Petruchio says, 'I will attend her here—And woo her with some spirit….' Take the next two classes, block the scene, rehearse—then do a walk-through for the class. Questions—find me."

We stood there for a few seconds. "I hope you don't mind working with me," Will said.

"You too—nobody wants to do a scene with the nun." I shrugged. "I don't blame them."

"It's okay, Sister—*Clare*. I don't mind. Honest. Some of my best friends are nuns." He said it like a line from a comedy. "Seriously, I would be honored to do a scene with you. You're good."

"That's—thank you. You're kind." Awkward pause. I smoothed out the pleats of my habit and opened the playbook. "All right then. Which role do you want to play, Petruchio or Katherine?"

We both laughed.

"That would throw Dr. Wickham for a loop, wouldn't it?" Will said.

"Knowing him—probably not."

We found a small rehearsal stage and read through the scene twice. Petruchio, a suitor, had to "tame" Katherine, the proud, unmarried daughter of a duke.

"Why don't we take a break—compare notes—start blocking?" Will asked.

We grabbed two chairs and sat down.

He looked up from his script and made direct eye contact with me. His eyes were the clearest, most penetrating brown I'd ever seen. I couldn't shake the feeling that we'd met before, though I felt sure I'd never known anyone with a beard.

"What do you do for kicks?" he asked, pushing a lock of hair back from his forehead. "I mean, besides memorize scenes from Shakespeare."

I had to look away—his eyes were mesmerizing.

"Nothing you'd find interesting." *What would be funny to him about our inside jokes or satirical skits?* "Sometimes at evening recreation we darn stockings or play cards."

"Do you go to movies? Do you ever…dance? Read books, listen to music?" He leaned forward. His arms rested on his knees, he squinted under the spotlight. "When you're not praying, that is."

"Our lives are cloaked in secrecy." I gathered my veil and covered half my face.

"Tell me. I won't laugh—I'm interested—trying to figure you out. Am I being too personal?"

"No. I understand, people are curious. We all look alike. We don't drive—don't eat in public. We only travel in pairs…."

"Wait a minute—you don't eat in public? I thought nuns had given up that practice years ago?"

"We're a semi-cloistered order. It's a long-standing custom."

"What's wrong with eating in public? Jesus wasn't shy about doing it."

"It's a custom. We don't act anything like a cloistered order anymore—it's just…."

"Haven't you ever thought of challenging the custom? I mean, any custom that's outlived its usefulness should be debunked, don't you think?"

"I'm under temporary vows. I need to toe the line," I said. "You wanted to know what I do for fun?"

"Sorry—I got carried away. Go on."

I spread the folds of my habit out like a fan. "Let's see…for fun, I read poetry—sometimes I write poetry."

"So do I. What else?"

"I play bridge with a few other sisters. Sometimes I work in a little garden."

Will sat up in his chair. "Those all sound solitary—except for bridge. It seems to me you're alone or secluded much of the time. That's not what college is all about. Don't you feel like you're missing out on the fun?"

He noticed my discomfort and rushed to apologize. "I'm sorry, I'm not trying to judge—it's just that…."

"I know," I said. "It doesn't seem possible that convent life could be satisfying. What about friends and fun and going out with guys?"

I picked up the playbook and glanced over our lines. My habit and veil made it impossible for us to play this charged and high-energy love scene with anything approaching honesty. Will-as-Petruchio should be pulling me-as-Kate towards him, to rough-house and flirt, to admire Kate's beauty, her fair locks of hair, her full bosom—according to the lines.

"It's okay," I said. "I don't expect you to understand. Not even my family does. Maybe we should get back to rehearsing."

"I didn't mean to pry. I'm just trying to get a feel for—to, you know, figure out—I don't know what the hell I mean. Sorry—excuse my language."

"Why don't we finish reading the scene?" *Could he tell how uncomfortable I felt? Was I revealing too much of myself? Why did I feel we'd met before?*

"I don't know how to play this next part. I mean, the lines suggest Petruchio gets a little rough. I don't think I could slap a nun around, no matter how good an actor I might be." He looked at me closely—almost staring.

"What?"

"Do you ever take off your veil and—headpiece? I was just thinking how much easier it would be."

"I'm afraid not," I snapped. My shaved head had long recovered, but it was not acceptable for public view. Rumors of changes to the habit—which Angela had predicted two years before—were beginning to surface. You could hear Bob Dylan's "Blowin' in the Wind" playing all over campus. Change was in the air—but it hadn't trickled down to our medieval habit yet.

"Someday," I said, as if revealing a secret, "and maybe not too far away, nuns will take off their veils and wear more modern clothing—so I'm told. When it happens, I'll be able to play Kate the way Shakespeare intended. In the meantime, we'll have to work with things the way they are."

We stood up and read through the lines again, blocking as we went. It felt awkward at first, but I allowed Will to grab my arms and shove me a little, and Will encouraged me to slap him in the face.

Will: *Come, come, you wasp, in faith you are too angry.* (He gets close, our eyes meet, he snarls.)

Me: *If I be waspish, best beware my sting.* (I snarl back, make buzzing sounds, point at his nose, as if to sting him.)

Will: *My remedy then is to pluck it out.* (He reaches for my heart.)

Me: *Ay, if the fool could find it where it lies.* (I block him with my forearm.)

Will: *Nay, come again. Good Kate: I am a gentleman.* (I laugh, disgusted.)

Me: *That I'll try!* (I slap his face—he is shocked, angry.)

Will: *I swear I'll cuff you if you strike again.* (He grabs my arm, I wriggle loose.)

Me: *If you strike me, you are no gentleman.* (I glower at him, walk away.)

Will: *Nay come, Kate, come—you must not look so sour.* (He taunts me. I fume.)

Me: *It is my fashion, when I see a crab....*
Where did you study all this goodly speech?

Will: *It is extempore, from my mother's wit.* (His bragging makes me laugh.)

Me: *A witty mother! Witless else her son....*

Will: *...Therefore, setting all this chat aside,...*
thus in plain terms, your dowry 'greed upon...
And will you nill you, I will marry you....
Here comes your father; Never make denial,
I must and will have Katherine to my wife. (He drags me off—I struggle, shout and cry.)

At the end of the scene, I was shaking. We looked at each other, then we laughed till we were out of breath. We turned around, to see other class members standing at the door of the rehearsal room. They broke into spontaneous applause. We both bowed.

All I could say was, "Thank you, Will. That was—wow!"

We sat down, caught our breath—snuck glances at each other—each time, laughing again. As we left the theater and walked toward the Student Union building, Will asked, "Where do you go now?"

"To the library, to study."

"No—I'm treating you to coffee in the Garden Room."

"Sorry—I can't."

"Why? You don't have a class, do you?"

"I told you, we don't eat in public—with seculars, that is. We eat in the Sisters' dining room. But thanks anyway." I turned to leave.

"Not so fast, Kate." He grabbed my elbow—as if we were still acting. "What are these ancient traditions for anyway?"

All I could think was: *What color are his eyes? Mahogany? Maple? Amber? They kept changing in the light.*

"Come on, be the first to break the rules."

"Do you want to get me thrown out?"

We stood in the café doorway.

"Do you think anyone cares? Who'll throw you out? It's a coffee, Clare."

"It's more than that—it's a century of tradition," I said. "I'm not about to...."

"Why not? Come on, sit." He pointed to a table in the corner. "Over there, with me. We'll pretend we're rehearsing lines. Better still, we *could* rehearse our lines."

I followed him, not only because he made sense. I wanted to be bold, to test the boundaries. Maybe playing Kate had given me courage. I sat down but couldn't stop glancing around the room, searching.

The Garden Room—a glass-enclosed café—was filled with students hanging out between classes. *Would someone see me, report me to Mother Regina or the college president?*

Will brought two steaming mugs of coffee to the table.

"Cheers," we said in unison.

"See—that wasn't so hard, was it?"

"No. In fact, it feels right."

"Good for you."

We locked eyes—I looked away first. Something about him—I'd felt it from the start—I decided to ask.

"Your voice sounds familiar. Have we met before?"

He held up his hands in surrender. "I cannot tell a lie. We have. You don't remember where?" He grinned and scratched his beard.

"Tell me!"

"We've actually met several times."

"Really?"

"Here's a hint: John Donne, Teilhard de Chardin, and Thomas Merton."

I felt goose bumps. I took a minute, studied his face. Suddenly, I remembered. "The Braille room. Bill? The seminarian....and in the library, Donne." I could feel my face turning red. "You read my poetry."

Will laughed. "Right. Great poem. And?"

"And?"

"I'm also the guy who tried to do justice to Chardin at that symposium." He flashed a smile. "You made Merton's words sing. I was envious. Merton's my guy. I wanted to speak for him...but once I heard you, I knew you were the right person to read him."

"It must be your beard," I said, embarrassed. "Sorry I didn't recognize you. Where are your glasses?"

"The miracle of contact lenses." He blinked. "Besides, people say I have a common face."

Common face? I thought. *Hardly.*

"I thought the beard would give me...*gravitas*."

I imagined Bill's face, remembered his sweet, shy smile. "I remember a very shy novice named 'Bill.' Why the name change?"

"I felt I needed a complete metamorphosis. I was Bill or Billy to most people in my life, but my Dad called me 'Will.' He's been gone a while."

"I'm so sorry. My friend Pauline went to school with you—she said he died when you were in high school."

"He did. 'Will' is a nod to my Dad. And 'Will' feels more... outgoing."

"You do seem different. Confident. You seem to know what you want," I said. "Or is that an act?"

"Being shy and withdrawn—that got me nowhere."

"I take it you're no longer a Jesuit?"

He shook his head. "After I left the seminary, I decided to step up and take control—like Petruchio—though not as rough." He took a gulp of coffee. "You don't think I'm too forward?"

"Me? No. You're...perfectly fine."

"You look like you're about to say something...."

His eyes—disarming. "I'm just thinking," I said, "what a coincidence it is, our meeting up like this."

"No such thing as coincidence," he said, draining his coffee mug.

Sun was pouring in the café windows, the warm glow highlighted Will's dark, wavy hair. We laughed and quoted lines back and forth from the play. I wished Jack could see me being a college student, having fun. But when one of my sisters, a science professor, passed through the lounge, she glared at me. I raised the playbook in front of my face, hoping she wouldn't recognize me.

"Something wrong?" Will asked.

"It's nothing." I hadn't been doing anything wicked but felt as if I'd violated all three vows, right there in the Garden Room. I took another sip, then stood up. "I need to go. Thanks for the coffee. See you next class."

"Hey, wait."

I didn't answer. *What would Pauline say when I told her I'd been playing a love scene with the heart-breaker!*

A few days later, Mother Regina called me into her office. "Sister, need I remind you that eating with seculars is forbidden?" Not even a *Please-sit-down.*

"No, Mother," I said, standing. "I know the rules."

She sat behind her desk, concentrating on a pen she was turning in her hands. "See that you observe those rules, then."

"Yes, Mother."

"You think, Sister Clare, that as Mother Vivian's novice, you can do as you please." She looked at me, her small, dark eyes squinting. "But you're wrong. You're no different than the rest of us. Remember that."

"Yes, Mother." My composure was giving way to anger—my jaw clenched, acid ate away at my stomach. Mother Regina was cut from the same cloth as Mother Loretta. I felt outraged, discouraged. *Oh, how I missed Mother Vivian!*

"You may go now, Sister."

I left without a word, resolving not to sulk in chapel and lick my wounds. What would Mother Vivian do? *Taming of the Shrew* in hand, I crossed the community room and went down a flight of steps to the visitors' parlor. Seldom occupied, it made a good rehearsal room.

I closed the door, opened my script and shouted my lines. I would be ready for Will in a few days, when we were due to perform our scene in class. We would be great. Dr. Wickham would finally see that I belonged in his acting classes. Mother Regina would not break me.

At first I ignored the knocking.

"Clare? Are you in there?" I opened the door to find Delores, looking worried.

"What in tarnation is goin' on? Sounds like you're murdering someone."

"I'm rehearsing," I said. "It's a raucous scene. Kate is—never mind." I invited Delores in. "What did you want?"

"An explanation, I guess," she said, sitting in an overstuffed chair. "I saw you come storming from Mother Regina's office."

"You followed me?"

"Don't sound so suspicious." Delores gave me a look that said, *Calm down.* "What happened?"

I told her the whole story—being seen in the Garden Room with Will, Mother Regina labeling me as one of Mother Vivian's novices.

"That's it," Delores sat up. "We're calling Mother Vivian."

"No! We can't. I don't want her to know any of this. We have to be bigger than that. You know that's what Mother Vivian would say."

"But it's unfair!" Delores shouted.

We sat in silence for a few minutes. Then a smile crept onto Delores' face.

"What? You look like you're cooking up another wild idea," I said. "No more petitions."

"Even better," Delores said. "A sit-in."

"Meaning?"

"In the Garden Room. If all of us decide to use the student lounge…."

"You're going to get us in trouble, Delores."

"Haven't you already done that, Clare?"

After my next psychology lecture, Audrey asked me to stay late. "Sit down, Clare."

I sat across from her desk in the empty classroom.

"Is something bothering you?" Audrey asked. "You look—I don't know—sad."

"Am I that transparent?" I told her about Mother Regina's accusations that I was "above the law"—privileged because I was one of Mother Vivian's novices. "I had hoped for change—

that our Community was modernizing, but all I feel is judgment. Mother Vivian taught us to be more open, more loving." I was fighting back tears. "Thank you," I said, "for listening. It's nice to have someone to trust around here."

"Your disappointment—it's valid, Clare," Audrey said. "But I can assure you that the change you talk about is coming. Some of us older folks just need more time."

"Time for what?" I blurted. "It's so obvious."

"The kind of change this Community is seeking won't happen overnight, I'm afraid—customs have been in place for centuries—it will mean a change in our culture."

Audrey moved to a student desk next to me. She placed her hand on mine. "Clare, dear, can you wait for the rest of us?" I looked into her kind eyes. "Can you be a leader? For your own classmates?"

I didn't want to be a leader. "Why me?" I almost laughed, I sounded pathetic.

"Others look up to you," Audrey said. "Surely you know that?"

I didn't—or didn't want to admit it. I didn't want the responsibility. But I remembered something Thomas Merton had written—something about emptying out our own small ego dreams so that we could be open to the plan God had in mind—from all eternity. I had no idea anymore what that plan was for me.

Audrey stood up. "Try to have patience with Mother Regina. She may be carrying her own private cross—we all are."

I was tired of being patient.

"If you want progress, go back to Mother Regina. Tell her how you feel. Find some common ground."

Was there common ground? We were sisters—members of the same Community. Could I bare my soul to Mother Regina? Would she listen?

I sighed. "I'll try, Audrey. Thank you for your kindness." I stood up. "Do you ever have coffee with your students in the Garden Room?"

Audrey laughed. "What a strange question. Of course. Why?"

"Just wondering," I said, and walked out the door.

A few weeks later, I knocked on Mother Regina's door and invited myself into her office. Her back was turned to me. She was wiping her eyes with her handkerchief. She looked at me.

"What is it, Sister Clare?"

"I'm sorry, Mother. I can come back—are you all right?"

"Sit down, Sister." She blew her nose. "If you'll give me a minute to…." She smiled but her eyes were red—her face sad.

I waited. "I'll just come back later."

"No…no. It's…I just had a call from the nursing home where my mother is." She blew her nose again. "She's not…that is…we just don't know."

"I'm so sorry, Mother." It hadn't occurred to me that Mother Regina had a mother.

"I'm all she's got—I'm an only child," Mother said. "She's failing—I need to decide whether to drive all the way to Cleveland…more *when* than *whether*…."

Neither of us spoke. She wiped her eyes a few more times.

I felt my heart crack open a little—I couldn't imagine being in her place. "Are you sure I shouldn't…."

"No. It's all right. Thank you for your patience." She struggled to smile. "What can I do for you?"

"I've come waving a white flag, Mother—figuratively speaking."

"You make it sound as if we're at war. Are we?"

"If so, I was hoping to call a truce, Mother." I swallowed hard. "I know some of us act differently—after our Novitiate year with Mother Vivian."

She shifted in her chair, cleared her throat. "I suppose I was hasty in my remarks, Sister. I didn't mean...." She looked away.

"I hope we can find common ground, Mother. I believe we're all after the same goals."

"You're brave to speak this way, Sister Clare. I wasn't wrong in seeing you as a leader." She looked straight at me. "I want nothing more than to work with you—with all of you."

"All of *us*? Who do you mean?" I wanted her to say it.

"All of Mother Vivian's novices, yes."

"I can only speak for myself—but that's what I want—without feeling I'm being watched."

"I see."

"I want to trust you, Mother."

"I understand." She reached her hand across the desk. "Here's my promise—I'll listen to no more gossip."

We shook hands—and held on for a few moments.

"I ask that same trust—and honesty—from you, Sister Clare."

"I'll do my best," I said, remembering Delores' threat to hold a sit-in in the Garden Room. I decided to mention that another time. One diplomatic victory at a time.

CHAPTER 22

As soon as I entered the campus theater, Will McBride waved me over to where he was sitting. "I was hoping you'd be in this Improvisation Seminar, Clare. I need a partner—thought we'd work together."

My heart raced. My cheeks felt flush. I heard myself spewing out false humility. "Look around you, Will, plenty of eligible co-eds. Wouldn't you rather...."

"Ah. The phony-baloney line: *Nobody wants to work with the nun.*" He wagged his finger at me.

"Point taken." Will made me forget I was wearing a habit.

Dr. Wickham barked out instructions to the class: "Partner up, people. Design a dance. Fifteen minutes. Visit the costume trunk for props, if you need to." He looked at me. "Sister—you're not getting out of this—I've seen your talent. That *Shrew* scene, both of you were splendid, but you...." He pointed at me. "Impressive."

I nearly fainted. Praise from Dr. Wickham? But now, a dance?

Dr. Wickham went around the rehearsal room handing out sheet-music copies. "Sister, and you—Will? Design a dance to this."

Will saw the terror on my face. "What's the song?"

I handed the sheet music to him.

His face turned deep red. "Ray Charles. 'I Can't Stop Loving You.' You know it?"

"I don't. It must have come out after I entered. We'll ask for a different song." *I was hoping for something like "The Surrey With The Fringe On Top."*

"Wait—I have an idea. C'mere." He led me across the hall to a rehearsal room. He sat down at the piano and started playing. "I'll sing it for you. It's easy."

Dr. Wickham is playing a cruel trick, I thought. *Well, I'll show him. This is theater—not real life. I can do this.* I sat next to Will on the piano bench and listened to his rich baritone voice. *Is there anything this guy can't do?*

Will's eyes went from the sheet music, to me, to the piano keys.

Each time he looked at me, I got lost in his eyes.

"Clare?" It took me a minute to realize Will had finished the song. "What do you think?"

"What do I think?" *It's a good thing I'm a nun, or I'd be in serious danger of falling head-over-heels in love with you*, I thought.

"Let's check out the costume trunk." Will brushed the lock of hair off his forehead and slid off the bench. "Ready?" He grabbed my hand and pulled me into the costume room. We rummaged through a trunk and found a handful of scarves and veils.

"We'll use these as our point of contact," Will said. "That way, we don't even have to touch—perfectly modest."

The last to perform, we got a standing ovation. Dr. Wickham admitted we were the most creative.

"Did you hear that applause?" Will asked, looping a scarf around me, his eyes dancing. He used the scarf to draw me close to him. "It was fun—we won the Improv Oscar."

I stepped back, uncomfortable. "You deserve the credit."

"Save your 'humble' act—it gets you nowhere in theater, Clare." He tugged again on the scarf, pulling me closer. "Have a little fun."

"I am." *I've never had such fun*, I thought. "Is there anything you can't do, Will McBride?"

We were so close…his eyes were sparkling; his smile was overpowering—I wondered if he knew.

"Wow," Will said, as he looked into my eyes.

"What?" I said. I could barely look at him.

"Your eyes are so blue, the color of sapphires." He reached out to touch my cheek, then pulled his hand back.

I turned away, felt the blood rush into my cheeks. "Don't," I said.

"There is one thing I'm going to try to do, bonny Kate."

My cheeks were burning, but I went along, to lighten up the moment. "Pray tell, what, Petruchio?" I said, and looked at him brazenly, hands on my hips, as Katherine.

"Coax you to take off that veil."

"Nay, Petruchio. Only I have the power to do that."

For senior thesis, I wrote, designed, and produced a children's play about unwanted Christmas toys, starring local second-graders. Theater students were my crew, and Will did the lighting. Pauline, who'd had to remind Will of their childhood grade school history, composed three songs and played the piano. From September until Christmas break, I practically lived at the college. Pauline—who stayed late to practice piano and violin—traveled back and forth from the campus to the House of Studies with me.

"Looks like you've hit it off with Will McBride," Pauline said as we walked home one evening. "I wish I could find another music major as helpful. This thesis work is killing my grade average. I haven't studied for a French test or read a single page in philosophy."

"Look at it this way," I said, "we're pouring everything into our majors. That's where we'll be working, once we graduate."

"How can you be sure?" Pauline asked. "Obedience, Clare. *Go where you are sent and do what you are told.*"

"You think they'd assign us to teach something we're not qualified for?"

"It happens all the time. In a few months, we'll have our diplomas, but we won't know the first thing about teaching—at least I won't."

"You'll figure it out, like the rest of us."

"Is that what you want?" Pauline asked. "Just to *figure it out*? Not me. I want to be good—not mediocre like some teachers I've had. What kind of teacher do you want to be?"

"All I've wanted is to do God's will." I paused. "My vocation led me here. God will do the rest."

"I wish I had that kind of blind faith. What if I'm sent to teach seventh-graders in Podunk, Pennsylvania? I hate seventh-graders. I remember *being* a seventh-grader. Dear God… worst year of my life."

"All the more reason for you to be their teacher," I said. "You'll understand and love them."

"I'll understand and hate them."

Pauline saw my disapproving glare.

"All right—I'll love them like God loves them."

We walked in silence. I'd been so caught up in theater, I hadn't thought beyond it. What if I got sent to teach elementary education?

We walked the rest of the way singing a hymn we'd learned in the Novitiate—the *Salve Regina* in two-part harmony. As we got to the front door, Pauline stopped.

"You didn't answer my question. You're going to be a teacher. What kind do you want to be?"

"A good one."

"Too easy," Pauline said. "You'd better come up with something better before you walk into the classroom on day one."

Pauline was right. I had no idea what kind of a teacher I would be.

Chapter 22

A week before graduation, Mother Provincial called each of us into the visitor's parlor—one by one, according to seniority—to give us our assignment and a blessing. Rumors circulated that this new Mother Provincial was on the same page as Mother Vivian, which raised my hopes—though not too high.

I knelt beside her, which was the custom when being sent to a new ministry. "You look nervous, Sister Clare Marie," Mother said. "Would it surprise you to learn that we want you to be the drama and English teacher at Marywood High?"

I swallowed hard, took a breath. "I was hoping…."

"Indeed." She smiled and handed me a piece of paper with my name, the assignment, and the place where I would begin a brand-new life.

"Marywood High has a long tradition of theater and drama. You know that, I'm sure, since you graduated from Marywood five years ago."

Was it only five years? It felt like a lifetime.

"Sister Helen is opening a drama department at our new high school in Pittsburgh, so we are counting on you to step in. You were one of Sister Helen's prized pupils, I hear."

"Sister Helen had many prized pupils—but, yes, I was one of her students."

"Then you are aware you will have big shoes to fill."

My stomach tightened. *On one hand, Sister Helen had a distinguished reputation; on the other hand, the theater department needed modernizing. Was I ready to do it?*

"I'll do my best, Mother." I was still on my knees. That same sense of smallness I'd felt while kneeling at the feet of Mother Loretta welled up in me.

"Of course. You're a Sister of St. Mary, after all. I wonder, Sister Clare, whether you'd ever be interested in working with the poor in our inner-city? The Brothers of St. Paul are looking for sisters to assist them."

"I've always had an interest, Mother. But for now, I'm excited to teach at Marywood."

Mother smiled and raised her hands over my head, reciting the stock blessing for beginning a ministry.

I walked into the community room, clutching my paper and motioned to Pauline. "Good luck," I whispered.

I flashed my assignment to my classmates, who celebrated with me that I'd be going "home" to my *alma mater*. In five short years, I'd been transformed from high school student to a Sister of St. Mary: teacher, drama director, grown-up, nun. I celebrated with Rosemary, who was going to be Marywood's new biology teacher.

Pauline returned from her meeting wearing a frown. She sat down next to me and handed me her assignment sheet. "Seventh Grade, St. Peter's, Celina, Ohio," she whispered. "Podunk," she added with a sarcastic laugh. "Didn't I predict it? Only difference is—it's Ohio, not Pennsylvania."

I was speechless.

Pauline turned to me with a rueful smile. "Okay—time to start my collection of choir music for seventh-grade boys."

"That's the spirit—you're going to knock them off their feet."

At dinner, Delores, Angela, and I sat together.

Delores announced she was being sent to teach first grade—to her hometown in Tennessee. "Daddy and Mama will be happy, I guess."

"You don't seem pleased," I said. Delores had hoped to get her master's in special education.

"It's bad enough that my loving parents are tottering on the verge of divorce. Even worse, my principal has—shall we say—a *reputation*. She taught me ninth-grade Latin."

"And?"

"I didn't make it to Latin II. She gave *harsh* a whole new meaning."

"Maybe she's mellowed?" Angela said.

"Maybe hell's frozen over," Delores said. "Still, I'm fixin' to bring Mother Vivian's spirit with me."

"You can do it, Delores," said Angela, who was being sent to Washington, D.C. for graduate study in theology.

"When you get to D.C., Angela, look up Sister Ellen," I said, "though her name is different now." I noticed their confused looks. "Ellen was the novice we all thought would die of homesickness, remember?" They did. "I had a letter from her a few weeks ago. She's working on a Ph.D. in psychology at American University."

"How do you know about her?" Delores asked.

"We've kept in touch a little. I hold her responsible—at least in part—for Mother Vivian's appointment as our Novice Mistress."

They were full of questions.

"Someday, I'll tell you the whole story."

Delores leaned in to whisper: "Speaking of stories—rumor has it Mother Loretta is going to be at our graduation."

My stomach did a flip. I stopped eating. My anger for Mother Loretta—buried for years—welled up. I had to take a long drink of water in order to swallow.

"She's back from the Philippines?" Angela asked.

"Temporarily," Delores said. "For medical treatment of some kind." She leaned in closer. "Word is, she wants to meet with us—if we're willing."

"Who told you this? What does she want?" Angela asked.

"If the sister who told me—and I can't reveal my source—is credible, Mother Loretta wants to reconcile with us."

"I don't believe it." Angela sat back in her chair and folded her arms across her chest. "Clare—would you show up for a meeting with Mother Loretta?"

"Of course," I said, "she's a member of our Community. If she wants to meet with us to reconcile, I'm willing—but if it's to argue her case, count me out."

The next evening, Mother Regina rang a bell in the refectory and told us to assemble in the community room. Once we were all seated, Mother Regina ushered Mother Loretta into the room. They both stood at the podium.

"Sisters, I know Mother Loretta needs no introduction, so I'll waste no time." Mother Regina found a chair along the side wall.

Mother Loretta looked around the room, taking in each face.

"Sisters," she cleared her throat several times. "I have rehearsed over and over what I might say to you all, given the chance." She moved from behind the podium—close enough to look each of us in the eye. "Now that I'm here with you—face-to-face, I can only think to say, *I'm sorry*." Her eyes clouded over, her strong voice weakened.

No one moved a muscle.

"That's it, Sisters—plain and simple—*I'm sorry*. As your Novice Mistress, I only knew to do what had been done to me. I know it's not an excuse—just a fact."

She looked at each of us in turn. I was holding my breath—my hands curled into a fist on my lap, my knees were trembling.

"*I'm sorry*—two words—and two more: *Forgive me*." A slight smile worked the corners of her mouth. "If I could believe in your forgiveness, then I know I'll be able to face the next...." She hesitated. "You might as well know."

She pulled out a chair and sat down next to the podium. This stern, proud woman was begging for our forgiveness—publicly.

I took a deep breath and willed my heart to open. This had to be worse than the penance she'd given me as a novice—thirty minutes kneeling before the Blessed Virgin.

"I'm being treated for cancer. It doesn't look good, but there is always the power of prayer, isn't there?"

We were dumbstruck.

Mother Regina stood up and moved to Mother Loretta's chair. "We will keep you in our constant prayers, won't we Sisters?"

"Yes, Mother," we answered in unison.

I glanced around the room. I wasn't the only one in tears. Without prompting, we all stood and applauded—never mind that Mother Loretta had forbidden clapping in the Novitiate.

She stood again and smiled. "Thank you, Sisters. You will never know what this means to me. My years in the Philippines, Sisters, among the poor...." She moved with Mother Regina toward the door. "I hope you will all have the opportunity. So humbling—such simple, loving people." She lifted her hand. "Good-bye, Sisters. I know this may be hard to believe, but I love each one of you."

We couldn't move for a long time. Later, I walked with Angela and Delores to our dorm.

"My head wants to believe her," Delores said, "but I'm not sure about my heart."

"I know—but I believe her sincerity," I said.

"Is it possible to have instant reconciliation?" Angela asked.

"The pain—the mistrust—it's deep. My head tells me I should open my heart," I said. "It's going to take time."

"I want to wear a cap and gown like the rest of the graduates," I joked to Pauline as we lined up according to our degrees on the college green. We weren't allowed to wear the colorful graduate hoods. We sat instead in the last row, behind the other graduates.

"You should have thought about that when you took the holy habit of religion," Pauline joked. "We're just the college's slaves anyway. All we're good for is to set up, serve, then take everything down again."

"At least we get to have punch and cookies with our families," I offered. "Someone else will clean up."

"You haven't heard?" Pauline snapped. "Tomorrow morning we're here, bright and early, to take it all down."

I didn't care how much mindless manual labor I'd have to do. I had earned a college diploma, ended up on the honor roll with an A-minus average, in spite of all the obstacles that came with living in a convent and meeting the obligations of communal life—in spite of the doubters, my former teachers and Marianne among them. Tonight, I would enjoy the celebration.

After the ceremony, I was standing on the edge of the crowd, searching for my family, when I saw Will waving at me. The sight of him made me blush.

"I have a present for you." He was acting like that shy seminarian I'd first met in the Braille room. He handed me a package wrapped in blue paper and tied with a white bow.

"You didn't have to get me a present."

"I wanted to give you something, to celebrate your bravery."

"My bravery?"

"The way you came to class prepared, always ready to work, no matter what Dr. Wickham threw at you. You knocked their socks off with your senior thesis. I thought it deserved a little something." He paused and smiled. "I hope you like it—I think you will. Open it."

Chapter 22

I untied the bow and unwrapped a slightly worn copy of Kahlil Gibran's *The Prophet.* I flipped open the cover to find an inscription from Will, but I was too embarrassed to read it.

"I hope you don't mind—a few markings in the book. Usually I don't write in books, but there are so many good lines. You don't mind, do you?"

"Mind? Gosh, no, Will." I looked up to see an anxious expression on his face. "I'm touched. What a wonderful gift."

"Do you have a copy? Do you know Gibran?"

"No and No." *I am going to miss your smile*, I thought. I held up the book. "I'll know him soon, though, thanks to you."

He moved closer to me. "I'm only here to give you this—I don't have a ticket—had to sneak in." We looked at each other. "Congratulations, Clare. I wish you luck. Where are you off to, by the way?"

"Marywood High."

"Drama teacher?"

"Plus English. Pretty exciting. You?"

"A few more semesters slugging it out here. That's what years in the seminary will do—you know, put you behind academically." He paused. "Behind in a lot of ways, I guess." He eyed me closely, his brown eyes sparkled.

"Have you declared a major?" I asked.

"Double major," he said. "English and Theology—at least that's my plan. Probably squeeze in some education courses."

"You're planning to teach?"

"I do hope to teach some day. Or maybe I'll be an actor, like you."

I laughed. "I'm not an actor, Will."

"Yes, you are, Clare, a fine one. When we did that *Taming of the Shrew* scene, you were so convincing, everyone forgot you were—you know."

"The nun."

"I forgot you were anything but a fine actor. Another thing…I think you've started a trend."

"A trend?"

"Haven't you noticed? Every day, more nuns are having coffee in the student lounge."

"I was trying not to notice—afraid I'd get blamed for inciting the masses. The credit is yours—you gave me the push."

Will leaned in and whispered, "I'll miss seeing you on campus." He moved aside to let an excited grad push by. "Working with you on your thesis, rehearsing, winning over Dr. Wickham, breaking the rules in the Garden Room—so many great moments."

My heart beat faster.

"I feel like I'm losing a best friend." He touched my arm. "I hope you feel the same." He stepped back and bowed deeply—a Shakespearean bow. "Good fortune, bonny Kate. Enjoy *The Prophet*." He turned and disappeared in the crowd.

"Wait! Will?" I waved after him but lost him in the crowd. "Thank you!"

"Who was *that*?" Marianne's voice.

I turned to see my family standing behind me.

"Just a friend—from my acting classes."

Marianne was staring at the book. I wrapped it and re-tied the bow.

"A present," I said. "From Will."

"Nice—isn't that nice, Mom?" Marianne said, standing on tiptoe to try to catch a glimpse of Will in the crowd. "A handsome man gave Maggie a present."

Mom nodded. "What's even nicer is Maggie's college degree, wouldn't you say, Marianne?"

Marianne was caught off guard—her pout and shrug spoke volumes, though.

"You followed your dream," Mom said. "You majored in theater—you did it."

I looked around to see Dad and Jack, beaming. I couldn't believe my ears. Not only was Mom recognizing my accomplishments, she was reminding Marianne that I had a four-year degree. I held up my diploma, tucked inside a blue leather case with gold lettering. I gave Mom a big hug. "That means a lot, Mom."

"It means a lot to me too, Maggie."

"Okay everyone, let's head to the Garden Room. I hear the punch and cookies are spectacular." Never mind that I'd be cleaning up the next morning.

PART THREE

July 1965 - May 1970

CHAPTER 23

Sister Corella, principal at Marywood, assigned me six freshman English classes. In the typical nine-period day, that left one period for prep, one for lunch, one for drama—I'd have to meet my other drama classes either before or after school. Some of my lessons and tests turned out to be embarrassingly simple, others were way too challenging. I fielded complaints and spent the whole year adjusting, readjusting, then adjusting again.

Drama classes were more fun. I created a new curriculum from scratch—which was only possible because I no longer had to observe lights-out at Grand Silence. The light in my cell often burned close to midnight that first year.

I produced and directed two plays during the school year. Working with all girls was a challenge, so I chose two of my favorites, *The Wizard of Oz* and *Alice in Wonderland*, thinking costuming would mask the fact that girls were playing the male parts. I hadn't taken into account the elaborate staging each play required.

Luckily, our janitor was a handyman, and I recruited art students to help build and paint the sets. Both productions were successful, in my humble opinion, though I got into trouble with Sister Corella—who was both principal and my superior—and some of the other faculty for letting my drama students stay late and make noise. Never mind that a record number of students participated in the school plays.

One positive thing: Rosemary and I, as the newest and youngest sisters, were selected to be drivers for our community.

Our driver's licenses had expired, so we needed to start from scratch. We both passed easily. It meant extra time after school. I didn't care. Driving restored a sense of freedom I thought I'd lost forever.

I looked back on my rookie year with mixed emotions. I congratulated myself on my major and minor successes, on all I'd learned, and forgave myself a number of blunders. I only hoped everyone else would be as forgiving.

One day as that first school year was closing, I was in my classroom looking for challenging monologues for my advanced drama class, when Sister Corella rapped on my classroom door and walked in. I stood up and offered her the teacher's chair.

"No, thank you. I won't stay long. I've been meaning to speak to you about this for months. The thing is," she went on, "I've had a complaint from one of the parents—about your choice of content for drama classes. It seems the parents felt the reading selections were—*too adult* for their daughter."

"Too adult?" My pulse raced and my hands began to sweat—a common reaction whenever Sister Corella spoke to me. I tried to sound calm. "Who complained?"

"That's not relevant—I just ask you to consider the maturity level of your students. There are girls who can't handle such mature themes."

"Would you like to see my list of plays and readings?" I said, trying to hide my defensiveness. "I can't imagine there are any pieces in my curriculum you'd consider offensive."

"Not *offensive,* exactly—at least I wouldn't use that word. Just—too mature. In the nearly twenty years Sister Helen was in charge of our drama department, there was *never* a complaint."

Of course not, I thought, *because Sister Helen—God love her—fed us Pablum. Nothing was ever challenging.*

"We don't want parents feeling unhappy about the education their daughters are getting here at Marywood, do we Sister?"

"No, Sister."

"Good. I'm glad we talked this over. I trust you'll be circumspect in future."

"I will do my best," I answered, trying to sound cheerful.

Sister Corella disappeared, taking with her any excitement I'd felt about beefing up my curriculum.

A few days later, when Sister Corella called me to her office, I expected another reprimand. I couldn't believe it when she said I'd been given permission to spend the summer living and working in the inner-city as part of an outreach project. I hunted Rosemary down in the biology lab to tell her.

"Didn't you answer a questionnaire from Mother Provincial about working with the poor?" Rosemary asked.

"I did—but that was over a year ago. I didn't expect to be *chosen*. Of course, Sister Corella took the joy out by reminding me that it was unusual for a sister in temporary vows to live outside the convent," I said. "But Mother Provincial approved, since I'd be living with women from other religious communities."

"Mother Provincial is a good egg."

Rosemary—so level-headed, I thought. "But then—as a warning—Corella emphasized I'd still be under her authority."

"Don't let her burst your bubble."

I read the official letter over and over. I'd be living in a downtown parish, sponsored by the Brothers of St. Paul, with twenty-five sisters from around the city. Up until the day I was to move downtown, I expected Corella to stop me—concerned I wouldn't behave myself outside the convent confines.

Safety was an issue downtown—race riots were erupting in cities across the country. It had been two years since the riots in Watts—a Los Angeles area—with police brutality and six days of looting and burning. Recently, the news showed riots in Cleveland, San Francisco, and Chicago. We wondered if it could erupt in our own city. I called Jack to see if he had any inside knowledge. He thought there could be bloodshed downtown.

No good news there, I thought.

I'd promised Sister Corella I'd contact the Brothers who were sponsoring the project. Father Mark, the program director, explained that while the inner-city was a poor neighborhood, there were as many poor Whites as Blacks—maybe more. They weren't the militant type.

Mom called, worried for my safety. "I'm praying my rosary every day. First, Jack crusades for civil rights in the South—now you're going to live in the ghetto."

Poor Mom—so many changes—although the new, "modified" habit was one change she could support. She was thrilled that we'd finally been given permission to wear it. During our last visiting day, I'd modeled the navy-blue dress—calf-length—and the shoulder-length veil—excited that I'd be able to wear it during my summer in the city.

"Finally—you can show your hair—at least on the top. How long is it?"

I took off my veil. "Short, Mom. It's easier."

Marianne was dying of curiosity. "Was it hard to make the change, Maggie? I mean, do you feel sort of naked?"

"I feel liberated, Marianne. And this habit is washable."

"Your old habits weren't washable?"

"There's a lot you don't know about convent life, Marianne." I realized I'd never told her we had two habits—one for first-class and visiting days, another for everything else—or that my everyday habit only got dry-cleaned twice a year.

"Whose fault is that, Maggie?"

For once I took her point—I'd kept a lot of secrets from her.

I arrived at St. Peter's—the parish and now-empty school where all the sister volunteers would be living for the summer. The Pastor met me. With his deep voice, his thick, white beard, and his brown robe, he reminded me of Old St. Nick.

Rosemary helped me lug my suitcase, books, and my favorite reading lamp up three flights of steps to Room 10, a former classroom. There were four single beds, each with its own chair and nightstand, each space separated by a hanging bed curtain—just like in the Novitiate. Faded blackboards hung on three walls, and large, un-shuttered windows opened to the hot, dusty street below, where trash piled up outside the dilapidated buildings and at night, drunks and streetwalkers roamed freely.

Every afternoon we celebrated Mass—like I'd never known it before—up close, in a circle around the altar. Father Mark—the celebrant—would invite us to extend our hands during the consecration—explaining that we all had priestly power to transform the bread and wine into the body and blood of Christ. Two of the Brothers—Jeremy, a seminarian studying to be a priest, and Victor, a brother in vowed life like us sisters—played guitar and led the singing. It struck me that women's voices could never achieve the depth and beauty of these men's voices—men who understood scripture and sang with their hearts.

I felt joyful—the way I'd felt on the day I entered the convent. For some time, I'd been silencing the fear that I'd lost that feeling—and with it, my vocation.

Every time Father Mark raised his eyes in prayer, it gave me goose bumps. I was inspired by his stories about the people he'd met in the inner-city—poor people suffering pain and loneliness, and how they impressed him with their courage and faith. I loved hearing male voices again. I realized how much I'd loved hearing Will's voice—how much I missed Jack and Stan—so strong, self-assured.

Sister Dorothy, a young Franciscan sister from across town, was one of my roommates. Every day, we walked the streets, greeting everyone we met. The Brothers of St. Paul at St. Peter's Parish wanted to get to know their neighbors, Catholic or not. We climbed rickety apartment steps and wound down dark hallways in search of the poor, the elderly, and the forgotten. We didn't have to look for the children—they found us.

"I came here thinking I needed to fix their lives," Dorothy confessed one night as we sat fanning ourselves on our beds. "I can't ignore their lack of material possessions, but they're also rich in simplicity and faith."

"I don't think I've ever felt closer to God," I said, "than when Miss Mary made scrambled eggs for us, even though her cupboard was nearly bare."

"And Mrs. Collier," Dorothy said. "Her tiny apartment crammed with library books about the American Revolution and the Civil War. She could have taught the course."

"My parents worry for my safety." I clicked off my reading lamp and lay back on my pillow. "I can't convince them what a sacred place I'm really in."

Long days were capped with evening recreation in the church hall, where people gathered for Bingo every Wednesday and Saturday. During the first week, Victor invited me to sit at his table and motioned for Jeremy to join us.

"Can I get you a beer? Pretzels?" Victor asked.

"I don't know. I haven't had a beer since my going-away party in 1960."

"Come on—what's your last name? Walsh? Irish, right? Irish, from Cincinnati, and you don't drink beer?"

"I used to, but...."

"I thought so. Here." He slid a bottle of beer toward me. "And pretzels. Can't have beer without pretzels."

"What about you?" I asked Victor.

"Jeremy's bringing more."

Jeremy showed up with two more bottles and sat down next to me. "Cheers!"

I took a long gulp of beer—it tasted better than I remembered.

"Now. Jeremy and I have a proposition. We hope you'll join the choir."

"Me?" I felt terrified—and thrilled.

"We heard you singing at Mass. Great voice. Strong. Good harmony. Do you play?"

"Play? You mean guitar? No. I pluck around on a banjo. But I didn't bring it."

"There's a banjo at our house," Jeremy said. "I'll bring it over, we can practice."

"I'm an amateur. There must be others who are musicians—I don't even read music."

"Hear that, Jeremy? Clare here is turning down an opportunity to perform with us. Come on. You're our second soprano. We've recruited a few others. You won't be alone."

Overnight, I'd become a member of "The City Voices," along with another sister who played guitar and sang alto, and a sister with a heavenly soprano voice who kept time rattling a tambourine.

After a few weeks living downtown, I had a deeper appreciation for what Jack was trying to accomplish. One evening, I called home and tried to explain it to Mom and Dad.

"Those people," Mom said, "they're lazy. If you work hard, you can make something of yourself—that's what we had to do."

"But Mom—you didn't experience discrimination like these folks."

"We survived the Great Depression—don't tell me about poverty."

I had to accept that they would never understand the challenges of being chronically poor and uneducated, or the stigma of suffering generations of discrimination.

Sister Dorothy and I got invited to a Baptist storefront revival where we stood up and witnessed for the Lord, to the delighted whoops and *Amens* of the congregation. That evening, we sat on our beds laughing for nearly an hour—bursting with joy.

With Father Mark and Victor, I sat down to a dinner of Irish stew in the squalid, one-room apartment of a notorious former streetwalker, while cockroaches traipsed over our sandals in broad daylight. We spent evenings playing Bingo with the locals, or learning Pinochle and sampling the locally-brewed beers with the Brothers. It took me no time to recapture my taste for a cold beer on a hot night. After choir practice one evening, Victor pulled me aside.

"Look what I've got! Five complimentary tickets to *La Traviata.* Mark said we could borrow the Plymouth. He's not interested in opera. Wanna go? The others in the Voices choir are up for it."

"Of course! I've never been to an opera."

"Really? A drama major and never been to an opera?"

"I had to read a few librettos in college," I told him, "but I've never seen a full-fledged opera. What's it about?"

"Opera plots are so juicy. *La Traviata*—Violetta leaves her former life as a courtesan to give herself to Alfredo. Alfredo's father considers her low-life, so to spare Alfredo humiliation, Violetta pretends to love someone else. In the end, love conquers all, and the two lovers are reunited."

Victor laughed. "You're wondering how I know so much about this, aren't you?"

"Actually, I am."

"My Mom is an opera nut. Typical Italian. She dragged me to a dozen before I was eighteen. Now I go willingly—when I can scrounge a ticket."

The five of us packed our sweaty bodies into the old Plymouth. Afterwards, we sang all the way home. One of the sisters, the soprano in our choir group, amazed us by belting out lines from the final aria, where Violetta begs Alfredo to love her.

That night I had a dream: Victor was trying to convince me to run off with him. It was too unsettling even to write about in my journal. I told myself it was *only* a dream.

Some nights, after choir practice, I'd steal off to my cubicle for solitude and a chance to read; but by the time I'd climbed the three flights, all I could do was fall into bed. Most nights, not even the incoherent shouts of drunks in the street, the shattering wine bottles, or the stifling heat kept me awake.

One night, I wrote a single sentence in my journal: *I have never been so happy.*

When it was time to leave the inner-city, I was torn between losing what felt like an ideal community, and getting back to my familiar life at Marywood High. As we packed up, I told Sister Dorothy that, in a perverse sort of way, I was going to miss this dormitory.

"Right—the heat, the odors, the noise, those three flights of stairs. We could write a book, couldn't we?"

"But only certain people would be allowed to read it—and *not* our superiors."

Victor was waiting outside on the sidewalk in front of the school. "Sorry we couldn't hire a band for a sendoff, Clare." He held onto my hand, which felt wonderful and uncomfortable, especially in the gathering crowd of people—a dozen brothers, a handful of priests, over twenty-five sisters, and the people who had come to pick us all up.

"We *are* the band, silly." I pulled my hand away—gently.

"When will I see you again?"

That felt like asking for the next date—it startled me.

"What I mean is...we have so much in common. It would be a shame not to continue our friendship, don't you think? You know, in the spirit of Vatican II, 'opening the windows to let in the fresh air.'"

While I told Victor I appreciated our discussions, and that it would be *nice* to get together some time, I imagined Sister Corella rolling out a welcome mat for someone like Victor. Hah!

"It's been great making music with you." Victor winced. "That didn't sound—what I mean is...."

I put him out of his misery. "Hey, I know, Victor. It has been fun—I learned a lot working with you and Jeremy. I thank you. My banjo thanks you. You wouldn't be interested in joining our convent choir, would you?"

Before Victor could answer, I felt a hand on my shoulder. I turned to see Father Mark.

"We all hate to see you go, Clare," Father Mark said.

I had such respect and admiration for Father Mark. I wanted to say the right thing. "I've had a wonderful time, Father. I'll never forget it."

"You're a natural. It's like you've been here before."

"Just a few mission trips during high school, Father. Our mission club sponsored them—we'd spend an afternoon at a community center, play Bingo with the old folks, or read to a group of kids."

"How was this summer different?"

"You helped us break through the façade. I learned so much, you taught me so much. I can't even begin to say...."

I felt short of breath, in over my head, longing for an escape. It was easier with Victor; he was a peer. Father Mark was—I couldn't even think of a word—a sage, a mentor.

"I'll say it again, Clare. You're a natural. I'm going to make sure we don't lose touch. We need people like you down here. Don't be a stranger. Otherwise I'll come and find you."

"No need for that!" The thought of this dynamic, attractive young priest calling on me at school made me dizzy. "I've met so many wonderful people," I said. "I'll be back to visit—if I can." I pointed to Rosemary pulling up to the curb in the school station wagon. "There's my ride." Rosemary hopped out and helped me load my things.

On the ride home I rambled on about the people, the places, the sheer adventure I'd been on. I didn't want to think about the work waiting for me back at school—retreat, class preparation, the books I hadn't read over the summer.

When we reached Marywood, Rosemary pulled the car into the parking lot next to Dolan House and switched off the key. She turned to me. "You know," she said, "I didn't see it before, but it all fits together now."

"Didn't see what?"

"You're being primed, Clare. I don't think you're destined to spend the rest of your days at Marywood. God is calling you somewhere new."

"You're scaring me, Rosemary. I'm not ready for a change that big."

"You should do some writing about this whole summer-in-the-city thing." We unloaded the car and carried my luggage into the house. Once I got caught up, I'd write it all down in my journal.

CHAPTER 24

I was re-reading *Romeo and Juliet*, preparing to teach it to ninth-graders, when I heard the receptionist page me—my bell was one ring, then three, then two rings. I was stunned to see Father Mark standing in the school lobby.

"Clare!" he shouted. "Sister here told me you'd answer your bell."

He gestured toward the sister at the receptionist's desk, who was eyeing me carefully. By this time, I had come to believe that my every move could be reported back to Sister Corella—whether that was true or not.

"Father Mark." I reached out my hand, to prevent him from hugging me. "What brings you here?"

He was wearing his clerical collar, rather than his full-length, brown habit. I led him out the side door—desperate to be out of reach of the sister-receptionist. It was late-afternoon, and in the fading sunlight, his hair looked a lighter blonde. Without the habit, he seemed thinner. He caught up with me and gave me a big hug.

"Let's not be so formal," he said. "I hope I'm not disturbing you?"

"No—I was just...." I held up the play.

"Reading." He smiled. "Not surprised. Can you spare a few minutes?"

"Of course. Let's walk to the rose garden—it's more private."

It was strange...downtown with the Brothers, I'd felt safe—to express myself, to show my feelings, sing, laugh, drink beer even. Having Father Mark drop in and hearing his voice in this convent environment felt jarring. I realized that here, I felt less safe. I had to work harder to be myself.

"I hope you're glad to see me," he said. "I was passing through, you might say." He looked straight at me. "Truth is, I've been thinking a lot about you—ever since the summer."

"Really?" The thought of Summer in the City made me smile. "What an unforgettable experience, Father."

"Mark," he corrected. "Please. Call me *Mark*." I moved down the gravel path, away from the school, out of range of—*who was watching?*

"Whoa. Slow down. Don't you want to know what I've been thinking? Why I'm here?"

I stopped at a grove of honeysuckle bushes that blocked our view of the school.

"You just said last summer was *unforgettable*." He moved closer. "You're not alone in that. I've been thinking…." He took a breath. "Okay. I'd like you to join us in the inner-city. You could live at St. Peter's. Get to know the people. Maybe start some classes—religious ed.—drama. I don't know. We'd work on the details. You'd be part of our parish team."

"Now *you* need to slow down." I tried to make it sound light but my heart was beating wildly. "I can't just move out of the convent and live downtown with a bunch of brothers and priests. I have a job—plays to direct, English classes to teach. I'm a Marywood faculty member, remember? A Sister of St. Mary."

"I did say we'd have to work out the details." He frowned. "Look. I think a couple of the other sisters are interested. Ruth, from the Sisters of Charity, and Dorothy—you two were quite a team."

I felt a sudden rush of jealousy. "They're leaving their ministries to work in the inner-city?"

He shrugged. "I said I *think* they're interested. I haven't gotten any further than that. I wanted to ask *you* first." I thought he was going to reach out and touch me but he sunk his hands in his pockets. "You're the best. The *crème de la crème,* as they say."

I blushed. "You're flattering me…Mark." We both sat down on a nearby bench.

He turned to face me, his hands open, as if arguing a case. "Think of it," he said. "Sisters and brothers, living in community, working together, just like the early Christians, the People of God, walking among God's poor. Living out our baptismal call. Isn't that the message that's coming out of Vatican II? Isn't that why you left home to become a sister?"

"I'm not sure anymore, to be honest. I entered right out of high school. Everything was simpler. The Rule was clear—cut and dried. Our days were all carved out for us." I felt I could be brutally honest—I could trust him.

"All you had to do was salute—I know. But we're living in a new era, thanks to Pope John XXIII. We're the ones who can help him open the Church windows."

I watched a family of sparrows flitting in and out of the bushes. I envied them their simple life. Since I had entered the convent, things had turned upside down, in great part due to the changes following the Second Council in Rome. I welcomed it. But it was also true that I had shaped my life—and my faith—around the convent structure and schedule. It was the core of my religious formation. Without that structure, would I be able to hold my life together as a religious sister? Without that framework, what would I become?

"I can see I've caught you off guard." He looked at me closely. "Look, I've prayed about this. It isn't going away. Promise me you'll consider it?" He placed his hand on my shoulder.

I was glad we couldn't be seen from the school. In the inner-city, we'd been free with hugs, but I felt sure Mark's touching me would be frowned on by many of the older sisters I lived with. I wanted to respond to him in some way, but I didn't dare. It was upsetting how easily he reached out and touched, laughed out loud, dreamed big. Men—they had all the advantages—all the power.

I tried to sound calm, rational. "First, you know it's not a decision I can make on my own."

He nodded.

"But, I'll *think* about it."

"Thank you, Clare," Father Mark said.

"I'll walk you to your car."

We said good-bye and I watched him drive away in the familiar, beat-up Plymouth. His question lingered: "Isn't that why you left home?" *I no longer knew how to answer that question.*

Father Mark's offer to join him in the inner-city was tempting—but that experience had already swallowed up six weeks of summer. I needed to prepare for the new school year.

The more Sister Corella censored my choices, questioned my curriculum—the more I tested the boundaries. I remembered what Jack had said, way back in the Novitiate, when he'd learned about my journal being confiscated: "Your obedience will be to yourself." Where the vow of poverty had seemed easy—I was learning that obedience was not. I tried hard to be a perfect Sister of St. Mary, but it was turning into a struggle between obedience to *them* and duty to *myself*. Now, there was the added problem of knowing what to do about Father Mark.

Back in my classroom, I was too distracted to go back to *Romeo and Juliet*. I picked up my copy of *The Prophet* and my journal. It was warm outside, a sunny day, but there was a breeze. I went out to the wooded area behind the school, sat in the shade of my favorite oak tree, and opened the book randomly. I read the passage about searching for God in the lightning and rain as well as in the beauty of flowers.

Seeing God in the flowers was easy. Seeing God in the lightning and rain, in the storms—that was harder. Just then, a large cloud blocked out the sun.

I opened my journal and wrote: *Was it wrong for me to fight against Sister Corella's judgments? What should I do about Father Mark's offer? Even if I couldn't work with him full-time, would I be allowed to drive to the inner-city on weekends?*

The cloud cleared, revealing the gorgeous late-summer sky. I took that as a message to trust my own judgment. I knew I'd need to stay faithful to meditation, otherwise the teaching and directing, the demands Father Mark was making, the current of opposition and criticism flowing from Sister Corella—all of it could overwhelm me.

"Clare? Is that you?"

I looked around to see Will crossing the lawn toward me.

"I thought it was you," he said, "but in that new, modernized habit, all you nuns look alike." His face brightened with a smile. Then, he did a sweeping bow and waved his arm. "Or maybe I should say: '*Good morrow, Kate, for that's your name, I hear.*'"

"*Well have you heard*, Will McBride—*but something hard of hearing. They call me Katherine, that do talk of me.*" I closed the book, stood up and turned a complete circle, modeling the new, long-sleeved, navy blue habit. "What do you think?"

"*The prettiest Kate in Christendom*," Will replied.

I blushed and curtsied.

"Huge improvement—I think we could do that scene from *Taming of the Shrew* without a hitch right now."

"No, kind sir, lest we be seen by the Sisters of St. Mary and they remove you hence too soon. Since you come hither, pray, tarry a while."

We both laughed. I stared at his face. Something was different.

"No beard," he said. "Is that why you're looking at me so closely?"

I blushed. "I can't say I miss it. You look good." *What was I saying?* "What are you doing here at Marywood? I mean, it's nice to see you, but…."

"Interviewing for a job—didn't anyone tell you?"

"No…I can safely say that I'd be the last person our principal would confide in." I tried not to sound bitter. "In fact, I didn't know there were openings—but I wouldn't. I've been gone all summer. What position are you applying for?"

"Religion. Junior level. And English, I think. I hope. If Sister Corella and the English department chair decide I have the proper credentials. Which I do, in my humble opinion."

"Lucky juniors."

"Hey, thanks. Appreciate your vote of confidence. I'm a bit nervous. You know—the typical pitfalls—first-time teacher. Young, unmarried male. All-girl school. Though my years at Mt. St. Mary helped me get over my fear of women."

"Fear? I can't imagine that," I said. "I thought you were over your shyness. You never seemed afraid of me."

"No—not you." He paused and locked his deep brown eyes with mine. "Never you."

I looked down, remembering that moment with him on the piano stool. *Those eyes.*

He broke the silence. "Go ahead, sit. Mind if I join you in the shade?"

We sat down under the tree.

"How are you adjusting to the habit change? The nuns on MSM's campus seem divided."

"Six of us—including my classmate, Rosemary—appeared in the community room in the modified habit early this summer. Some of the older nuns walked out—some in tears. Others refused to acknowledge us."

"Wow. Upsetting."

I nodded. "In the end, curiosity and the vow of obedience won over, I'm happy to say." It was a quick summary. It had been a traumatic few months, for those of us wearing the experimental habit. "Compared to the traditional habit, this dress is a vast improvement."

"What about the students? Shocked to discover you have hair and feet?"

I rolled my eyes—remembering Dr. Wickham's frustration with me in acting class. "The ones I've seen so far accept it as natural—our response to the Vatican Council's call for modernization. Most of the girls seem interested in bigger issues—the war on poverty, racial equality, ending the Vietnam war. Once they got over the shock, they weren't that interested—in my hair or my feet."

"I'm glad they've got their priorities straight."

"It's surprising to see how quickly some of us mothballed our habit—considering it was a 150-year tradition. Some insist on pulling the veil and headband down to their eyebrows, with no intention of *ever* revealing their hairline. The rest have eased into the change in stages."

"You? How do you feel?"

"Relieved, but I have to admit—at least at first—I was a little sad to see the old habit go. I loved it—in spite of everything."

"It's symbolic of a lot of other changes going on. I've been reading up on the documents from the Vatican Council. What's the one for sisters?"

"*Perfectae Caritatis,* Latin for 'Of Perfect Charity.' Believe it or not," I said, "the bishops approved it by a vote of 2,321 to 4. I'd love to know where those four bishops live, wouldn't you?"

"You've read the book by Cardinal Suenens, *The Nun in the World?*"

"That book has been a catalyst for so much good! We heard recently that Mother General is about to announce permission for us to eat meals with seculars in public, and visit our families at home."

"You mean we could have a cup of coffee, without committing a mortal sin?"

"We could. I could be sitting down to Thanksgiving or Christmas dinner with my family this year—first time in seven years."

Will looked out over the campus, with its small houses tucked among the clusters of trees. "You live here?"

"Yes," I pointed across the lawn to our two-story, white-frame house. "With Rosemary and another sister—on the second floor of that little white house. Dolan House, named after...."

"Mother Mary Dolan—don't forget, I'm a diploma-carrying graduate of your esteemed college."

"Congratulations! Gosh, I'm sorry. I lost track. I would've sent you a card." I held up *The Prophet.* "You were so nice to give me this book."

"No apology needed—but if I get the job, you'll have to treat me with a little respect."

"When will you know?"

"End of this week. They're interviewing a few others. Say a few prayers for me? I want this job. It feels right."

"I will. Pray, that is." Assuming Will's opposition to war, I guessed he was also hoping to avoid the draft, as long as he was a teacher. "Let me know—call the school, ask for me. Everybody has a paging bell. I usually hear it."

"You'll know. I'll be the one hauling cartons into the building. You won't be able to get rid of me."

It felt so right sitting under the tree with Will. I didn't want him to leave, but I couldn't think of anything to say.

"We've actually known one another a long time, you know?" he said. "Do you ever wonder why our paths keep crossing?"

"I'd call it a coincidence, but you said once you don't believe in coincidence."

"Correct."

We both fell silent. We sat, staring out over the lawn, at the trees, looking up at the clouds against the blue sky.

"Remember that symposium?" Will asked. "I saw you, but you didn't see me."

I got up my nerve and looked at him. If he was joining our faculty, I needed to get used to his good looks without my stomach doing flips. "I did. Well—sort of. I was too nervous to look at anyone or anything but my notes," I said. "Pauline recognized you—from school, but you didn't remember her."

"I noticed only you. I mean, someone who loved Merton as much as I did…."

"I'll say this much—the 'new you' I met in Acting class was just fine," I said. "You were kind to me. You didn't have to be. Playing Petruchio to my Kate—me wrapped in the habit—that had to be awkward."

"At first it was. 'Nobody wants to work with the nun,' you said. You were wrong. One person did."

"Why?"

"I told you—some of my best friends are nuns."

I groaned.

"Truth is, I wanted to get to know you. We *both* had fun."

I nodded. "You have a knack for turning everything into a game. I laughed more in those classes than I did during the two years I spent at the House of Studies."

"It felt comfortable. I hope I wasn't too—I don't know—familiar."

"I wanted to slug you after you dragged me into the Garden Room—I was spotted by one of the faculty."

"I'm sorry I got you into trouble. But look at the good that came from that. Your own version of a civil rights sit-in." Will picked up an acorn and turned it around in the palm of his hand. "We were great friends—unless you were stringing me along. Were you?"

I looked at him—his wavy hair shone in the sunlight. He swept that wayward lock of hair off his forehead. My heart skipped a beat. "No—I wouldn't do that."

We watched a pair of squirrels chasing each other up an oak tree.

"So," Will said, "what have you been doing for fun without me?"

"My first year here at Marywood, I've had nobody to play with—all I've done is plan, teach, correct papers, conduct play practice. If you join the faculty, you'll see what I mean."

"You mean *when* I join the faculty." He tossed the acorn to me. "Remember the dance we created—with the veils and scarves?"

"How could I forget?"

"All the times I asked you to be my partner, I thought for sure you'd say no."

"I was grateful you asked," I said. Right then, I felt immense gratitude for Will—the way he'd offered his friendship. "I need to give you credit for the good grades I got in those classes."

"We were a team." Will pointed to *The Prophet*. "You read it?"

"What? Of course." I leafed through the pages. "I love it. I use it all the time for meditation." I chose my words carefully. "I liked finding your markings and notations on the pages…like reading it with a partner. It was a thoughtful gift, Will. Thank you."

"Good." He picked up the book, read the inscription he'd written, then handed it back to me. "You're welcome." He looked away, out toward a row of sycamore trees. "Did you like what I wrote inside?" He sang the few lines from the Ray Charles song he'd written in the book.

I couldn't control my blushing.

"As long as we're being honest…you don't have to answer this, if it's too personal."

I could feel him eyeing me closely.

"Go ahead. Ask me. Why did I leave the seminary?"

"Why did you leave?"

"They threw me out."

I laughed.

"No, really, I was asked to leave. Before you ask why, think about it." He used his fingers to count off. "I'm more interested in drama than dogma; I detest patriarchal power; I take liberties with the Mass rituals; I had nothing in common with most of the guys I was with in seminary—except that we'd all been altar boys; and I'm not cut out to live a celibate life. For starters."

"I could say the same things. Except for the last one." I tossed the acorn at him and he caught it.

"I guessed as much," he said. "Too bad about the last one," he mumbled.

I ignored his comment. "How did that go over with your family—being asked to leave?"

"As long as we're being honest?" His laugh sounded nervous, unsure.

"I'm sorry—you don't need to…."

"It's okay. I probably need to talk about it." He stretched his legs out and crossed his feet—he wore Jack's brand of loafers, Weejuns. "My family—which consisted at the time of my mother and my uncle—a priest—neither of them were very happy with me. My Dad had been sick for years with Parkinson's. They think it began with a head injury he sustained in an automobile accident when I was about four. His dying wish was that his only son would be a priest."

"I'm so sorry, Will. Has your Mom recovered?"

"You might say that. She remarried—a widower with a daughter. Mom finally got the girl I was supposed to be." He crossed and uncrossed his feet. "So basically, I'm still the family failure."

"That's ridiculous. You're not a failure. Look at all you've accomplished."

"In college credits, yes. I'll give you that. I started out with a double major—English and Theology—then I added philosophy, making it a triple major—for all the good it'll do me. Plus, I'm in the process of earning credits in education and a certification in teaching—let's call that a minor—though it's actually major. Confusing, isn't it?"

"Thoroughly." I had been leafing through *The Prophet.* "You've given me a great gift with your friendship, Will," I said. "I hope you get the teaching job."

"I *will* get the job," he said. "And if I'm half as good in the classroom—and on stage—as you are, I'll no longer feel like a failure."

"You a failure? Never. You flatter me—you haven't seen me teach—I think I'm getting better at it, now that my rookie year is over."

He slipped the acorn into his pants pocket, then reached forward, picked a dandelion, and examined it. "I'll let you know what I think of your teaching credentials, once I've seen you in action." Will knelt, then stood up, clutching the dandelion. He gathered his blazer and slung it over his shoulder, then turned, bowed, and handed me the dandelion as if it were a dozen roses.

"Farewell...*Sister*," he said. "I trust we two shall meet hither—anon." He turned and stretched his arms wide, as if embracing the entire campus landscape.

I watched him walk quickly—practically sprint—across the lawn toward the parking lot. He looked back and waved, got in his car, and drove away.

CHAPTER 25

Rosemary and I were walking across the Marywood campus one night, after locking up the school.

"How is that new teacher working out—Will McBride?" Rosemary asked. "He seems to know you."

"He was in my theater classes at Mt. St. Mary's. Actually, Pauline knew him from grade school." I left out the fact that I'd met him in the Novitiate library on several occasions. "Nice guy—we sort of became friends. The girls like him."

"Big surprise." Rosemary laughed. "He's young, good-looking, and—most important—he's wearing pants."

"I know. That's something we'll never have to worry about—I mean, that one of the girls will have a crush on us."

"You think not?" Rosemary said. "Think again. This is the sixties."

"You don't mean...?"

"Why not? If two men can fall in love, who's to say two women can't? Why do you think we were warned within an inch of our lives—all during formation—about Particular Friendships?"

"The dreaded PF," I groaned.

"As far back as Plato, human beings were aware of the Law of Attraction. Newton pointed out the physics of like being drawn to like...."

"Rosemary, you never cease to amaze me. You're such a scientist. You learned about this in biology class?"

"Yes and no. Yes, the anatomy text referred to studies in gender preference. You'd be surprised. Back to biblical times, human beings have been experimenting with gender." Rosemary stopped to admire the nearly-full moon. "Can you pick out Orion?" She pointed upward at a cluster of stars. She was teaching me the constellations.

"There," I said, pointing. "There's his belt."

"Perfect. You're getting good at this." We walked quietly for a moment. Then she turned to me and said, "Remember Mother Vivian's first lectures? Her shocking—now groundbreaking—talks about sex?"

"I didn't understand attraction in *that* way," I said. "I just thought…I'm not sure now what I thought."

"Don't worry. If one of the girls falls in love with you—just let me know, we'll talk. 'Forewarned is forearmed.' I don't believe ignorance is bliss."

We crossed the school parking lot, past my beloved oak tree, its leaves white with moonlight. A squirrel scurried past us on the sidewalk.

"You hinted there was another way you learned about love between two women, Rosemary?"

"Lesbianism, Clare. Or female homosexuality. Might as well use the correct term."

"I don't think I'm ready for either of those words yet. But do you feel like telling me?"

"I had two old-maid—I should say *unmarried*—aunts," Rosemary said. "They lived together. My mother's sisters, or so we were told. Turns out only *one* of them was my aunt. The other was her lover—her life partner. I found out when my *real* aunt died. The other aunt, not a blood relative, dropped out of the picture. One of my cousins told me."

"How sad."

"I don't know what happened to her. Considering the stigma homosexuality still is, they were courageous to do what they did."

We reached the front porch of the house. "Anytime you want another biology lesson, just let me know."

"I bet Sister Corella would say our discussion was 'for mature audiences only.'" We laughed as we climbed the stairs. "I wonder how Sister Corella would have reacted to hearing Mother Vivian's lectures?"

"Scandalized! What about the Pre-Cana marriage classes? I haven't thought about those in years. Have you?"

"Not much." That wasn't the truth. I had questions I was too embarrassed to ask even Rosemary. What did two women do for sex? Did they just hug and kiss? Did they sleep together? For that matter, what did two men do for sex?

I knew one thing—I was not a lesbian. I loved many of my sisters, but not *that way.* I was attracted to men—beginning with Stan. I found other men attractive—Victor, Father Mark—though not romantically. Then there was Will. I felt...something... deeper for him.

I took the call in the school office. Jack was on the other end. "You're coming with me. You can bring your friend Rosemary—or whoever else wants to come. I know how you nuns like to travel in twos. But you, little sis, are coming."

Jack was organizing a rally for voting rights on the University's campus—along with other University newspaper staff members. They'd chosen this day, March 7, 1967, the anniversary of what was known as 'Bloody Sunday.'

I still remembered the shock when we'd turned on the TV in the House of Studies, in 1965, to see marchers being beaten by police. They were trying to cross a bridge in Selma, Alabama, on their way to the state capitol. It was the first time I'd ever seen nuns marching side-by-side with Blacks. In less than six months, Congress had passed the Voting Rights Act.

"All right, Jack," I whispered, "I'll go." I didn't want everyone in the office to know I'd be going to a protest rally—especially on a school night. We—if Rosemary would join me—would have to be discreet about slipping out after vespers and supper.

"Count me in!" Rosemary said. "At least we'll be able to take a stand. I don't care who sees us."

"Okay. We're partners in crime."

"Think of it this way," Rosemary said, "would Mother Mary Dolan go, if she were alive? I say she would."

We had been re-examining the letters and writings of our Foundress—amazed at how far ahead of her time she was. She'd advocated for the poor and homeless, the disenfranchised in Ireland, long before it was acceptable. She'd been a thorn in the side of many a politician—and clergy—during the late 1800's. Yes! Mother Dolan would go. So would we.

"I've got to be there early," Jack said. "Amy will pick you up at your convent—not the front entrance. Don't want to upset Mother Superior."

Amy was petite and quiet—until she started talking about Jack. "He's so dedicated to civil rights—he inspires me," she said as we walked to the University campus stadium.

I hadn't been on these grounds since Stan had taken me to a basketball game. It felt strange to be back as a nun, representing my religious order and everything it stood for—whether I intended it or not. I prayed I wouldn't be seen by anyone I knew. *You may be grown up, but you're still a bit of a coward, Clare*, I thought.

"Look! We're not the only sisters here." Rosemary pointed into the bleachers, as we entered the arena. We saw sisters from other orders spilling into the stadium.

"Hey, sis!" Jack was weaving through the crowd. "Don't look so forlorn. You're safe here." He guided us to seats in the front row near the speaker's stand. "I've saved these for you. If you're lucky, the TV cameras will pick you up," he laughed. "That should make Mother Superior happy, huh?"

"No! We don't need that."

"Don't worry—they'll be focusing on long-haired hippies—you don't fit that bill. But seriously, they'll focus on the speaker."

Jack rushed off to usher two men toward the speaker's stand. He tapped the microphone and welcomed the crowd, then introduced a Black clergyman who'd been injured during the Bloody Sunday march.

"You cannot be silent, you cannot be distant from this struggle any longer," the speaker said.

When it was all over, the crowd rose to sing "We Shall Overcome." I was moved to tears at the sight of so many people holding hands and singing. Rosemary was crying too. The two speakers and people from other civil-rights organizations led a procession across the floor and out one of the main exits.

It was nearly dark as we waited for Amy in the parking lot. She and Jack walked hand in hand toward the lot. They stopped under a streetlamp. Suddenly Amy put her arms around Jack's neck and kissed him. I watched as Jack kissed her back. It was sweet.

"You survived, didn't you?" Jack was laughing by the time they reached Amy's car. "What did you think?"

I rushed to hug him. "I'm so proud of you, Jack."

"Good, little sister. You should be. But the big question is: What are you going to do to make voting rights a reality?"

I was speechless.

"No need to answer right now. I know you're already doing your part as a teacher. I'm just glad you could be here." He glanced at Rosemary. "You too, Sister."

"Call me Rosemary, Jack." She reached out to shake his hand. "This was great. Thanks for getting us here."

During the ride home, we listened to Amy chatter about the good work Jack was doing, how proud she was.

"I hope we don't run into anyone when we get home," I said. "Technically we didn't have permission to go to this rally."

Amy laughed. "You know what Jack says…*Better to act first and apologize later.*"

"It looks like we may be doing a lot of apologizing in the days to come," Rosemary said.

That night, I had a hard time getting to sleep. I'd seen Jack in a new light. He was coming into his own as a leader. I replayed the evening like a filmstrip—the packed stadium, the crowd holding hands and singing, the inspiring speakers, my brother and the woman he loved, kissing under a streetlamp.

Play practice had run later than usual; I was rushing to get a quiz run off before vespers. The mimeo room was crammed with copy machines, a paper cutter, a hole punch, and other equipment. It was one of the busiest spots in the school during the day, but it was almost evening, so I was glad to find it empty.

I clamped the vocabulary test onto the drum of the ditto machine, checked the settings and the paper level and threw the lever to start it. I was lost in thought, problem-solving how to block a scene from *The Glass Menagerie*. I wasn't aware of anyone else in the room until I heard him clear his throat. There stood Will, smiling from ear to ear.

A bolt of heat shot up my back. "Oh my God! You scared me." I could feel my face flush. "What are you doing here?"

"Looking for you." I was curious—and cautious—wondering who might see me alone with him. *It's okay*, I told myself. *I can handle this. We're colleagues. I know why I'm here. Nothing wrong.*

Before either of us could say more, the ditto machine—unreliable and quirky on a good day—started spitting copies and spilling them onto the floor.

We both stooped down to pick up the papers.

Will's shoulder pressed against mine, sending another bolt of heat up my spine.

I turned my head away, sure I was blushing. I could feel him breathing. It fascinated and frightened me to be so close, so connected to him physically. *This is different than the play-acting we've done together*, I thought. He put his hand over mine—held it down for a few seconds—stopping me from scooping up the papers.

I didn't resist his touch or the fact that he was—however gently—controlling me.

"Let me get these," he said, with a tone that said he was in charge.

I felt him take a deep breath.

"Why don't you check that crazy machine, I'll do the floor work."

I was relieved to hear his let's-just-make-everything-light-and-funny voice. I stood up and turned off the ditto, leaving a copy dangling from the steel drum in mid-air.

"I'll sort these out later," I told him, shuffling the papers he handed me and setting them on the worktable. "What did you want?" I asked. "I'm due in chapel in a few minutes."

"It can wait—now that I think about it." He sighed. "Yeah, it can wait."

There was something about his eyes—mischief or confusion—I wasn't sure.

"Come on, tell me," I coaxed.

"Nope. It's—forget it. I've made up my mind. It can wait."

"Okay." I turned toward the table with my pile of copies, shuffled them into my folder. "I guess I'll see you later." I turned back to look at him.

He hadn't moved. "Tomorrow." He pointed at me. "Tomorrow I'll be ready to tell you."

We stood opposite one another in the cramped copy room, the alcohol fumes from the ditto fluid making me feel slightly light-headed.

He was watching me closely—or so it seemed—looking for some other sign, or waiting to see what I would do or say next. I felt he could climb inside my head. That disturbed me—and excited me.

"I *do* have to go," I said, squeezing around Will to reach the door. We brushed against one another, I felt his elbow in the center of my back, his thigh brushing against mine. I swung open the door and stepped into the hallway. I heard the door slam behind me. I did not dare turn around to see if he was following.

I ran down the flight of steps to my locker, stashed my papers. I stood in the hallway outside chapel for a few seconds. I needed to breathe, calm my beating heart, shake off the touch of him, focus on evening prayer. I dipped my fingers in the holy water, made the sign of the cross, tapped my forehead, chest, left and right shoulders, then slipped into my pew near the front of the chapel. I knelt on the kneeler and reached for my Choir Manual.

The psalms were a baseline to my other prayer, worship, and liturgical practices. There was something about them—their poetic rhythm, the rich imagery and slightly melodramatic language, the life-or-death subtext, the utter honesty, humility, and audacity of the writer. These ancient prayers had become my friends, often coinciding with my own dejection or discouragement, triumph, or celebration, buoying me up with belief in God's fidelity and strength.

I had come to the psalms as a beginner, but now I embraced them. I stood when the cantor began chanting the opening lines, answered the refrain in unison with my sisters, bowed and sat as we chanted: *"With those who are honest you are candid, my God."*

Was I being honest with myself? What did it mean, this electric jolt I felt, just being close to Will? *"With strength from you, Lord, I charge the enemy...."* Charge the enemy? Who? The sisters I live with? Surely not, though lately I'd been feeling that way.

I'd overheard two older sisters talking about me recently. I'd stopped outside the community room to listen. They were saying something about my behavior being "...dangerous...and shameful, just shameful." Their words were like a slap in the face. Is that what they think? Maybe I was my own worst enemy. Maybe I was encouraging Will. Or Father Mark. No. I didn't think so.

Recently I'd come across the paper I'd written for my Psych class in college—a review of Erich Fromm's *The Art of Loving*. I remembered being encouraged by the idea that when individuals cultivate loving relationships, they contribute to development of the self. I'd taken a copy of the book from the college library at the time—without ever signing it out—and had never returned it. I reasoned that it was community property, so it was acceptable. I promised myself that—some day—I'd return it. Instead, I brought it with me to Marywood and reread it often enough that I knew some passages by heart.

I imagined the book was still suspect in the eyes of some of my sisters. But Rosemary and a few others—even Audrey—

had read it, and it turned out that Will could practically quote it verbatim. "*Growth and happiness*," the book said, "*is rooted in one's own capacity to love.*" I had devoted my life to loving *God* with my whole heart and soul. But wasn't every Christian supposed to do that? Wasn't I also called to love my *neighbor?*

Couldn't I care for Will, or Father Mark, or Victor, human being to human being? It didn't have to be exclusive or erotic. But it was love just the same. If so, what *kind* of love? Was I feeling pure, unselfish, platonic love?

So many unanswered questions. *What did Will want to tell me? Were my actions shameful—or was I practicing the art of loving as described in Fromm's book? Where could I go for the answers?*

To God alone. My thoughts drifted back to the final words of the psalm: "*Your way is perfect…tried in fire.*"

CHAPTER 26

Weeks had passed since Father Mark's surprise visit. I hadn't told anyone about it—not even Rosemary. Together we'd survived the ups and downs of the Novitiate, the turbulent years at the House of Studies, and now, high-school teaching. Rosemary had hinted that maybe I was being "primed" for inner-city work. I didn't want to think about that.

I certainly hadn't told Jack, who would have come up with a hundred reasons for me to accept Father Mark's offer. To give up teaching and move downtown was such a leap that I couldn't comprehend it—even though I was intrigued by it.

Then Father Mark called again. I took the call in the linen closet-turned-phone-booth—one of the few private spots on campus.

"Have you been thinking about my offer?"

"Yes, Father. Sort of...."

"How many times do I have to say: *Call me Mark*. Do you have an answer?"

"I need more time. If I ever do move from Marywood, from my life here as a teacher, to live and work in the inner-city—and I'm not saying I will—I want to be sure it's for the right reasons."

"Why don't you come have dinner with us some Friday night? You can get another close-up view of community life in the inner-city—as if you needed a reminder."

"I'd have to bring another sister with me."

"Great! We have a big round table. Deal?"

"I'll have to check with Sister Rosemary. When do you need to know?"

"Sooner the better. Victor shops at the market on Fridays."

Rosemary loved the idea. "I'll finally get to meet everyone!"

We drove downtown the following Friday. I had butterflies in my stomach, though I tried not to let on to Rosemary.

Victor answered the door wearing a light blue tee-shirt and jeans. I hardly recognized him without his brown robe and cowl collar. He smiled, his dark eyes glistening. He wrapped his arms around me in a hug that nearly took my breath away. "Welcome to the slums," he laughed. "Don't judge the book by its cover, though. Wait'll you see what Jeremy and Maury have done with this dump."

I introduced him to Rosemary, who also got one of Victor's bear hugs. "Any friend of Clare's is a friend of mine." He led us up the creaky wooden stairs to the second floor and down the narrow hallway to a cozy living room, where Jeremy was setting out a snack tray.

Jeremy came across the room and hugged me, then shook hands with Rosemary. "You'll excuse Victor here, for not dressing for dinner." Jeremy laughed as he indicated his own robe. "He just got back from the market. We dress down, otherwise we get hit up for God only knows what."

Victor defended himself. "Not that we're ignoring the poor, mind you, but we all need a little anonymity now and then."

"No explanation necessary," I said. "You're looking at two people who understand the power—and the curse—of living in a fishbowl. Our religious habit, modernized as it is, still draws attention."

Jeremy was a bit reserved, while Victor was outgoing. "Guess which one of us is German, and which Italian?" Victor had joked, not long after I'd met them. I envied the freedom they felt. It had taken years for me and Rosemary to feel that free with one another.

Father Mark peeked into the room, an apron tied around his waist. Otherwise, he wore all black. He'd removed his clerical collar.

"Don't criticize," he said, pointing to the apron, "unless you're willing to take my place in the kitchen next to Brother Maury." He smiled. "Apparently good cooks are messy cooks. Maury is both," he added, "as you can see from the marinara sauce I'm wearing."

Rosemary shook hands with Mark and Maury. "I've been so looking forward to meeting you, Father Mark. I've heard so much about your work here."

"Clare's been avoiding us, Rosemary, did you know?" he said. "Has she told you the big plans we have for her?"

I turned to see Rosemary's quizzical expression.

"She doesn't know," I said. "Why don't we talk about it later?"

Rosemary and I were both impressed with the beauty we saw all around the apartment.

"I love that colorful Batik tablecloth, and the bouquet of fresh flowers, the candles...is this the way you set the table every day?" Rosemary asked.

"Actually," Victor said, "it is. Maury believes in bringing beauty into our ordinary lives, don't you Maury?"

The slightly overweight Maury laughed, his cheeks flushed. "Life is too short," he said, "not to make it beautiful."

I couldn't help contrasting that with our convent upbringing—the austere refectory table, the silent meals, the clank of utensils, the tepid dishpans, the hurry to finish and move on to the next thing. I ached for this richer life the brothers were living.

Rosemary and I drank red wine and raved about Maury's sauce, and later, his banana cream pie. It was like reliving the previous summer—in the company of men who sang and laughed, who enjoyed cooking and a colorful table, who talked easily about their love of God and their desire to serve the poor.

"I've tried to explain to Father Mark," I said to the brothers and Rosemary, "that I can't just pick up and leave teaching to move to the inner-city."

"What do you think, Rosemary?" Father Mark asked. "You've got to admit it's a great idea."

"I can see the attraction," Rosemary said, looking around the table. "But I don't think our superiors are quite ready for this. Maybe in a year or two?"

As the evening wore on, each of us took a turn telling what had made us decide to enter the convent or seminary. We all agreed our life stories would make a great movie.

During our drive back to Marywood, Rosemary and I talked about the evening—what a good cook Maury was; how funny Victor was; what a good musician Jeremy was; how Father Mark's laugh rang in the rooms; how his prayer practically gave us chills.

"Jeremy is teaching science at St. Peter's," Rosemary said. "He asked me to help him write up a curriculum."

"How perfect, Rosemary. Maybe we could figure out a way to go downtown together—I'd really like to visit some of the people I met over the summer."

"Remember what I said, Clare, when I drove you home from the inner-city last summer?"

"You told me you thought I was being called to something new," I said.

"Now I know why."

I hadn't seen much of Will since our impromptu meeting in the mimeo room. It was as if he'd gone into hiding. Whatever he'd had on his mind must have been resolved—he hadn't mentioned it again.

I was finishing up play practice in the theater. I'd risked directing *Pride and Prejudice*—I was recruiting actors from the neighboring boys' high school and wasn't sure I'd find a suitable Mr. Darcy.

We'd been through several weeks of rehearsal, and I was relieved that the boy I'd cast for the part was showing promise.

I tugged the ropes to close the red velvet curtain. They glided smoothly with just a gentle pull. I loved the swaying motion, the click of the pulleys high up in the stage rafters, the way the weighted curtain floated an inch or so off the polished floor, swishing like a giant, pleated skirt. My faithful student stage manager had turned out the lights and gone home, leaving me alone on the stage. *My stage,* I thought. *My theater.* Though in religious life, nothing was ever *mine.*

The first time I heard Mother Loretta say that we needed to strike the word "mine" from our vocabulary, I didn't question it. Now that I was professed, I was questioning *everything*—with the possible exception of the vow of poverty. Referring to my things as *ours* was not as hard as it sounded, once I'd gotten used to the colloquialism.

But this place—this theater—was different. This felt like *my* space. I'd had my first acting role on this stage, my first leading role in a play here. This is where I first knew I was good, that I had acting talent, that I could take words and use them to influence or control others, to reel people in and touch their hearts. I felt lucky to be back here directing plays, living my dream of performing, even if I was not the leading lady.

Dr. Wickham had loved to drag out the costume trunks and challenge us to grab a piece of clothing, then turn it into an improvised scene—alone or with a partner. "Acting is all improvisation," he'd said. "If you learn that much, I'll feel like a success."

I'd wondered then whether I could wrap myself in something, without desecrating the holy habit. I'd decided I could. I'd played along and rediscovered a sense of freedom in wearing a costume—besides the obvious costume of the religious habit.

I looked at the costume trunk I'd created here at Marywood. I kept it handy on the left wing of the stage outside the curtain, filled with wigs, hats, scarves, and drapes of all kinds—ready to use in my drama classes. As difficult as Dr. Wickham could be, I had to thank him for that idea.

I opened the lid, pulled a royal blue scarf from the trunk, and thought about the dance Will and I'd created in Dr. Wickham's improv class to the song, "I Can't Stop Loving You." I looked out at the dark auditorium—I was alone. The stage was lit only by the safety lights in the ceiling.

I swirled the scarf around in the air and sang a few lines of the song. It felt freeing to twirl, bow to my imaginary partner (Will), pantomime my broken heart, and drop the scarf at the line about feeling blue. I picked up the scarf and hugged it to my chest, then turned to drop it back in the trunk.

That's when I heard it. Applause. A bolt of heat went up my spine. I peered into the dark auditorium. Will was walking down the aisle toward the stage.

"Brava!" He was still clapping when he arrived on stage. "I give you an A+ for that. You must have had professional help putting that scene together."

"You've been spying on me," I said, embarrassed and a little angry. I felt the hot flush stinging my cheeks.

"You're cute when you're blushing."

"Stop it!" I closed the costume trunk and straightened my veil. "What are you doing here?"

"I was waiting for you. I have something I want you to hear."

"Now? I need to get to chapel for vespers."

"Just a few minutes. C'mere." He motioned me to follow him out the side exit, into the classroom reserved for study halls and club meetings. "Sit down."

"You're being a bit mysterious, aren't you?" I loved his playfulness, though I tried not to let on.

Will pulled his guitar from a corner, and looped the strap over his shoulder. He began strumming—his singing and playing were breathtaking. More than good. I felt the chords of his guitar vibrating, his words made my heart beat faster.

His lyrics were about finding a home, about being able to travel into winter, knowing love and spring would come. I didn't catch all the words, but I knew enough about song lyrics to identify this as a love song—and not to spring.

My ears were ringing, my heart was pounding, my face was even more flushed.

Will cleared his throat. He stood, holding his guitar, and looked at me. His slender body was outlined by the sunlight streaming in the window behind him. "What do you think?"

"It's beautiful." *Did he write that? Who was he writing about? Did it matter?*

"The words came to me after we…anyway, I got inspired and stayed up most of the night writing it. You like it?"

"I do. It's…it's beautiful." I was not going to ask what or whom the song was about. He'd have to tell me.

"Aren't you curious to know what inspired me?"

Mind-reader! "You'll tell me, if you want to."

Will set his guitar down and crossed over to sit in the chair across from me. "Well." There was a careful pause; he was almost whispering. "I think...I've met someone." This was nothing like the impetuous Will I knew.

"You *think* you have? Is that good? Do you want to say more?"

"Not just yet—don't want to spoil it. You'll find out soon enough. In fact," he looked me in the eye again, "you'll be the first to know." He reached into his back pocket and handed me a piece of paper folded into a small square.

"What's this?"

"The lyrics. You're a writer. Have a look. Feel free, give me suggestions."

"I couldn't." I pushed it back at him.

He insisted. "Seriously, I'd like to know your thoughts. I've got a few more where this one came from. Someday, who knows? I might go public." He placed the paper in my hand and held it there for a few seconds.

"I'm honored." I pulled my hand away. "Thank you. I'll have a look." I tucked the paper in my pocket without looking at it. "I'm afraid it'll have to wait, I've got to get to chapel." I was desperate to remove myself, this felt too intimate.

Perhaps Will's gesture—resting his hand on mine—was meant to be casual, but I felt an electric charge, like the one I'd felt in the mimeo room, go through me.

In the doorway, I turned to him. "I feel privileged that you shared your song with me, Will."

He didn't respond. He raised his hand. *Was he blowing me a kiss? No,* I thought. *He was only waving. Must've been the light.*

I was nearly running by the time I reached chapel. I knelt in my usual spot, took up my prayer book and joined in the opening psalm. *"Shout joy to the Lord...Sing a new song...with ten-stringed lyre...."*

I loved the psalms, but tonight at vespers Will's music rang in my ears. I fingered the folded paper in my pocket but put off reading the lyrics until later, when I was alone in my cell. What should I feel? Was this a love letter? Who was Will writing about?

His words and music circled inside me. Once again, Will had left me wanting to know more but afraid to ask.

Chapter 26

Spring Came Early—Will McBride

Spring came early
I should have seen her coming
She blew in with a smile
and shining eyes of April blue

Then came summer
I should have felt it blossom
It opened with her words
the laughter in her voice

Home came easily
I should have known I'd find it
I felt it reach and touch me
the moment Spring came calling

Each new meeting
I have a deeper knowing
that Spring has come for me
and I am finally home for good

Shall I tell her
I've always felt it growing
Or did she know already
the moment that we met?

Home came calling
across the spinning seasons
and love came calling,
came calling to me.

CHAPTER 27

"I take it you'll be back at the House of Studies this summer—to make final vows—is that right?" Will had waited until the other teachers at our lunch table had gone. He slid his tray to my end of the table and sat down next to me.

It had been a whole week since he'd sung his song to me and seen my little dance—a whole week without another word about it. I'd been avoiding him. What was I supposed to say? His question about my plans for final vows told me he kept close tabs on me. I was flattered—and rattled—by it.

"I'm asking because I have an idea—a proposition for you."

I almost laughed out loud. "A proposition?"

"Before the school year's out, I'd like to talk with you. I have a teaching idea."

"Uh-oh. I've heard about some of your off-the-wall ideas from the juniors."

"Guilty." He raised both hands in surrender. "But seriously, here's what I want you to consider—a team approach for juniors—combining religion, English, and American history. Before I pitch the idea to Sister Corella, I need just the right team member. Interested?"

"Whoa. That's a lot to take in."

"But you like the idea, don't you? I can tell. I've tempted you, haven't I?" Will leaned in closer, so our conversation would not be overheard. "Don't turn me down."

I hesitated, knowing I'd find the time. Team teaching with Will—too good to be true. Sister Corella had a soft spot for

Will, but would she allow me to drop some of my freshman English classes and switch to juniors? Could I continue my drama classes, play rehearsals, and now the school newspaper? Something would have to give. I wanted to make it work, but I didn't want to look too eager.

"I don't know, Will. Maybe the timing isn't right."

"Not to worry. It wouldn't go into effect until next school year. We'd have a whole year to plan—I just want to get the ball rolling." He picked up his tray as if to go but stayed in his seat. "Clare?"

"I'm interested. Why don't you propose the idea to Sister Corella and let me know what she says?" Sister Corella had been my worst critic, but she had given me permission to work in the inner-city the summer before. Maybe she'd turned a corner on my behalf.

"Perfect! I'll handle the Boss, do not worry." He smiled. "Thanks, Clare. There isn't anyone else I'd rather work with."

I could feel myself blushing.

"Come on, don't pretend you didn't know that."

I changed the subject. "Do you have enough history credits to teach the American history part of this seminar you're proposing? History's not my field, you know."

"This summer, I'm going back to Mt. St. Mary's to pick up more graduate credits in American history—it'll give me enough credits for a teaching field."

"You're ambitious! I'm impressed." *We'll both be on campus for the summer.*

"We'll both be on campus—maybe I could treat you to a coffee."

Mind-reader, again. His smile made me smile. "I'll be busy, Will," I said. "I wouldn't count on it."

We stood up and took our trays to the clearing station. Just then, Sister Corella interrupted, recruiting Will to help put away the folding chairs in the gym.

Will raised his eyebrows and leaned in to whisper, "Women can't resist my brute strength and muscular physique."

I laughed out loud. I watched him follow Sister Corella down the hall in a mock march. Just before they reached the door, he turned and gave me an exaggerated salute. *Working with him? Pure pleasure.*

Will and I set aside Friday afternoons to meet and plan our team-teaching project, with the working title, Seminar. We carried an unused bookcase from a storage room on the ground floor and created a corner in my classroom.

Will opened a box labeled "SHAKESPEARE" and unpacked a hardcover collection of plays, stacking them on a middle shelf.

"These are beautiful," I said, running my finger along their embossed leather spines.

"Now it feels official," Will said.

I noticed three boxes labeled "U.S. CIVIL RIGHTS." I turned to Will. "You've been collecting these?"

"Ever since my first American history course. Did you know that one of the champions of the Freedom Riders in the late fifties is a pastor here in our city?"

"You need to talk to my brother Jack about the Freedom Riders. He was almost one of them. Thank God, he didn't get chosen. As you probably know, it didn't end well."

"Is this the brother I met in the Braille Room that day?"

"Yes."

"Why don't you introduce me again?"

"Someday," I said. *But not now,* I thought. Jack would fall in love with Will—and matchmaker that Jack was—he would assume I was doing the same. For now—it was best not to introduce them.

Will opened a box labeled "MAGAZINES" and pulled out editions of *LIFE* and *TIME*, one with Martin Luther King, Jr. on the cover, another with President Johnson. He picked up a *NEWSWEEK* from August 30, 1965, showing American soldiers in a convoy—guns drawn—riding down the middle of a Los Angeles street. The headline read: "*The Riots In Color—Los Angeles: Why?*"

Will held up the magazine. "We can read *The Scarlet Letter* and talk about Hawthorne's use of symbolism, or…we can use it as a springboard to talk about social isolation, class warfare. We could even have the kids rewrite the novel and set it in our own time. Today's outcasts could be hippies and anti-war protesters." He paused, then walked toward me. "See, Clare, we can do something really big here. We can follow that calling you talk about—together we can shake people up."

I was excited. I was stepping out of my comfort zone, and that felt exhilarating. It was the same kind of uncomfortable joy that had made me so happy working in the inner-city. I thought about all the hours we were putting into the project. "I just hope we get enough juniors to sign up for this course. Otherwise…."

"Listen to you," he scolded. "O ye of little faith. We'll be turning students away, trust me."

My teaching and directing was demanding, but I'd accumulated notes and tests, handouts and filmstrips, small-group projects, and enrichment reading lists. Sometimes it felt like cheating—using the same materials over again. Would my teaching get stale? I made a point of introducing a few new pieces here and there—that kept it fresh enough. I had figured out shortcuts for grading papers—more time to meet with Will. Even with resistance and criticism from some of the older sisters, I finally felt I was in the right place.

"About a dozen of us are meeting in the community room most weeknights after dinner," I told Will one day during our planning time. "We watch the nightly news—it's almost another form of communal prayer."

"I get it," Will said. "You're lucky to have that community. I'm watching it all alone. Maybe someday you could join me for dinner at my house."

I ignored his invitation. *Was he serious?* "We watched a special program on the war," I said. "What do you know about the Tet offensive?"

"A ramp-up in fighting and bombing—my oversimplification—but it'll mean more troops. The war that started as a battle in the jungles in the 50's has turned into all-out warfare in the major cities of Vietnam."

"It's so upsetting," I said. "The invasion of our embassy in Saigon, five hundred Americans dead in a week—that's just Americans. Protests across college campuses—I don't know what to think."

Will and I talked about the U.S. Army major's statement: "It became necessary to destroy the town to save it." We were outraged—but encouraged when Walter Cronkite on CBS News advised the government to negotiate their way out of the conflict while it still seemed possible to do so honorably.

"What are your feelings about being drafted?" I asked him.

"You know I'm a patriot, but my teaching job will keep me out of the draft, Clare—it'll give me the chance to be sure our students know the truth."

"What you're doing here is more important to the future of our country than fighting Communism in the remote villages of Vietnam."

"Not to mention the destruction and pain we're inflicting on innocent civilians. I'm wondering about your brother. If he's not a full-time student, he could be drafted at any time."

"The thought of Jack picking up a rifle makes me physically sick."

"I'm sorry I brought it up." He touched my shoulder.

I wanted to lean into him—of course I couldn't do that.

In March, Will and I watched as the presidential primaries unfolded. Senator Eugene McCarthy nearly defeated President Johnson in the New Hampshire primary, thanks to what was dubbed "The Children's Crusade," a group of college students who cut their long hair and switched to conservative dress, to appeal to voters other than their hippie counterparts.

Jack and I talked about the possibility of Robert F. Kennedy entering the presidential race. By the end of March, President Johnson was delivering a television address to the people, saying the U.S. would limit bombing in Vietnam. At the end of the address, he shocked the nation by saying he would not run for reelection.

In mid-February of 1968, we watched a strike by sanitation workers in Memphis turn ugly. The all-Black strikers were attacked by onlookers, and within weeks, Martin Luther King traveled to lead a march in support of the workers. This only caused more violence, and King scheduled another march for April 8, arriving in Memphis a few days before. The next evening, as King stood on a balcony of his motel, he was shot and killed.

Our new Superior at Marywood—now known as the Community Coordinator—scheduled a prayer vigil for the following evening.

Chapter 27

"Sisters," Sister Irene, my local coordinator, said, "we must pray for peace and calm. Much is at stake in our country."

I prayed with the other sisters—thought about the Blacks I'd met in the inner-city. I couldn't stop thinking about Jack's involvement in civil rights issues—how he kept saying I should do more. I worried that Jack (or Will, or Stan) might be sent to Vietnam. Troop limits had been lifted—25,000 new reservists were called to action, thousands more were drafted. So much for President Johnson's promise to reduce the number of troops. Each night footage of dead soldiers being lifted onto helicopters flashed on the TV screen.

Holy Week—with its solemn rituals of Holy Thursday, Good Friday, and Easter—was about to begin, but I felt distracted by the chaos going on in so many cities across the nation. Even in my city, there were reports of fires and disturbances. During my years in the Novitiate and House of Studies, I'd loved Holy Week—a time for silence and prayer building up to the Last Supper, the Way of the Cross and devotions, and the Easter Vigil with its incense and music—a promise of resurrection and new life.

This Holy Week was different. Will had connections to a group who'd been planning a march downtown to commemorate the Way of the Cross. Victor and Father Mark had called and invited me to the same march—a candlelight vigil beginning at Music Hall and ending at City Hall a few blocks away. Led by the Brothers, there would be prayers for peace and justice. In another part of the city, near the University, Jack was leading a protest march, but we decided we'd be safer in the company of the Brothers.

Sister Irene advised us not to take part in these or any other public events. "You may feel drawn to these events—but they could turn violent. It's not proper or prudent for us as religious to be part of this."

I disagreed strongly, and so did Rosemary. Other sisters saw it as a matter of obedience—if our superior said we shouldn't go, then we shouldn't go. Will had agreed to drive us, along with another lay teacher from a neighboring boys' school. Without telling anyone, we snuck out of our house at dusk after the services on Holy Thursday.

I spotted Father Mark in the crowd when we arrived at the park across from Music Hall. He greeted me with a big hug. Before I could worry about whether others might be shocked, Mark was hugging Rosemary and thanking us for coming. We picked up tapers from a table set up by volunteers.

Will caught up with us and announced he would be leading one of the groups. "Follow me," he shouted, as we lined up to have our tapers lit.

The glow from hundreds—maybe even thousands—of candles was a thrilling sight, snaking along the downtown streets, around corners—for blocks ahead and behind. I could see the faces of mostly Whites, but also some Blacks, shoulder to shoulder, united in purpose.

This, I thought, *is why I was called to religious life. This is why I said yes to poverty, chastity, and obedience. This is how I will love the world—by giving myself to the cause of justice.*

The procession had been singing "We Shall Overcome." At the first stop, I saw Father Mark standing at the steep, wide steps of First Presbyterian Church, microphone in hand. "Today we celebrate the anniversary of the passage of the Fair Housing Act. Let's make history and end this War in Vietnam."

The crowd cheered.

I felt my heart cracking open with love—for Father Mark—for Will, his face shining in the candlelight, his hair falling over his sparkling brown eyes.

Next to me, Rosemary, tears trailing down her cheeks, had dripped candle wax all over her fingers and the skirt of her habit. We looked at one another. I loved Rosemary too.

Across the city, Jack and Amy were marching too. I missed Jack and wished he could be with me. The love I felt for them all was wonderful and terrifying.

Rosemary and I said nothing to anyone about our act of disobedience. But somehow, Sister Irene found out. On Easter Monday, she called us into her office.

"I am disappointed in you both, for violating my directive," Sister Irene scolded. "I won't say how I learned about it—only that I hope it won't happen again—for your own safety."

This made me more paranoid. Who reported us? What else were they reporting to my superiors? In the end, I didn't care who was watching. The message I kept getting during morning meditation was that I should listen to my heart and follow my conscience—wherever it would lead me.

CHAPTER 28

It was a Saturday afternoon, and Will and I had just returned from a visit to the Art Museum—to do some research for our course. I was sorting through the brochures we'd brought back, thinking about which works of art might work with various themes.

"It was such fun to browse the museum without having to supervise a bunch of kids, wasn't it? And that surprise picnic in the park—how did you manage that, Will?"

"Just one of my many talents," he joked.

"Well, thank you," I said, "That was really special."

"My pleasure," Will said, as he wrote on the blackboard at the front of the classroom. "Here's a question for you: 'How do you know when you've made the right decision?'"

"For our Big Decisions unit, I take it?"

"We'll include writers, philosophers, and poets; theologians and saints; founding fathers and members of Congress up to the present." He put the chalk down and turned around. "How did *you* know?"

"Know what?" I picked up my red pen and started correcting papers—only half-listening. When I looked up from my stack of essays, he was standing over me across the worktable, staring at me with those transparent brown eyes.

"How did you know that becoming a nun was the right decision for you?"

I sighed. "How much time do you have?" *Which version of the story do I want to tell?*

"I'm just asking. Because, after all, it's a life-changing decision. I think about my own decision to enter—then leave—the seminary. I'm wondering. How did you get to the point where you knew becoming a nun was the right thing to do? Didn't you ever question it?"

"Never." *I am always questioning it*, I thought.

"Never? That's hard to believe." Will pulled out a chair and sat down at the table, folding his hands, as if to say he wasn't leaving until he got a better answer.

I pictured the slide-show of scenes leading up to my "big decision."

"Okay," I said, looking up from my stack of essays. "Let's start with the Catechism. You get to heaven if you love God with your whole heart and soul. Given the choice between hell and limbo, heaven was definitely where I wanted to end up. I knew that as early as first grade."

"That didn't mean you had to join a convent, did it?"

"For me it did. Before the enlightenment of Vatican II, that's exactly what it meant. Think about it: woman as Eve-the-temptress, or woman as the Virgin Mary. Which would you choose?"

"You were that clear about it—even as a girl?"

"Is that a stretch for you?" I could feel my pulse rising. "My choices by the time I was in high school came to: wife-and-mother; nurse; teacher; nun. I asked myself which would bring me closest to God."

It was an oversimplification, I knew. But it really was the driving force behind my decision to enter the convent.

"Then there was the reality of being *called*," I said. I was feeling defensive, even with Will. "Stories in religion classes warned that if I ignored that call, I would never be happy. I might get to heaven, eventually, but my life would be miserable." I shifted in my chair and doodled on a notepad with my red pen. "Didn't you hear about women who chose to marry instead of following their vocation to the convent? Terrible things happened to them: disfigured children, death and destruction, wasted, unhappy lives. I wasn't going to risk that."

"When did you know you would be a nun?" Will asked. "Was there a specific moment?"

I told Will about kneeling at the communion railing after Mass on Christmas Day, how I'd felt called to give myself to God. "It was almost as if I heard the voice of God asking me to give myself completely," I said. "Maybe it was my imagination… maybe not. I don't know. Anyway, that's when I decided. In that moment, I said *yes*."

"Over and done at sixteen?" Will asked.

I hadn't intended to tell this story to Will. I had told it to Stan and he had not taken it seriously—would Will understand? Aside from Mother Provincial, I hadn't shared it with anyone else.

Will reached across the table and grasped my wrist with such force that I dropped my pen. "Are you sure, Clare, that your decision at sixteen is still binding, ten years later?"

"Why wouldn't it be?" I slipped my arm from under his hand. My hands felt sweaty. I wiped them on my habit. I was sensing the danger I had put myself in by telling Will the truth about myself. "God doesn't change His mind. Why should I?" *Just because you left the seminary doesn't mean I should leave the convent.*

"But you were only sixteen—you didn't know what you know now. You've grown up. Your theology has developed. Now, you know there's more than one way for you to love God. You can love God through other people."

"I've never stopped loving other people—I just love God more."

But was that true? Had I outgrown that notion of being called that had seemed so attractive to me, so central to my decision? Being called had made me different—special. In fact, because I believed in that calling, I could lay all my troubles and trials in God's proverbial lap. Even on the day I'd entered, I'd told myself: "God wants me here." I said it as I waved good-bye to my family, watched Mom wipe away tears, knowing I might never return home. Those first days of strangeness, the rules and regulations that dictated self-denial and silence, the separation from my friends and everything familiar to me: All that was God's will. *But was it? If it was not God's will, what was it for?*

"How do you really know?"

"What?" I had been lost in thought. I tuned into him. I should have shut down the discussion, but I was in too deep.

"Here's what I'm thinking," Will said. "Big decisions are made over and over, not just once. We change—our decisions change. Like evolution—we evolve, our decisions evolve. You're reading Teilhard de Chardin. Isn't that what he says about evolution? Isn't that what you think?"

The scenes kept clicking in my head. Reception Day, when I was eighteen, and received the holy habit of religion. How that day had started out with anticipation and excitement—the dream of being clothed in the habit and white veil, the status, the moment of supreme holiness. How, in fact, Delores and I had both felt like running—but didn't. How wearing the habit was not a magical garment—I was just as self-centered and judgmental as always.

Was God in the challenges I'd met in superiors? They misinterpreted my initiatives—accused me of being full of pride, bold, lacking in humility. Was all this God's will?

It must be—or what was the point? Hadn't I learned to practice obedience, the virtue of trust in God? If so, why was

I so uncomfortable? Why were Will's eyes so irresistible—the touch of his hand on my arm like an electric shock?

My heart was beating fast. I picked up my pen and focused on the paper I'd been correcting. "Listen, I'd love to talk more, Will," I said, "but I need to get these papers done. Let's call it a day here, okay? Don't you need to get going? We can pick this up next week."

"Is that how you deal with the big questions?" Will said it with a smile, but he remained seated across from me. "Keep working? Stay busy?"

"Duty calls," I mumbled, unable to look at him, afraid he would see the tears gathering. "Are we good for now?"

"We're good. We're really good. We're doing God's will, aren't we?" He stood up and moved away.

My hands were sweating, I was shaking, but I tried to sound casual. "Not funny, Will. Now get out of here and let me finish."

Will slipped on his jacket and stood at the door, not moving.

I knew—without looking up—that he was still there. I could feel him looking at me. "What now?" I finally asked, my head bent into the papers.

"Just...we're not done with this. Not by a long shot." He closed the door behind him.

In that instant, it could have been 1960. Stan's parting words to me were virtually the same: *We're not done with this...not by a long shot.* Stan and Will both seemed determined to challenge my dedication to my vocation.

Minutes passed before I could look up. My tears left water drops on a student essay. I laughed through my tears when I noticed the essay's title, "What it Means to Say Yes."

"You'd think, wouldn't you," Rosemary said to me one evening during our rounds of locking up the school building after a PTA meeting, "that the assassination of Martin Luther King might have brought us all closer together. Instead, I feel more alienated than ever from most of the sisters in this community." She stopped in the empty ground-floor corridor and looked at me. "How can that be?"

"We feel the need to speak out—they believe their role is to pray and suffer in silence. We see public protest as the path to peace. They're falling back on those three words: *Jesus was silent.*"

Rosemary protested. "They're forgetting the angry Jesus in the temple. They're conveniently skipping over all the times Jesus exposed the religious establishment and called them hypocrites." She was close to tears. "This tension—this anger between the young and old in our convent feels like—I can't describe it, but I feel it growing. We need to find a way to bridge the gap."

I had no solution to the tension—I was contributing to it—but I couldn't help it. "I won't back down," I said.

The corridor echoed: *I won't back down.*

"I'm noticing the divide among my students too," Rosemary said. "I hate to admit it, but most of them are Whites who don't appreciate what it means to be Black."

"I know—they just want the riots and trouble to go away, so that everything can return to normal—whatever they imagine normal to be."

During the final weeks of the school year, Will and I worked creating study guides and packets that wove the explosive current events into our Seminar curriculum.

Before he left one night, he sat down across from me at the table in the rear of my room. "I'm only going to say this once—then I'll be quiet...."

I tensed up. "What?"

"Look at me. Please."

His eyes had such power over me—I looked, then had to look away.

"Just…be sure this is what you want—these final vows, I mean."

I nodded. "I'm sure."

"Okay. That's all I have to say. I'm done."

Soon, in August, all of us in my profession class would return to the House of Studies for our final profession. I'd submitted a letter to Mother General just before Easter, requesting perpetual profession. We were all waiting for word of our acceptance.

Rosemary and I were doing our usual lock-up of the school building one evening. "I don't mind saying this has been a rocky couple of years," I said. The halls were dark, so I knew it was safe to talk freely. "But I'm not giving in to Corella's criticisms—I can tell from my students that I'm doing the right thing in my classes."

"Sometimes I feel we're being spied on—it's unnerving." Rosemary bolted the gym door. "I heard from Pauline—rumors—two in our group aren't making final vows. One met a Jesuit priest while she was getting her master's in philosophy at Loyola in Chicago," Rosemary said. "Apparently, they're more than friends—getting married as soon as he gets permission from Rome."

We moved on to check the cafeteria windows.

"She's asked Mother General for dispensation from her vows?" I was thinking about what I'd have to do if—God forbid—I ever….

"At one point, I might have felt scandalized…not anymore."

"And the other sister who's leaving?"

"Joining the Carmelites."

"A cloistered order? That's defying the trend."

Rosemary locked the bookstore while I checked the business office, and then we headed for Dolan House.

"There was a time when I thought I could've lived a contemplative life," Rosemary said. "Silence, prayer, working with nature…things I love. But I think I've chosen the right path."

"Me too, Rosemary. We're women of action!"

We walked back across the yard in the dark. Rosemary stopped, pointed to the sky.

"Can you find Virgo? Look for a woman carrying a grain of wheat and a walking staff."

"I see it! What's Virgo's story?"

"She stands for every famous and powerful woman in Roman mythology—Minerva, Diana—the Greeks called them Athena and Artemis." We gazed at the woman outlined in stars. "They call Virgo *Goddess of the Moon*."

"Think of all the women who've come before us, Rosemary. I hope we don't disappoint them."

"How could we?"

We walked the rest of the way to Dolan House in silence.

Just before final exams, I picked up a note in my mailbox in the school office: *Call Sister Audrey*. My teacher and friend during college was now a member of the General Council, at the Motherhouse in Pittsburgh. At first, I was happy to have a message from Audrey; on second thought, I wondered why she would be calling me, just before the time when word of acceptance was due.

"Sister Clare, I'm so glad you called," Audrey said when I reached her by phone. "Are you somewhere you can talk privately?"

"I'm in the phone room, Audrey—couldn't be more private. It used to be the linen closet, so it's lined in cedar—completely soundproof."

Audrey laughed, then cleared her throat. "I think you know part of my job here on Council is to oversee approval of profession of vows—temporary and final vows." There was an awkward silence. "Clare? Are you there?"

"I'm here. What is it?"

"I've been reading the evaluative reports on you, and frankly, I can't believe what I'm reading. I can only say that it doesn't sound like the Sister Clare Marie I've known, not in the least." Another silence. "Can you enlighten me?"

"There have been some difficult times, Audrey, I admit, but I'm still the same person—honest." *How weak was that?*

"We don't have a lot of time—so this is my suggestion: If you truly want to profess final vows with the Sisters of St. Mary, then it would be best for you to write a letter to Mother General, expressing your desire to do just that. Make it as specific as you can. Write about your willingness to practice your vows. About your desire to be a vital part of the Community."

"But what are my superiors saying, Audrey? How can I defend myself?"

"It's confidential, my dear. I shouldn't even be calling you. In fact, you can never reveal that we've had this conversation." Audrey paused but I could hear her breathing. "Listen, Clare. I know you. You have what it takes, in spite of what we're reading in these evaluations. But if you have any doubts—or if you discern that your desire to live out the vows is not genuine—then you need to say so now. Because final means final. You understand that, don't you?"

"Of course, Audrey. I understand. I'll write Mother General today." I could feel my knees shaking—my hands trembling. "Thank you, Audrey. I don't know what to say."

"Take it to prayer—take it to God. Write what's in your heart. God will do the rest. I need to go now, dear. We won't speak of this again. God bless you, Clare."

The wooden ladder-back chair dug into my spine. I sat there, trembling. The bell rang—students shuffled to class along the corridor. Luckily, my next period was a free bell. I slipped out of the room, down the hall, and into my chapel stall. I gazed at the crucifix hanging over the tabernacle.

How much energy should I waste being angry with Sister Corella—the obvious source of my damning evaluations? I would resist the temptation to storm into Corella's office and demand an explanation. That was impossible anyway—I'd promised Audrey I wouldn't reveal that she'd called me. Maybe I should just chuck it all, pack up my trunk with the best of my teaching materials, and ship it off to my parents' house, where I could collapse on my bed and cry my eyes out. Except I remembered that my bedroom was now Mom's sewing room, so I couldn't even do that.

"You have what it takes," Audrey had said.

Damn it, I do have what it takes. Am I going to allow the small-minded jealousy of a few to jeopardize my vocation as a Sister of St. Mary?

I would write the letter. I would beg if I needed to—not beg—but at least reassure Mother General and the Council that I had the desire, the will to live out my vows as a faithful Sister of St. Mary. Or else what had the last eight years been for?

I slipped into the typing room. A small class of juniors was practicing a speed test. No one noticed me sit in the last row of typewriters. The room hummed and vibrated with the cacophony of keys hitting keyboards.

I took a piece of paper from the box near the door, rolled it into the IBM Selectric, and typed the date, *May 2, 1968*, then began: "Dear Mother General, I write to tell you about my desire to serve as a Sister of St. Mary for the rest of my life…."

CHAPTER 29

Jack dropped in for a visit one day after school. I led him outside to walk in the garden, away from snooping ears and eyes.

"Amy and I are getting married some day, Megs." Jack stopped walking and looked at me. "Having that kind of love in my life—it's totally changed me."

Jack's face lit up describing how he and Amy had first met, how they'd gone for drinks at the local hangout in Oxford during their Freedom Summer training. How they'd talked and talked for hours about everything—favorite writers, musicians. "She's a Dylan Thomas freak, just like us. And Brubeck—she loves Brubeck—even Lenny Bruce."

I had no idea who Lenny Bruce was but didn't let on. I was a fan of Dylan Thomas—so was Will. It was amazing how much Will and I had in common. I still wasn't ready to share Will with Jack, though.

"Has Amy said yes? Have you set a date?" We sat down on the bench under the rose arbor.

"I haven't asked her—in so many words."

"Jack—ask her—don't beat around the bush."

"I'm not—I think she knows. But we've both got a few years of school to finish. Then there's the draft looming over me. A wedding seems a long time off." He looked at me as if he were a doctor examining a patient. "Do I detect a sad face, little sister? What's going on?"

"It's nothing."

But it was something—I was remembering my recent conference with Sister Irene. *"Sometimes I think I'm being called to work with the poor downtown," I'd said, floating the idea to see how she would react. "Leave teaching, Sister Clare?" she'd said. "That is not possible—you're needed—you're a vital part of this school." That was that—I'd had to refuse Father Mark's generous offer inviting me into community with the Brothers—though I did sneak away there some Saturdays. "We'll keep plugging away at it," Father Mark had said. "These things take time."* I knew that if I weren't a Sister of St. Mary, I'd have to choose between my dream careers and the call I felt to be in 'the world' working for justice, like Jack and Amy. That thought made me uncomfortable…but I needed to stop wondering. Had I made the right choice?

Jack and I moved from under the rose arbor and continued along the path. "Something's on your mind, Megs. What is it?" He put his hand on my shoulder. He stared down at me, and even though he had assumed his typical position of authority as my older brother, my protector, my boss, there was the hint of a smile. "Come on. Margaret Ann…." When Jack called me by my full name, he was hard to resist. "You can tell me."

I'd always maintained a fierce loyalty to my religious calling. What went on between me and the sisters I lived with was private; I'd been careful not to share it with my family. If I told Jack anything, I might break down—he'd be even more worried.

Jack dropped his hands to his sides. "Look, I know you're always accusing me of trying to talk you out of this convent thing. But when I see you like this, what do you expect? Where's happy-go-lucky Megs? I want to see her singing, acting, laughing. When is she coming back?"

I put on my best smile. "I'm fine, Jack. I'm just tired. Months of play practice…I'm behind in my classes. I just need to catch up, I'll be fine." I would be fine—once I'd heard that I'd been accepted by Mother General. The disgrace of rejection was too terrible to imagine.

I desperately wanted to confide in him. I knew if I did, I would turn a corner—and there would be no going back. We walked back toward the school building. Once we neared his car, I hugged him.

He spoke in a low whisper. "Don't look now, Megs, but there's a nun standing at the window, staring down at us."

"Oh, no." I sighed and pulled away. "I can just imagine the stories. . . ."

"Stories? What do you mean? For Christ's sake, I'm you're brother."

"*They* don't know that. You could be any man, as far as they're concerned." I glanced up at the building, feeling as if I'd been caught making out on the school playground. Whoever had been looking out the window had disappeared.

Jack smirked. "Don't you feel slightly wicked?"

"It's not funny." I punched him in the chest. Not hard, but enough to let him know I was serious.

"Spies, eh? Poor little sister."

"You don't know the half of it."

He leaned in. "You could get in my car right now and never return, Megs. What kind of a life...?"

I imagined what that would feel like—driving away from Marywood—away from everything that had become so familiar to me—away from the emotions that sometimes overwhelmed me. For a split second, fleeing felt exhilarating. But I knew it wouldn't last long.

"We're out of time, Jack. I'm fine. Now go on. Tell Amy how happy I am for the both of you. Amy's one lucky gal."

"You got that right."

I leaned against a tree and watched Jack walk to his car. He turned and flashed a smile. "Call me, you hear?" Then he drove off.

Two weeks after I mailed my letter to Mother General, my *word* arrived in the form of a letter, signed by Mother General and the General Council—including Sister Audrey. I skimmed over the letter—searching only for: *. . . we approve your request to profess perpetual vows as a Sister of St. Mary. . . .* I didn't bother to read the rest.

I wanted to wave the letter in the air and do a victory lap around the campus. I had won! I owed it to Sister Audrey, of course, so I called to thank her.

"You don't owe me anything," Audrey told me. "You wrote a good letter—you expressed what was in your heart. That saved you."

I had to laugh. I'd written a good letter. As early as I could remember, I'd wanted to be a writer and now my talent had saved me. No one must ever know, I knew that. It was too humiliating anyway. But oh, how I wished I could walk into Sister Corella's office, lay the letter before her, and say, "See? You can't beat me down."

Four days before Marywood's graduation, Robert F. Kennedy was shot and killed in Los Angeles while campaigning for the Democratic presidential nomination. We watched the grisly scene of the Senator lying on the floor of the hotel kitchen, blood circling his head like a crimson halo, his eyelids flickering. The image played out on TV screens, followed by his funeral and the grim, stoic faces of the Kennedy family.

It had been five years since the shock of President Kennedy's assassination. It had only been four months since Martin Luther

King's assassination and the unrest that had followed. Jack and I (and Will and the other faculty members) had placed our hopes in the younger Kennedy brother. We sunk into a sadness and depression that was impossible to shake, even in the face of graduation celebrations.

Rosemary and I took this somber mood with us to the House of Studies, as we anticipated two months of preparation for our perpetual profession of vows. The number of us making final vows was down to twelve. As much as I wanted to share with my classmates the struggles I'd experienced during the past few years, I promised myself I would not be negative. I'd made the commitment to put my heart and soul into professing my vows for life. I had put it in writing to Mother General.

I heard enough disturbing stories to compensate for my own, though. Only one of the twelve in my class could say that she'd had two good years in a row—and that was because her superior was young enough to understand younger sisters—she'd gotten management training from college courses she'd taken on a secular campus. It didn't hurt that her convent was located so far away from the Motherhouse that the powers-that-be in the Motherhouse knew little of what went on there.

The summer passed quickly. Between retreat and lectures with Mother Regina, I carved out time to catch up with Pauline, Angela, and Delores.

Something was different about Pauline—I couldn't pinpoint it. She told me all about her seventh-graders and the music programs she'd pulled off. "I thought I'd hate the kids—and some days I did. But most days, I loved them. How is that possible?"

One afternoon, Pauline had a visitor—a dark-haired woman she introduced as Annette. "Annette taught sixth grade this year," Pauline said, "just across from me. She got me through the year—no doubt about it."

Annette smiled broadly. "It was the other way around, Polly, and you know it."

They locked eyes the same way I'd seen Jack and Amy look at one another.

"You were great," said Annette. "Don't deny how much those kids took to you." She turned to me. "Everyone did."

Annette's bronze tan and athletic build suggested she'd spent the summer outdoors. She had driven all the way from what they both affectionately called "Podunk," just to visit Pauline—whom I had never before heard referred to as "Polly."

After a few minutes, Pauline said she was going to show Annette the campus, and they walked off together.

I watched them go. About a half block away, Annette took Pauline's hand, and I winced when Pauline did not refuse it. They leaned into one another, their shoulders and heads pressed together as they walked. Then, they leaned away from one another and dropped their hands to their sides. I felt clenching in my stomach. Suddenly I knew—Pauline and Annette had fallen in love.

What did I feel? Jealousy? Anger? Yes—but sympathy and curiosity too, though I didn't want to admit it. What did it mean that Pauline was in love—or at least infatuated—with another woman? But it was not mine to interfere. If Pauline—or *Polly*—wanted to tell me, she would. If not, I would look the other way. Who was I to judge her? I couldn't inflict on Pauline the kind of suspicion and judgment others had laid on me—I had close friends too—though many of them were *men* (Victor, Father Mark, Will, even Jack).

When Angela and I took evening walks, she filled me in on Church renewal. Angela had mellowed, but was no less liberal in her viewpoints.

"We're moving in the right direction, Clare," Angela said as we walked past the college admin building. "The modified habit, focusing more on serving the poor, the updated theology classes—even the fact that our campus is now co-ed: all good, in my opinion. When you and I can say Mass, then we'll know we've arrived."

I confessed to Angela that my wings had been clipped when Sister Corella had confiscated my driver's license.

"Why'd she do that?"

"It's too long a story. I haven't shared it with anyone except Rosemary, it's too embarrassing."

"Come on—I love your stories."

"Once upon a time," I joked, "I drove sweet old Sister Miriam to her eye doctor downtown. I parked at a meter, which expired, and Cincinnati's finest had the school station wagon towed."

Angela chuckled. "Hilarious."

"By the time we got back to Marywood—with detours to the police station and the impound lot—it was nearly dark. We'd missed vespers, supper, and evening prayers."

"And Corella wasn't overflowing with forgiveness and understanding?"

"Hardly. She confiscated my driver's license on the spot—which made it impossible for me to continue visiting the poor in the inner-city. Figure the logic on that one."

"How did Sister Miriam take it?"

"Said she'd had the time of her life…once her pupils were no longer dilated."

Angela and I laughed.

"Miriam and I were friends for life after that. Unfortunately, she's one of the few in her age bracket I've won over."

"Y'all didn't kill anyone, did you?"

I laughed. "Good heavens! Of course not."

"Then ask for your license back, dummy!" Angela shouted. "Use your voice, for God's sake."

"I refuse to beg," I protested. "Okay, that's my pride talking. But too often, I feel like I'm being treated like a child."

"You've made it through another year of teaching with flying colors, Clare. You've been to civil-rights rallies. You've directed plays. You're a big girl." She picked up a shiny stone that caught her eye along the path. "Here—put this in your pocket—for bravery. Get that license back. Make your case."

Angela was good for me. Maybe I would ask, once I was finally professed. What could it hurt? Then again, maybe Corella treated me like a child because I acted like one.

I discovered during my summer catch-ups with my friends that not everyone had a positive story to report. Delores' principal had decided to make her life miserable. "She's suspicious of every little thing I do or say," Delores told me one evening, when we'd decided to take one last walk around the college campus. "I don't think I can go back and live there."

"Maybe she'll be transferred," I offered. "Do you know?"

"She'll be there. She's already sent me a note with a list of things I need to give her once I get back."

"Like what?"

"Like…a year's worth of lesson plans. Like a list of all the books I've read this summer to prepare for the school year. Shall I go on?"

Corella had given me a hard time—but nothing like this. "Why is she doing this, Delores?"

"You know how I am." She had her 'disgusted' look on her face. I loved her for it.

We passed the Student Union building—the site of Delores' successful sit-in in the Garden Room. "Remember your threats to petition Mother Loretta? You are so ahead of your time," I said.

"I was all gung-ho about Vatican II and pushing for renewal of religious life." She laughed softly. "I thought the rest of them would be ready. Boy, was I wrong. They weren't the least bit interested in studying the Vatican Council documents. They were shocked that I wanted to go hear speakers and attend rallies to promote civil rights. I was definitely *persona-non-grata*."

"Couldn't you talk with her? Try again?"

"Honestly, Clare? I don't think I can do it. Besides, she's gotten half the other sisters in the house to go along with her. I've talked to a few of them—they went right back to her with my comments." Delores was close to tears. "I'm fixing to throw in the towel—just so you know."

"Delores, please don't."

"It's too hard. These are supposed to be my sisters—not my enemies."

"Have you talked with Mother Provincial?"

She nodded. "Mother says I should think of the future—keep trying."

We sighed together and started back toward the House of Studies.

"So, darlin', if one morning I don't show up for prayers in chapel, you'll know." Delores took my hand and squeezed it hard. "I hate goodbyes." She sighed. "It just hasn't turned out the way I hoped. You know what they say—*final means final*."

We sat on the back steps of the House of Studies for a while without saying anything, both of us weeping silently.

"I'll pray for you, Delores," I said finally. "After all we've been through, I would hate to see you give up now. You're too good. You are. The world needs you."

"Maybe it does. But maybe not as a Sister of St. Mary," Delores said. "I don't think I can wait until those gals back home are ready to change. I've got to face that possibility. Maybe my superior is God's instrument—not to preserve my vocation—but to show me the door. Ever think of that?"

"I've had my moments when that thought occurred—beginning with Mother Loretta in the Novitiate, and now with Sister Corella. But something keeps me bouncing back."

Even though there were some who didn't accept me, I was looking forward to a new school year. Delores' words—and Audrey's—reverberated: *Final means final.*

During our weeks at the House of Studies, we read and studied the documents from Vatican II, and shared our favorite spiritual reading books. We planned our profession ceremony and wrote invitations to our families.

Mother Regina had mellowed, no longer calling us "Mother Vivian's novices." Our "truce" had turned into peaceful co-existence.

Every afternoon a Jesuit theologian lectured on the Spirituality of Religious Life—informative, but I longed for discussion—a way to translate the conflict and turbulence we were living. We had to find our own way to relate to one another and make sense of all that was happening to us. Sometimes we had evening discussions, other times afternoon one-on-ones in the parlor.

One day, when Pauline was playing her violin in the parlor, I came along to listen—for old time's sake.

"What do you think of the latest from Mother General?" Pauline asked.

"You mean that we can go back to our baptismal names? I'm thinking I might do it—if I'm Margaret Ann, then I can ask everyone to call me Maggie."

"You'll always be Clare to me." Pauline set her violin gently in its case. "To the rest of us too. It just fits."

"You knew me in high school as Maggie," I said.

"But not the way I know you now, as Clare," Pauline said.

"I'd love it if you'd all try. You'll get used to it." I followed her back to the community room. "Besides: What's in a name?"

"You and your Shakespeare."

In the evenings, a few of us gathered with our copies of Teilhard de Chardin's *The Divine Milieu.* Rome had censored Chardin and had even silenced him as a teacher, which only made his writings more popular. We weren't sure we understood his *expansive view of the universe and the evolution of spirituality,* as it was described by critics, but we wanted to know more. The fact that Chardin saw the evolution of the universe as an act of love—not law and order—intrigued me and filled me with hope. I loved that the Church was changing, but it wasn't happening fast enough for me. We all looked to Angela to fill us in on the latest theology.

"Being on Catholic U's campus was mind-blowing—marching next to the Berrigans," Angela said, as we walked to campus one evening. "I took every political science course possible."

"It's inspiring to see priests like Phillip and Daniel Berrigan—and Merton too—preaching peace, not war. What'll happen to them, Angela?"

"They'll probably end up in jail. Some say they're peace-makers—the Catholic bishops call them traitors."

"It must be exciting to be part of it." We went into the student café and sat at a table.

"I'm dabbling in an old boy's network, a male-dominated society. Catholic theology—the Catholic Church in general—it's all about patriarchy. I'm a voice crying in the wilderness."

"But what a voice! Though I think you've lost some of your Southern accent," I said, hoping to cheer her up.

"It's hard not to be discouraged, especially after the last few months we've been through. First Martin Luther King, then Bobby Kennedy."

"We'll support one another, Angela, we'll get through this. Once you're finished with your degree, where will you go?"

"Probably back here, to teach at the college." She propped her elbows on the table, cradling her chin on her hands—I noticed she'd been biting her nails. "What I'd really like to do is study canon law—if I want to compete with the boys in Rome."

"That's the spirit!" I looked up to Angela—I could never measure up to her.

After we finished our coffee, Angela said, "I guess we'd better get back."

We walked side-by side, shaded by trees lining the path. "You'll always be my good friend, Clare."

"You mean *Maggie*."

We both laughed.

"Life would be empty, somehow, without you, my friend."

"Likewise," I said.

We hugged for a half-minute. I felt tears coming. I wanted to tell Angela about the damning reports I'd gotten from Corella, my principal—or so I assumed, since I'd never been allowed to read them.

Angela stepped back and noticed my eyes filling up. "You okay?"

I sighed. "I'll fill you in another time. I've missed our talks—you keep me in line."

"Nobody's tougher on yourself than you are, Miss Perfection."

I looked away—at the red-brick buildings, the manicured lawns—avoided looking her in the eye—it would only bring more tears.

"Look, I could unburden a lot of negativity about my experience at Catholic U. You've got stuff to unload too, right?"

I nodded.

"Let's lift one another up without dragging ourselves through other people's mud. Agreed?"

I nodded. We walked the rest of the way, whistling "We Shall Overcome."

The Archbishop officiated at our final profession ceremony, preaching his usual sermon about women having a special place in the Catholic Church, and religious life being the jewel in its crown—without allowing women any power or a seat at the table.

I paid attention to the details of the ceremony, felt the thrill (and not a little relief) at receiving the silver ring—the sign of my perpetual profession. The Archbishop—in the person of Christ—placed the ring on the ring finger of my left hand. I had chosen a motto to be engraved on the inside, along with the date: 8-16-68 *Fiat*—a single word in Latin, but when translated into English it spoke volumes: "Let it be done unto me," the Blessed Virgin's response to the Angel Gabriel, when she'd been told she would be the Mother of God. *Fiat voluntas tua.* "Let it be done unto me according to Thy will." During my years as a Sister of St. Mary, I'd consistently longed for that kind of trust, that level of faith, that willingness to be God's instrument.

I watched the Archbishop and the priests in their vestments, and the altar boys in their red cassocks trimmed in white. Even as a child I'd wanted to be one of those boys. They swung the censer, spreading the incense in smoky swirls, and carried the candles up the aisle of the cathedral. I envied them their place in the sanctuary—given to them simply because they were male.

At the closing of the profession ceremony, I lay with my classmates, face down, prostrate on the floor of the cathedral. Even then, I was thinking about power. "You have what it takes," Sister Audrey had told me. It was up to me to use my power.

While it was a joyous occasion, we took part in it under a cloud. Delores had decided she would not continue. Only when her place was vacant on the morning of the ceremony did we know. Over these past eight years, I hadn't bargained on losing her.

Once the celebration was over and our families had gone home, we packed up and returned to our ministries—teaching, nursing, studying. If and when we returned to the House of Studies in the future, we would be there as perpetually professed sisters. We had finally reached adulthood in religious life—though most of us were in the second half of our twenties or beyond.

One day everything is temporary; the next day you are perpetually professed, I thought. It would all be different—now that I wore the ring—now that I was in it for life.

CHAPTER 30

Back at Marywood High, I was busier than ever. Our Seminar class was a year away—but Will and I met regularly to plan. I opened the fall semester with *Little Women* as the school play. It had eleven strong female parts and only three male parts. By the time I double-cast the play, almost everyone who wanted a speaking role had one. My English and drama classes were going well. I was allowed to drop one English class and add a journalism class—I had a loyal group of girls as my newspaper staff who'd actually petitioned Corella to schedule a class during the school day.

I applied for a Wall Street Journal grant to attend a journalism workshop, which would take me one step closer to a teaching certification in journalism. I had my final profession behind me. Finally, all was right with the world.

Will and I didn't see much of one another during the school day, except at lunch time. Not that I was exclusive. I tried mixing it up with different people during the week, but other teachers also had their favorites. I didn't always settle at a table with him—but often enough to make it something to look forward to. Even when we didn't sit at the same table, I felt some strange comfort knowing Will was in the room, catching his animated face in the corner of my eye, hearing him laugh, or hearing others laugh at some story he was telling.

Sometimes we would go through the cafeteria line together, then deliberately split up and plunk our trays on different tables. Other times we would wander all through the faculty lunch room, playing the musical chair game, then end up together at the one empty table near the door. It was fun. We never spoke of it.

With Will, I didn't need a lot of words—though we were both good at them. I wondered: *Is this what a soul mate is?* Amy had said Jack was her soul mate. I'd heard that term in the Pre-Cana classes too, back in the House of Studies, when John had said Sylvia was his soul mate.

We'd been warned often about intimate friendships during our formation. I suspected now that this caution against getting close was rooted in a fear of lesbianism. The picture of my good friend Pauline walking hand in hand with Annette flashed in my memory. Was I doing the same thing—creating a PF with my teacher-friend? Was it just an innocent friendship? Wasn't God alone my soul mate? After all, I'd been called to this life by God.

Yet…here was Will. We laughed at the same things, loved the same music and books, gravitated to the same poets, could almost finish each other's sentences. We'd grown so close during theater class and then we'd drifted apart. Now, here he was again, a part of my life in a big way.

I believed God had been guiding my life decisions and calling me to follow this path of religious life. Why, then, was Will appearing at every step of the path? Was he part of the plan? If he was—and I believed he was—what was I supposed to do with him? God would show me the way. In the meantime, I filled my days with work.

"As soon as our new Mother Provincial moved in, good things started to happen," Rosemary said. "Have you noticed how approachable she is?"

"I used to be terrified of the old one," I said. "I'll bet she regrets the day she sent Mother Loretta to the Philippines and installed Mother Vivian as Novice Mistress."

Chapter 30

"Best day of my life," Rosemary laughed, as we walked from the school to Dolan House. "You know how they say Pope John XXIII opened the Church's windows and let the fresh air in? That's what Mother Vivian did for our Novitiate—for me."

I told Rosemary how—years ago—Sister Ellen had vowed to report Mother Loretta. "I'm not sure she did, but…."

"She probably wasn't the first," Rosemary said, "or the last."

Rosemary stopped to admire a caterpillar crossing the walkway. "I'm glad to have this new Community Coordinator—a more civilized title than *Superior*."

"What do you think of her idea—forming smaller communities for each of the houses on campus?"

Rosemary was ecstatic: "What a breath of fresh air! I loved when she said: 'Institutional life is deadening—let's bring it to life.'"

"Creating a close community with twenty-five people is impossible." I said. "We traipse to the school's third floor for community recreation, down to the ground floor refectory for meals, back to the chapel on the school's first floor. Then out to the houses to sleep. It's exhausting."

"I'm trying to imagine a community of four or five living together," Rosemary said. "Think about it, since we entered, we've only known institutional living with anywhere from twenty-five to a hundred women."

"How will we decide who'll be in these smaller communities?" I asked. "You can feel the tension. Won't it cause even more division and friction?"

A few days later Sister Irene gathered us in the community room. She laid out a series of blueprints of each of the houses. "Walk around the tables once, so you can see all the bedrooms. Each available room has a number, with a space next to it. Write your name next to one of the numbers. That will be your room—and your small community—for the coming year."

I chose to stay in Dolan House and so did Rosemary. Two other sisters would be joining us in Dolan House. I didn't know them as well as I knew Rosemary, but they were philosophically and theologically on the same page. Both were older by about ten years. I knew I could benefit from their wisdom and seniority—they might even give me an air of legitimacy. I was grateful they wanted to live with me—and hoped they knew how to cook—not one of my talents.

"This moving and redecorating is going to eat into our free time," I complained to Rosemary.

"It'll be fun," she said. "We'll have this drab dormitory looking like the little white frame house with the blue shutters it wants to be."

"Soon you'll be saying it needs a white picket fence."

"We'll scrub and paint the kitchen," she said. "It's primitive, but everything works. My family has some old pots and pans they want to get rid of."

"I'll recruit my Mom—she loves making curtains. She could wallpaper the first-floor bathroom in no time. I think she'll donate a few lamps and pillows."

Rosemary's family donated a sleep sofa. Our other house-mates contributed an old black-and-white television set and a coffee table. We joked that the décor was "Early Salvation Army."

Sister Irene helped us come up with a monthly budget. "I can't believe I'll actually have an allowance," Rosemary said.

I agreed with Sister Irene when she said: "If we're to live like the poor, the way Jesus did, then we need to take a good look at our own resources—be responsible for using them."

Some of the older sisters who'd worked for years with no pay thought it was time for the community to take care of them.

"I can see their point," I told Rosemary, "except our vow of poverty doesn't have an expiration date, in my opinion."

"I know," Rosemary said. "Even some of the middle-aged sisters balked at living off an allowance, said they were being treated like grade-school kids."

"If they spent a week downtown, and saw what it's like to have little or nothing, they'd think differently," I said.

With my new small community, we divided the cooking and shopping, housecleaning, gardening, and the budget management. We took turns leading evening prayers. Once a week—usually on Thursday nights—we planned a special dinner where we shared what was going on in our lives and encouraged one another in our common mission.

This made community life more meaningful, compared to the institutional lifestyle we'd been living. The whole Marywood community—all twenty-five sisters—still met in chapel for Mass and to chant the Divine Office, and most times I got to chapel in the late afternoon for vespers with all the sisters. But my morning meditation and evening prayers—which I shared with my three housemates in Dolan House—more and more became the center of my prayer life.

A week or so after we'd converted to small communities, Will joined me on my way to lunch. "I hear you've turned Dolan House into a home—with a living room and kitchen—curtains even," he said. "Does that mean you're entertaining visitors?"

I laughed. "We haven't given it much thought. What did you have in mind?"

"Nothing…I just thought that since we'll be doing some planning together, you might invite me in sometime. Wasn't hospitality one of Mother Dolan's special qualities?"

What was Will suggesting? I had to be careful. "I have three housemates, you know. I think the classroom is just fine. If you're lucky, we might invite you to our open house."

"Great, Clare. When's that?"

"When we finish painting and re-decorating—maybe never at the rate we're going. Oh, and by the way, it's official, you can call me *Maggie*. I've gone back to my baptismal name."

"You'll always be Kate to me," Will said. He bowed deeply and was gone.

CHAPTER 31

The school secretary found me in my classroom, grading essays. "Emergency phone call—your mother, you can take it in the office."

I rushed to the phone. "Mom? What's wrong?"

"It's Jack—he's gone—we think he might be fleeing the country." She was crying—she handed the phone to my father.

"Dad—for heaven's sake—what's going on?"

"We don't know. Yesterday, the draft notice came—today he's on his way to Canada—that's the best we can determine." He let out a long, deep sigh. "Amy called to tell us."

"Is she with him?"

"No. She's at her apartment. One of Jack's friends has a contact—a draft-dodger in Toronto—he thinks that's where Jack is headed. Amy's trying to get ahold of him."

"I thought Jack was safe from the draft—student deferment."

"Doesn't look like that's the case anymore. He's twenty-eight and still in college—that makes him a 'professional student' in the Army's eyes. I'm afraid there's no way around it—unless he doesn't pass the physical. Either way—he needs to come home." Dad was breathing heavily.

"Dad? Are you okay? What can we do?"

"I'm all right. Look, I don't know all the details. I tried to convince your mother to wait until we knew more. But you know how she is."

"Dad—I need to know. He can't stay in Canada indefinitely, can he?" I couldn't stand the thought of Jack as a fugitive. "I've heard the stories—draft-dodgers—they get arrested if they try to come home."

"We all know Jack is opposed to this war—to any violence. But I know my son—he won't shirk his duty. Give him a few days—he'll be back."

"I hope you're right."

His voice cracked. "I just hope there's a way to avoid Vietnam."

I heard Mom in the background. "Who else is there?" I asked.

"Your sister, Jeffrey, and Jennifer—they came over right away. Marianne is getting dinner going. Thank God for grandchildren—a welcome distraction."

I had to give Marianne credit. "Put her on, will you?"

"Maggie?" Marianne sounded surprised that I'd asked to speak with her.

"How are they doing—Mom and Dad?"

"They seem to be taking turns being the strong one." She shouted at Jeffrey to watch Jennifer. "Are you okay, Maggie? About Jack?"

"We'll stick together, won't we?"

Silence.

"I'm glad you're there, Marianne. I'm sure it means a lot."

"Thanks, Maggie." I pictured her untwisting the coil of phone cord so it was long enough to stretch around the corner into the kitchen pantry. "Ever since '62, when Jack spent two nights in jail in Tennessee…."

"What? Why?"

Marianne was whispering. "Demonstrating for civil rights. Mom and Dad didn't want to tell you. Then he risked his life to cover a story about James Meredith—the first Black student at the University of Mississippi."

"I didn't know."

"Then he *had* to be at the March on Washington in '63—you knew about that, didn't you?"

"I did. He came back on fire, lecturing me that I needed to know what's going on in the world." Jack had sneaked his Joan Baez and Bob Dylan albums to me in the House of Studies. "Little by little, I'm going to radicalize you," he'd said. *You've done your job*, I wanted to say. *I am a radical. Now—come home*! "Let's talk tomorrow, Marianne," I said. "Hopefully we'll know more then."

At dinner, I told Rosemary and my other housemates.

"Isn't there someone you can contact?" Rosemary asked. "Someone who knows the ropes on this?"

Actually, there was. Stan. He'd been in the service for the last—what?—over seven years. Stan knew Jack inside-out. "There is…one of Jack's closest friends. He's in the Navy, probably knows what Jack will be facing."

"Perfect. Call him."

"I can't." What would Stan do with a phone call from me? I was even more curious about my own reaction to hearing Stan's voice. "I don't have his number," I said.

"Then write him a letter," Rosemary said.

Once the idea of writing Stan was *out there*, I was already composing it in my head. If anyone could talk Jack out of this, Stan could.

"Jack will probably be back home in a day or two," Rosemary said. "You never know—he could report, be rejected for poor eyesight—or flat feet."

"Wishful thinking. His eyesight and his feet are just fine."

"But he's studying journalism, isn't he? I have a cousin who's a Public Information Officer—in Seattle or somewhere—for the Army. Maybe your brother could end up there, avoid Vietnam completely."

"Or maybe the President could end this war that no one is calling a war, before it takes any more lives." I was no longer willing to suppress my anger: *This is my brother we're talking about!*

"Think positive—but write Jack's friend too—for peace of mind. What's his name?"

"Stan." Just saying his name made me shiver. Then I reminded myself: *Stan is ancient history—I've grown up—so has he.* He'd be grown up enough to put the past behind him too. Maybe he'd already heard from Jack.

We said evening prayers in the living room around a lighted candle. Later, I sat at the desk in my room, staring at a blank piece of paper. I pulled out Stan's last letter—Jack had delivered it to me—it had Stan's current address. Stan had said he wouldn't write again until he heard from me. For more than three years he'd written, then given up. What a lousy friend I'd been.

I began the letter with an apology for never writing, then begged Stan to reach out to Jack. I imagined Stan opening a letter from me. Would he get the wrong impression? It no longer mattered. It was worth the risk.

Before I could mail the letter, Jack had returned and was sitting with me on the front porch of Dolan House. "I couldn't do it, Megs—I wanted to run—but I couldn't."

I was so glad to see him, my heart beat faster, my eyes filled with tears.

He rubbed his hands together. His left knee was constantly jiggling. "You should see how those guys are living in Canada, scared of their own shadow, separated from their families, never able to go home again. The Canadians are great, welcoming—giving them shelter, food. But it's like living underground."

"Is that what brought you back?"

"That—and the fact that, plain and simple, I love my country…."

"You don't need to tell me…." I rested one hand on his knee to quiet his shaking.

"I talked with Stan—did I tell you?" He gave me his look. "Am I allowed to mention his name?"

"Yes—you're allowed." I jabbed him with my elbow. "I have to believe Stan has moved on. In fact, I wrote him about you—but I didn't get a chance to mail it."

"You wrote Stan?"

"I did—but you came home, so I didn't send it."

"That's progress." I laughed at how determined Jack was to fan a dying ember.

"What did Stan tell you?" I asked.

"*Work the system*—that was his advice."

"Meaning…?"

"Stan told me about Advanced Individual Training—AIT—said I need to make sure my commanding officer knows I've been in college, studying journalism. Maybe I can qualify for Defense Information Officer School—DINFOS. Otherwise they're going to send me to AIT Infantry."

"Meaning?"

"Combat." He lit another cigarette. "By the way, you don't have to worry about Stan going to Vietnam."

"Why?"

"He said his three-year posting will keep him in Norfolk. He seems happy." He cleared his throat and sat up. "Looks like he might have a steady girl."

"I'm happy for him."

Jack frowned.

"I'm relieved Stan's moved on," I said. "When are you going to believe that? I hated thinking he was wishing for something that was never going to happen."

"I can tell you still care about him. You can't fool me."

"I do care about him—I always will. How could I not? It's just…I wish you could understand that I've made final vows. I'm not carrying a torch for Stan anymore."

"It's never too late, Megs. I'll bet Stan would appear on this porch tomorrow if you asked him."

"It is too late. I've made my decision—final is final. Can we please…?"

"Okay. Let's change the subject. What were we talking about?"

"Your advanced training. I want to hear about it." *And move the spotlight off myself*, I thought.

Jack's nervousness faded as he talked about the prospect of avoiding being assigned to a combat unit in Vietnam. "First, I can get advanced training in journalism—photography, public relations."

"What will that mean?"

"If I do go to Vietnam, I hope I'll go there to write stories, take photos, do PR for the Army—no guarantee though. If I get into DINFOS I'll be in training for fourteen weeks; then I'll be assigned someplace stateside for another six months." He stopped pacing. "I'll probably end up in Vietnam, Megs."

"I pray daily that doesn't happen. But then, you were all set to be a Freedom Rider, weren't you? You could have gotten yourself killed in the South just as easily."

"You make it sound like I have a death wish. What I care about is life—equality—freedom. I'll tell you a secret: If I can write and expose the evils of war—this unjust war—then it'll be worth going to 'Nam."

"Please don't say that to Mom and Dad—or Amy."

"I haven't—I won't." He looked at his watch. "I've got a lot to do before I report for basic training. Mom and Dad, Marianne and the kids—not to mention Amy—I need to spend time with them."

"Poor Amy." I hugged Jack longer and harder than I ever had. "I'm proud of you." I swallowed and smiled through my tears. "You scare me—but I'm proud of you."

He whistled all the way to his car. Was it Bob Dylan's "Mr. Tambourine Man?" He waved and sped away.

Once Jack left for basic training, I made a point of meeting as often as I could with Amy. In good weather, we'd go to a nearby park—or she'd drop by the school. We'd compare notes from Jack's entertaining letters—he was a better writer than I was. He phoned Amy once a week, she'd share his most recent news.

"Jack says there's a big war offensive coming—that we should watch the news—as if we weren't already," Amy said one afternoon in my classroom. "Training is intense, but he likes the guys he's with."

"Dad said Jack got accepted into the training program in Indianapolis. Will he have time at home before he has to report?"

"Three whole weeks!" Amy shouted, her dark eyes flashing. "It's called Defense Information Officer School—DINFOS. His letters are full of acronyms."

"That means he'll be home over New Year's. Thank God! His last letter said the next phase could last until April or May of '69. The longer he's in training...."

"...The longer we can keep him out of Vietnam." I could see the worry lines on her face. She tucked her long, dark hair behind her ears. "The thought of Jack picking up a gun, training to kill people. It's so...."

"He says that if he can write and publish the truth—stories of the guys sent to fight—then maybe it's worth it." I walked to the rear of my classroom to put away some teaching materials.

Amy followed me. "I know you're right—but it's hard." She blinked away tears. "I miss him. If it weren't for my student teaching—those first-graders are sweet." She laughed. "And funny. They're my life-savers."

We both sighed. The room got quiet.

"Maggie—could I ask you about…."

"Anything."

"Stan. Jack's told me a little about the two of you and—I was wondering…."

"Stan was my first love." I blushed. I wanted to tell Amy—to tell someone. "He was my life for over two years. Back then, Stan was everything."

"You loved him."

"I thought I did. It was innocent. We were—I was—so immature. Stan was more mature, I see that now. We were figuring out what to do with our lives."

"You chose the convent."

"And Stan chose the Navy. He wrote to me for years—saying he loved me—hoping I'd leave."

"Tell me about him—do you mind? Jack thinks so much of him."

"Stan was more like a friend than a boyfriend—at least at first. I was a sophomore—Jack and Stan were about to graduate."

She worked her hair into a pony tail. "What was he like?"

"Good-looking, clean-cut, sandy hair, athletic."

I could see Amy nodding—maybe picturing Jack, except with lighter hair.

"But it wasn't just his looks—he met everyone, eye-to-eye—he leaned in to people." *Just like Will does.*

"Jack introduced you?"

I nodded. "Before long, we were holding hands, gazing into each other's eyes."

"Awww," Amy said, "how romantic. He sounds like a great person."

"He was—is." I realized I had unconsciously put him in the *dead* category, along with drop-outs from the convent. "My parents worried about my dating a non-Catholic," I said. "He balked at the suggestion that I might convert him. He'd had a bad experience with the Church."

"One more reason for him to be upset at your joining the convent."

I stopped—I hadn't considered that before.

Amy's face softened. "You did love him—didn't you?" she whispered.

"He planted a good-bye kiss on me that I still feel sometimes," I said.

"You're blushing, Maggie!"

"But that was as far as it went. Being in love in the fifties was...innocent."

Amy sighed. "The sixties—look what these years have done to us."

"Sometimes I imagine meeting Stan. I can still see his face clearly. I'd like for us to be friends. Jack says Stan is serious with someone."

"Don't you ever wonder—does your life have enough love in it to fill you up?"

I started rooting through my student folders—this subject was too raw for me.

"Sorry. I didn't mean to pry. It's just—the love I feel for Jack—I want everyone to experience that kind of love."

"Don't apologize, Amy. Here's a secret I have a hard time admitting, even to myself: I want that kind of love too. But I have to trust God will provide it."

I saw the question on her face—her pursed lips and drawn eyebrows. "I don't expect you to understand," I said. "Stan never did—neither does Jack."

One afternoon, I stopped Amy before she could cross the threshold of my classroom door. "Keep your coat on—we're going shopping!"

"Great! Where to?"

I told her the good news—Mother General had just given us permission to wear "street clothes" instead of our modified religious habit. "I'm hoping you can steer me in the direction of some cheap stores."

"Wow! Did you see that change coming?" Amy asked.

"Yes and no," I said, slipping on my coat. "Rumors—we were afraid to believe them. We'd been asking for this for over a year—part of our ongoing effort to modernize."

"I know a good thrift shop—not far from here. Great bargains on clothes. I'm a regular."

"If you don't mind, Rosemary would like to come too."

Amy loved the idea. We stopped at the biology lab and picked up Rosemary.

"This is more fun than sitting around reading Jack's letters," Amy said. "Don't tell him I said that!"

"Our lips are sealed," Rosemary and I said, in unison.

Over the next few weeks, we made several trips to the thrift store, using our monthly spending money. After dinner one night, Rosemary and I modeled our sweaters and blouses (fifty cents apiece)—straight skirts (one dollar each)—and blazer jackets (two to three dollars each) for our housemates. For ten dollars and change we'd each gained nine articles of clothing—which Rosemary and I traded off to create some lovely ensembles.

Not many of the Sisters at Marywood chose secular clothing over the modified habit—many were still upset they'd had to give up the original medieval one. It didn't take long for me to see that our wearing "real" clothes was causing friction.

I didn't care—it was an experiment—approved by Mother General. Besides, I felt—more normal. I hoped that once the other sisters got used to the idea, they'd go along. For some it was just one more reason to judge me.

Jack's Army training kept him so busy, he started limiting his letters mostly to Amy and my parents. But I wrote to him—made my letters upbeat—plays I was directing, visits with Marianne's kids, class projects my students were doing. I reassured him I was watching the nightly news—and praying for him.

I didn't mention Stan—or Will McBride. What could I say? I didn't tell Jack my principal was still giving me fits about my choice of plays—and insisting on censoring the school newspaper before it went to print. Jack would have lectured me to stand up for myself. I wondered if he was doing the same for himself in the Army.

I did have one bit of good news. The Wall Street Journal scholarship I'd applied for months earlier had come through. In late July, I'd be off to Chicago for a week-long workshop. I'd encouraged Victor to apply too. If he won, we could go together—what fun that would be.

As the Sisters of St. Mary continued to change with the times, we were all overjoyed to learn we'd been granted permission to visit our families. I decided to work on getting closer to Marianne. One Saturday, I set aside time to take Jennifer to a park.

I was met at Marianne's front door by a rambunctious Irish setter puppy.

"Finnegan! Down!" Marianne shouted, as she let me in.

I scratched the puppy's ears. "He's beautiful, Marianne."

"Mom and Dad are still mourning Danny's passing—well, we all are."

My heart sank. "I didn't know."

"Yes, well…Mom and Dad didn't want to talk about it." She held the honey-colored dog's collar as we walked into the kitchen. "Anyway, the kids are over the moon with Finney." She opened the back door and Finney bounded out into the garden. "So cute," Marianne said as she shut the door.

I realized how distant I'd been from my own family. My beloved Danny had died and I hadn't shared the sadness with them.

"Jennifer's getting ready," Marianne said. "I'm fixing dinner."

I don't know what started it, but before long, Marianne was talking about her own place in the family. "It's no secret you're their favorite, Maggie."

I rolled my eyes.

"Don't look at me like that. I've always known it. Jack too—of course, because he's the boy," she said, chopping the ends off her carrots with gusto.

"Marianne, that's not true."

"But I was the one who got all A's—and don't think it came easy." Another carrot fell prey to her knife.

"I never thought...."

"I was the one who got the scholarship, and the nursing degree, *summa cum laude*, I might add. *That* wasn't easy either."

"No one ever said...."

"I married a *doctor*, Maggie." She pointed her knife at me. "Now that part was luck, I admit. Ted turned out to be a great guy and a good father, on *top* of being a good breadwinner."

"Marianne, you don't have to...."

"I'm the one who's given them grandchildren." She chopped some celery loudly, then slammed her knife down.

"Marianne...."

"Still, I can see it. *I'm not blind.* What's a person supposed to do in this family to...." She sat down at the kitchen table and covered her face.

"Marianne," I pulled up a chair next to her and put my arm around her. "You're wrong in thinking I don't look up to you—I do—I always have. Even as a kid I admired your accomplishments—wished I could be more like you."

"I try so hard," she sobbed. "So...hard."

"You don't need to try—you're perfect just the way you are."

"*You* say that? *Perfect*? You? Who chose a life of perfection? How can you know?"

"You're right, Marianne—I can't—only if you tell me.

She wiped her eyes, blew her nose, and sat up straight. "It's... I'm fine. I'm sorry I got so...so emotional."

"You don't need to apologize. If anyone in this family is a failure, it's me. There's no way I can fill your shoes. Can't you see that?"

"I'd like to, Maggie." She looked at the vegetables and the cutting board. "I'd better get on. I'll check on Jennifer."

I wondered how we could have grown up with the same parents and still see our place in the family so differently. I was beginning to feel hopeful that Marianne and I might be friends after all—though it wasn't going to be easy.

Over Christmas, Jack was home on leave. I kept my conversation light. I didn't mention that a student's older brother had returned from Vietnam missing an arm; that another student's cousin had come home in a body bag; that we'd been to too many funerals for young men. I didn't mention the body count, broadcast on the nightly news.

Jack spent most of his time with Amy—who could blame him? Mom and Dad had begged him to spend time with them, Marianne complained that the kids wanted to see their uncle. How could I compete?

I longed to tell Jack how complicated life was as a nun—how I saw the path toward Church renewal so clearly, yet many in my community were dragging their feet—even blaming me for their confusion and discomfort. I loved my vocation but couldn't always love some of my own sisters. I wanted to tell him I hated the war but supported his part in it. I kept silent.

In the midst of all this, news reached us that Thomas Merton—my beloved spiritual writer and monk—had died—accidentally electrocuted after giving a lecture on Marxism and Monasticism in Thailand. How ironic that this staunch warrior for peace was flown home to his Trappist Monastery in Kentucky aboard a U.S. Air Force plane—his coffin lined up next to U.S. soldiers killed in Vietnam.

After dinner, I called Will—he loved Thomas Merton too.

"I heard," Will said, then fell silent.

Neither of us could speak for a long time.

"Thanks for calling," he said finally. "I love—I appreciate it."

We hung up together.

Later that evening, our little community lit candles and prayed—each of us reading some of our favorite Merton quotes, tears falling. We'd lost a spiritual giant. The year 1968 had been the worst year I had ever lived through. Nothing indicated 1969 would be any better.

Chapter 31

A few months later, Will and I were meeting in my classroom to plan our Seminar curriculum. We were sitting across from one another when he stood up, stretched his arms over his head, and cleared his throat. "How about a break? I have something...to tell you…." He seemed a little unsure of how to go on.

I looked up from the *TIME* magazine I was reading—February 28, 1969—with President Nixon on the cover, promoting his latest war offensive.

"What's your news?"

"I have a date."

I set down the magazine and looked at him. "A date? Who with?" What was I supposed to say? Did he want my approval?

"We met at a singles dance—a few months ago. She knows you. You two were in drama club together. Brenda." He waited, expecting me to react. "Brenda Taylor."

Brenda Taylor. She knew what she wanted and went after it—including leads in the school plays. Brenda had been president of the Honor Society and a member of the prom court. She'd had the audacity to complain that she'd been passed over for queen.

He stood there, looking at me.

I wanted to tell Will that Brenda had gone after—and won—the ultimate trophy—most Mary-like to crown the Blessed Virgin during the May Procession. How was it possible that Brenda, the most ambitious girl in our class, hadn't landed a husband?

"Brenda Taylor." I tried not to sound ironic. I wanted to sound happy—or at least neutral. It was only a date, after all. *But dear Lord: Brenda Taylor?*

"I'm picking up something…. Not: Gee, that's great, Will! Not: What a bad idea, Will. Something in between, maybe?"

"No, no—I'm happy for you…I guess. I mean—I haven't seen Brenda in years—she actually came to visit me when I first entered the convent." *She never came back though, thank the Lord.* "What's she doing? She was off to Northwestern."

"She got a Ph.D. She's a professor of education at the Mount."

So, I thought, *she's going after Will.*

Suddenly I connected the dots: That song Will wrote must be about Brenda—not me. That would explain why he didn't bring it up again. Had he been using me as a critic? Of course—it made sense. *How stupid of me.*

"Guess where I'm taking her?"

I could care less where he took Dr. Brenda Taylor on a first date.

"To the art museum—like you and I did, remember?"

So, the wonderful trip we'd taken, to the art museum—to do research for our course—was a rehearsal? We'd strolled the museum galleries, taking notes and picking out which ones we'd take our students to. Will had surprised me with a picnic lunch in the park across from the museum—complete with checkered tablecloth and candles. The tactic worked for me, why not try it again on Brenda Taylor? *What was he was doing?*

I tried to gather my thoughts. *Am I jealous of Brenda? Ridiculous. I'm a nun. I don't date, certainly don't own Will, have no say over who he dates or where he goes.* But that had been *our* moment, that beautiful afternoon in the museum and the park, and here he was, duplicating it with *Brenda Taylor?*

My heart was beating fast—my mouth was dry. I stopped listening—until I heard Will say how great it would be to have Brenda join our faculty parties.

What was wrong with me? I looked down at my tightened fists. *I had to get away.* Just then, the call bell rang in the hallway. "That's my bell." I scooped up my folders.

"We'll talk later?"

"Sure." I practically ran out of the room. I brushed away tears. The last thing I wanted was for anyone to see how immature I really was.

Every evening, the TV news spewed bombs and bloodshed. I didn't understand the politics—all I saw was the bloodied bodies of innocent Vietnamese children on one hand, and throngs of American student demonstrators on the other. My students became more confused and depressed, as their uncles, brothers, and cousins came home injured and shaken—or not at all.

Jack's letters to Amy and me trickled off—I wondered if he was being censored. Soon he would learn where his new assignment would be. I prayed night and day for his safety.

CHAPTER 32

"Sister, I'd like you to spend some time in prayer on the topic of charity in community." I was meeting with a spiritual director—a Jesuit priest—once a week now. I'd never had a *real* spiritual director before. My Mistresses of Formation—Mother Loretta, Mother Vivian, and Mother Regina—were not my spiritual directors, they were my superiors. Spiritual directors were supposed to be objective, neutral—unlike my superiors, whose role included regularly passing judgment on me.

"Your foundress, Mother Dolan, wrote a brilliant chapter on charity in your Rule," the priest said. "Why not take her writings and make them your meditation for the next few months?"

"I can recite that chapter by heart, Father," I was proud to say—though I probably sounded defensive to him.

"Reciting is different than meditating," he said. "Sit with the words—one sentence at a time—repeating, letting the words sink in. When they've become a part of you, then you'll be better able to practice the virtues embedded in the words."

Each morning I did as he directed. After a few weeks, he asked if I noticed any changes in my attitude.

I sat across from him in the little office. "I leave meditation determined to be charitable," I told him, "but before the day is over, something derails me—Sister Corella calls me to her office to complain my drama students are too loud—or that parents don't like what or how I teach their children. Or I hear two sisters whispering about me in the lunch line—things like that. It's been going on so long, I didn't realize until recently how heavily it weighs on me. I'm suffocating." I shifted in my chair, aware I was probably sounding like a chronic complainer.

"Can you see the good in your sisters, in spite of their weaknesses? What would it take, to look past their failings?"

"A miracle." I laughed—though I felt like crying. "I'm supposed to be charitable, but the sisters in my community aren't. How is that fair?"

"If you could see these as opportunities—not setbacks—then fairness wouldn't matter." He leaned forward in his chair. "How determined are you to persevere in your vocation?"

"Very determined!" I nearly shouted. "I've read and re-read the Rule. How did Mother Dolan and her sisters live the words of the Rule *to never dispute…and avoid all suspicion?*"

"I'm sure it wasn't easy for them either."

I looked down at my silver ring—evidence that I was a perpetually professed sister of St. Mary. That ring meant everything to me. I was surprised to find myself holding back tears. "I don't know what to say, Father. I want to be worthy of my vocation—I want it with all my heart, but…."

"Have you thought about giving yourself some distance?"

"Distance? What do you mean, Father? I live in a fishbowl."

"Exactly. I mean, literally, distance. Doesn't your order grant temporary leaves?"

"Leave the convent? That's not what I want."

"I'm suggesting you ask for some time away. Talk to your superior—tell her what you're feeling. Ask for guidance. It's possible a temporary leave will give you the perspective—and peace—your soul is seeking." He paused. "Will you do that?"

"I'll do my best, Father."

The next day, I reached Mother Provincial by phone. A few days later, I was sitting in her office, trying to hold back tears.

I got right to the point—afraid I'd lose my courage. "My spiritual director said I might need some time away from the Community."

"Tell me more." Her calmness surprised me, put me at ease. I was not the first to ask for a leave of absence.

"I can't avoid conflict in the Community, Mother," I told her. "I don't agree with the older sisters—or my superiors—on much of anything. I know they disapprove of me, but I can't help it. I'm discounted, ignored. They think I'm too young to know anything—at least, that's the way I see it."

"What are you doing that causes such disapproval?" Mother seemed genuinely interested.

"As you can see, I don't wear the habit to teach in, for one thing," I said. "I usually wear what I'm wearing today—street clothes—you know, skirts and blouses or simple dresses—we do have permission to experiment with secular clothing."

"You're correct—we do. I assume you dress modestly?"

"Of course!" My principal didn't think so, but I didn't say that. "I feel more comfortable when I'm not wearing the habit, which feels like a uniform of rank to me. I know I'm upsetting the older sisters."

I waited for Mother to interrupt or comment, but she listened quietly.

"I still meet occasionally with the brothers I met in the inner-city," I said. "I think some of the sisters disapprove of my friendships with men." I didn't bring up my friendship with Will—I wasn't sure if anyone else knew how close we were—or if it mattered. The truth was, I had no desire to give it up.

Mother listened, without showing emotion or disapproval. "Do any of these conflicts seem large enough that you feel you should give up your vocation?"

Her words made me shiver. "I hope not."

"Are these issues so impossible to resolve that you think you must leave?" She didn't wait for my reply. "Is there more to your struggle—something deeper than giving scandal to our older sisters?"

I could not look Mother in the eye. I could not say, "Yes, there is something deeper." I could not put my feelings into words—not even in the privacy of my journal. I had made final profession—promised to love God alone for the rest of my life.

I would not allow myself to say: *I was wrong. I've changed my mind; I want to be loved, exclusively—to be held. I want to know how it feels.*

Would it ever be enough to love and be loved by God alone? I had to answer yes—to trust in my vocation. My vows had to count for something—for everything. *Didn't they?*

I thought for a long time before replying. "Mother, I value religious life, and I've cherished my vocation as a gift from God—a calling. But lately I seem to be a cause for scandal, or at least disapproval. It's making me and everyone else unhappy."

Mother sat back in her chair, her chin resting on her folded hands, her eyes closed. "If you are sincere about your vocation—and I believe you are—take my suggestion, give it the time it deserves."

I felt both curious and uneasy—Mother Superior's *suggestions* were generally a matter of holy obedience.

"There is a seminar this summer I want you to attend, a course on religious life at Villa University. You'd live on campus, immerse yourself in study and prayer, learn all you can about this life you've embraced. Then, after you've completed, we'll talk again."

I had no choice. On the bright side, a month on a college campus, out from under the watchful eyes of my detractors, sounded like a gift from heaven—or at least a nice vacation.

"Yes, Mother," I said, like the obedient novice I had once been.

I went to the *Institute on Religious Life in the 20th Century*—listened to the presenters, read the literature, talked with sisters, priests, and brothers my own age. No one criticized my clothes, my ideas, my theology, my politics. I was brought up to date on the latest in theological and philosophical thinking. Merton and Teilhard de Chardin—my favorites—were required reading.

On weekends, I came back to Dolan House, excited to share the experience with Rosemary and my other two housemates. I felt hope filling my heart—I walked around with a smile on my face. *Mother Provincial was right*, I thought. *It's all going to work out.*

I returned in time to re-pack for the two-week journalism workshop at Loyola University in Chicago—all expenses paid, thanks to the Wall Street Journal Grant I'd won. I was thrilled to hear that Victor's grant application had also been successful.

I'd kept in touch with Victor, who was teaching at a boys' high school sponsored by his religious community. He was the advisor for their school newspaper. Way back in February, we'd both applied for this two-week intensive course in Chicago.

"We could drive together," I said. "If you think that would be okay."

"Sure," Victor said. "I just need to clear it with my superior."

I didn't even think to do that.

Sister Irene gave me permission to go without question. From the time she'd been appointed the local Coordinator, I'd sensed that we'd get along well. I was amazed that I was actually having a good relationship with someone in authority.

Sister Corella was still my principal—I had to answer to her for school matters, but I was glad I didn't need her approval to attend this workshop—though I hoped she'd be glad I'd won an education grant. I was determined to earn enough credits to pursue what was becoming a new vocation: life as a journalist. I had proven myself in theater—I wanted to do the same as a writer.

Victor picked me up at Dolan House and we headed off in the Friary's beat-up Plymouth. "Hah! If this old jalopy could talk," Victor said.

"It's a good thing she can't," I said. "We've had some good times, haven't we, Victor?"

"You're talking as if the good times are over." He was tuning the car radio—trying to find something other than country-western music. "I like to think they're just beginning."

"I have such good memories from that summer in the city."

Victor handled the highway with ease, his dark eyes on the road, a cigarette dangling from his lips. He laughed. "Good times, weren't they? You really learned how to play that banjo."

"I'd never known such freedom."

"Freedom: a relative term."

"True," I said. "When I entered—putting on that postulant outfit at seventeen—I believed I'd be free to love only God—that once I handed myself completely over to God, all would be well, that I would find true freedom."

"Now, what?" Victor asked. "Nine years later, you're less free? Is that what you're saying?"

"Choices have consequences—they can bind you forever, in a way that feels anything but freeing." *How depressing I sound*, I thought.

Chapter 32

We listened as the radio played everything from Peter, Paul and Mary to Elvis to the Beatles. Sometimes we sang along, sometimes we talked—about putting out a high school newspaper, the challenges of living downtown, all I'd learned at the Institute on Religious Life, even Brother Maury's Italian wedding soup recipe.

After the first full day of sessions at the University, Victor convinced me to take in the local color, so we walked to a bar a few blocks off-campus. A live band was playing—the singer was a handsome Black woman with a bluesy voice. We found a table in the corner and settled in.

"Have you found happiness, Victor?" I asked, after the waiter had brought a bottle of chianti and two glasses to our table.

Victor had been watching a young man and woman at the table next to us—obviously in love—their hands clasped tight, bodies leaning in, gazing at one another. The man was running his fingers through her long, blond hair, as she laughed softly.

"Happiness?" Victor shifted his attention away from the couple. "Trick question?"

"No trick." I wished I hadn't brought it up. "Sorry—none of my business."

He nodded toward the couple. "I haven't found *that* kind of happiness. Have you? Is there a guy in your past with a broken heart? Or is that none of *my* business?"

"I've never talked much about it." I swallowed a mouthful of wine. "There was a guy. But I haven't seen or talked to him since…I left home."

"What happened to him?"

"He joined the Navy. He was my brother's best friend—for years Jack played matchmaker." I didn't mention Stan's stream of letters. "I hear he's dating someone—a nightclub singer, no less. I have to admit, I do wonder sometimes if *he's* happy."

"I may be reading between the lines, but you're wondering whether religious life is going to make *you* happy? Can you be truly human if you don't experience physical love? It's the contrast between Erich Fromm's idea of loving relationships in *The Art of Loving* versus St. Thomas Aquinas' view of love as being platonic—or Neoplatonic, I think was his term. Physical love versus spiritual love."

"Our theology and philosophy courses were all so traditional," I said. "They all say man is inherently evil—that we constantly need to safeguard ourselves against our humanity, our tendency toward sin. My intuition tells me that the doctrine of original sin is flawed."

Victor raised his eyebrows. "That's a little daring, isn't it?"

"I don't believe in original sin, but I've never said so out loud before. I can't defend my belief—my intuition—with credible arguments."

"A bit on the heretical side, are you?"

Victor saw the concern on my face.

"Don't worry," he said. "I'm not going to tell anyone." Victor shifted in his chair, took another sip of wine. "I'm in the same place myself."

"You've read *The Art of Loving*?"

Victor nodded.

"That book made such a difference for me," I went on. "I wrote a paper on it in college. I'm not an expert. I just know that, after reading it, I felt liberated. But also, afraid."

"Of what?" Victor refilled our wine glasses.

"If we are free to embrace life, and resist authority, then the whole religious life structure, the monastic life, the top-down patriarchy would have to be rejected." I realized I sounded radical. "If I believe in that kind of freedom, how can I live this religious life I've chosen? What happens to my individuality if I sacrifice my identity for the whole?"

"I think it's possible," Victor said. "I just don't know how yet. Fromm says we need loving relationships; to be creative—feel we belong—see ourselves as unique individuals *and* as part of a group. Can't religious life help us do that?"

"I think it can," I said. "But only if there's drastic change. I think it's different with women. Men can live together in a more detached way. Women—we can't live together without entanglements, suspicions, jealousies, games."

"Games? What do you mean?"

"See? You don't even know what I'm talking about. That proves my point! You men."

We laughed as we both noticed the couple locked in a kiss.

Victor sighed.

I focused on the candle flickering between us—reached in to touch the dripping wax. Its light gleamed in my silver ring. I remembered the public vows I took. I couldn't wipe out the image of Stan's last kiss.

"Cigarette?" Victor tapped the pack on his palm—two cigarettes popped up. He held out the pack. "Been trying to quit, but the smoke here is driving me crazy."

Victor was just being polite, I don't think he thought I'd actually take a cigarette. I'd given up smoking the day I entered the convent, but in the last few months, I'd been tempted to smoke. Maybe it was the stress. I took one.

I would never smoke in public back home, of course—but I was a stranger here. I was wearing secular clothes—modest, but not religious—few people would even suspect I was a nun. What difference would it make? What could a cigarette hurt, far from the judging eyes of my superiors?

"I don't normally do this." I had to lean into him, to be heard over the singer, who—as it happened—was singing, "Light My Fire," the big hit by The Doors. "Nobody knows me," I said, glancing around the dark café lit by candles and low hanging lights. "So, I guess it's okay."

Victor drew out a package of matches and lit my cigarette. He looked amused. But then, he was male. Plenty of priests, brothers, and seminarians smoked. Nuns smoking, though, was another thing altogether.

"Sister," he asked in a serious tone, "I see by the way you just inhaled, this isn't your first time. Fess up: When did you smoke your first cigarette?"

"Go ahead, make fun." I enjoyed Victor's playful side. "Are you a reporter for *True Confessions* magazine?" I asked. "Or am I on *Candid Camera*?"

He pretended to hold a microphone up to me. We both laughed.

"Sophomore year in high school," I said, blowing a slow puff of smoke just over Victor's head. "Peer pressure. I wanted to be like my with-it girlfriends. I wanted to be original—no one in my family smoked—except my brother Jack, of course."

"You? A rebel?" He was joking—he'd tagged me as a rebel the first day we'd met.

"In small ways—nothing bad. I drove my parents crazy with smoking, but they didn't say I couldn't, I never had to hide it. I was grateful for that."

I enjoyed smoking—something about striking the match, that wicked sulfur smell, the *snap* of the cigarette tip igniting, the tobacco and paper giving itself over to flame, inhaling the warm smoke, holding my breath, forcing the smoke back out into the air. I liked the sound of it passing over my lips—the gentle *whoosh.* It gave me a feeling of power and control. Maybe even a sense of risk, lack of care, as if blowing smoke into the air told the world that, while I could be serious, I was a rebel.

"I accepted that I'd had my last cigarette the day I entered the convent. Now here I am, years later...."

"I've been a smoker since high school—I'm not proud to say. I've tried to quit a hundred times." Victor knocked ashes off his cigarette, using the edge of the ceramic ashtray. "I'll go a week without a cigarette, then the smoke from one of the other Brothers will find its way to me." He opened his nostrils and crunched up his long, straight nose, his dark eyebrows arching. "Next thing, I'm bumming cigarettes. Like a bloodhound, I track it down. I wonder if I'll ever quit for good."

"You can quit," I said. "Anybody can. I did. Just stopped—didn't miss it. Ten years without a cigarette, not even a craving." *Not for a cigarette, anyway.*

"Until now." Victor smiled. "The craving is back, isn't it?"

"I wouldn't call it *craving*," I said, focusing on the amber tip of my cigarette, the smoke curling up and winding around Victor's smoke trail, like one spirit searching out another. "I could stop anytime. I don't consider this"—I held up my cigarette—"falling off the wagon."

Victor laughed out loud, leaned his head back. "We'll see," he said, running his long fingers through his hair and sucking in one last drag before stubbing out his cigarette.

"I can quit!" I felt my defiance rising, from somewhere in my gut, heating up my chest and charging up my throat. I felt angry at Victor, judging me, accusing me of being weak.

Victor sat upright in his chair. "Hey, it's okay, Clare."

He looked me straight in the eyes, always uncomfortable for me, especially where men were concerned. Victor had beautiful, dark eyes.

"Don't take me too seriously." Victor reached for my hand, then seemed to think better of it. He flicked an ash off the table instead. "I'm incorrigible. I think you know that. But you. You're...." He sighed.

I was a little afraid of what he might say next.

"What I mean is," Victor said, "it's clear to me that you can do anything you set your mind to. Including giving up smoking."

"You know something that might surprise you, Victor? It's not clear to *me* that I can do anything. That's not the message I got from the world, growing up. Be a teacher, a nurse, a wife and mother, or a nun." I said *nun* and heard disdain in my own voice. Was that true? No, of course not. The convent was the "higher path," everyone knew that. It certainly hadn't been an easy choice.

Victor cocked his head to one side. "You sound regretful."

"It's a calling." I chose my words with care. "I didn't choose this life—it chose me. Regardless of the outcome, the obstacles, I have been *called*. I know God will give me whatever it takes to live this life." I crushed my cigarette in the ashtray. "Regret? No, Victor. Never. I'm constantly in awe of my vocation."

"In awe, yes," Victor said, "but questioning it too, it seems to me. No life should be taken for granted, should it? Isn't there room for exploration? Examination? Questions?"

"Would we be sitting here in LaBamba's, smoking cigarettes and drinking chianti if I didn't think that?"

We both laughed—a nun and a brother of St. Paul, bound by vows of poverty, chastity, and obedience, having what in society's norms was a *date* at a Chicago college bar.

I fingered the matches. "Remember the matchbook covers that used to say: *So You Want to Be a Writer?* During my teens, I wanted so badly to be a real writer, that I answered one of those ads, in a ladies' magazine. When they wrote back that they loved my writing sample, and sent me a packet to enroll in their mail-order writing course, I was hooked."

"Did you enroll?"

"No. It cost money. My Mom said it was a hoax. My sister laughed. I threw out the packet and never mentioned it again." *I was competing with Marianne, even then.* "Instead I chose a vocation that was possible for me, even praiseworthy, although not everyone approved of my vocation either."

"But you've never given up the dream, have you?" Victor said. "That's why we're at this journalism workshop. I have you to thank for convincing me to apply for the grant. 'It'll look good on your resume,' you told me."

"On both our resumes," I reminded him. We drained the last of the chianti from our glasses.

"Listen, Vic—may I call you Vic?" I was feeling the tongue-loosening effects of the wine. It felt good.

"Call me anything…just be sure to call me," Victor said, mimicking Groucho Marx. "That was a favorite joke in my family." A frown clouded his angular face. "I hope you don't think I'm flirting with you—it's just a joke."

The word *flirt* brought me down to earth, back from the heady euphoria I had been feeling, the buzz that results from wine and nicotine combined. The question I was about to ask him had vanished, and in its place, that dark warning about crossing a line descended. "Let's get back to our dorms." I stood up and slid my chair back. "I've got some writing to do for tomorrow's session—you do too, by the way."

Victor took my cue and stood, towering over me. His tone had shifted to polite, his hands hung straight at his sides. But he didn't take his gaze off me, and for a moment we locked eyes.

"You're a good buddy, Clare. I value your friendship. Let's never spoil it, okay?"

"No, let's not," I said, formal smile, lips tight. "I value you too, Victor."

I couldn't hold his gaze for more than a few seconds. "Okay, back to work. I hear they lock the women's dorm early. By the way, I've gone back to my baptismal name, so you can call me *Maggie*."

He smiled. "*Maggie*—I like it."

We walked back to campus under the shade of tall oak trees, past ivy-covered stone buildings. A silver moon, hours short of being full, was low in the darkening sky. The air was musty, damp. We kept a measured distance, our bodies close but never touching, walking with purpose toward the dorms. Neither of us broke the silence that held us.

We stopped once to gaze at the moon. Victor tapped the pack on his palm; two cigarettes popped up. He held out the pack to me. I took one, Victor the other. He struck a match and held the flame for me, the flickering light cast shadows on our faces. The flame almost burned his fingers. We walked, smoke trails winding together behind us, the red embers dancing in the falling darkness.

CHAPTER 33

I returned home to Dolan House in mid-July—in time to watch Neil Armstrong walk on the moon. The year 1969 was only half over, but it felt like an entire epoch to me. Each evening we'd turn on the TV, not knowing what to expect: the ravages of war, student protests, a three-day music festival in the Catskills of New York State. Half a million young people flocked to a dairy farm, where they camped out and danced in the rain and shouted *Peace, Love, Rock 'n Roll!* I heard some sisters *tsk-tsking—a veritable orgy!* I secretly wanted to be there.

We got hopeful news—the first troop withdrawals from Vietnam—but when Jack came home on leave, he announced that he was, in fact, being sent there.

"I'll be in a secure place—in Long Binh—doing radio and TV programs for the Army," he told us, as we sat around my parents' kitchen table, wiping our eyes and blowing our noses.

When it came time to say good-bye, I couldn't stop crying.

"Come on, little sis." He lifted my chin. "I need you to cheer up the troops here at home."

"I'll try." I nodded. "You'd better come home safe or I'll never forgive you."

He laughed. "I said something like that to you—when you left home, didn't I?"

"How am I going to get through the next year, Jack?"

"Keep writing, Megs."

"You know I will. You've taught me to be true to myself as a writer."

Over the next months, Jack's letters were interesting and upbeat. He had to be witnessing horrific scenes: wounded soldiers, terrified Vietnamese women and children, rotting livestock, a countryside stripped of everything. Instead, he wrote of heroic rescues, humanitarian acts of kindness, bravery, and humor.

"You're a good writer," I wrote to him. "I'm proud of you."

"So are you," he wrote back. "When are you going to use your talent?" Jack never gave up on me—I loved him for it.

Jack's last letter announced that he was being discharged early—something about being given "a drop" in days, so that he could enroll in classes and finish his degree. We didn't care why. It was early March on a school day—busy—but I couldn't miss seeing Jack get off the plane. Will and Rosemary volunteered to take my afternoon classes.

The whole family was at the airport—including Amy—with WELCOME HOME signs. A few of his college buddies showed up with musical instruments—a trumpet, Jack's own saxophone, and a harmonica—and played "With a Little Help from My Friends" over and over. It might have been the only song they knew.

He was wearing his Army uniform—khaki shirt and black tie, olive green jacket with bars and medals pinned above the pockets, along with his name: WALSH. His dark hair was short—he carried the olive green folded cap. He was beyond handsome.

We all had a turn hugging him—Amy first. I saw sobs shake my brother—I had never seen that before. When it was my turn, I looked in his eyes. Something was different. There was a new sadness. He looked into each of our faces, as if he were searching for something. He moved more slowly, took deep breaths.

He's going to need some time, I thought.

Chapter 33

Jack moved back into his old apartment in time to enroll in classes at the University, determined to study law. Whenever he wasn't in the law library or taking part in marches and rallies, he was at Amy's. She had a roommate, so I guessed Jack was not staying overnight, but of course, no one asked and Jack never volunteered—they were adults, after all.

Rosemary and I had talked about contraception—that "the pill" was becoming more and more popular—even among Catholics.

In a rare moment, I'd had an honest conversation with Marianne, during which she'd revealed her views about family planning.

"Ted and I don't intend to have more kids," she told me, matter-of-factly. "I don't know what you know about contraceptives, Maggie, but trust me—the Church hasn't a clue, if they think *anyone* is using the rhythm method."

The pill was safe, and she, as a nurse, had no qualms about using it. "I've advised Jack and Amy to do the same. He's got too much to do before settling down to raise kids—if ever. I told them—don't make my mistakes!"

"What mistakes?"

"You know." She was folding laundry into piles of socks and underwear on the dining room table. "Falling for the line that the little woman is subject to her husband. Not that I bought it. But boom—boom—there we were, two kids." She stopped folding. "I didn't mean to dump on you—you probably don't know what I'm talking about."

"You'd be surprised, Marianne."

I told her about the scene in the confessional I'd overheard when I was a teen—the one between the unfeeling Monsignor and Mrs. Bennett. "If I'd had anything to say about it—if the pill had been available then—I would have handed her a pack."

"There you go, Megs." Marianne laughed. "You've come a long way."

"We all have, Marianne."

More reassurance that the two of us—just maybe—could get along.

Will and I had launched our Seminar, after a whole year of preparation. It felt right to be with him—laughing, creating, comparing notes. As the school year wore on, I was surprised to see how demanding it was to teach a course with another person—even Will.

My schedule was as full as ever. I had to move the Fall play to early November, which upset our planning times. Will organized outreach projects for his junior religion classes during the Thanksgiving and Christmas seasons—another schedule adjustment for us. When exams came in late January, we experimented with a new way to evaluate and test our Seminar students—through interviews, projects, and group reports. Sister Corella was skeptical, but as usual, Will won her over.

It was mid-March when I realized I hadn't heard Will mention Brenda in months. One day after class I got up my nerve to ask, "How's Brenda?"

"Fine." He was sorting through some books in the back of the room.

"Just…fine?"

"I said *fine.*" He turned to face me. "Why do you want to know?"

My heart beat fast, my mouth went dry, I clenched my teeth. "Just being friendly. Is that a crime?"

"Come here." He motioned for me to come to him.

I hesitated, then walked to the rear of the room. "What?"

He took my hands in his and looked straight at me. "No one is ever going to take your place, okay?"

A hot flash spiraled up my spine. My cheeks felt like they were on fire. "I didn't mean...."

"Brenda is…fine. You are…." He let go of my hands. "*You.*" He turned back to the stack of books. "Let's leave it at that."

I went over to the window. An unexpected snowfall had blanketed the ground the night before. *What did he mean? No one would take my place?* I couldn't leave it alone.

"Does that mean...I'm not allowed to mention Bren....?

He dropped his book and started laughing—a little at first. He turned and grabbed the nearest chair. Soon, he was laughing uncontrollably—like in acting class when we'd find something hysterically funny.

"What's so funny?" I couldn't help laughing too—not sure why, except almost everything Will did made me laugh. I leaned into the window sill, I was laughing so hard.

It took us a while to catch our breath.

I wiped tears from my eyes and looked at him.

He was looking at me too. "You're my soul mate, you know that?"

I had to look away—I concentrated on the snow-covered leaves outside. "Am I?"

His breathing had returned to normal. "You know you are."

I nodded, thinking: *Maggie, that's the first step down the road of no return.*

Jack stopped by the convent one Sunday afternoon. It was a warm spring day so we walked around the Marywood campus.

"It's not my business, Megs, but you've lost weight, haven't you?"

"A little—it shows?" I knew it did. In fact, I'd lost more than a little. When I went shopping for clothes with Amy, I discovered I'd dropped two sizes—something I hadn't noticed wearing the loose-fitting habit.

"I know better than to discuss a lady's weight—still, sis…." He snapped off a forsythia branch in bloom and examined it. "Is something going on?"

"I'm fine. Besides, I can afford to lose a little." Jack still had dark circles under his eyes—he looked tired. "What about you? Have you readjusted to civilian life?"

"You know—the occasional nightmare—some of the photos I shot in 'Nam—the images—they won't fade. Not that they should." He peeled the yellow forsythia flowers off the branch, one by one, dropping them on the ground. "They spit on me, you know? When I landed in California, people were protesting outside the base, screaming and throwing rocks at the bus. The bus dropped me off at San Francisco airport, and they were there, spitting and hollering. They looked just like me, Megs."

I wanted to scream, *What? People spit on my beautiful brother?*

Jack lit a cigarette, took a long drag. "Many Veterans have it worse. Every day, I count my blessings—keep working to end this war."

I pulled myself together. I needed to be strong for him. "But you got into law school—that's great!"

"I'm going to form a Viet Vets support group on campus. Some of those guys are really messed up. There's already a Vietnam Vets Against the War group. You can be sure I'll join that."

"Will it help—I mean you—help you?"

He gave me a tender look. "I think so. We'll include spouses and families—in case you want to look into it."

"I would love to—anything to support you. By the way, good news: I'm driving again." Jack was one of the few people I'd told about how I'd lost my driver's license.

"What did you have to do—beg on hands and knees?"

I laughed. "There was a time when I would've had to—but my Coordinator said yes—no hesitation. Either she didn't know about the whole car-towing fiasco, or she chose to overlook it."

"A simple mistake—letting the parking meter expire. When I get my law degree we'll sue Sister Corella."

"Very funny. Anyway, maybe now I can spend a little more time with Father Mark in the inner-city.

"You loved it there. Ever think of moving there? You told me one time you'd never been happier."

"Someday, maybe. Like you say: *The Times They Are A Changin'.*"

"I'll help you move—say the word."

We had done a complete circle around the school, back to Dolan House where he'd parked his car. He hugged me and rushed off to meet Amy.

I went to protests and peace marches with Father Mark and Victor. My students wrote letters to the editor encouraging an end to the war. Sister Corella and some of the other faculty members said it wasn't my place to take a public stand—it was unpatriotic and inconsistent with my status as a Sister of St. Mary. This made no sense. I saw Jesus as the ultimate advocate for peace. I kept up with current events. My time among the poor had awakened me to injustice on all kinds of levels. I'd learned more about the history behind the war by listening to Will. I wasn't willing to be quiet. Not anymore.

Will and I had been teaching a series in our Seminar on writing and media and had arranged to have the local newspaper delivered to each of our students.

On the first morning of the series, I picked up the newspapers and carried them to the classroom. The front page pictured a young woman with her arms outstretched—her face in anguish—kneeling over a young man in a pool of blood—apparently dead from a gunshot. Others—they appeared to be students—stood around or were caught by the photographer in the midst of running. The headline ran: "4 Kent State Students Killed by Troops."

Will arrived and saw me hunched over the newspapers. I turned to him. "Have you seen this?"

He scanned the photo, the headline. "I heard about it on the radio, couldn't believe it."

"We can't give these newspapers out," I whispered, slumping into a desk. "This is terrible. What are we going to do?"

"We most certainly *will* give these out," Will said. "After all we've been saying about *the media is the message*, we have no choice but to look this square in the face—to read and discuss this with the girls."

I took a few deep breaths. "Of course, you're right." I put a newspaper on each of the desks. Then I went to the front blackboard and wrote: "Who? What? When? Where? Why? How?" "What is the message?" "What is your response?"

The students arrived and found their seats. Their enthusiasm for getting to read the newspaper—a goof-off class to some—switched to horror when they saw the front-page photo and read the headline. Some had already heard about it. Most of them, like me, had missed the news altogether.

Some cried. Others just stared at the front page. We divided the students into groups, directed them to explore the questions on the board and write down their responses.

Student organizations were calling for a nationwide strike. Would our college president encourage students to strike? Should our school newspaper be interviewing students to see how their families felt about all this? Would Sister Corella censor such writing?

Will and I listened to the girls—some cried, others worried about brothers or cousins.

"I don't know what's right anymore," one girl said.

"I just want this to stop—nobody's listening," another girl said.

I feel the same way, girls. If I'd ever thought I knew what is right, I didn't know it now.

At vespers that evening, I turned to the psalms of David—looking for comfort and inspiration but finding none, as we chanted: *"Man is like a breath, his days, like a passing shadow."*

PART FOUR

June 1970

CHAPTER 34

I*'ll just say it—Please may I keep my ring?* I sat outside Mother Provincial's office, twirling the silver band on my ring finger. It had been so long since I'd had a real appetite, the ring was loose.

The hall was empty. A stream of sunshine highlighted the gold stars in the oriental carpet and picked up specks of dust floating to the polished wood floor. Mother opened her office door and smiled. Her navy-blue habit hung unevenly on her slight frame, her salt-and-pepper wave of hair spilled from the black veil with its white rim around her face. I was immediately conscious that—in my slim navy shift dress—I was out of uniform.

Mother waved me into her office and gestured to a chair facing her. There was little point in small talk. We both knew why I was there—to make official the year of exclaustration—living outside the cloister—that I had requested to help me decide whether I would return to religious life or leave for good.

"It was only last year you sat in that same chair."

"You sent me to the summer institute on religious life." I did not want to sink into crippling guilt, but I could feel it overtaking me. "We both hoped I'd come back with new purpose."

Mother nodded. "Now, you must realize my role is different."

I noticed the documents spread out on her desk. "Yes, Mother." I stuffed down my tears. "I'm ready to sign the papers. But before we do," I said, leaning forward, "I wanted to ask—may I keep my ring? It would mean a lot to me if...."

"For the next year, you can keep the ring, Sister," she answered as if this weren't the first time she had been asked.

"Whether you wear it will be up to you. But remember, this will be a year of discernment. You're still a vowed member. The only difference is that you'll be living outside the cloister." Her gaze felt kind. "If you decide, after this year, to be dispensed from your vows and leave for good, you will return the ring."

It was hard to hear—and probably hard for her to say.

"I see."

I didn't have access to the entire Code of Canon Law, that cumbersome and legalistic system that spelled out the hierarchical structure of the Roman Catholic Church and governed every aspect of religious life. But I knew what I had taken on when I'd first pronounced my vows. Only two years earlier I had promised to be faithful for the rest of my life—and now, here I was, considering the possibility of being dispensed from that promise.

"You know the regulations," Mother said. "By the end of this year, you could request a dispensation from your vows—leave and not come back." Her words made me shiver. "Or after one year, you could request up to two more—regain your balance, come back fully restored, ready to live your vows in community."

"I think a year will be sufficient."

"You're a respected member, Sister. You're admired as a teacher—you follow your convictions—others look up to you. You have great leadership potential."

It had taken me nearly a decade—not only to *hear* that kind of praise—but to believe it. "Thank you, Mother. My life feels—like all the threads are unraveling. I hope I can weave them back together."

Mother handed me a copy of the statement from canon law. "This spells it out—for your records."

"You've been a good friend, Mother—I'm grateful for your kindness. I know this isn't easy for you either."

Chapter 34

She pushed the legal document aside and reached her hands across her desk, her palms up. I unfolded my hands from my lap and clasped hers. Neither of us spoke.

"Are you *sure*, Sister?" A tear fell and spread on her glass-top desk.

My eyes filled up. "I need this time." The words caught in my throat. "I'm smothering. Some days…I feel as if I can't breathe." I pulled one hand away to wipe tears from my cheeks. Mother snatched tissues from the shelf behind her and passed one to me, then dabbed her own cheeks, blew her nose. "If you're sure, it's time to sign this," she said. She sat up straight, picked up her pen—I heard it move across the document as she signed—then she slid the paper and pen to me.

A cardinal sang outside the open window. The clock on Mother's desk ticked. I picked up the pen, noting that I needed to sign both my religious and secular names. I wrote them slowly, noticing the flow of the fountain pen—reminded of the one I'd shown up just after entering and had never seen again.

"Shall I send a copy of the papers to your parents' home address?"

"I don't have a place of my own yet—so yes, thank you." *I had wanted this to be mine alone to bear.*

"There is something else." From a desk drawer Mother retrieved a white envelope labeled, *Sister Margaret Ann Walsh, SSM.* "I realize this isn't a lot, but I hope it will help get you started, until you are drawing a salary. You can read the terms later."

I held the envelope without opening it. How much money could the Community possibly give me? I didn't want to show either disappointment or pleasure. What did she mean by "terms?" I didn't want to be obligated to the Community. I knew it was my fierce independent streak—the thing that got me in trouble in community life. But still, I was without a job—and determined not to move back home with my parents—so I accepted the gift and put the envelope in my pocket.

"Thank you, Mother. I am grateful, for everything. You've been so kind." I stood up.

She stood too and came around her desk, arms extended. As we hugged, I felt her delicate bone structure beneath her habit. Was she well? Overworking? Stressed from being Mother Superior—having to sign exclaustration documents for young sisters she admired?

She stepped back, and in a tone I could only call formal, she said, "I hope you'll keep in touch and let me know how it's going. It would be wise to continue with your spiritual director. Goodbye, Margaret Ann. God bless you."

Those words were the signal, it was time to go. She'd dropped my title, *Sister.*

"Goodbye, Mother." I said. I turned around. Without looking at her, I opened the heavy door, crossed the threshold, and closed the door behind me. The click of the lock echoed in the empty hallway. I walked down the steps to the front door. There was no one at the front desk. Were all the sisters busy, or did they know to make themselves scarce?

They're dead to us now. Sister Julia had said it on my first night in the convent. *Would I be dead to everyone?* I was grateful that there was no one there, no one to sit in judgment of me, no one to feel alienated from me—as I would feel toward them.

Outside, the sun was shining, a warm breeze was blowing. I heard the same cardinal singing. Jack was waiting in the front circle in his red Ford Fairlane. I slipped into the passenger seat—he knew to say nothing—good old Jack. He passed me a white handkerchief.

I cried for five minutes or longer—sobs and heaves—coming from down deep—I must have sounded like a wounded animal.

Chapter 34

Jack sat there, his hand on my shoulder. Finally, I sat up, wiped my eyes, and took a deep breath. "I got to keep my ring," I said, looking over at him, smiling—thinking how much I loved him. "For now, anyway."

"Good. What next?"

"Take me home—that is, back to Dolan House. My housemates won't find this news surprising, but I need to tell them it's official."

"I have a better idea." Jack started up the car, looked at his watch. "Just after four. It's five o-clock somewhere. Let's get a beer. I know just the place."

"I hope you're treating. I'm broke, you know." I had forgotten about the envelope in my pocket.

As Jack pulled away, I looked at the stately Motherhouse. *So many memories.*

"Remember the day—almost a decade ago—when we drove here? When I...." I had to stop or I'd be crying again.

"How could I forget?" Jack held the steering wheel tightly. "Strange, isn't it? Everyone *but* you felt like crying. Today—it's the other way around."

"It's a mystery, Jack."

"Yeah, yeah." The year in Vietnam had made him cynical.

As Jack's car entered late-afternoon traffic, I lay my head back, closed my eyes—burning still, from crying—and sighed. "I can't believe it's over—just like that. Ten years of my life—in a matter of minutes."

Jack drove the car up a narrow street and backed into a tight spot in front of a little café.

"Where are we?" I'd dozed off—the sleepless nights were catching up with me. I felt exhausted, my legs felt like rubber, from fear and relief.

I followed him into an empty bar—it was early. The linoleum floor was sticky with spilled beer. He led me onto the back porch, it had a stunning view of downtown and the river valley.

"How did you know about this place?"

"College, dear sister." He pulled out a chair, sat me down. "Remember? I went to college—this is a favorite hangout. There's a lot about my life you don't know—might as well begin here."

Jack ordered two local beers on tap, picked out some tunes on the juke box.

I gazed out at the city. We clicked our glasses. The beer tasted good.

Jack leaned back in his chair, taking long gulps, admiring the tall buildings, the Ohio River snaking by, the bridges spanning it.

"This is a different view of the city," I said. "All I saw that whole summer was broken glass, poverty, drunks and hookers, a lot of displaced people without hope." I looked toward the river and took a gulp of cold beer. "I'm beginning to think there's fun to be had out there."

"Careful now, Sister—you don't want to go overboard—the ink is still drying on that document."

"Oh my—what an experience. An *Indult of Exclaustration.* Who knew I was that important? This is serious, Jack."

"I know that, Megs."

"It's *exclaustration*—I'll be living outside the cloister."

"But you haven't climbed over the wall—is that right?"

"You could say that," I laughed. *Though with a little coaxing from Will, I could be tempted,* I thought.

We sat looking at one another for a few seconds. The jukebox was playing "Good Morning Starshine" from the musical, *Hair.* Jack had picked it out. As I listened to the words, a rush of love for him swept over me. I nearly broke into tears.

It dawned on me that Jack wasn't smoking—I'd been thinking how good a cigarette would taste right now. Maybe Victor was right—about the craving—maybe it was back—or maybe it had never left me. I asked Jack if he had a cigarette.

"Hmm?" He seemed absorbed in thought.

"Cigarettes. You're not smoking?"

"No." Jack frowned.

"Because…."

"Amy doesn't like it. The smell, mostly, I guess. She's convinced it's a health hazard. She's been doing research. Did you know that cigarette companies deliberately jacked up the nicotine to make it more addictive, and then disguised it with menthol? The bastards."

"You'd give up cigarettes for Amy? That's...."

"I'd give up a lot for Amy—in case you haven't noticed."

"I have noticed." I envied Jack and Amy—they were soul mates. We sat, listening to the music.

Jack broke the silence. He pointed at the envelope sticking out of my pocket. "What's that? Secret documents? A million dollars? Aren't you going to open it?"

"I guess I should. I think it's a check—not sure." I broke the seal and unfolded a check made out to *Margaret Ann Walsh*—no *Sister—Five hundred dollars and no cents.*

I passed it to Jack.

"Pittance," he said.

"I guess it is—but I wasn't expecting anything."

"Maybe a couple month's rent," he said, "if you're lucky." Jack noticed the letter inside the envelope. "What's in the letter?"

"I don't know. Let's see…." I read it quickly.

Jack was watching my face. "What's with the frown?"

"It's a loan," I whispered. "A year to repay it." I stuffed it into my pocket. "Oh well." I took another sip of the beer.

"Are you kidding me?" Jack shouted. "Ten years of your life, not a dime in return, a loan?"

"Don't." I raised my palm. "It's okay—really. The Community can't afford to dole out money to every sister who decides to take a year's leave."

Jack appeared ready to argue, then dropped it.

I studied my glass of beer, watching the bubbles pop in the amber liquid. I could feel Jack watching me. "You're taking this whole loan thing calmly," he said.

"I'm too tired to argue. I'm thinking about what to do with the check. I'll need to open a checking account—maybe apply for a credit card—though I don't have a credit record—that I know of. Look, I know Dad thinks I should move home, but you understand why I can't do that?"

"Don't worry about Mom and Dad—I'll explain—I handled them when I moved out. It isn't as if they don't know how independent you are."

"I have so much to do, Jack. I'm thinking of the list of people I have to tell. The sisters in my community—Rosemary and my housemates. I broke the news to Sister Irene—she was understanding, said I could stay at Dolan House as long as it takes to find an apartment. Still have to tell Corella, my principal."

"The mean one?" Jack asked.

"I don't think she's mean, the two of us are just miles apart. She'll say, 'Two years ago, I saw this coming, but you refused to hear it.' Maybe someday, we'll reconcile. Do oil and water ever blend together?"

"Not in my experience. Who else?"

"Victor, Father Mark, the other Brothers." *Will.* "Jack, I'm scared."

"Of course you're scared—it's all new. But have you ever stepped away from a challenge? Not the Margaret Ann Walsh I know. You can do this." He drained his glass and held it up to me. "Another one?"

"I really shouldn't—I'm out of practice."

"Come on, you're only going to celebrate an *Indult of Exclaustration* once in your life—if for no other reason than it's impossible to pronounce."

He strolled up to the bar and ordered another round, to the Beatles' singing, "Here Comes the Sun."

Back at the table, Jack and I both started to loosen up. I felt more relaxed with each sip.

"I need to find a job…." I said, thinking out loud. "Something in journalism."

"Hey," Jack broke in. "There's an opening for a Production Assistant at TV-7 posted in the journalism office at the University."

"I don't have TV experience."

"You have six years in the classroom—teaching writing, directing plays, publishing school newspapers—that should count for a lot. Then there's all your post-grad courses in journalism." He raised his hand and pointed at me. "My journalism prof knows the production manager at Channel 7. Maybe he'd put in a good word for you—if you want."

"Of course! I need all the help I can get."

We drank in silence, listening to the music.

I looked at my watch. "Jack! We've got to go. I'm meeting with my community for dinner—I'm the cook tonight."

"Pity the poor community."

I grabbed his arm to keep from swaying.

"Easy does it, Sister!"

"You're a corrupting influence, Jack." I stopped. "Thank you, big brother—for being with me. You can't know how much it means."

"Don't underestimate me, Megs."

We walked to his car. I rolled down the window and felt the breeze cool my burning cheeks. It blew my carefully-combed, shoulder-length, page-boy haircut in all directions. I thought: *I'm free—as free as the rules of exclaustration allow.*

I leaned my head back and closed my eyes. *Dear God—what am I doing?*

CHAPTER 35

"You'll move back in with us," Dad said, when I went for dinner the next evening. "This is your home."

"Maggie's got a life of her own now, Ed." Mom was stirring spaghetti sauce at the stove. "She's going to need some privacy—a place of her own."

I lifted a prayer of thanks to Jack—he must have had *the talk* with my parents—or maybe Mom finally saw me as a person.

As if reading my thoughts, Mom said: "Maggie's an adult—her own person." She slid a fistful of spaghetti into a pot of boiling water and looked at me. "You've proven yourself, haven't you—not the way I would have done it. I never did think the convent was a good idea—but you've made it work. College degree, high school teacher, theater director—all those plays—even your volunteer work downtown. You should be proud of what you've accomplished."

"Thanks, Mom." I walked to the stove and hugged her—we were both near tears. "You understand, don't you, why I can't continue teaching at Marywood?"

"I do," Mom said. "You need some distance. You'll figure it out, Maggie. I have no doubts—not anymore."

My father piped in. "All we've ever wanted is for you to be happy, Megs. I used to think the convent suited you to perfection—but it is up to you."

"I've disgraced the Irish side of our family, Dad. Can you forgive me?"

"Don't be daft. We couldn't be prouder."

I wouldn't expect him to say otherwise. My heart burst with appreciation for them both.

I set the table.

Mom left the kitchen and reappeared holding a small box in her hand—Stan's ring. "I've been saving this." She put the box in my hand. "Your sister had her eye on it, but it belongs to you—I guess I held out hope that you and Stan would...."

I held the ring box. "Stan is seeing someone—that's what I heard."

"We heard he's getting married." Mom whispered the next news: "There's a baby on the way."

"A baby?" My heart beat fast, the blood rushed to my head, my temples throbbed. I sat down at the kitchen table. "When did you hear this?"

"Today. One of my bridge ladies knows Stan's mother. Sounds like he's moving back in with her for a while."

I held onto the ring box. "Good for him."

"Anyway, you can decide what to do with the ring during your year of—what's it called, again?"

"Exclaustration."

They both repeated it.

For dessert, Mom had baked the family favorite—pineapple upside-down cake. "Dad and I think you should tell your sister right away," she volunteered, "that is, if you haven't already. Why not give her a call?" Mom gave me that pleading look. "She could come over. It would mean a lot to her."

"I don't know—I wanted to tell you first, by yourselves."

"You did," Dad said. "But your sister—sometimes she feels a little left out in the cold."

I called Marianne. She must have been camped out next to her phone.

"I'll be right over!" In minutes, she was through the front door. "I just want you to know that I'm here to support you." She hugged me and stepped back as if to survey the damage. "Mom and Dad said you were coming over—I kind of *guessed* what it was about." She paused. "We're not bli...."

How happy I was that she stopped herself mid-sentence—no longer asserting that she knew more than I did.

"Listen, whatever you need, say the word—Ted and I want to help. The kids—they'll be happy to see more of their Aunt Maggie."

"I'll be fine, Marianne, thanks. I just need to sort things out."

"We have a family pass to the YMCA—you can use it anytime. There's a great exercise class I've been taking—you'd like it—we could go together."

"I think Maggie needs a little time, Marianne," Dad said, stepping in to rescue me. "Join us for some upside-down cake."

I laughed to myself. Upside-down suited my situation perfectly.

"Maggie wants to find her own place," Mom told Marianne. Then she turned to me. "I've got some material that would make lovely drapes—or slip covers. The three of us can shop the flea markets—it'll be fun."

"I've got my eye on a small apartment near the University—cheap but clean—on the bus line. You can put your seal of approval on it—both of you. I don't know how I'm going to pay for it."

"You'll find a job—with your talents...." Marianne caught herself giving me a compliment. "And your brains and good looks."

I smiled at her. "I haven't received a paycheck since my job at Woolworth's during high school—talk about starting over."

We ate Mom's cake in silence, our forks scraping up every last crumb.

Mom spoke up. "Dad wants you to use the VW—the old Chevy is too hard to manage."

"I can drive a stick—you taught me, Dad, remember?"

"Nothing to do with your driving abilities—the VW's a stick too, you know. It's just that the VW is more reliable—saves on gas. It makes the most sense."

"You're all too wonderful." I went around the table and hugged all three of them.

Those years when I'd been deprived of my driver's license had made me dependent on other people. Now, my own car—borrowed but mine (*to my use*)—that was too good to be true.

Back in my room at Dolan House, I opened the ring box. The opal glistened in the lamplight—beautiful as ever. The gold was untarnished. I slipped the ring on my right hand. It fit perfectly.

"Oh Stan," I whispered, trying to imagine him married to someone else. I tucked the ring away in a drawer. Which ring might I wear—my silver ring signifying perpetual profession, this opal ring signifying my first love—or neither?

A few days later, the phone rang at Dolan House—it was early evening. I answered it.

"Dolan House—Sister Margaret Ann speaking."

"Hello, Maggie."

Even after ten years, I knew his voice.

"Stan." My hands trembled—I heard my voice go weak.

"You recognized me." He laughed softly. "You sound the same—maybe more mature. Maybe we both do."

How had he gotten the convent number?

He read my mind. "Your Mom gave me your number—hope you don't mind."

How could I? "I hear you're moving back...back home.... You know how rumors fly around here."

"Got in yesterday. I have an interview with General Electric tomorrow morning—an opening in their engine maintenance department. I could write the book on that." He cleared his throat. "I was wondering if I could see you?"

"I don't know…." *Did I want to see him? Of course I did.*

"I could pick you up tomorrow afternoon. There's a coffee house near campus I used to go to when I was in night school. It's quiet—private."

"I'm not wearing the habit, Stan, so…." *So what? Why did I even say that?*

"I know—your Mom mentioned. I'm in civilian clothes too. What do you say? About four tomorrow?"

I couldn't think of a reason to put him off. "Do you need my address?"

"I've driven by—I know where it is."

We sat across from one another in the Campus Coffee Bar. We couldn't stop looking at one another in amazement.

"Ten years." Stan was grinning. "You look—more beautiful than I remember." He stirred his coffee repeatedly. "All I had was that prom picture—for all those years."

"I'm sorry I didn't write, Stan. I wasn't allowed for the first three years. Then…it just seemed kinder for me not to."

"Kinder?"

"We were never going to…I didn't want to lead you on. Whatever Jack has told you about my leave of absence—that's what it is—a temporary leave. I haven't leapt over the wall."

"Yet." He still had that same winning smile. He sipped his coffee without taking his eyes off me.

I inhaled the coffee aroma—it was comforting. "Tell me about your—your fiancé? What's her name? How did you meet her?"

His smile faded. "Gail." He leaned in close. "I'm going to tell you the truth, Maggie. What do I have to lose?" He picked at his paper napkin, twisting it between his fingers.

"The truth about what—about Gail?"

"She isn't what I thought she was." He leaned back in his chair. "I'm not what she thought I was either, I'm sure." His eyes went dark.

"What's happened, Stan?"

"A big mistake—and now a baby on the way." He leaned in again, staring into his cup. "She doesn't want to get married—doesn't want the baby. I need to find a lawyer. I have rights as the father."

"How terrible." My heart ached for him. "What will you do?"

"I tried to make it work—for the baby's sake—but it's hopeless. She's into this rock band she sings with." He looked away, combed his hair with his fingers. "Turns out she was already thick with the drummer. I was just…a diversion."

"What does your Mom say?"

"She's been so good, Maggie. She understands what it's like to make a poor choice. But she's raised me well—and I plan to do the same for this kid."

"Isn't there a chance you and Gail could work it out? Don't you love one another?"

Stan's laugh was bitter. "I should've seen it—but all I saw was…." He had twisted his paper napkin to tatters. He drained his mug of coffee. "That's my tale of woe. How about you?"

"My tale? I need to find a job—and an apartment. I need to leave Will—that is—I need to *tell* Will, the guy I'm team-teaching with."

"Will? Who's Will?"

"He's a friend...." I suddenly had a hard time getting the words out. "He's...we've created a special seminar course for juniors together."

"What's he like? This guy you're teaming with?"

"He's...great...you'd like him." *He's my soul mate. He's taken your place,* I thought.

"How long have you known him?"

"We met in college—he befriended me actually. We just—hit it off."

"Something tells me this guy is pretty important to you." He looked at me close. "I'm right, aren't I?"

We both smiled—I read sadness in his eyes.

"Should I tell you the truth, Stan?"

"What have you got to lose?" he asked.

"I don't know—I'm hoping I haven't already lost you as a friend."

He sat up straight and reached across the table. "Give me your hand."

I obeyed.

"I promise—you'll never lose me as a friend." He squeezed my hand—then let it go. "Tell me something: Did you read *any* of my letters?"

"I did. All of them."

"Remember how I ended each one?"

I nodded. "*I'll always love you.*"

"I'm just wondering: If you had written, would you have said the same?"

I took his hand again—I felt no jolt of heat, no sparks, only the comfort of knowing I had Stan's friendship.

"I'll say it now: I'll always love you—as a friend." I smiled at him. "You were my first love, you know."

"But not your last—I can see it in your face." He dropped my hand, looked away, then back. "I guess I'll have to settle for your friendship—for now. I'm going to need a friend like you, Maggie."

"Jack—he loves you too, Stan."

"Yep. He's said he'll find me a good lawyer. You two—you're family."

We sat. I finished my coffee. I felt sad for him—and angry with this woman, Gail, for mistreating him.

He looked at his watch. "Ready? I probably need to get you back to your convent."

We didn't say much on the drive back. I was struck by the sacredness—the sweetness of our reunion—after all these years.

I'd put off telling Will for as long as I could. He'd lose the other half of his teaching team—that would hurt. Did he suspect it? Without knowing, he gave me the perfect opening.

"I have a surprise for you," he whispered one afternoon as we finished up work in the classroom.

"A surprise?" He knew I hated surprises.

"Sit here." He led me to the teacher's desk, then pulled a small box out of his pocket and held it up to me.

"What is it?" I could see it was a ring box—similar to Stan's.

Will flipped the lid, revealing a diamond ring. "It's a little impulsive—but what do you think?" He handed me the box.

"About what?"

"The ring. Do you like it?"

"Who's it for?" I couldn't think who'd be getting an engagement ring from Will—certainly not me. Ever since I'd made final vows, I'd faced the fact that I'd never receive a ring from him—or anyone.

I glanced at my silver ring—my final profession ring—just to remind myself of my obligation.

"Who do you *think* I'd be giving a ring to?"

Dear God—he's not going to ask Brenda Taylor to marry him? I was glad I was sitting down. My legs felt weak, wobbly. It took a few seconds to catch my breath.

"Is it—it's for Brenda, isn't it?"

He didn't answer. I took that as a *Yes*.

"Will—you did it. You got Brenda a ring." I was finding it hard to breathe. "I didn't...."

He waited—he was searching my face—leaning in close.

"Well...that really is a surprise...totally unexpected." I felt my soul leave my body altogether and flit upward, like a moth smashing itself against the buzzing fluorescent ceiling lights. I tried to focus on Will's face—the eagerness in his bright eyes—that lock of hair that had fallen onto his forehead—my hand holding the ring box—the glittering diamond peeping out from inside the white box.

Eventually, I felt myself re-entering my body, and heard myself say, "I'm happy for you. I guess I didn't realize you two were...."

"I wanted to run it by you."

"Why me?"

"Because I...because you're my...." He paused, stumbled over his words. "...My best friend. Because you're...a woman...even though you're a nun." His face turned red. "It's just...I mean, women...understand these things."

I understood nothing—especially engagement rings. I especially did not understand Will. What was he doing? Did he have any idea?

"That's it," he said as he took the box from me, snapped it shut, and slipped it into his pocket. "That's the surprise. I just...I wanted to see if...how it'd go over."

"It'll go over, all right," I said, trying to mask the irony in my voice. "It'll definitely go over. Brenda is one lucky gal." *What was I saying?* I seemed to have a habit of turning away rings and turning the men I loved over to—let's face it—other women.

I prayed silently: *God, this is cruel. Must you do this to me?* I had done as God had asked—chosen God alone—trusting no man's ring could ever satisfy me.

Will picked up his things and turned to go, then turned to me. "Promise we'll always be friends." He sounded sad.

I nodded. "Always." My voice almost squeaked…more tears were on the way—I swallowed, breathed hard.

I gathered my courage. "Can you stay a few minutes? I have a surprise for *you*—at least I think it might be a surprise. Sit down."

Will found a chair and sat, facing me. "A surprise? Shoot."

"A few days ago, I signed papers that will allow me to take a year's leave of absence. It's called 'exclaustration,' which means…."

Will interrupted. "I know what *exclaustration* means." He stared at his folded hands. "Would you say that again?"

"A few days ago, I signed papers…."

"That's what I thought you said. Are you telling me you're not going to be teaching here next year?"

"Will…I can explain."

"You're telling me, with less than two weeks of school left, that you're not going to teach Seminar with me next year?"

I nodded. I could see the anger rising in him.

"What the—what do you think you're doing, Maggie? We've been building this program for two years. You can't back out on me now."

"But Will…I have to." *Just being around you is tearing me apart.*

"You have to…." He stood up and walked toward me. I couldn't move from behind the teacher's desk. He plopped his hands on the desk and leaned in, our faces nearly touching. "I'll tell you what you have to do, Maggie. You have to…."

He stood up straight, his eyes still locked in mine. "Jesus, woman. Do you have any idea what you're doing? You think you can…."

Now I was angry. "I had hoped for a little sympathy from you—a little understanding. I thought—I guess I was wrong." I knew he'd be upset about my leaving, about having to find another teacher—but I didn't expect him to be this angry.

He started pacing around the room. "Let me refresh your memory, Maggie. Two years ago—two—before you took final vows—I asked you if you were *sure*…remember? I grilled you—I reminded you how we grow out of certain decisions and into others. What did you tell me?"

I couldn't answer.

"You said you were *sure*. Remember?"

I nodded, watching my tears drop onto my desk.

"Now—two years later—two years of planning, dreaming, creating together—you tell me you're not so sure."

"I'm sure of one thing, Will. I can't keep doing what I'm doing."

"What's that supposed to mean—you mean working with me?"

I nodded again. "It isn't your fault. It's me. I need to get completely away. I wish…."

"*You wish*…that's a good one, *Sister*. Why the hell couldn't you have…?" He held onto the back of a chair, then sat down facing me. He twirled his tie, ran his fingers through his hair, sighed heavily. "I am so angry." He looked out the window. "If you want to know the truth, I always hoped…." He looked back at me—his eyes sad, his face ashen.

"Hoped what?"

"Forget it. Now I've got to find someone else."

He went to a shelf, picked up a box of magic markers, and threw them across the room—they scattered in all directions.

"Will, please." I had never seen him this angry. I started to cross the room, intending to pick up the markers.

"Leave them," he shouted. Then, more softly, he said, "I'll get them. I'm not done throwing things yet."

"Where do you want me to stand—until you *are* done throwing things?" I hadn't planned it, but I could see a smile creep onto his face. I'd made him laugh a little.

"Stand in front of the blackboard," he said, turning to a bookshelf. "I'll throw every play on this shelf at you." His smile spread across his face—it never failed to melt my heart.

"I'm standing here," I said. "Have at it. I deserve every book you throw at me."

"You could have told me earlier, before—but it's done." He was standing in front of the bookshelf holding the collection of Shakespeare plays—he grabbed one. He held it up, so I could see: *The Taming of the Shrew.*

"What are the chances?" Will asked, and threw the book at me.

I sidestepped the flying book; it landed on the floor with a thud.

"If I played Petruchio now," Will said, "the violence would not be acting, believe me. It would be real." He threw another book—it hit the blackboard. "What's Petruchio's line?" he asked, hurling another book. "*My tongue will tell the anger of my heart, or else my heart, concealing it, will break?*"

"That's Katherine's line," I said, ducking the book. "I'm so sorry, Will."

"We've been a hell of a team, haven't we?" He lobbed one more book at the blackboard, then sat down and slumped forward, elbows on his knees. "I don't want to do this without you. You must know…."

"You'll find someone else." My legs were shaking but I found the strength to come from around the desk and stand over him. I followed my impulse to reach out to him—I rested my hand on his shoulder.

He looked up at me—his eyes half-closed. "I'm too angry to—I'd better go."

I let go and stepped back.

He stood up, gathered his briefcase and sport coat, then set them down and turned to face me.

I was close enough to push that stray lock of hair off his forehead—I decided to do it.

He put his arms around me and kissed me. I didn't resist.

Heat coiled up my spine. Bells rang in my head. The electric jolt I felt whenever Will and I touched pulsed inside me.

He held me tight and whispered, "You have no idea how long I've wanted to do that." He held my gaze, touched my face softly, ran his finger down my cheek. "Beautiful, sapphire eyes," he said tenderly. Then, he stepped back. "Remember—friends. Always." He moved toward the door. "Friends," he repeated, and then he was gone.

I found the nearest desk and sat down. My whole body was tingling. I looked around the room—his scent, his touch, the sound of his voice, the stacks of his favorite books and records—I wanted to preserve them all. I didn't have the strength to pick up the markers and books he'd thrown. I couldn't fight back my tears.

Suddenly I felt his presence at the door.

"My briefcase…sport coat…." He pointed to the chair where he'd left them. He fought back a smile. "I can't even manage a good dramatic exit, can I?"

"Will…." I wiped away tears. "I'm sorry."

He picked up his briefcase and coat. "Me too." He sighed. "This time I'm really gone." He turned and was out the door.

Our time together was over—he was going to marry someone else. We could never be just friends. I put my head down and sobbed.

His words kept circling in my head: *I don't want to do this without you.*

After that, our dealings were business-like, formal. Until the school year was over, I avoided being alone with him. It was too painful—probably for both of us, but certainly for me.

CHAPTER 36

I had written to Sister Audrey, my faithful mentor. Would Audrey forgive me? Of course—she'd understand better than most. My spiritual director had known for weeks. I was grateful that he was willing to continue to guide me, even though I couldn't pay him.

I couldn't face the faculty members or the older sisters—not yet—well, except for Sister Miriam, who had been my passenger and partner-in-crime during the infamous car-towing escapade that had cost me my driver's license.

"I have something to tell you, Miriam," I said, as I led her outside to the rose arbor. "I wanted to do it without anyone else around."

"Oh my, yes, dear," Miriam agreed, "the walls have ears."

We walked, her arm on mine, and sat under the rose trellis. I explained that I had been trying to decide for months—that I'd asked for a leave of absence.

"I understand," Miriam said. "Some of these sisters have made your life miserable, I know that. I wish I could help."

"You've helped, Miriam, believe me." I squeezed her frail hand. "More than you'll ever know."

"If you decide to come back after a year, I hope I'm still here to welcome you with open arms. If you don't come back, I'll pray for you—just like I do now. You have so much to give the world, dear. Don't be afraid to go out there and try."

"I'll always be grateful to you, Miriam." I did not try to stop the tears. "You're one in a million."

"We both are," the old nun laughed. "That's why we hit it off so well."

I didn't want my students to know about my decision. I wanted to avoid any disruption—and didn't want to have to explain myself to them. School would be over soon. Given the rumor mill, I knew they'd find out soon enough.

I imagined telling Victor: I planned to visit him at his school. At first, he'd act surprised—then admit that he was more or less expecting it. I'd thank him for being such a good friend and promise to invite him—along with the other brothers and Father Mark—to my apartment where I would cook dinner. We'd drink enough wine so as not to notice my lousy cooking skills. In parting, he would hug me and I would cry—I'd been crying a lot lately. I would suggest we go to an opera sometime. I would miss Victor. Maybe we'd stay in touch, maybe not.

Then there was Father Mark. I would drop by St. Peter's downtown. He would be sympathetic: "Your community doesn't appreciate you," he'd say. "Move downtown and work at the parish—you can teach and do outreach—we could find you a place to live."

My intuition told me I needed to make a clean break—to explore what else was "out there" for me. Mark had been a constant friend; I couldn't imagine not including him in my new life. But I knew not to count on it; he was a priest focused on his mission. I wondered if he'd want to stay in touch, if I no longer worked with him in the inner-city.

Finally, I needed to tell Mother Vivian. She met me in the visitor's parlor at the Novitiate. I'd been back there for reception and profession ceremonies, but we hadn't had time to talk. We hugged for a long time. "You don't need to tell me. I can see it in your face, Sister," she said.

"What do you see, Mother?"

"Sadness, but also courage and conviction." We stood facing each other in the parlor. "I want you to know that whatever you decide, you'll always have my love and admiration."

"Thank you, Mother." I wiped away tears. "If I do have courage and conviction, I learned it from you."

She laughed. "No, dear. You've had it all along."

"You've always seen something in me that I don't see in myself," I said. "How can I ever thank you?"

"By becoming the loving person you're meant to be." She led me to the front door; we hugged again. "I hope you'll keep in touch," she said, tears falling.

"I'm not dead to you, Mother?"

"Good heavens! You were my first batch. I'll never forget you."

"I haven't had a minute these last few weeks," I told Rosemary as we washed the dinner dishes one night. "Finishing grades, packing, waiting in line in banks—I feel like I'm neglecting my Community." The thought that I'd be leaving Rosemary made me sad. "I've failed in my vocation, Rosemary—I've failed you, our house mates, everyone in our profession group. I tried so hard." I was scouring the pot I'd burned making scalloped potatoes.

"You're not a failure, Maggie—no one believes that." She took the pot from me and rinsed it out. "You're following your conscience—and your heart—how can that be a failure?"

I dried my hands and picked up my ring from the windowsill. "At least I can keep my ring—for now." I examined the motto inscribed inside. "*Fiat*...what does that even mean anymore?" I watched Rosemary putting away the dishes. "I've forgotten your motto, Rosemary—tell me again."

"'*Micah 6:8.*' The reference—there wasn't room for the whole quote."

"Which is...?"

"*Act justly, love mercy, and walk humbly with your God.*"

"Beautiful."

I dried the glasses; she put them away. "You are *living* your motto, Rosemary." I laughed. "I almost said *perfectly*...but I'm trying to eliminate that word from my vocabulary. How do you manage to stay so faithful to your vows, to your motto?"

"I've never really wanted anything more than to walk with God—this life helps me do that. Even as a little girl, I was in love with nature—still am. Teaching biology feels like the right calling for me."

"You didn't need to join the convent for that."

Rosemary put the last glass away and we sat down at the kitchen table.

"No—but it helps," she said. "Less distraction—more time to focus on *my* God—the God of Creation. I know living in community can be a pain sometimes, but overall it supports me." Rosemary dusted the philodendron on the table with her finger. "I don't think I told you—I've been spending more time helping Jeremy set up his science lab downtown at St. Peter's. I feel more and more at home there. Who knows? Maybe I'll end up living in the inner-city some day."

"Father Mark used to say I was a 'natural' there, but really, you belong there even more." I pulled a few wilted leaves from the plant. "I still don't know where I belong. Do you think I've lost my focus?"

"You're on a path. Your search outside the convent—that takes courage." She finished dusting the plant and looked up. "You're showing us what it means to love."

"Me? How?"

"You and Will—surely you can see that he's...?"

"I'm trying not to think about him...."

"Why? There's more than one way to *walk with God.* Remember Pre-Cana? Mother Vivian's lectures?"

"Is it that obvious?"

"To me it is. You two have chemistry...seeing you together in the cafeteria...you light one another up."

I had to laugh. "I like that image. Leave it to you, Rosemary, to explain it in scientific terms." *No wonder I always feel sparks whenever Will and I are close.* "He's furious with me," I said. "For him, the light's gone out—he's giving Brenda a ring."

"Oh, Clare," Rosemary said. "*Maggie*, I mean—I'll never get used to your name change!" She got up from the table. "Come with me," she said, and pulled me through the house. She opened the door to the front porch and guided me to a rocking chair. "You should talk to Will," she said.

The setting sun was blazing orange in the western sky.

We sat down in separate rockers side by side and rocked quietly, listening to the music of chirping crickets and the creaking of our rocking chairs.

"Will came here a few days ago," Rosemary said. "I'm not supposed to tell you—we had a heart-to-heart."

"Will came here? Why?"

"Just...talk to him. Tell him how you feel."

"It's over—he said as much. I quote: 'Now I have to go out and find someone else.'"

"Talk to him."

A group of teen-agers whizzed by on their bikes, calling after one another, laughing. "Rosemary…I can't believe he came here. What did you say to him?"

"Pretty much what I'm saying to you."

"He was so angry with me. You think there's still hope?"

Rosemary rested her hand on mine. We stopped rocking; the creaking ceased. "I don't think—I know. But only if you talk to him."

"I'll try." *Once I'm settled,* I thought, *my mind will be clearer—my heart—that's another story.* "You're such a good friend, Rosemary."

"I know." She squeezed my hand. "I also know you need support right now, to get you through this. And I know where to get it. I'm going to make a few phone calls. Delores and Angela—even Pauline—are standing by to pitch in."

"They're busy, Rosemary. I'll be okay."

Rosemary laughed. "Looked in the mirror lately?"

CHAPTER 37

"We're coming to Cincinnati." Angela was calling from D.C. "I'm catching the pre-dawn Greyhound. Classes are over here at Catholic U—I'm free. Rosemary's picking me up at the station. I'll be at Dolan House by tomorrow night."

"Angela—I'm fine. Jack's helping me move. I don't want you to…."

"Pauline's driving down from Podunk. Delores is driving up from Tennessee. It's a done deal. Rosemary's made all the arrangements. Don't even think about refusing us. What else am I going to do with my monthly allowance but spend it on a bus ticket?"

When Delores left the Community in August '68, she'd left her former ministry (and the principal-from-hell) to teach first grade in a public school in Nashville. We'd kept in touch, by phone, through letters, but I hadn't seen her for two years. I saw Pauline more often—Community Assembly meetings over the summer—special feast days when she'd drive down from northern Ohio. Having them all stay with us in Dolan House: a dream come true.

By the time all four of my best friends were sitting around the dining room table at Dolan House, I was a fountain of tears.

"I've been crying non-stop," I told them, as we toasted with a bottle of red wine. "Tonight, they're happy tears, because I have all of you here to support me."

They lifted their glasses and shouted: "Hear, hear!"

"I have another reason for toasting," Angela said. "I just got permission from Mother General to go on for my doctorate in theology."

Our oooh's and ahhh's rippled around the table.

"It's a pipe dream now, but my brother...."

"The priest!" we all echoed.

"...Yes, smarties, my-brother-the-priest predicts the door might be opening for women to study canon law."

"You've been saying for years you'd need a degree in canon law to compete with the boys in Rome," I laughed.

"Here's the best part," Angela said. "It means I get to study for a time in Rome! Don't weep for me, sisters. I'll be starting off with an immersion course in Italian—in late Fall."

Delores squealed with delight. "I'll see you there, Angela!" She raised her glass again. "I was supposed to keep it quiet until it's official, but...I've applied for a fellowship to study the Montessori Method of Education." Delores tapped her glass with Angela's and grinned. "In Rome—starting in the Fall. If all goes well."

Delores and Angela jumped up and hugged one another; the rest of us followed suit.

Rosemary, ever practical, asked, "Delores, how's your Latin? Didn't you flunk it in ninth grade?"

"My cousin is tutoring me. He sailed through four years of Latin. Maybe I'll meet a dashing young classics professor in Rome and learn Latin that way."

We all laughed and toasted again.

Quiet settled over us. Pauline said she had some news. "Maybe you already heard—about Mother Loretta?"

The mood shifted from celebratory to somber.

"She died this morning in the Philippines...where she wanted to be buried," Pauline said.

We all joined hands.

"May she rest in peace," Pauline said. "She's probably playing Beethoven right now in heaven."

Heads nodded.

"What she did—publicly asking for our forgiveness—I'll never forget that," Angela said.

"I can only hope to have that kind of courage some day," Rosemary said.

We held hands for a few more minutes.

Finally, Delores lifted her glass again: "To Mother Loretta!"

We clicked our glasses together. "Mother Loretta," we all said in unison.

I looked around the table. "I don't deserve you beautiful women," I said, wiping my cheeks with my dinner napkin.

"You are so wrong—we all deserve one another. We're a Community," Delores said, "no matter where life takes us. You know, Maria Montessori wrote that the job of education is to establish lasting peace. That's my goal too."

"You may have left the Sisters of St. Mary, Delores," I said, my wine glass held high, "but we're still joined in a bond that will never be broken."

The next day, Jack arrived with a moving van. We loaded the boxes, pieces of furniture, my trunk, and assorted lamps into it. Jack carted out an old wardrobe with a missing door—which I'd scavenged from the basement of one of the convent buildings—and loaded it into the van.

"At first I felt a little guilty about stealing this," I admitted to everyone, "but then I thought, *I'm doing the convent a service by saving them the cost of removing it.*"

"No one is going to miss this old thing," Jack said. "It was full of moldy clay pots and covered in cobwebs."

"I can hear Mom already," I said. "'We'll strip it down, paint it a bright color. It'll be fun!'" Mom and Marianne had promised to come over all next week to help me paint and decorate, while Amy kept Jeffrey and Jennifer entertained. *What a great family!*

Jack brushed his dusty hands on his jeans. "You know how Mom loves a project. You'll be hers for the next year, at least." He shut the back of the van. "We'll meet you at the apartment after we pick up the stuff Mom's been storing in the basement. You gals better do some push-ups and stretches to get ready for those three flights of stairs."

"Three flights!" Pauline protested. "I'm out of shape, Maggie. Did you have to choose an apartment on the third floor?"

"On my budget? Yes."

"We can do it," Angela said. "With the miles I clock walking across a college campus every day—a few flights of stairs is nothing."

"Remember our first night in the Novitiate?" Delores asked. "I complained I needed to run around the block? Look at these extra pounds. I still do." She picked up one of the boxes. "Let's get cracking!"

I looked at my strong, smart, dedicated friends—and started crying again.

After an hour of huffing and puffing up and down the steps of my new apartment, we'd worked up a sweat. "I've got lemonade in a cooler," I said. "Let's take a break."

We sat under a maple tree on the grass outside the apartment building—a four-story red-brick (in a row of buildings just like it) with a small front yard bordered by bushes needing trimming. Drivers whizzed by, their horns complaining that the moving van was blocking a traffic lane.

"I'd better get this van back," Jack said. "We can load the small stuff in our cars. I'll pick up Amy later—she can help with unpacking."

Chapter 37

We watched the van disappear, happy to catch our breath before moving the rest of the stuff up the three flights.

Just then a car pulled up and parked in front. Stan waved, got out, and walked up to us. "Maggie—I thought you might need some help."

"Stan, hi!" I said, hugging him. "Let me introduce you. These are my closest friends—Angela, Delores, Pauline, and you met Rosemary when you picked me up." I could see Stan getting used to the idea of nuns dressed in tee-shirts and pedal-pushers.

Everyone stood up and shook Stan's hand. They all looked stunned. I had never told them about Stan—except Rosemary who'd met him briefly the week before. I was amused at their sudden shyness, their "Nice to meet you" greetings, and their stares—Stan was as handsome as ever.

Stan helped carry the heavy stuff—including my trunk, two overstuffed chairs, the coffee table, the book shelf, and boxes of books up the stairs.

Delores pulled me aside. "Who is this gorgeous guy and why didn't we know about him?"

I laughed. "My high school sweetheart, Delores. We're just friends."

"Not according to the way he looks at you, Maggie." Delores mimicked a love-sick face. "He'd like to be more than a friend, trust me."

Angela overheard our conversation. "The most beautiful blue-green eyes I've ever seen on a guy—not that I've done extensive research." She grabbed my arm. "Maggie—that guy is nuts about you."

"Not anymore. He's already taken—expecting a baby, in fact."

"Impossible," Delores said. "He's married to someone else? Huge mistake—on both your parts."

"Actually, he's not marrying her. He plans to fight for custody." I saw the confusion on their faces. "It's complicated."

"A single father—I'll say it's complicated," Angela said. "Big legal issues. Maggie—you could be just what he needs."

"It's not meant to be. I've got this year of exclaustration ahead of me. Besides, if I do give my heart to a guy, it won't be Stan."

"There's someone else?" Angela and Delores said in unison.

I nodded. "But I can't talk about it right now."

"Obviously," Delores said. "But you're going to tell us."

"I will. You'll need to give me a little time." *Besides...I've already lost him to another woman.*

"We'll leave you to sort this stuff out," Angela said. "Come on sisters, let's head back to Dolan House, have some lunch."

I noticed them sharing a wink with one another. *They think I want to be alone with Stan!*

"Can we bring you something, Maggie?"

"No, I have a sandwich, thanks."

"Okay," Rosemary said, "we'll be back in the afternoon with more stuff."

"Speaking of stuff—whatever happened to your vow of poverty?" Pauline joked, as they went out the door.

Stan stood in the midst of the unopened boxes, running his fingers through his hair, still streaked with blonde and wavy as ever.

"Half a peanut butter and jelly sandwich sound tempting?" I asked.

"Sure." He pulled two chairs into the center of the living room. We munched our half-sandwich and washed it down with lemonade.

"I've been thinking," Stan began, "about our meeting last week." He'd finished his sandwich and was looking at me intently.

"What about it?"

"I gave up too easily." He set his glass on a nearby box. "I was determined to fight for you ten years ago. Why should I give up now?"

"It isn't going to work, Stan. We've both moved on."

"I don't care if there is another guy in your life—what's his name?"

"Will."

We sat across from one another, knees nearly touching. He didn't take his eyes off me. His strong hands were planted on his knees.

"When I told you I love you, I meant it as a friend," I said. I saw the same hurt in his eyes I'd seen ten years ago.

"We had something beautiful," he said. "Why couldn't we have that again?"

"How can I say this without hurting you?" I put my hand on his hand. "Years ago, I realized our romantic relationship was over. I've grown up. My heart belongs to someone who is probably the closest I'll ever come to…a soul mate. Whether I leave the convent for good or not—my heart will always belong to that person."

"To Will?"

I nodded. "I'm sorry."

Stan pulled his hand away. He sighed and blinked away tears.

"It wouldn't be fair to you, Stan. I'm not that seventeen-year-old girl anymore."

"I'm not the same either, Maggie. How important is that?"

I shook my head. "It means everything. Think about all you've been through—and the struggle you have ahead of you. You deserve someone who is fully committed to you. I will be here to help you—just not as your wife." I swallowed hard and fought back tears.

Stan stood up and looked around the room, as if he'd just woken up in a strange place. "I guess I'd better go. I was hoping against hope—but you're right. It was all over your face that this other guy is the one." He walked to the door. "If you change your mind—if he changes his mind—you know where to find me."

"Stan… wait." I hugged him. "Soon you'll have a child to raise. I'll be there to help. We have history—we'll always be close."

He put on a brave smile and opened the door. "Easy for you to say." He closed the door gently behind him.

I leaned against the door and let the tears fall. "When, O God, will I ever stop crying?" I shouted, as if I were reciting the lines to a whole new psalm. I wiped my eyes and blew my nose on the only thing available—a roll of toilet paper. I flashed back to those days in the Novitiate when I'd escape to my favorite toilet stall to cry. *Some things never change, even when everything does.*

CHAPTER 38

I stood in the front room of my new apartment—my first full day in my new home. It was summer in Cincinnati and hot. I had worked up a sweat. I was wearing Marianne's hand-me-downs—a tee shirt and Bermuda shorts. In fact, I had a whole closet filled with clothes from Marianne, for which I was eternally grateful. I brushed my hair back into a short ponytail and tied a piece of yarn around it. I took a good look around the room. The daybed from Mom and Dad's basement, with its gaudy floral upholstery, made a half-decent couch. I fluffed the pillows and propped them up against the wall—it needed painting—all the walls needed painting. *Later*, I thought, *after my first paycheck*.

So much would happen after that first paycheck. I had two job leads: One was as a copywriter at the local newspaper. The other was at TV-7—in the production department—both on the lowest rung of the ladder, but a beginning. I would know more after I'd had the interviews.

First, I needed a phone, so I'd been listening all day for a knock at the door from the phone company repairman. I took another look at the old wardrobe I'd scavenged from the convent basement. Mom and I—and maybe even Marianne—would turn it into a work of art. In the meantime, I stuck the hand-me-down, portable black-and-white TV with rabbit-ear antennae and snowy reception on the bottom shelf.

I was grateful for every item I had—everyone had been so generous. I laughed to myself—the eclectic collection of furniture gave new meaning to *early Salvation Army*. I looked at the Naugahyde easy chairs. They were a color that could only be described as *Pepto-Bismol* pink—throw-aways from Amy's parents. I draped one of the chairs with an afghan Mom had crocheted in red, green, and yellow circles. Like the daybed, the afghan was a little on the loud side, but I loved it because Mom had made it.

I hadn't tackled the galley kitchen yet, so I picked up a paring knife and pried open a box labeled "Glasses." I made room on the kitchen counter—it was stacked with unopened boxes labeled "Dishes," "Utensils," "Mom's Old Pans & Lids," and "Fondue Set"—a cast-off from a cousin who had never even opened the box. One of the many things I'd learned in the convent was how to set a proper table for dinner, but I knew practically nothing about cooking. One of my aunts had donated a crockpot. "You can make *anything* in those things," she told me.

We'll see, I thought.

It was already late afternoon—cold cereal and milk for dinner.

It took me a while to recognize the doorbell—an unfamiliar buzz, like one of those trick gizmos that gives you a shock instead of a handshake. I peered through the security peephole, expecting to see the phone repairman. A hot flash shot up my back. I opened the door halfway.

"Hello, Maggie." Will stood in the hallway, holding a large cardboard box in his arms.

"I wasn't expecting—how did you…?"

He set the box on the floor and pushed the stray lock of hair off his forehead. "I would've called first, but Rosemary told me you're getting settled and don't have a phone."

I looked down at my hands. I was still holding the paring knife. "I must look a wreck. I was just…." I waved the knife toward the front room where boxes were scattered on the drab green carpet.

Will kept his distance in the hallway. He didn't crowd or push in, but he was firm in his stance, as if to say, "This time I'm not walking away." He spoke just above a whisper. "You look good... to me. I like you in a ponytail." He glanced at my knees. "I've never seen you in shorts."

"They're my sister's...." I was sure I was blushing—my cheeks and earlobes on fire, my heart pounding.

He kept his gaze on me. "Aren't you going to invite me in?"

I hesitated, knowing that the way I answered his question could weigh on me for a long time—possibly forever.

He pointed to the box on the floor. "I have a housewarming gift for you."

I couldn't think straight. "I don't know, Will."

"I need to see you, talk with you. Couldn't let things end the way they did." He took a step closer. "I'm betting everything I've got that you feel the same." He took another step closer.

He was so close I could feel his breath, smell his aftershave.

"So, I can come in?"

My plan was that I would get my bearings—a routine with my spiritual director, meaningful work, time for prayer and reflection. I'd pictured writing in my journal, walking in the park near the University, visiting the brothers downtown.

Instead, here before me was the person who'd told me plainly that I was his *soul mate*. I was tingling with emotions—drives I'd been suppressing for years. I wanted to fulfill those desires...to feel it all. I could say none of this to Will.

If I invited him in, would I be able to send him away? What would happen to my fidelity? To my vows? What would become of the years I'd invested in religious life? I'd promised we'd be friends—but nothing I was feeling told me it would stay there.

Had he been sent by God—like some archangel? Who needed me more, God or Will? Was Will the one I should be binding myself to for life? Would a union with Will bring me closer to the perfection I sought? If I closed the door on him now, would I lose him for good?

"Maggie?" He whispered my name with such tenderness, I felt faint. He took my hand and gently removed the paring knife. "You weren't planning to use this on me, I hope?" He slipped the knife into his shirt pocket with one hand, cradling my hand with the other. "Not that I don't deserve it."

He waited for me to speak. I watched him breathing, in and out. "I'll tell you what. I'll come back. I can see you aren't ready for me. Am I right?"

"No, I—yes—I mean no."

"No, I'm not right? Or yes, you're not ready?"

"We're doing it, you know? We're playing that word game."

"Yes." His brown eyes, usually dancing with mischief, were serious and steady. "Except it no longer feels like a game. The stakes are higher, wouldn't you say?"

All I could do was swallow and nod.

"So. I can come in?"

"I wish I could offer you something—my pathetic little fridge is empty." Then I remembered. "Wait! Jack left a six-pack here when he helped me move. There might be some left. Would you like a beer?"

Will nodded, never taking his eyes off me.

He set the box down in the living room and followed me into the tiny kitchen. I felt him close, the warmth of him, heard his breathing. I opened the lone bottle of beer and handed it to him.

"We'll split it," he said.

I unwrapped two glasses, dropping the packing paper to the floor.

He poured half the beer into one glass, half into the other. "Cheers!"

"Cheers," I whispered, afraid to look at him. Did he notice my hands were shaking?

"To us." He stepped closer. "Don't worry—I know what exclaustration means—the restraints you're under." He swallowed the beer in one gulp. "But I've also done my homework. The wording is actually *up to a year*—but it can also end *early*—even after a few weeks."

"You looked up canon law?"

"One of my former seminary professors is a canon lawyer. I checked it out with him." He set his glass on the counter. "I owe you an apology for my magic-marker, Shakespeare-hurling tantrum."

"I deserved it," I said. "I should've told you about my decision sooner."

"Yes, you should have." He removed the knife from his shirt pocket and set it on the counter. "I forgive you. But I'm not going to apologize for that kiss. I should've done it long ago."

I blushed and slid around him into the living room. "Show me what you brought me. From the looks of the box, I'd say it's a case of red wine?"

"Ah-hah! Packages can be deceiving." He picked it up and handed it to me. "Open it."

"It's heavy—it rattles a little. What is it?" I sat down on the daybed, and holding the box on my knees, I tore off the tape. I opened the box flaps to uncover a metal pot. "A pressure cooker!" I laughed out loud. "My Mom had one of these."

"Mine too—she passed it on to me—it's an ingenious little machine."

"I remember Mom's used to explode, spewing beef stew all over our kitchen. My Mom's a great cook but she never mastered the pressure cooker."

"I *have* mastered it." Will held it up and turned it around, as if it were a crystal ball. "My beef stroganoff is a thing of beauty."

"You can cook?"

"Better than you—according to local legend. Rosemary told me."

"There's so much I don't know about you, Will."

He looked a little hurt. "All you needed to do was ask. You spent a lot of time avoiding me." He scolded me with his finger. "Those days are over."

I felt giddy, light-headed.

"About my gift—you might guess that there are multiple layers of meaning to the word, *pressure*—I will enlighten you about the hidden meanings. But first—you have to remove the lid."

"There's more?" I balanced the heavy pot in my lap and looked at Will. "My heart feels like this cooker—ready to explode."

"Look inside." He sat down next to me.

"You're full of surprises, aren't you?"

"And you're not?"

"*Touché*." My hands were still shaking. I loosened the clamp on the handle and lifted off the lid—at the bottom lay a small velvet pouch.

Will saw the confusion on my face. "Open it."

I pulled on the drawstring. Out slipped a ring. Not the diamond ring he'd shown me—this one looked like an antique—gold with a blue sapphire in the center and tiny diamonds around it.

"I don't understand." I looked for some explanation in his face. His eyes were wide with anticipation.

"It's my grandmother's engagement ring," he said. "My mother was saving it. She gave it to me last week after I told her I thought I'd lost you for good. She's hoping for a daughter-in-law."

"It's…exquisite."

"Sapphire, to match your eyes."

"Oh, Will. But...what about the diamond you showed me a few weeks ago? What about Brenda?"

"I bought that ring two years ago. On the installment plan—for you—only you—hoping, believing that I'd win you over—that you'd decide to leave the convent for me."

"But you told me that ring was for Brenda."

"No. You assumed—I didn't say *who* it was for."

"Oh, Will."

"The truth is, I'd given up hope that the two of us would ever…I was so depressed. I came close to giving the ring to Brenda."

"Wasn't she disappointed?"

"Brenda? After our little scene in the classroom…I drove to Brenda's apartment. I sat in my car holding the ring…I couldn't go in. That kiss…*our* kiss. You kissed me back, you know. That sealed the deal. I knew there would never be anyone but you—not that I haven't tried getting over you." He put his arm around me. "Try it on—Grandma Celia's ring, I mean."

"Will—I can't." I held up my left hand. "As you can see, I'm already wearing a ring—my profession ring."

"It's all right," he drew me closer to him. "God is not going to mind." He looked at me. "I know these things—don't ask me how—I just do." He took his grandmother's ring from me. "If it fits—then we'll know it's God's will."

"What if it doesn't fit?"

"That's why God invented jewelers."

We both laughed.

"Remember Kate's lines in the last scene of *The Shrew?*" Will asked.

"I do. She says: '*My hand is ready.*' I think I'm feeling the *pressure*," I said.

What had Mother Provincial said when I'd asked if I could keep my ring? *Whether you wear it or not is up to you.* I slipped off my silver ring and set it on the coffee table.

"Wait—let's do this properly." He got down on one knee. "Maggie—Margaret Ann Walsh—convince me you don't love me as much as I love you."

I looked into his eyes. Mine were brimming with tears—his were bright and clear.

We both held our breath.

I surrendered my hand to him. "My hand is ready."

He slipped the ring on my finger.

"It fits!" He let out a breath and took my hands. "You're shaking. Please—say something—anything."

"I don't—love you—as *much* as you love me."

He looked confused—almost wounded.

I ruffled his hair and slid my forefinger down the bridge of his nose. "Now it's my turn to quote Petruchio: '*I love you ten times more.*'"

He looked relieved. "Won't we have fun... trying to see who wins that contest."

We walked to a small café just around the corner from my apartment for pizza. It was summer break at the University, so the café was empty. For the first time, I felt safe being with Will without being scrutinized.

With every movement of my hand, the ring caught my eye. "I have to ask," I said. "What did you do with the other ring?"

"Did you know those things are returnable—even after two years? It never came out of the box. Which ring do you like better?"

"You don't need to ask."

We held hands. The pizza wasn't great but we didn't care. We raised our mugs of beer and toasted: *To us.*

"I hate to break the spell," I said, "by bringing up a sore subject."

He sat back in his chair. "Let me guess. What am I going to do about the Seminar?"

I nodded, afraid to look him in the eye. "I'm so sorry...."

He reached across and lifted my chin. "Hey. Look at me. Remember when I said no one could ever take your place?"

I nodded again, daring to look him in the eye. *Please don't tell me Corella's hired Brenda Taylor.* "Well? Who *is* taking my place?"

"The good news is, I am." A grin worked its way across his face and lit his eyes.

"I don't get it." *I'm not in the mood for jokes, Will.*

"I'm going to teach your drama classes and direct the plays. I'm adding one of your English classes to my already full load of theology and history classes."

"You're not teaching Seminar? Who is?"

"Yet to be determined. I've given Corella a few good leads." He picked up my hand and kissed it. "See. It's taking two to replace you." He watched my face. I tried not to smile, but it was hard when Will was smiling. "What do you think?"

"I'm not sure," I said. "I need to let all of this sink in."

"That makes two of us," Will said. "There's a lot of sinking-in to be done." He examined the sapphire ring on my finger. "I'm still trying to absorb the fact that, after all these years, you finally said 'yes.' You did, didn't you?"

"This is the first time you've asked me!" I protested. "You expected me to read your mind?"

"Yes! You're my soul mate. I knew it the first time I saw you. Didn't you?" Then his face turned serious. "Maggie...I couldn't force you to give up your vocation—not that I didn't come close. It had to be up to you."

"I know," I said. "I love you for that. Speaking of mind-reading...the song, the beautiful lyrics, *Spring Came Early*. Who was that for?"

"For you, Maggie. Only you."

"I hoped so."

We both laughed.

Outside, the streetlights had switched on. We crossed the busy street, hand in hand. Everything around us seemed to glow in the twilight. We climbed the three flights to my apartment.

"I think it's better if you don't come in," I said.

"I know." He touched my cheek. "Tomorrow I'll show you how to use that pressure cooker. I shall dazzle you with my stroganoff."

"*Is that the way to kill a wife with kindness*?" I said, realizing in quoting *The Shrew* that I'd said *wife*.

He tucked a stubborn lock of my hair behind my ear. The gentleness and familiarity of his gesture nearly brought me to tears. "*We will have rings and things and fine array…*," he said, "*so kiss me, Kate.*"

"You want me to play the part, here in the hallway?" I asked.

"We're not play-acting anymore, Maggie." His eyes sparkled. "But yes, I want you to."

I closed my eyes, kissed him gently, then opened my eyes. "You need to know I'm not like Kate," I said. "I'll never be obedient…ask my superiors."

"Sometimes I think I know you better than you know yourself." He backed away, bowed deeply, then stood and looked into my eyes. "I almost forgot. Look again in the box I brought. There's one more little present—a talisman." He took my hand. "Good night, my Kate," he said, "we'll meet again on the morrow." He let go, stepped back and disappeared.

I listened to his footsteps—heard him singing Ray Charles' "I Can't Stop Loving You" all the way down the three flights. I ran to my bedroom window—saw his car headlights flash onto the low-hanging branches of the maple tree in front—then watched the red taillights trail away.

What else did he leave in that box? I removed the packing paper and found a small envelope. Inside was an acorn—our acorn—and a note: *I've kept this all these years, hoping this day would come. Let's plant it and see what grows! Yours always, Will.*

I scanned my apartment. Unopened boxes and newspapers were scattered on the floor—my silver ring was still on the coffee table.

Stay grounded, Maggie, I told myself. *You have so much to do before you give yourself to Will alone.* From my first day in the convent, the psalms had guided me. I turned to them.

I cleared the table in the dining room and spread out the linen hand towel my great aunt—the nun from Ireland—had sent me for final profession. She'd embroidered a gold chalice entwined with bright-green ivy on it. It would be my altar cloth.

I searched for the box I'd packed my candles in and found the beeswax candle—a gift from my housemates at Dolan House. I lit the candle and set my silver ring in the center of the cloth.

Then I found the book of psalms Angela had given me—a modern-day translation—and randomly chose a psalm:

You who fear Divine Love's abandonment:
Feast your eyes on the table before you,
Open your heart to Love's invitation.
Seek no longer. You're already home.

THE END

ACKNOWLEDGEMENTS

I am forever grateful to the countless writers at *Women Writing for (a) Change (WWf(a)C)*, a community of women and girls (and some men) in Cincinnati and across the country, who have listened patiently while this story took shape.

I am indebted to *WWf(a)C's* founder, Mary Pierce Brosmer; to Karen Novak, my first real editor; and to a number of writers in small groups: Bronwyn Parks, Lisa Hess, Jenny Stanton, Mary Ann Jansen, Mary Jo Sage, Karen Jaquish, Jane Pugliano, Sally Schneider, Andrea Nichols, Sarah Hayward McCalla, Linda Busken Jergens, Christy Schmidt, Sarah Huffner, Vivien Schapera, Laurie Lambert, Diane Debevec, and *so many more.* Thank you all.

I'm grateful to the Ohio Writing Project teachers and writers, especially Tom Romano, Diane Rawlings, and Darby Lyons. Gratitude to Josip Novakovich, who kept asking: *What if…?*

Thanks to Ken Keener, who read an early draft and gave valuable feedback; to Marilyn Herring, Nan Fischer, Myra Saladino, Peg Fox, and Carren Herring for early encouragement; and to Vicki Vondenberger for insights on canon law.

Thanks to my parents, Art and Dot, and to my entire family for their support, including my niece, Cecily Lambert Claytor, for her artistic talent and time. Kudos to the members of CLDP4 for creating my first public reading.

Deep gratitude and cheers to Michael Ireland, my intrepid editor, for her insight, expertise, insistence, and gentle holding of my feet to the fire. I've learned much from her.

Thanks to Publisher Jesse Krieger and his Director of Publishing, Kristen Wise, for believing in the story.

I'm especially grateful to my husband and fellow writer, Forrest Brandt, who read drafts, listened to rewrites, encouraged me to keep going, and served as my historic consultant throughout.

Finally, I acknowledge and salute religious women everywhere for their inspiration and courage to walk the imperfect path, wherever it leads. They continue to inspire me.

CREDITS

I gratefully acknowledge the many poets, authors, philosophers, composers, and playwrights whose words or titles appear throughout the book. Each has been a source of inspiration and enrichment.

Artists: The Beatles; Ray Charles; The Everly Brothers, Johnny Mathis, Galt MacDermot, James Rado, Gerome Ragni and Giuseppe Verdi.

Authors and Publications: Teilhard de Chardin's *The Divine Milieu;* Erich Fromm's *The Art of Loving;* Kahlil Gibran's *The Prophet*; Thomas Merton's *No Man Is an Island* and *Seeds of Contemplation;* Maria Montessori's *The Absorbent Mind;* Plato's *The Symposium;* William Shakespeare's *The Taming of the Shrew;* and Cardinal Suenens' *The Nun in the World.*

Other resources referred to include *The New Baltimore Catechism*; various Reception and Profession Ceremonials; *Perfectae Caritatis* (issued by the Second Vatican Council); and the Code of Canon Law. Psalm references were taken from the World English Bible; the closing verses are entirely the author's invention.

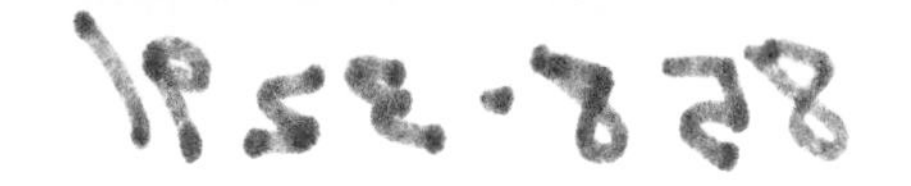

AUTHOR BIO

Kathleen Wade has enjoyed a thirty-year teaching career. She served for ten years as Executive Director of Women Writing for (a) Change, and most recently as Director of a leadership-development program for women religious. Her poems and essays have appeared in many anthologies. She lives with her husband in Cincinnati.

CPSIA information can be obtained
at www.ICGtesting.com
Printed in the USA
LVHW02s0525140218
566507LV00003B/3/P